Delores Fossen, a *USA Today* bestselling author, has written over one hundred novels, with millions of copies of her books in print worldwide. She's received a Booksellers' Best Award and an *RT* Reviewers' Choice Best Book Award. She was also a finalist for a prestigious *RITA®* Award. You can contact the author through her website at deloresfossen.com

Debra Webb is the award-winning *USA Today* bestselling author of more than one hundred novels, including those in reader-favourite series Faces of Evil, the Colby Agency and Shades of Death. With more than four million books sold in numerous languages and countries, Debra has a love of storytelling that goes back to her childhood on a farm in Alabama. Visit Debra at debrawebb.com

MAVERICK DETECTIVE DAD

DELORES FOSSEN

MURDER AT SUNSET ROCK

DEBRA WEBB

MILLS & BOON

First Published in Great Britain 2023
by Mills & Boon, an imprint of HarperCollins*Publishers* Ltd
1 London Bridge Street, London, SE1 9GF

www.harpercollins.co.uk

HarperCollins*Publishers*
Macken House, 39/40 Mayor Street Upper,
Dublin 1, D01 C9W8, Ireland

Maverick Detective Dad © 2023 Delores Fossen
Murder at Sunset Rock © 2023 Debra Webb

ISBN: 978-0-263-30732-0

0723

MIX
Paper | Supporting
responsible forestry
FSC™ C007454

This book is produced from independently certified FSC™ paper
to ensure responsible forest management.

For more information visit: www.harpercollins.co.uk/green

Printed and Bound in the UK using 100% Renewable Electricity at
CPI Group (UK) Ltd, Croydon, CR0 4YY

MAVERICK DETECTIVE DAD

DELORES FOSSEN

Chapter One

The moment Everly Monroe pulled her SUV to a stop in front of her house, she spotted the bloodstained box sitting on her porch.

Her breath stalled in her throat.

Even though she was a good fifteen feet away from the box, she could see the smears of the rusty-colored blood on the side of it. Well, maybe that was what it was. It certainly looked like it anyway.

Forcing herself to breathe, Everly called 9-1-1. Since she lived in the small ranching town of Silver Creek, Texas, it wouldn't take long for the sheriff, Grayson Ryland, to send out a deputy. Probably only a couple of minutes considering her house was less than a half mile from the Silver Creek Sheriff's Office, but she figured those minutes were going to feel like an eternity.

What the heck was going on?

Who'd put that box there?

Everly kept the SUV's engine running, and she glanced around to see if she could spot who'd left the box. She had neighbors on both sides of her and across the street, but no one was out and about. Most had no doubt already left for work. Her, included. And she likely wouldn't have found the box for hours if she hadn't forgotten her lunch. After she'd dropped her daughter Ainsley off at day care, she had decided to swing back by the house and pick it up before going into her law office on Main Street.

At the reminder of her two-year-old daughter, Everly's heartbeat kicked up, and she quickly pressed in the number for the day care. The owner, Sara Cordova, answered on the second ring.

"It's Everly," she said, well aware that there was too much breath in her voice. "I, uh..." And Everly trailed off while she tried to figure out how to say this.

"Ainsley is fine," Sara assured her. The woman had obviously picked up on the concern. "She's in playgroup right now."

"Good," Everly muttered, and she repeated it while she tried to steady herself. "This could turn out to be nothing, but someone might have left me..." She trailed off again. "...a possible threat or something. It's probably nothing," she emphasized.

"Oh." There was concern in Sara's voice now, too. "Should I do a lockdown of the building?"

Everly hated to overreact, but she didn't want to regret underreacting either. After all, she'd been a defense attorney for six years now. She was certain that she'd managed to rile certain people who'd been involved in some of her cases. People who might want to scare her.

Or worse.

The handful of threats she'd gotten over the years had never extended to her child or to anyone except her, but Everly didn't want to take the risk that it was different this time.

"Yes, please," Everly told the woman. "Do the lockdown,

and as soon as I've talked to the sheriff, I'll let you know what's going on," she added right before she ended the call.

It was only a couple of minutes later when Everly saw the Silver Creek cruiser turn into her driveway. Still clutching her phone, she got out of her SUV just as Grayson exited the cruiser. He was tall and lanky, and even though he was in his late fifties now, he still managed to look in charge merely by stepping onto the scene.

He also wasn't alone.

Everly required a deep breath of a different sort when Detective Noah Ryland got out from the passenger's side. Since Grayson was Noah's uncle and they both lived in Silver Creek, it wasn't unusual to see them together. But because Noah was a homicide detective in nearby San Antonio, she doubted it was customary for Grayson to bring his nephew to respond to a 9-1-1 call.

Especially this 9-1-1.

After all, Noah and she had spent more than a decade just avoiding each other. Wide berths were their norm. Him showing up at her house wasn't something he'd ever done before.

Like his uncle, Noah was a Ryland through and through. Black hair, sizzling gray eyes and the handsome face that always sent a jolt of alarm, and heat, through her. She figured no man could actually be too good-looking, but Noah always seemed to put that theory to the test.

Thankfully today, it was easy for her to push aside his looks and the inevitable attraction he stirred inside her. A pull that she figured would always be there since he'd been her first lover, way back when they'd been sixteen. A lifetime ago.

And he hadn't been her lover since.

Not after what'd happened that night.

Nothing to do with the actual sex. No. It was the aftermath that had led to a horrible nightmare that still haunted her. Always would. And she doubted Noah had been able to put it to rest either.

Since Noah had on well-worn jeans, a gray shirt and Stetson, she guessed that he wasn't on his way to or from work. She'd caught glimpses of him in the homicide detective mode, and when he was on the job, he wore what would be called business casual. But even when he was in a suit jacket, Noah had always somehow managed to look just as much cowboy as cop.

Clearing her throat and attempting to do the same with her head, Everly motioned toward the porch. "That wasn't there when I left to take Ainsley to day care about thirty minutes ago. I dropped her off, stopped at the café to get a to-go cup of coffee and then drove back here to pick up something I'd forgotten. That's when I saw it on the porch. I didn't touch it," she added, well aware it'd be something they'd want to know.

Both Noah and Grayson looked at the white cardboard, bloodstained box that was the size of a container usually meant to store files. But neither man seemed surprised it was there. However, there was deep concern in both sets of those cowboy cops' eyes.

"I got a box, too," Noah said, his gaze connecting with hers again. "It was delivered to the ranch this morning. That's why I was at the sheriff's office when Grayson got your 9-1-1 call."

The ranch, as in the Rylands' sprawling Silver Creek Ranch where Noah, Grayson and many other members of their family lived. Now her own concern went up another significant notch. Not because it'd been delivered to the ranch but because it'd been delivered at all.

"Who left it and what was in it?" she managed to ask.

Noah dragged in a long breath, and he glanced around. Another cop move. Both Grayson and he were keeping up a steady surveillance of the area.

"A courier from San Antonio delivered it," Noah explained. "He's being held at the sheriff's office, but it appears he was just doing his job, that he didn't have any part of what was inside."

The icy chill sparked. And spread. "What was inside?" she muttered.

"You should get Everly into the cruiser," Grayson insisted before Noah could answer. He took out his phone and fired off a text. "The county bomb squad is still here in town, and I'll have them come over and take a look."

"A bomb?" Everly blurted out. That icy chill got even colder and went straight through her entire body.

"There wasn't any kind of explosive in the box left for Noah," Grayson quickly assured her. "But we should check, especially since it appears yours was delivered more than an hour after his."

Even though her mind was still whirling and she was close to panicking, Everly had no trouble following that. The person who'd sent these boxes would have had plenty of time to add a bomb to hers as a way to escalate this.

Whatever *this* was.

She was about to press Grayson on what was in the box, but he glanced at Noah and then tipped his head to the cruiser again. Everly also had no trouble interpretating that. The person behind this could still be around, and they were all standing out in the open.

"Maybe you should get inside, too," she murmured to Grayson as Noah and she headed to the cruiser.

"In a minute," the sheriff said, and he started walking closer to the porch.

"Sara Cordova from the day care called Grayson just as we were pulling into your driveway, and she said you'd asked them to go on lockdown." Noah threw that out there. He opened the back door of the cruiser, got her in and followed, dropping down on the seat next to her. "Is Ainsley all right?"

That got her attention off Grayson and back on to Noah. It shouldn't surprise her that he knew her daughter's name. In a small town, everybody knew pretty much everything, but the fact he'd brought it up made her wonder if there was something more she should do to make sure her baby stayed safe.

"Sara said Ainsley was okay. Why?" Everly pressed, and her heartbeat was starting to thud in her ears. "Did something bad happen at the day care?"

"No." He was quick to answer, but his forehead bunched up. "But when Grayson learned your daughter was there, he sent a deputy just in case. *Just in case*," he repeated when he no doubt saw the panic in her eyes. "The day care is locked down, and once the bomb squad arrives and has a look at that box on your porch, I can drive you over to see your daughter. I can't do it now because I don't want to leave Grayson here without backup."

"Because backup might be needed," she stated, letting the full effect of that sink in. Still, she had to make sure her baby was okay. "I need to see my daughter."

"And you will. Soon," he assured her. His voice was calm, cop-like, but she could see the emotion stirring in his eyes.

"Is there anyone else Sara will contact about the lockdown? Ainsley's father, I mean," he clarified a heartbeat later.

Going back to that small-town deal again, Noah likely knew the answer to that was a Texas-sized no. Ainsley's father and her ex, Philip, had left Silver Creek, and Everly, shortly after she'd told him she was pregnant. He'd moved in with a girlfriend Everly hadn't known about, and Philip had then filed for a divorce that'd been finalized while Everly was still weeks away from delivering their daughter.

"I just figured Ainsley's father might be alarmed if he gets a call from Sara," Noah added.

"Philip's not in the picture," Everly settled for saying. "And there's no one else for Sara to call. As you know, I don't have any family other than Ainsley." She paused and tried to prepare herself for any answer she might hear to her question. "What was in the box delivered to you?"

Noah hesitated a moment. "Bloody clothes. Specifically, a dress and women's shoes. They're on the way to the crime lab, but they seem to match missing items from a murder I'm investigating."

Everly hadn't been able to stop herself from coming up with a mental list of what might have been the contents of the box, but her first guess sure wouldn't have been bloody clothes. In some ways it was a relief since she'd imagined all sorts of things, including a dead animal.

"A murder that happened in San Antonio?" she asked.

He nodded. "Five days ago. Her name was Jill Ritter, age forty-two, and she had a sheet for child neglect and drug-related charges. She went missing shortly after finishing up a shift at a diner in San Antonio where she worked, and her body was found yesterday on the side of a rural road miles away from where she lived."

Everly's stomach jolted at hearing those details, but she needed to know more. Because it would help her understand why a box had been left for her.

"Jill Ritter's cause of death?" she asked.

"She bled out from a gash to her femoral artery." He motioned to his thigh to show her the location of that particular wound. "She'd been drugged and her clothes removed, but there were no signs of sexual assault." He stopped, sighed. "No evidence left at the scene. No suspects. No contact from the killer. Until now, that is."

Yes, because leaving a box with the victim's bloody clothes was definitely contact. But why? And why draw her into it since she had no involvement whatsoever in Noah's investigation?

She watched Grayson as he used his phone to take pictures of the box on her porch. Meanwhile, Everly tested out the dead woman's name by repeating it aloud to see if it spurred any connections. It didn't.

"So, what does Jill Ritter's murder have to do with someone sending me a bloody box?" she pressed.

"That's what I'm here to find out. I haven't had the case long, and I need to learn everything I can about her and what's going on." He opened his mouth but stopped when a van turned into her driveway. "Bomb squad," Noah explained.

Three men hurried out of the vehicle. Emphasis on *hurried*. One of them headed toward Grayson while another began to take out equipment. The third pulled on a blast suit made of heavy body armor. Obviously, he was assuming the worst, that they were dealing with explosives.

Again, Everly tried to rein in her too-fast breathing and heartbeat. Tried to rein in her fear as well, and while she watched the bomb squad spring into action, she tried to focus on the murdered woman, Jill Ritter. If the box on her porch had a connection to Jill, then there was likely also a connection to her. One that involved Noah and perhaps some past legal case.

Everly had most of her work files stored in a secure on-line account, and while she volleyed glances at the bomb squad, she used her phone to log into it. There was a search function so she typed in the woman's name. And came up with nothing.

"Did Jill Ritter use any aliases in the past six years?" she asked.

"Not that I've found. She had a brother, a couple of exes and two kids who are now teenagers." Noah rattled off those names, one by one, and Everly searched for each of them.

Still nothing.

She was about to ask for the names of anyone associated with the woman's criminal past, but she stopped when the now fully armored bomb squad member approached her porch. He had a shield in one hand and a small device in the other.

"He's got a portable scanner," Noah said with his gaze fixed on the man. "It'll x-ray the contents of the box to see if it's safe."

Grayson and the other two members of the squad moved back behind some shields while the one lumbered his way up the porch steps. Once he reached the box, he moved the scanner over it while he peered at the screen. Everly was too far away to see exactly what was on that screen, but several moments later the man gave a nod before he stepped back.

"All clear," he shouted.

Everly automatically moved closer to the cruiser window,

waiting to hear what was inside the box, but the man didn't say anything about that. Instead, he lowered his shield and stepped aside when his comrades and Grayson moved in, going onto the porch with him. Since the four were now huddled around the box, Everly couldn't tell what they were doing.

Shaking her head in frustration, she reached to open the cruiser door, but Noah put his hand over hers to stop her. "Wait," he insisted, and the glance he made around the yard reminded her that while the box might be all clear, their surroundings might not be.

She looked down at Noah's hand that was still over hers and silently cursed that his mere touch could trigger so many memories. Both really good ones, and really bad ones, too.

While he locked his gaze on hers, he drew back his hand. No cop's poker face for him now, and in that instant she knew that she wasn't the only one in a battle to forget they'd once ever been involved. But it was only for an instant before Noah pulled it all back in.

When she caught some movement from the corner of her eye, Everly's attention snapped back to the window, and she saw Grayson approaching. He opened the door a couple of inches and peered in at them.

"No bloody clothing," he said, looking at Noah. "There's only an envelope. I'm leaving it in place so the CSIs can photograph it and process it. They're on their way."

"An envelope?" Everly questioned.

Grayson nodded and turned his phone so she could see the screen. "I took a picture of it. I don't know if there's anything inside the envelope, but there was a message handwritten on the outside."

There was something in his tone, in his eyes, that had

Everly bracing herself for the worst. Good thing, too, because she soon discovered that some bracing was definitely needed.

She saw the photo of the envelope. Saw the smears of blood on it. And the message that tightened every single muscle in her chest.

Everly, you're next.

Chapter Two

Noah got two bottles of water from the break room vending machine and headed back toward Grayson's office where Everly was waiting. Too bad he couldn't give her a shot of something stronger, something to settle her almost certainly jangled nerves, but he doubted that settled nerves would happen for her anytime soon.

Everly, you're next.

Considering that was almost certainly a threat from a killer, unsettled nerves were the least of her worries. Noah was hoping he could do something to help with that, which meant going back over all the details of Jill's murder to see how, when and where it intersected with a Silver Creek lawyer.

Of course, Everly wasn't just a lawyer, wasn't just from Silver Creek. She'd been his high school girlfriend, and he needed to figure out if that played into this. It was possible someone wanted to use her to get back at him in some way, though he couldn't imagine why they would have gone so far back into his past. He'd certainly been involved with other women since then. Plus, he had plenty of family and family connections.

Not exactly a comforting thought that a murderer could use one of them to serve up a twisted form of justice.

Noah rounded the corner and immediately spotted Deputy Theo Sheldon who was taking a box of Kleenex from the supply closet. He wasn't a blood relative, but Theo had lived on the Silver Creek Ranch since he'd been a kid. After both of Theo's parents had been murdered, Grayson had brought him to the ranch to live with him and his family. So, in Noah's mind, that made Theo family, too, and therefore he was another of those connections a killer might use.

Then again, a killer might not want to go after a cop head-on when there were much easier targets.

"Heard about the bloody boxes," Theo greeted. He studied Noah's face for a moment as if checking to see if he was okay. "I just had a short chat with Everly. She's shaken up some."

"Yeah, she is." Noah nearly left it at that, but he knew that Everly and Theo were friends so he decided to start the digging. "Any chance her ex could be involved in something like this?"

Theo certainly didn't jump to dismiss it. "I haven't seen Philip since he left town, but I could ask around and see what he's been up to."

"Do that," Noah said after giving it a few seconds of thought. "It could turn out to be nothing, but at the moment, nothing's pretty much all I've got. I need to pull at any and all threads."

"Will do." Theo handed him the Kleenex. "I was getting these for Everly so why don't you take them to her? She looks as if she might need them."

Noah cursed. Everly definitely had a right to shed some tears, but he was hoping she could win that particular battle and stave them off. Seeing her cry would only add to the cuts they were both already feeling, and it wouldn't help them focus. Right now, focusing was a necessity.

He took the box of tissues from Theo and started toward Grayson's office again. A route he knew oh so well. This particular building had been constructed thirteen years ago, when Noah had been seventeen, and it'd replaced the old sheriff's office. Silver Creek might be a small town, but the council had put a lot of money into the new facility, and the place still had that "shine" to it with its glossy gray tile floors and slick white desks.

Everly was exactly where he'd left her, in the leather chair next to Grayson's empty desk. Empty because Grayson was with the courier in one of the interrogation rooms. That interview probably wouldn't last much longer, but Grayson had said he'd be heading back to Everly's afterward and that Noah was to use the office as long as needed.

"Thought you could use some water," Noah said, setting one of the bottles next to her. He put the tissues on the desk as well but was still holding out hope that she wouldn't have to use them.

"Thanks," Everly muttered. She opened the water and drank deep. "Anything from the courier or the CSIs?" she asked.

Noah shook his head and sat at the small side desk where he'd already set up his laptop that one of the hands had brought to him. "It's early still. We could have something soon."

She made a small sound that made him think she was clinging to hope that it was true. "I called Sara at the day care again. I considered going and getting Ainsley, but it's probably not a good idea for her to be here. Plus, she might be upset at having her routine interrupted."

Noah figured she needed to spell all of that out to stop herself from going to the child. If Everly did press doing that, he'd need to talk her out of it. At least until he knew if it was safe for her to be out and about.

"Usually, I meet with clients at my office or in one of the interview rooms. This is my first time in here." She took another long drink of water, and her gaze skirted around the room.

Small talk, maybe to try to rein in those tears that were indeed pooling in her eyes. Except it might be more than that. She had been in Grayson's office in the old building. *That night.* They'd both been in Grayson's office then. Not for a visit either but to give an official statement of what had happened.

The accident.

That's how folks referred to it on the rare times it came up in conversation. Noah thought of it more of a fast trip to hell. One that would haunt him forever. He had no doubts, none, that it would do the same to Everly. So, it was possible that her being here was triggering some memories she'd rather not have sparked.

"I spent a lot of time here before I joined SAPD," Noah admitted to get his mind off that trip to hell. "Here, at the old building where I worked part-time and in my dad's office in San Antonio." Where his dad, Lt. Nate Ryland, had been a cop. His dad was retired now, just as Grayson would soon be, and the next generation of Silver Creek lawmen would step up to the plate.

She nodded, blinked back the tears. "Why is this happening?"

Small talk was apparently over, and rather than try to

soothe things that couldn't be soothed, Noah rolled his chair
closer to hers and met her eye to eye. "That's what I intend to
find out. Here's what I know so far. There was no envelope
in the box sent to me. Just the dress and the shoes, and the
blood is still being processed to see if it's Jill's. Also, there
was nothing inside the envelope left at your house. I got a
text about that when I was in the breakroom."

"No note," Everly said under her breath. "Just the threat
written on the outside."

Yeah, just the threat. *Everly, you're next.* For three little
words, it had certainly packed a wallop. And it had also
spurred a whole lot of questions.

Noah opened Jill's case file on his laptop, pulled up the
woman's picture and turned the screen so that Everly could
see it. "You didn't recognize the name, but maybe you've
seen her before?"

Setting her water aside, Everly moved closer. So close that
Noah caught her scent. Not perfume. Soap, maybe, and beneath it was all Everly. A scent he had no trouble remembering even after all this time. Fourteen years. Because those
memories were strong, he had no trouble remembering that
she tasted as good as she looked. And he'd certainly done a
lot of tasting back when they'd been together.

She'd changed, of course, from that sixteen-year-old girl
who'd been his first lover. *His first love*, he mentally corrected. Because he had indeed been in love with her. Her
dark blond hair now hit her shoulders instead of cascad-
ing down her back, and she'd added the right amount of
curves to her body. The face was the same. Beautiful and
the kind of face that got a lot of attention when she walked
into a room.

The eyes though were her big change. No longer carefree. Those deep blue eyes showed the troubles and strains of being a single mom who had now been seemingly targeted by a killer.

"I don't recognize her," Everly finally said. "Why was she murdered?"

That was the million-dollar question, and he didn't have anywhere near a million-dollar answer. "Her body was only discovered yesterday so I'm at the preliminary stage of the investigation. I don't have any suspects, only a few persons of interest. Jill's drug dealer and a couple of ex-boyfriends."

With Jill's drug abuse and checkered past, it was going to take him a while to work through everything to narrow down a motive and then suspects.

Noah paused and decided to lay this all out for her in the hopes that she'd hear something he might have missed. "Jill was on and off drugs since she was a teenager. She lost custody of her daughter, got clean and messed up enough to lose custody again."

"She abused the girl?" Everly asked.

"Yeah. Abuse and neglect. Nothing that required the girl to be hospitalized, thank God." But enough to ensure she'd need a whole lot of therapy. "The daughter is twenty-one now, and she has an alibi for the time frame of the murder. She was at a movie with a group of friends."

Everly stayed quiet a moment. "Tell me about the drug supplier and the exes."

He pulled up the photos of the three men. Mug shots, and Everly could no doubt see that all three looked like the thugs they were.

"They've all been arrested multiple times for assault and other charges," Noah explained. "These are men who use their fists to settle disputes. Other than the cut on her thigh that severed her femoral artery and a slight puncture mark where the killer drugged her, Jill didn't have any other injuries."

Noah knew Everly was trying to wrap her mind around this, trying to make the pieces fit. Since he was doing the same, he pulled up Jill's arrest record and went through it. Again. In the past twenty-four hours, he'd read and reread it at least a half dozen times.

And then something hit him.

Not the words of the previous police reports. But what wasn't there.

"No jail time," Noah muttered.

Of course, he'd noticed that before, but now he had to wonder if it was important. Jill had been arrested three times. Once as a juvenile for possession and use of drugs, and she'd been sent to court-mandated rehab. There'd been another drug arrest five years later as an adult, followed by more rehab that'd kept her from seeing the inside of a cell. A third arrest for neglecting and abusing her daughter which had led to the child being removed from her custody. Jill had gotten yet more court-mandated counseling and probation for that one.

"No jail time," Everly repeated, her gaze skirting over the screen to read the reports.

Noah saw, and felt the exact moment that Everly froze, and he could have sworn that everything in the air came to a dead stop. He hadn't expected her to pick up on the same thread he had, but that's obviously what she'd done.

"I didn't get jail time," she added. Both her tone and expression went stark.

"Because it was an accident," he quickly reminded her.

Everly shook her head. "I was the one driving that night."

"And I was the one who distracted you."

He'd done that by kissing her while she was driving back from the make-out spot by the creek where they'd had sex. So, yeah, they'd both been distracted, careless even, and because of it, a woman was dead. During that distracting kiss, Everly had swerved into the oncoming lane and had hit Helen Fleming's car. Helen, who hadn't been wearing a seat belt, died at the scene.

"Is it possible that what happened fourteen years ago is the reason I got the threat?" Everly came out and asked.

"Not likely." But since it was one possible explanation for what was going on—*one thin possible explanation*—Noah opened the statewide crime database. He'd already checked it for victims matching Jill's description and the method of her murder and had gotten way too many hits that he was still going through. Now he added a search for murders that'd happened where the victim had received a box from an unknown sender.

And he got two hits.

That put a knot in his gut, but he had a quick look at both cases. One male murdered in the Houston area and a woman in Kerrville, about an hour away from here. Both had died from stab wounds. Both had been drugged. Both, stripped of their clothes. Just like Jill.

Hell.

"The man, Delbert Washington, was killed two months ago," Everly said, reading it along with him. "There's no photo of the box he received, and one wasn't found at the scene. His neighbor reported he'd gotten one because the delivery guy had left it with him when Mr. Washington wasn't home. That happened the day before the victim was killed."

"Here's the description of the box itself." Noah pointed out, causing his gut to tighten even more. Because the description matched the one left on Everly's porch. Still, he reminded himself that it could all be a coincidence. "There was nothing in the box."

However, there had been something in the second box, the one delivered to the female victim, Winona Billings. It had contained a typed note with one sentence, "You'll die for what you did."

So, a threat very similar to Everly's.

After he did some silent cursing, Noah again went searching through the database, and this time he dug into the pasts of the two victims. It didn't take him long to find connections he hadn't wanted to be there.

Bad connections.

Eleven years earlier, Delbert had received community service and probation for an incident in a bar fight that had left a woman dead. During the fight with another man, Delbert had shoved the woman out of the way, and she'd landed on some broken glass.

"She bled out," Everly said, and this time her voice cracked. "A cut to the femoral artery like Jill."

Noah didn't bother to try to reassure Everly that this could still be a coincidence. Instead, he went to Winona's background.

Bingo.

About ten years before she'd been murdered, when she was still a minor, Winona had been driving under the influence when she'd hit a pedestrian. The person had lived but had been seriously injured and was now disabled. Winona had been convicted and had done only a couple of weeks in juvie lockup.

For several moments, the silence stayed thick and heavy between them. Obviously processing it. Or rather trying to do that.

"Did Jill receive a box?" Everly asked, her voice stabbing through that silence.

He was about to answer no, that a box like that hadn't been found at her residence, and Jill hadn't reported receiving one. Instead, he took out his phone and called Hank Dubois, Jill's landlord.

"Detective Ryland," the man said when he answered. He'd obviously seen Noah's name on the phone screen. "Did you find Jill's killer?"

"Working on it. Mr. Dubois, I need you to think back to the days or even a week before Jill's death. Do you know if she happened to receive a package she hadn't been expecting? Or maybe you saw a box left outside her apartment door?"

"I didn't see a box," he answered without hesitation, "but she came by the office here and complained about it. Somebody had put a box filled with broken glass on her doorstep. It was the kind of glass from a car windshield, and she said they'd poured ketchup or something on it."

Everly made a soft sharp sound, and she pressed her fingers to her mouth for a moment.

"What'd Jill do with the box?" Noah pressed. "And was there a note or anything else inside it?"

"She didn't mention a note, only the glass, and I'm pretty sure she tossed it in the dumpster. She said something about kids playing a stupid prank." The man paused. "Was it a prank?"

"I'm not sure," Noah settled for saying. And he wished

like the devil that he'd known about the box sooner so he could have tried to retrieve it from the trash. "Get in touch with me if you remember anything else that might help," he added.

Noah ended the conversation so he could text Grayson to have him ask the courier if he'd also delivered anything to Jill's apartment. He intended to follow that up with a call to the courier company, but his phone rang before he could do that.

"It's Kevin Kendall," Noah relayed to Everly.

They both knew the man. They'd not only gone to high school with him, but Kevin was also now the head of the CSI team.

Noah had a debate about whether or not to put the call on Speaker. A debate that quickly ended when he realized that even if it was bad news, this was something Everly had the right to hear.

"Kevin," Noah greeted. "Please tell me you found something I can use."

The man certainly didn't jump to answer, but Noah had no trouble hearing Kevin's heavy sigh. "We found something," he verified. "After we'd bagged the dress from the box delivered to you, I saw some writing along the entire inside of the hem."

Noah had certainly looked at the dress, but he hadn't taken it out of the box, hadn't examined it because he hadn't wanted to contaminate possible evidence.

"It appears to have been written with a black marker," Kevin went on. "It's smudged in a couple of places, but it was still easy enough to read."

"What did it say?" Noah pressed when Kevin paused.

The CSI cleared his throat. "It said, *The law didn't pun-*

ish her so I made her pay for what she did. You and Everly will pay, too." Kevin muttered some profanity. "It looks as if we might be dealing with a vigilante killer."

Chapter Three

Vigilante killer.

Those two words repeated in Everly's head. So did the threat that had been written on the dead woman's dress.

The law didn't punish her so I made her pay for what she did. You and Everly will pay, too.

Two hours ago when she'd first seen the box on her porch, Everly had been clueless as to what it had to do with her. But now she knew. Well, she knew a part of it anyway. Someone wanted Noah and her dead, and it went back to the car crash when they'd been sixteen.

The wreck that'd killed Helen Fleming.

Correction—the wreck *she* had caused that had killed Helen Fleming. The only part Noah had in it was that he'd been unfortunate enough to be a passenger who'd been kissing her at the time she'd lost control of the vehicle.

While she paced Grayson's office and waited for Noah to finish up his latest call, the memories of that night came at her like hurled knives. A hot summer night that'd cooled down because of a long, slow rain. Her, behind the wheel of her mother's car, a vehicle they'd used because Noah's truck had a dead battery, and she'd picked him up from his part-time job at the sheriff's office.

It'd been an incredible evening, eating the burgers they'd gotten from the diner, and they'd capped it off by having sex in the backseat of the car. Unplanned and not especially comfortable but still amazing.

In hindsight, Everly could see that the amazing part of it had left her giddy and light-headed. She hadn't had a drop to drink, but she certainly hadn't been focused on her driving either.

Even now, she could hear the squeal of the brakes when she'd tried to stop on the rain-slick road. Could feel the muscles in her arms and hands turn to iron as she tried to keep the car in her own lane. And she could still feel the sickening dread and shock when the car had slammed into Helen's. The sounds of metal tearing through metal, followed by the stunned silence of realizing what had just happened.

Both their lives had turned on a dime that night, and Everly would never be able to forgive herself for what'd happened. Apparently, the killer wasn't going to forgive her either. But why wait all these years to make her pay?

At that thought, she took out her phone again to call the day care and tell them she was on her way to pick up Ainsley. It wasn't the first time Everly had had that particular thought, and like the other times, she dismissed it again. The day care was on lockdown with not one but now two deputies stationed there, and Everly not only knew the lawmen, but she also trusted them. Besides, bringing Ainsley here would likely upset her.

Along with perhaps put her in danger.

It was possible the killer could try to use Ainsley to get to Noah and her, but if that was the case, then it was best for her daughter not to be out in the open. At least not until they had a better handle on this.

"I should hire a bodyguard," Everly muttered under her breath. She'd been thinking out loud, but Noah obviously heard her because his head whipped up, and his gaze snared hers.

"I can put you both in my protective custody," Noah said the moment he ended his call. "Then, I can tap some resources from SAPD."

Everly didn't intend to turn down any and all security measures, but she needed to think this through. Protective custody would mean close quarters with Noah. Uncomfortable close quarters. But she had to think of her baby first, and if that meant being uncomfortable around her former flame, then so be it.

Noah could no doubt see the concerns in her eyes, and that was probably why he walked closer, but Everly didn't think it would help for her to spell out the obvious about the close quarters. That's why she went with trying to put the focus back on the investigation.

"Did you learn anything from that phone call?" she asked. She wasn't even sure who he'd been talking to, but from what she'd gathered, it was someone at San Antonio PD.

"No. I was just updating my lieutenant about what's going on. She'll give any assistance she can and will flag the crime lab to expedite processing the bloody clothes, the note and the boxes."

That was good. Even though the evidence might not tell them who was responsible, it could point them in the direction they needed to go. Of course, Noah would probably say there was no "they" in this, that he didn't want her involved in the actual investigation, but Everly intended to be part of it every step of the way. Her daughter's safety was at stake, and that meant finding the killer was now a top priority for her.

Noah turned back to his computer. "I'm just starting some searches to find out if there have been other murders that match…" He trailed off, and she followed his gaze to see the reception area where one of the deputies was running a security wand over a man in a wheelchair.

"You know him?" Everly asked.

Noah shook his head. "But I think I just saw a picture of him when I was going through the database. If I'm not mistaken, that's Jared Jackman."

Everly drew a blank on the name. "Who is he?"

"He's the person Winona Billings hit with her car."

The accident that'd left the man permanently disabled. That got Everly's attention because she seriously doubted it was a coincidence that he was here in Silver Creek. Maybe he too had been contacted by the killer.

She hadn't read the details about Jared in the database, but she guessed that he was in his late thirties or early forties with just a touch of gray at the temples of his dark brown hair. He was also obviously in shape with wide muscled shoulders and a toned chest, something she had no trouble seeing because he was wearing a snug dark gray T-shirt.

Everly heard Jared ask the deputy if he could speak to Noah Ryland. "I'm Detective Ryland," he said heading toward Jared. Everly followed him.

"Good. I was hoping I'd catch you here. I called your office in San Antonio, but they said it was your day off. I didn't have your number so I did an internet search and found out you lived in Silver Creek. Since your uncle is sheriff here, I figured he'd know where I could find you."

He shook hands with Noah once he'd cleared security, and his gaze shifted to Everly.

"This is Everly Monroe," Noah explained. "She's a local attorney."

Everly had no doubts that Noah had chosen his words carefully when adding that last bit. No way would he bring up the bloody box to their visitor. Not yet anyway. But it might come into play if Jared actually had information about any of this.

Jared tipped his head in greeting before he shifted his attention back to Noah. "We need to talk," the man insisted.

Noah made a sound of agreement and motioned toward Grayson's office. "Is this about Winona Billings's murder?" Noah came out and asked once they were inside.

Jared followed a nod with a heavy sigh, and he maneuvered his wheelchair so he could shut the door. "I heard she'd been killed and found out you were the lead investigator on another murder, Jill Ritter. She died the same way Winona did."

Everly wondered how the heck Jared had pieced that together so quickly. Then again, she suspected the discovery of Jill's body had been all over the news, and since Jared would have likely gleaned any and every detail he could about the murder of the woman who'd left him disabled, then it might not have been so hard for him to see the connection.

She looked at Noah though, to see if he was thinking along the same lines. Or if he was considering that Jared might have gotten his info from some other source. Such as the killer.

"The press reported Jill's cause of death," Noah said, responding to her unspoken question.

"Yeah," Jared verified. "And the reporters talked about her criminal history. Do you have a suspect?"

"I can't talk about specifics of the case," Noah informed him.

It didn't surprise her that Noah had dodged the question. That was standard procedure, but the response seemed to frustrate Jared. He shook his head, muttered something under his breath.

"What do you know about Winona's and Jill Ritter's murders?" Noah pressed.

"More than I want to know," the man said on another heavy sigh.

Noah shifted, just a fraction, but Everly caught the movement. He'd angled his body so it'd be easier to draw his gun. If that became necessary. Because Noah had obviously just come to the same conclusion that she had.

That Jared could be the killer.

"Wait," Noah insisted when Jared opened his mouth again. "I'm going to read you your rights, and then if you decide to continue without the presence of a lawyer, you can tell me all about what you know."

Jared didn't get angry while Noah recited the Miranda warning, and he didn't seem especially alarmed that he might be on the verge of being arrested. He just sat there and waited for Noah to finish.

"I don't need a lawyer because I didn't kill Winona or that other woman you're investigating," Jared said the moment that Noah was done. "I haven't killed anyone." Obviously, he wasn't going to exercise his right to stay silent. He tapped the armrests of his wheelchair. "Even if I'd had the inclination to end a person's life, I wouldn't have been able to manage it, now would I?"

Everly heard the raw bitterness in his voice, and she supposed she couldn't blame him. After all, he couldn't walk because of his injury.

"Before the accident, I was a high school football coach," Jared went on. "I was pretty good at it, too, but I had to give that up. Just couldn't keep up with all the physical demands of being on the training field and traveling to the away games."

"And you blame Winona for that," Noah stated, and since he hadn't readjusted his stance, that meant he probably wasn't convinced yet that Jared was innocent of killing at least two women.

"Of course, I do," the man readily admitted. "She was to blame, but that doesn't mean I killed her. The way I see it, a bigger punishment for her was having to live with what she'd done. Now that she's dead, her punishment is over. I'm still having to live with what she did."

Yes, there was plenty of bitterness all right, but Everly could understand the point he was making about why it was better to have Winona alive. However, like Noah, she still wasn't convinced they weren't face to face with a killer.

"What do you know about Winona's and Jill's murders?" Noah repeated.

Jared sighed again. "I debated whether or not I should come in because this might turn out to be nothing. I really hope it's nothing," he added in a mumble. "But I'm in a support group for victims of violence or trauma. Peace Seekers, it's called. Yeah, it's a wussy-sounding name, but it's helped me. We meet once a week at a civic center in San Antonio, and we had a meeting last night. Anyway, I'm concerned about one of the members."

"A member who might have had some part in killing these women?" Noah pushed when Jared didn't continue.

"Maybe." Jared cursed under his breath. "His name is River Parnell."

The name meant nothing to Everly, and judging from the way Noah shook his head, it didn't ring any bells with him, either. That would change though. Noah would no doubt do a thorough investigation on the man. So would she.

"Tell me about River Parnell," Noah insisted.

Jared gathered his breath. "He's in his early twenties and is in the group because his mom murdered his dad when he was a kid. The mom got off, claiming self-defense, but River believes she set it all up so she could collect on some life insurance money." He paused again and met Noah's gaze. "River's one very angry young man. Mad at the whole world, if you know what I mean."

Noah made a sound of agreement. "Do you know his mother's name?"

"No. But River said she was killed in a car wreck a few years ago. I don't know that for certain," he quickly added, "but River likes to go over the details of her death. He says she didn't suffer or pay nearly enough for what she did."

All right. So, that would work as a motive for a vigilante seeking justice.

"River knew about Jill Ritter and Winona?" Noah asked.

"He knew about Winona and what she did to me," Jared readily admitted. "I guess you could say I'm an angry man, too, because I talked about it a lot. And River also knew about Jill Ritter because Jill's daughter, Megan, is in the support group, too."

Sweet heaven. Of course, it could be a coincidence, but it was a solid connection that needed investigating.

"Megan talked about her mom, about the things her mom had done to her. After I heard about Jill being murdered, I got to thinking about Winona's death. I also did some thinking about River and how he might have, maybe, listened to what we said and decided to do something about it."

Noah stayed quiet a moment, obviously processing that. "Who else is in the group?"

Jared gave a quick shrug. "I only know a couple of people's names. Most don't say or they use nicknames, and not everybody shows up regularly to the meetings. Like I said, I know Megan Ritter, and when she came to the meeting last night, she said her mom had been murdered. I read the news stories online, and one of them mentioned you were the lead detective on the investigation. That's how I knew to get in touch with you."

Well, that explained why he was here, and by coming forward, he'd just corroborated the most likely motives for Winona's and Jill's murders. It twisted at her that she was in the same category as they were. And even worse, she was responsible for a woman's death while Winona's and Jill's victims were still alive.

"Who runs the Peace Seekers?" Noah asked Jared.

"Daisy Reyes. She's a counselor. I don't know anything about her because she doesn't get into her own personal stuff. I do know that River Parnell doesn't live in San Antonio," Jared went on. "He's mentioned he lives on his grandparents' ranch. I'm not sure where that is though."

"I'll find his address, and I'll be talking to him," Noah assured him. "I'll be talking to Daisy Reyes and everyone else in the group. Other than Jill Ritter's daughter Megan, do you recall anyone else mentioning anything about a murder? Did River say anything about the two dead women?"

"No, nothing." Jared shook his head. "I hope I'm not causing trouble for him if he didn't do anything wrong."

"Don't worry. I'll sort that out." Noah paused. "Does the name Delbert Washington mean anything to you?"

That was the man murdered in Houston. The one who'd been responsible for a woman's death during a bar fight.

Jared repeated the name under his breath, frowned. "No. You think he's in Peace Seekers?"

Noah made a noncommittal sound, but Everly knew what he was thinking. Since Delbert was already dead, murdered, then it would be more likely that someone connected to his dead victim was in Peace Seekers. Well, if that case held pattern with the other two.

Groaning softly, Jared leaned forward a little. "Look, I hate putting this kind of suspicion on River, but I didn't want to just sit back and wait to see if somebody else got killed."

"You were right to come forward," Noah assured him. "I'll investigate and get back to you if I learn anything." He handed Jared a notepad and pen that he took from Grayson's desk. "Just write down your contact information and any of the members' names you do know. Also, make sure to call me if you remember anything else that might help."

"I will," he said as he wrote. "Am I in danger? Because I'm not exactly in a position to defend myself." Jared quickly tacked that on to his question.

"I don't think you're in danger, but you shouldn't try to contact River or anyone else in the group. I'll do that. I also won't mention to River or to the others that I've spoken with you. I'm asking you to do the same. Don't tell any of them that you came to see me. Not until I've given you the okay to do that."

The next breath that Jared blew out seemed to be one of

relief. There was a good reason for that. If someone in that group was a killer, then that person might object to someone setting the cops on him. If Jared followed Noah's instructions, it would help keep him safe.

Noah took the notepad from Jared when he'd finished writing and set it on Grayson's desk. "I'll just see Jared to the door," Noah muttered to her.

Everly didn't waste any time. The moment Noah and Jared were out of the office, she looked at what the man had written. His address, the address of the Peace Seekers meetings and some names.

Daisy Reyes, the counselor.

Megan Ritter, the daughter of the woman whose murder Noah was now investigating.

River Parnell, the suspect Jared had just handed to them.

Bobby, last name unknown.

Everly took out her phone, did a quick search on the Peace Seekers, and she went to their website. There was a picture of a pastoral setting of Texas wildflowers, followed by an invitation to attend if you were a survivor of violence or trauma. The only contact info was for the counselor, but there were also numbers for a suicide help line and other support groups. What was missing was a list of any members which didn't surprise Everly. Groups like that didn't usually advertise that sort of thing.

When she heard footsteps, she looked up and saw Noah making his way back toward her. He was on his phone, apparently leaving a voice mail for someone to call him ASAP.

"I was trying to get in touch with Daisy Reyes," he informed her after he put his phone away. "I got her number from the dispatcher, but she didn't answer. I left her a message."

"Good. Though she might not cooperate if she thinks this will violate counselor-client privilege."

The look he gave her was all cop. "And she might cooperate if she realizes one of her support group members is a killer." He tried another call. "I got River's number from Dispatch..." Noah explained, but she heard the call go to voice mail. He left another message for River to call him ASAP before he looked at her phone, at the Peace Seekers webpage she still had on the screen. "Anything on there that'll help?"

"Not at first glance, but they might have a social media page, a way for members to stay in touch in between meetings."

"Let's hope so because I'm not buying that all of this is happenstance, not with Jill Ritter's daughter and Jared in the same group."

She would have quickly agreed with him, but his phone rang, and Everly hoped this was the counselor who could start giving them some answers. But it wasn't.

"It's Grayson," Noah relayed to her, and he put the call on speaker.

"I'm out at Everly's house, and the CSIs went through her backyard." Grayson immediately said. "They found a body."

Chapter Four

A body.

Noah felt the sickening dread wash over him. Dread not just for this new victim the CSIs had found but because of the stark terror he now saw in Everly's eyes. The bloody box had been bad enough, so had the info that Jared had given them, but apparently that had been just the beginning of this particular nightmare.

"Who's dead?" Noah asked Grayson, praying it wasn't a friend or a family member.

"Not sure yet. There's no ID on her, but it's a woman. Her clothes have been stripped off, and the cause of death appears to be from a knife wound in or around the femoral artery."

Hell.

Beside him, he heard Everly make a hoarse sound, and as if her legs had lost all their strength, she dropped down into the chair. The color drained from her face, but that only lasted a couple of seconds before the panic set in.

"Ainsley," she muttered, and with her fingers trembling, she sent another text. No doubt to Sara at the day care.

Noah knew he'd soon have to take Everly there to get her daughter, but he needed to deal with a few other things first. That included getting any and all details about their latest victim.

"There are two deputies with Ainsley," Noah reminded Everly in a whisper. "She's safe."

He resisted the urge—no, the need—to pull Everly into his arms to try to give her some reassurance. But considering there had been four people murdered, a hug wasn't going to give her much of anything. The only thing that would help was for him to find this killer and put him or her away in jail so that Everly and her child would no longer be in harm's way. Since he was also likely on this killer's hit list, it'd keep him and his own family safe as well.

"Can you describe the woman?" Noah asked Grayson. Because even though his investigation was at the preliminary stages, he might have done a search on someone matching her description.

"She's in her late twenties or early thirties. Black hair, brown eyes," Grayson readily provided. "About five foot three, around a hundred and twenty pounds. I can't see any distinguishing marks or tats on her body."

Nothing from his searches immediately jumped to mind, but Noah would definitely take another look.

"Other than the wound and a small puncture mark on her right shoulder," Grayson went on, "there are no signs of violence. No defensive wounds. She doesn't appear to have been dragged to her current location, and it's clearly not the site of the murder. Not enough blood."

So, she'd been killed elsewhere and brought to Everly's. Maybe the killer had done that when he'd dropped off the box. If so, that was gutsy of him to place a body there where the neighbors could have noticed. Then again, the body could have been there all night.

That wouldn't be a comforting thought to Everly. To know that the killer had been so close to Ainsley and her.

"Does the dead woman appear to have been a junkie?" Noah asked Grayson.

Because Jill had definitely looked like a drug abuser, and now that he'd seen photos of the other victims, Delbert Washington and Winona Billings, Noah knew that a veteran cop would recognize the signs of someone who'd lived a hard life.

"No," Grayson answered. "She looks as if she was healthy."

Yeah, healthy before someone had murdered her. So, it obviously wasn't a hard life/drug or alcohol abuser that had caused the killer to single out this woman. Then again, Everly and he were damn healthy, too.

"The CSIs have already gotten the dead woman's fingerprints," Grayson went on a moment later. "We might get a hit on them. You should go ahead and see if there are any missing persons reports that might be a match."

"Will do," Noah assured him, and he moved his laptop closer so he could get that started. "I had a visitor while you've been out."

And he filled Grayson in on what Jared had told them and his new working theory for this investigation. A theory that so far pointed to three murders connected to this vigilante killer and perhaps the support group. Specifically, to a member, River Parnell.

After hearing Jared's account and concerns, Grayson muttered some profanity that let Noah know his uncle had had no trouble following that theory straight to Everly and him. Considering both of them had gotten boxes, they were now the killer's targets.

"Let me know if there's any way I can help," Grayson added. "How's Everly?"

She evidently heard Grayson's question because she looked at Noah the same moment he looked at her. Their gazes connected. Held. And he saw exactly what he expected to see. The tornado of emotions barreling through her.

"Everly will probably feel better once she can see Ainsley," Noah decided on saying.

"Hold off on that a little while longer," Grayson advised. "I don't have the manpower right now to give you a backup escort, and I'd rather the two of you not be out alone on the road."

Neither would Noah. Even though the day care wasn't far, the killer could no doubt figure they'd be headed there and could lie in wait. No one wanted bullets flying or an attack happening near all those kids.

"Once I'm back in the office, that'll free up Theo to drive with you first to the day care and then to…" Grayson stopped, muttered more profanity. "I'm guessing your house on the ranch. Yeah, I know Everly won't like that, but the CSIs aren't going to be finished with her place today."

Everly's mouth tightened, confirming that no, she wouldn't like going to the ranch, but Noah would have to convince her that was the safe thing to do. He didn't want Everly out of his sight, and if they were at the ranch, he'd have plenty of backup between his family and the ranch hands.

Noah ended the call with Grayson and turned to Everly. He was fully prepared to launch into an argument as to why Ainsley and she needed to stay with him. But she spoke before he could say anything.

"It'll be just for the night," Everly muttered. "Just until I can make other arrangements."

He'd take that. For now. But Noah didn't intend to back down when it came to keeping her in his sights.

Before he dived into the missing persons reports and the other background checks he needed to do, Noah sent a text to his mom, Darcy, who was also a retired district attorney, and he asked her to get someone to set up a temporary nursery at his house. She didn't question him as to why he needed that. Probably because his dad, Nate, had already gotten updates from the CSIs or even Grayson. Added to that, getting nursery items wouldn't be a problem since many of his cousins had young children.

His mother merely responded, It'll be ready. Stay safe.

With that done, he shifted his attention back to Everly. Since he could practically see the nerves firing off her, he decided to give her something else to focus on. After all, there was work that needed to be done, and it might be hours before they could go pick up Ainsley.

"I'm going to set up a search in the missing persons database," Noah let her know, "but why don't you use Grayson's personal computer to get started on the background checks for River Parnell and Daisy Reyes?"

He motioned to the laptop on the small table behind Grayson's desk. Unfortunately, Noah couldn't allow her to tap into official records and such, but he figured Everly had plenty of resources to help. Then, he could fill in the rest.

Everly nodded, and without hesitating, she went straight to the laptop. He'd been right about the work settling her. Well, as much as that was possible under the circumstances. She immediately sat down, opened the laptop and started typing.

Noah did the same, but he frowned when he put in the dead woman's description and came up with a goose egg. No missing persons reports filed for anyone like that in the past week. So, he broadened the search, going back a month. Still nothing. And that meant it was possible that no one had realized the woman was missing. Or maybe no one cared that she was gone. Jill's body hadn't been found for days, and yet there hadn't been a missing persons report on her either.

Noah tried to push aside the image of Jill's body. Tried also not to think that the killer wanted to do that to Everly. But Everly and he had an advantage that the other victims likely hadn't had. They knew someone wanted them dead. That meant they could take steps to make sure it didn't happen. Necessary steps. Because Noah didn't want anyone dying because of a vigilante killer who thought this was the way to get justice.

"I have some preliminary stuff on River Parnell," Everly said, snapping his attention back to her. "I have access to several PI databases, and I used those to learn that he's twenty-five and is employed by Images, a PR company that builds and hosts websites for businesses. He does indeed live on his late grandfather's ranch near Bulverde and works remotely from there."

That was a lot of info for only a couple of minutes of searching, and Noah latched on to the Bulverde location. That was only about a twenty minute drive from Silver Creek. Hell. If this was their man, the vigilante, then he was damn close.

"River obviously loves social media and posting on blogs on the internet," Everly went on. "I did a Google search, and I'm pulling up some of the pages now." She stopped and read whatever it was she'd found. "It's a rant about the corrupt criminal justice system." She put *corrupt* in air quotes.

Noah set his missing persons search on auto and went to stand by her so he could see the next page she'd found. Another blog, and River had left another rant about his mother getting away *scot-free* with murdering his father.

Since Noah wanted to see if that was anywhere near the truth, he used Grayson's desktop computer to search for details about the case. He got an instant hit.

"'Six years ago when River was at college in Austin,'" Noah read out to Everly, "'his father, Vance, did indeed die from a fatal gunshot wound to the chest. His blood alcohol level was five times the limit at the time of his death.'"

Everly looked back at him and lifted her eyebrow. "Did River's mother actually kill him?"

"She's the one who pulled the trigger all right." Noah kept reading. "'During the investigation, River's mother, Jackie, claimed she'd thought her estranged husband was an intruder and that he hadn't responded when she'd called out to see who'd broken down her door. So, she ended up shooting him, saying that she had been afraid for her life.'"

Everly sighed. "Yes, I can see where River might have thought it was murder. And it might have been. Estranged?" she repeated. "I'm guessing they were going through a messy divorce?"

"Definitely. Friends and neighbors verified that. Verified, too, that Vance was prone to drinking, and that Jackie was prone to cheating. They had a history of breaking up and making up."

He'd thrown that out almost casually, but after hearing his words, Noah thought of Everly and him. It didn't apply. They had no such history. But they had indeed broken up, and every time he was around her, like now, his body wouldn't let him forget that he was very much open to the making-up part.

Something that probably would never happen.

Because whenever Everly was around him, her thoughts probably went in a whole different direction. For her, he was a reminder of that night when they'd accidentally killed a woman.

"River has a record for assault," Noah went on, forcing his attention back on the work. "It happened during a heated argument at a party."

Which didn't necessarily prove the man had a violent streak. It could have been a one-time deal, maybe an argument that had gotten out of hand. Still, the assault charge didn't play in his favor.

Noah sent the files about River to his own computer, and he'd pore over them later. For now, he did a search on Daisy Reyes, and the moment her background info came up, he spotted something. And he groaned.

"Daisy Reyes is the daughter of the woman killed in the bar fight by Delbert Washington," Noah relayed to Everly.

That got her more than just glancing at him. She stood and looked at the screen. "Mercy, that's not a good connection."

No, it wasn't, and of course, it made Daisy their new person of interest. She could have killed Delbert out of revenge for her mother's death and then continued her vigilante cause. Or she could even be using the other murders to cover her tracks.

"I need to get my hands on records for Delbert's murder," Noah muttered, already emailing Houston PD to request the files.

Hoping that it would cause someone there to put a rush on it, he added that it was pertinent to his current murder investigation. Since Delbert's case was still unsolved, maybe it wouldn't take too long for the request to go through. If he didn't have the files though by midafternoon, Noah would have his lieutenant make a call to speed things up. The sooner he had info, the sooner he could do something to stop another murder.

"Here's something interesting on one of River's social media rants," Everly said. "Megan Ritter commented on it." Everly gave Noah another glance, and there was fresh concern in her eyes. "A post about the corruption in the courts, and Megan said, and I quote—'The courts are filled with people who don't give a damn. They don't care who gets hurt. Something has to be done to stop the injustice.'"

Noah definitely didn't like the tone of that. It was possible that Megan was just trying to be supportive of River, but that *something has to be done* could mean she'd taken matters into her own hands.

"You're positive Megan's alibi is airtight?" Everly asked, obviously considering exactly what he had.

Noah nodded. "She was at the movies in San Antonio with a group of friends. Security cameras confirm it. And there isn't anything to indicate that Megan hired anyone to do the job." He stopped, shook his head. "Of course, she could be working with River or someone else."

Everly made a sound to indicate she was giving that some thought. "Could one person have done the murders and moved the bodies? I mean, were there drag marks or something to indicate someone could have done it alone?"

"No drag marks on Jill, and if there'd been any on this latest victim, Grayson would have mentioned it. I'll check on Winona and Delbert to see if there were any. But to answer your question, yes, it's possible one person could have done this if they were strong enough to lift or had some way of moving an unconscious person. The drug the killer used on Jill would have incapacitated her within minutes."

"Minutes," Everly repeated in a mutter, and she shuddered. She was no doubt imagining just how it'd all gone down. "I have to protect Ainsley," she added, and even though her voice was mostly breath and little sound, Noah heard her. He felt the sickening dread from her fear.

"And you will. We will," he added.

She looked at him. "By going to the Silver Creek Ranch." She paused, gathered her breath. "Ironically, I have good memories of that place. I certainly went there enough when we were in high school. But the good memories could possibly trigger the bad ones. It took me five years of therapy just to be able to cope with the bad ones. And sometimes, the coping doesn't work. Sometimes, it all comes back."

Yeah. It was the same for him. He'd had the therapy, too, because his mom had insisted, and it'd helped. But nothing washed away the bone-deep guilt. Nothing. Guilt that had to be even worse for Everly.

He'd known about her therapy, but what she'd just left out was that she'd had a mental breakdown as well. That'd happened shortly after the accident, and her doctor had sent her to stay at a mental health hospital in San Antonio. Since Noah hadn't had any contact with her when she'd been there, he didn't know how it'd gone. Well enough for her to get out, eventually. However, she hadn't returned to high school but had instead finished her courses online.

Noah heard the footsteps heading toward the office, and he automatically got to his feet, going into defensive mode.

No threat though. It was Deputy Ava Lawson. Before becoming a Silver Creek deputy, she'd been a cop at San Antonio PD so Noah knew her. Knew, too, that she was darn good at her job.

"I thought I heard Grayson say this was your day off," Noah said to her.

Ava nodded. "Noah, Everly," she greeted. "But I spoke with Grayson, and he filled me in on what's going on. If you're ready to go to the day care and then the ranch, I can follow you as backup."

"Yes, please." Everly got to her feet, too. "I really need to see my daughter."

Ava made a sound to indicate she understood that. "Grayson suggested Noah and you use one of the cruisers." She handed Noah the keys. "There's one parked just out back."

Good idea about the cruiser, but Noah immediately thought of something. "When we pick up Ainsley, we'll need a child's car seat."

"Grayson already thought of that, and on the way over here, I called the daycare, and Sara said she could lend you one."

That was good, too, because it meant they wouldn't have to go back to Everly's to get hers from her vehicle.

Noah saved the searches they'd already started, and he shut down his laptop and gave it to Everly. She didn't ask why he'd done that because she no doubt knew he'd want to keep his hands free in case he had to draw his weapon. He prayed it didn't come down to that, but it was best not to take the risk.

They hadn't even made it out of the office when his phone rang, and he saw Grayson's name flash on the screen. Hell. Noah hoped this wasn't another round of bad news.

"What happened?" Noah asked the moment he answered.

"We got a quick hit on the fingerprints of our latest victim so we were able to ID her," Grayson replied just as fast. But then he paused. Sighed. "Daisy Reyes, the counselor at Peace Seekers, is the dead woman."

Chapter Five

Daisy Reyes.

Even though Everly had never met the woman, she had seen the DMV photo of her that Noah had pulled up after Grayson had given them the news.

That Daisy was apparently the latest victim of the vigilante killer.

Everly hadn't seen any pictures from the crime scene, thank goodness, but her imagination was working too well today, and she had no trouble conjuring up the images of the woman lying dead in her backyard. A location where the killer had no doubt placed her as a way to torment Noah and her.

It was working.

It was hard to think of anything else but the danger that could be heading straight at them.

Ainsley giggled at something she saw in the little book she was "reading," and Everly tried to latch on to the joyful sound of her daughter's laughter. Tried to let it anchor her. That and the fact that Ainsley didn't seem to be afraid or worried that she was in her car seat in the back of a Silver Creek cruiser while Noah drove them to the Ryland ranch.

As promised, Deputy Ava Lawson was behind them in

a second cruiser, and she was no doubt keeping watch just as Noah and Everly were doing, but they were on an extremely curvy country road where someone could lie in wait for them.

In the front seat and behind the wheel, Noah continued to make brief eye contact with her in the rearview mirror while he took a call from San Antonio detective Jake O'Malley. Everly didn't know the cop, but before they'd left the Silver Creek Sheriff's Office, Noah had called O'Malley and had asked him to run a thorough background on Daisy and the Peace Seekers support group.

"I've got that info you wanted on Daisy Reyes." O'Malley started the moment Noah took the call. Because he'd used the hands-free, the cop's voice poured through the cruiser.

"Good but keep it G-rated," Noah advised him. "I have passengers in the cruiser."

"Will do," O'Malley answered as if that were no big deal. "Daisy Reyes was thirty-two. Never married, no kids. She got her master's in clinical psychology from Baylor and at the time of her death was working for a domestic abuse shelter. She ran Peace Seekers on her own time."

"Did anyone at her work realize she was missing?" Noah asked.

"No. She had three days off and wasn't due into work until tomorrow. From what I can tell, she didn't have close friends outside work."

So, that would explain why no one reported her missing. Then again, maybe the killer hadn't had her that long.

"Her father's unknown," O'Malley went on, "and as you mentioned, eleven years ago her mother was killed in a bar fight by Delbert Washington who's now deceased. Delbert was charged with negligent homicide, but he worked out a plea deal to get probation and community service."

It was ironic that Delbert's sentence of no jail time had likely been what had led to his murder. Had he served time, he might still be alive.

And that only brought back more bad memories of the car crash.

No jail time for her was the reason both Noah and she were now on this killer's radar.

"You asked me to look for any instances when Daisy was arrested or under investigation, and I found nothing," O'Malley continued, drawing Everly's attention back to the conversation. "Either we're dealing with a copycat, or else there's another reason this vigilante did this to her."

Everly was going with option number two.

"What about a list of members of the Peace Seekers?" Noah pressed. "Anything on that?"

"No," the other cop readily admitted. "I'm working on it, but it'll be harder to find that now that Daisy's been murdered. She might be the only person who knew all the members."

Noah sighed. "Yeah, and that might have been the motive for why she became a victim. I've already spoken to one member, Jared Jackman, and I plan on speaking to another, River Parnell. According to Jared, there's a guy named Bobby in the group so if you see that or any of its variations pop up, let me know."

"Will do," O'Malley assured him.

When Noah ended the call, he glanced at her in the mirror again. No doubt to see how she was handling all of this. She wasn't handling it well.

"I won't fall apart," Everly assured him. Not as long as Ainsley was around anyway.

She wasn't sure Noah believed that, but he shifted his attention from her as they drove through the massive gates of the Ryland ranch. Actually, *massive* applied to the ranch itself, and even though the front part of it was acres of lush green pastures, she saw the houses and outbuildings scattered seemingly everywhere. Everly had no idea how many people actually lived here, what with his uncles, aunts and cousins, but it was like a small town.

It'd been years since she'd been here. So many memories, and Everly tried to tamp down her racing heartbeat and too-quick breath. A situation like this could be a perfect storm for the mother lode of flashbacks. She was terrified for her child's safety and worried about being a killer's target. Added to that, she'd be sharing close quarters with a man who could trigger those flashbacks simply because he'd been part of the nightmare ordeal all those years ago.

"I've already told my dad and Uncle Mason to keep watch as to who comes and goes from the ranch," Noah explained. Maybe because he was trying to reduce the wariness he saw in her eyes.

"There are a lot of ranch hands," she muttered. And she suspected there were also plenty of deliveries and visitors.

"Yes, but all the hands have been vetted," he assured her. "They'll keep a lookout for anyone suspicious."

She didn't doubt that, but it'd be impossible for them to stop any and all threats. Everly saw proof of that as she watched several men unloading horses at what she knew was his uncle Mason's section of the grounds. Since Mason was a former deputy, he was likely being cautious, but someone—the killer—could slip in with such a delivery and disappear onto the ranch.

Definitely not a comforting thought.

"How good is the security system in your house?" she asked.

"Good," he quickly verified as his gaze skirted around. He took the turn off the main ranch road and onto an even narrower one. "My mom and dad are there now with Hudson Granger, the tech who handles security for the ranch, and he's installing some new equipment."

It probably shouldn't have surprised her that a ranch this size would have its own security specialist, and while it might seem over-the-top, there were a lot of homes, prized livestock and equipment here. Added to that, the Rylands were rich so those homes probably had expensive items in them.

More proof of the size of the ranch, Noah drove for at least another mile before he reached the end of the road. The trees were thicker here with the waters of the shallow creek winding through them. Beyond the creek were the woods with trees still thick with leaves even though they were showing the first signs of autumn. Not exactly close to the road, but it would be a good place for someone to sneak onto the ranch.

"The fences are all rigged with security cameras and motion detectors," Noah explained after he'd followed her gaze.

Good. She wanted any and all measures to keep Ainsley safe.

Everly turned her attention back to the road, and just ahead she spotted the house with the white stone and pale gray wood exterior. According to talk she'd heard, he'd had the place built shortly after he'd finished college, and while it was his primary residence, he also owned an apartment near his work in San Antonio. A reminder that Noah was rich as well, but then she suspected most of the Ryland offspring had trust funds.

There were two silver SUVs that sported the ranch's name on the side parked in Noah's driveway. The vehicles probably belonged to his parents and the tech, but Noah didn't park near them. He used the app on his phone to open the garage door, and he drove inside. He immediately lowered the garage doors, a reminder that while the fence was secure, there could be a sniper in those idyllic-looking woods.

Ainsley laid aside her book, and she looked around the garage. "Ome?" She meant *home*, and Everly had to shake her head.

"A vacation," Everly lied. "We're going to have fun and play here for a while."

Ainsley probably didn't understand vacation though Everly had taken the girl to the beach. But she clearly got the "fun and play" part because her little face brightened, and she began to try to get herself out of the child seat.

Everly helped with that after she'd gotten out of the cruiser. She scooped Ainsley into her arms just as someone opened the door that led into the house. Everly instinctively pulled Ainsley closer to her, but it wasn't a threat. It was Noah's mother. Darcy.

Considering the size of Silver Creek, Everly ran into Darcy now and then, and they usually settled for a polite hello, but Darcy offered her a beaming smile today. One that was no doubt meant to try to reassure her that all was going to be just fine.

"Everly," Darcy greeted. She went to her and hugged her,

and she extended the smile to Ainsley. "And this must be your daughter. She looks like you."

She did, and there were so many times Everly was thankful for that. She would have loved her child no matter what, but it was nice not to look at Ainsley and see her ex's features.

"Grayson said we couldn't get anything from Everly's house, but everything here is set up," Darcy added to Noah, and she slipped her arm around Everly to get them moving inside. "I might have gone a little overboard with the playroom though."

Noah groaned, but he kissed his mother's cheek, obviously letting her know that was okay. There was a lot of love between Noah and his family. Always had been, and Everly figured that had helped him get through these past fourteen years.

They went inside the house into the open living room and kitchen that managed to look both modern and cozy at the same time. Noah had gone with a farmhouse kitchen, complete with a large dining table.

"Want to find some toys?" Darcy asked Ainsley, and when Ainsley muttered a yes, Noah's mom led them to a large bedroom that had obviously been converted for a two year old. There were a toddler bed, books, stuffed animals and lots and lots of toys.

"Mom," Noah muttered on a sigh. "You definitely went overboard."

"I did," Darcy readily admitted. "Lots of family helped, and I had Leah come over and make sure it was kid safe." Leah was the daughter of Noah's uncle Kade, and she had a son just a little younger than Ainsley.

"Thank you," Everly told Darcy, and she'd obviously need to thank others who'd helped set all of this up.

Ainsley immediately squirmed to get down, and the moment Everly stood her on the floor, the little girl took off to explore her new stash.

"Your dad's on the back porch with Hudson," Darcy told Noah. "They're dealing with the new cameras."

"I'll check on them," Noah said. He turned but then stopped to make eye contact with Everly. She was pretty sure he was silently asking if it was okay for him to leave her for a couple of minutes, and she nodded. The cameras and other security stuff were important.

Even if that meant being left with Darcy.

"Noah's worried about you," Darcy murmured after Noah had left. "And I'm worried about both of you. Nate's trying to downplay it, but I was a cop's wife for more years that I care to count so I know when things have to be taken seriously. We're all taking this very seriously."

"Thank you," Everly repeated, and she watched her daughter scurry from one new toy to the other.

"Don't worry," Darcy went on, "Nate and I won't be underfoot. We'll leave as soon as the security is in place, and we're just up the road if you need anything." She motioned to the room across the hall. "That's the guest room, and there's an attached bath and sitting area that you can use as office space."

That required another thanks. Obviously, Noah and his mother had thought of pretty much everything.

Darcy laughed when Ainsley found a stash of blocks that caused her to giggle and spill them all out on a play mat. "It's nice to be around kids," Darcy remarked. "I miss the toddler stage."

Everly knew that Darcy didn't have grandchildren, and that none of her three kids were married yet. Noah's sister, Kim, was an assistant district attorney, and their younger brother, Hayden, was a marshal.

"I hope Ainsley and I don't disrupt Noah's life too much," Everly commented.

"You won't," Darcy assured her. "Noah loves kids." She stopped, her eyes widening a bit as if she couldn't believe what she'd just said.

And because of small-town gossip, Everly knew the reason for the woman's reaction.

Noah had been engaged five years earlier to a fellow SAPD cop, and he and his fiancée lost their child late in the pregnancy. Apparently, the loss and grief had been too much for the relationship because they'd broken up.

When Noah and she had been teenagers, Everly recalled him talking about how one day he'd like to be a father. Very unlike most teenage boys. So losing his child would have been a very deep cut. Everly totally understood that, now that she was a parent. She couldn't imagine losing Ainsley. And just like that, she got a slam of the fear that she might not be able to keep her baby safe.

Everly had to fight to tamp down the roar of panic, and the sound of voices helped with that. Noah and his father, and a second later, they came into the room. As Darcy had done, Nate greeted Everly with a welcoming smile and turned that smile on Ainsley.

"The security cameras are all set up," Nate assured her. "They're aimed at the windows and doors so you'll still have privacy once you're inside." He pointed to the trio of cameras mounted on the sides of each of the windows in the room.

"Inside because it'll make it harder for someone to tamper with them," Noah explained.

Since the panic was still right there, just beneath the surface, that gave her another jolt. Noah must have noticed it because he discreetly touched his hand to the back of hers. Just a touch. But it was enough to remind her that Everly didn't have to do this alone.

That was both good and bad news.

Good, because she needed Noah and his family's help. Bad, because that touch brought back all the memories of when touching each other had been their norm. A norm that had always generated a lot of heat. Despite everything going on, that hadn't changed, and that's why Everly silently cursed.

Being this close to Noah was not going to be easy.

But for a whole lot of reasons, she had to resist this heat. She couldn't deal with the constant reminder of the past. Another reminder, too, that she didn't exactly have a stellar track record when it came to relationships. The proof of that was Philip who'd basically rejected his own child before she'd even been born. Ainsley deserved better than that, and while Noah wasn't Philip, Everly didn't want to bring the possibility of that kind of turmoil into her little girl's life. Especially now, where they had the turmoil from the danger to face.

"Look," Darcy whispered, motioning toward Ainsley.

Her daughter was cuddling a stuffed horse on the bed, and she was falling asleep. It was her usual nap time, but Everly had thought the excitement of all the new toys would keep her awake. Apparently not.

"Here's a baby monitor," Darcy whispered, picking up the

handheld and giving it to Everly. "I can watch her though, if you've got work to do."

"Thanks, but I'd rather stay close," Everly answered. Though she might borrow a laptop from Noah in order to continue researching their persons of interest.

"I understand," Darcy assured her. "But if you change your mind, let me know. Also, Leah said she can send over her nanny if needed." She patted Everly's arm. "We'll help in any way we can."

That brought on another round of heartfelt thanks from Everly, and after they'd said their goodbyes, Noah walked his parents to the door. Several moments later, he came back to join her in the doorway.

"I've locked up and set the security system," Noah let her know. The corner of his mouth lifted when his attention landed on Ainsley. "How long will she sleep?"

"Normally about two hours. Not sure she'll be out that long though, since she's obviously out of her usual routine. When she gets up, she'll want a snack so I need to see what you have in the fridge."

"My dad said Mom stocked it. There are four kinds of milk. Four," he added with a sigh. "There's also plenty of fruit and toddler crackers and such."

Everly sighed, too. It was harder for her to keep up this barrier between Noah and her when both he and his family were bending over backward for her.

"I'll help keep her as safe as possible," Noah murmured while he kept his gaze on Ainsley.

"I know you will, and I thank you for that." She paused. Had to. Because Noah was standing so close to her that it was causing that heat to stir again. "Maybe we can work until Ainsley wakes up?"

"Absolutely." He didn't hesitate, but Everly thought she saw some hesitation in his eyes.

Noah motioned for her to follow him to the guest room across the hall. It was huge, decorated in a soothing pale green, and his mother had been right about it having a seating area. One already set up with a desk and a laptop.

"Maybe you can focus on social media sites to help us ID any members of Peace Seekers," Noah suggested, and Everly gave him a quick nod. "Let me grab my computer, and I'll join you."

Noah left while she settled in at the desk. Since she didn't want to dwell on the thoughts of Noah and their situation, she set the monitor so she could easily see it, opened the laptop and got started right away. Everly had only been at it a couple of minutes when Noah returned with not only his computer tucked under his arm but also a plate with two sandwiches, potato chips and two bottles of water.

"Mom really stocked the fridge," he commented. "Good thing because you missed lunch."

She had, but Everly wasn't sure her knotted stomach could handle food just yet. Noah dived right into his sandwich while setting up his laptop on the side of the desk next to hers. When he abruptly stopped eating though, she glanced over to see what had snagged his attention. Judging from his somber expression, it hadn't snagged it in a good way either.

"My lieutenant got the lab results expedited for the boxes we got," he explained while he continued to read the report he'd pulled up on his screen. "The blood on the clothes left for me belongs to Jill. However, the blood on the box you received doesn't. The lab will run tests to see if it belongs to Daisy."

Everly had to take in a long breath and try to loosen those knots that were tightening even more. Because if the blood wasn't Daisy's, it could mean there was another victim. One who hadn't been found yet.

She almost managed to bite back a groan. "The killer probably believes there are plenty of people who need punishing. That means, he has so many to choose from."

"Yeah," Noah softly agreed. "And that's why we need that members' list for Peace Seekers." He checked the monitor, no doubt seeing that Ainsley was still sound asleep, and took out his phone. "I'm calling Megan Ritter and then River Parnell. I'd rather have a face-to-face with them, but this will do for now."

Everly agreed. Talking to both of them in person would be better, but it was critical that they get info fast. She didn't know what kind of plan the killer had for Noah and her, but she doubted they had a lot of time.

"I spoke to Megan yesterday," Noah explained. "*Briefly* spoke to her. She wasn't at home for me to notify of her mother's death so I called her. She was at work, said she didn't care what'd happened to her mom, that she hadn't seen her in years. I pressed for her whereabouts, she gave them to me and the alibi checked out."

Noah made the call, put it on Speaker and a groggy sounding woman answered on the third ring.

"Yeah?" she said, and she made a noisy yawn.

"Megan?" Noah asked.

"Yeah," the woman repeated. "Who is this? If you're calling for me to come in early for my shift, it's not going to happen."

Since Everly had researched Megan's social media accounts, she knew the woman worked as a hostess at a busy San Antonio River Walk restaurant.

"This is Detective Noah Ryland," he explained. "We spoke yesterday."

Megan muttered some profanity. "Look, I told you I didn't want to hear anything about my so-called mother. I don't care if her killer isn't caught—"

"The person who murdered Jill killed another woman," Noah interrupted. He didn't give her Daisy's name, maybe because the notification of next of kin hadn't been done.

"For real?" Megan asked, and she no longer sounded groggy or annoyed.

"For real," Noah verified. "In fact, I believe the killer has murdered at least four people they believe didn't get punishment they deserved."

Megan stayed quiet for several seconds. "So, the killer isn't going after innocent people," she concluded.

"The victims didn't deserve to be murdered. Maybe jail time, *maybe*," he emphasized, "but not murder." Noah paused. "I also believe the killer murdered someone they were just trying to silence, and that's why I need your help."

Megan paused again. "You think I know who's doing this. I don't."

"Maybe you know more than you think. I believe there's someone in the Peace Seekers who can help with the investigation. What are the names of the members in the group?"

The woman made a sharp sound of surprise. "You think the killer could be in the group?"

Everly definitely thought that. Or at least it could be someone connected to the group, but Noah clearly wasn't ready to spell that out to Megan just yet.

"I believe someone in the group has information that'll help me," Noah explained. "Tell me the names of the members."

"I don't know them all," she readily admitted. "Some only show up for a meeting and never come back. Some only use their first names or a nickname."

That meshed with what Jared had told them, but Noah continued to push. "What about a man who calls himself Bobby?"

"Bobby," she repeated. "I don't know his name."

"Why is he in the group?" Noah asked.

"I have no idea. He's still carrying a red card."

Noah frowned. "A red card?"

"Yeah. When a new member shows up, they can take a red card from the table, and that means they don't want to talk or have anyone ask questions. Most ditch the red card after a meeting or two, but Bobby hasn't."

"How long has he been coming to Peace Seekers?" Noah wanted to know.

Megan made a noncommittal sound. "A couple of months or so."

That sounded like the perfect arrangement for a vigilante killer to find targets. He could listen to all the gripes and grief and then add the offenders to his hit list.

So, how had Noah and she gotten on this guy's radar?

Had someone in the group mentioned them? Was the killer also scouring other sources to find his victim? Maybe. In this case, Everly thought the way the killer was getting his info would definitely lead Noah and her to identifying him.

"Give me the names of others in the group," Noah told Megan.

This time, Megan huffed. "Look, I'm not comfortable spilling this. You should talk to the counselor, Daisy Reyes. If anyone gives you a list, you should get it from her."

And they would have done just that if the killer hadn't gotten to her first. Noah though, didn't spell that out.

"Remember, this person killed someone who was innocent," Noah reminded Megan. "Your help can maybe stop someone else from dying."

"Maybe someone like my mother who deserved to die?" Megan snapped. "Thanks but no thanks. Goodbye, Detective Ryland." And with that, she ended the call.

Noah sat there for a moment, staring at the phone, no doubt processing what Megan had just told him. With her alibi, Megan obviously wasn't the killer, and Noah had already said there was nothing to indicate she'd hired someone to off her mother. Still, Megan probably knew more that could help them.

"I'll arrange for Megan to be brought in for an interview," Noah finally said. He looked at her. "I'll need to do that one in person so I can press her. By then, too, I can tell her Daisy's been murdered. That should shake Megan into spilling what she knows."

"I'd like to be there to hear what she has to say," Everly blurted out before she realized what that meant. Noah and she would be out and about, where the killer could possibly get to them.

And maybe that wasn't a bad thing.

If Ainsley was tucked away safely here at the ranch with lots of protection so that this monster couldn't try to use her, then maybe the killer would come directly after her.

"No," Noah said. "You're not going to make yourself bait."

Either he had ESP or else he knew her far better than

she'd expected. Well, she knew him, too, and he'd see the logic of this once she made it clear.

"We can't just shut ourselves away," she said. "Because this snake will just keep killing. He wants us. *Me*," Everly emphasized. "And while I'm not especially eager to cross paths with him, the threat to Ainsley and others has to stop. *We* have to stop it, and we can do that by going to interview Megan, River Parnell and maybe even Jared. We push away at them until they tell us who this Bobby is."

Noah kept his narrowed eyes pinned on her. "I'm not going to let you use yourself as bait," he spelled out.

Everly swiveled her chair around so they were face-to-face, eye to eye. "Bait with backup. When we go to the interviews, you could bring a deputy or another detective with us. One who'll stay out of sight, maybe like laying low on the backseat or something. We could wear Kevlar," she added.

It still twisted at her stomach to consider doing this, but the fear and worry were only going to skyrocket until the danger to Ainsley was over. The way to end that danger fast was to catch the killer and put him away.

Noah stayed quiet, obviously considering all of that, and he cursed under his breath. "I'll think about it," he finally said but didn't get a chance to add more because his phone rang, and Everly saw a familiar name on the screen.

River Parnell.

"Detective Ryland," River snapped the moment Noah answered. "I just got a call from Megan. Why the hell would you scare her like that?"

Noah gathered his breath before he spoke. "I scared her because I told her the truth. That a serial killer murdered her mother, and they might be connected to Peace Seekers."

River certainly didn't jump to deny that. "You want the membership list for the group," he finally said.

"I do," Noah verified, "and if you don't have an actual list, I'll need any names you know."

River's groan was low but still plenty loud enough for Everly to hear. "Let me talk to Daisy about that, and I'll get back to you."

Again, Noah didn't spill about Daisy being dead, but if River was their killer, he already knew that. "We'll talk," Noah insisted. "For an official interview. I'll get in touch with you to give you a specific time. And FYI, it's your right to have an attorney present during that."

Now River cursed. "Am I a suspect?"

"What do you think?" Noah countered, and he hung up. He looked at Everly again as he put his phone away. "Tomorrow morning, you and I—and a backup lawman—will pay River a visit."

Some of the tightness eased inside her, but it was quickly replaced by the realization that Noah and she were about to put themselves in the direct path of a killer.

Chapter Six

While Noah loaded the breakfast dishes into the dishwasher, he refused to keep dwelling on how much of a mistake it was to set Everly and himself up as bait. That's because he'd already spent most of the night doing just that, and since he couldn't figure out a faster way to draw out a killer, he'd chosen to focus on the logistics of making this trip to see River as safe as possible.

He hoped he'd succeeded.

In addition to bringing along his cousin, Deputy Theo Sheldon, who'd stay out of sight, Noah had made sure they were both armed with backup weapons and extra ammo. He'd gone with Everly's idea, too, of them wearing Kevlar. Even though the killer had never shot any of his victims, that didn't mean they wouldn't do just that if the opportunity came up.

Noah had to make sure an opportunity didn't happen.

That meant getting Everly inside with River after Noah had checked to make sure the man wasn't armed and ready to gun them down. After all, River was a prime suspect with means and motive. If the man didn't have alibis for the murders, then Noah could add opportunity to the mix.

Means, motive and opportunity were the law enforcement trifecta when it came to suspects.

Noah was hoping this interview would give them lots of info, including the names of the others in the Peace Seekers, but that might not even be necessary if River let something slip that could lead to his arrest. Then, Noah could get Everly back to her daughter.

Back to her life, too.

He silently cursed the gut punch that gave him. Part of him, a big part, didn't want to let go of the connection they had again. A connection forged by danger and fresh attraction, but he also didn't want to be the reason for more nightmares for her. He'd certainly be a reminder of the past, and he was going to have to accept that might never change.

His mental pep talk took a nosedive when Everly came in. Yeah, there was fresh attraction all right, and Noah couldn't stop himself from noticing the way her blue pants and a loose top were nearly the same color as her eyes. It was an outfit that one of the ranch hands had gotten from her house the night before after Grayson and the CSIs had given them the all clear for someone to go over and get some of Ainsley's and her things. Two suitcases full, but Noah was betting that Everly was hoping the items wouldn't be needed, that she would soon be able to go home.

But he rethought that, too.

He wondered if she'd ever think of the place as a safe haven again. After all, a murdered woman had been dumped in her yard. Would she ever be able to look at the yard, or the porch, and not remember the grisly things the killer had left for her in those spots?

"You'd better not be changing your mind about this," Everly said, obviously noting his expression. She tugged at the Kevlar beneath her top. "Because it's taken everything inside me to leave my daughter with your folks and Ava while we try to put an end to this. It's the right thing to do," she tacked on to that.

"It is," he agreed. Yes, he had doubts, plenty of them, but he had even greater doubts about them doing nothing to stop more killings.

"How's Ainsley?" he asked though Noah was certain he already knew the answer.

He'd seen her at breakfast, had listened to her babble and giggle about her new toys. The babbling and giggling had continued when his parents and Ava had arrived, and the little girl obviously thought of this as a great adventure.

"She's reading a book with your mom," Everly answered.

"Mom's good with kids," Noah reminded her when he saw a flash of the nerves in her eyes. "And Ava will keep watch." The deputy would do that on a laptop that Hudson had set up so she'd been able to monitor all the new cameras. "Added to that, the gate will be locked, and the ranch hands have strict orders. No visitors, no deliveries."

There were other security measures, too, such as having some armed hands patrol the fence line. His uncles and cousins would be on alert as well and would be looking for anything and anyone suspicious. In other words, they'd turned the ranch into as much of a fortress as it could be.

"It'll be okay," Everly murmured, and Noah was 100 percent sure she was saying that to steady her nerves. He wasn't sure though that the assurance was working.

He went to her and took hold of her hand. Even that simple gesture was a risk because it was still touching. Added to that, they were close and standing face-to-face. Mere inches apart. And that was the problem with having been lovers in the past. Even under the circumstances, their bodies could rev up in a snap.

She sighed, but she might as well have shouted from the rooftops that the heat was still there. Worse, Everly's gaze dropped to his mouth, and he wondered if she was remembering how they'd once kissed. He certainly was. Remembering it and wanting to do it again. He resisted though and got some help in that area when his phone dinged with a text.

"It's Theo," he relayed. "He's in place on the backseat of the cruiser." Theo had done that with the vehicle parked in the garage. That way, if anyone had them under long-range surveillance, they wouldn't know another cop was with them.

"It's time to go," Everly muttered. He saw her gaze zip to the playroom, and she was no doubt considering going in to say another goodbye to Ainsley, but she shook her head. "She might start crying if she sees me leave. She does that sometimes, and I might not be able to take it if it happens today."

No, that wouldn't be a good way to start this trip. Thankfully, a short trip. Noah already had River's residence in his GPS. The man lived on a small ranch only about twenty minutes away. So that River would have a chance to get a lawyer, Noah had told River when they'd be arriving. It was a risk, since the man could use the time to set up an ambush, but Noah hadn't wanted to drive out to River's ranch only to find him not at home.

Again, Noah tried to push aside all the worry about what could go wrong, and Everly and he got in the cruiser to start the drive. Behind them, Theo moved onto the floor behind the backseat to prevent someone from seeing him and finished a call from Grayson.

"Grayson said I'm to let you know that the CSIs have finished processing the crime scene at Everly's but didn't recover any evidence other than the body and the bloody box," Theo relayed. "Also, SAPD CSI went through Daisy's place, and it'd been ransacked. Her laptop and phone were missing."

None of that surprised Noah about the missing items. The killer wouldn't have wanted to leave anything behind that could ID him, and Daisy might have not only had the membership list but notes about members as well.

"The forensic techs will try to find out if Daisy used a storage cloud for files about the Peace Seekers," Theo went on. "And your lieutenant at SAPD will send out a detective this morning to talk to Daisy's coworkers and neighbors to find out if they saw or heard anything. Or if they know if Daisy received a suspicious box."

That was a necessary thread to tie off, but Noah wasn't expecting much since Daisy had worked at a domestic abuse shelter where plenty of things were kept confidential. Still, Daisy might have shared some small facts about the Peace Seekers they could use. Added to that, if she'd gotten a box, a neighbor might have seen it. But Noah was still thinking Daisy was the exception to the killer's MO.

"When will you talk to Megan?" Everly asked, but she wasn't looking at him. Like Noah, her gaze was firing all around them. Looking for a killer.

"This afternoon if the meeting with River goes off without a hitch." A hitch being plenty of things from a killer striking to River's arrest. "Depending on how things go, Megan is coming to my office at SAPD. I thought the official setting might tone down her venom and make her more cooperative. Just in case she knows more than she's saying about the members of Peace Seekers." He paused. "Again, depending on the outcome of this meeting, you can go with me to San Antonio and observe the interview."

Everly hesitated. Then, she nodded. "That's when you'll tell her about Daisy being murdered?"

"Yes, and that might shock her into cooperating, too." He could use that now that Daisy's next of kin had been notified.

Since there was no direct route to the ranch where River lived, Noah had to thread his way through the rural roads. He was well aware that anyone who'd have them under surveillance could have anticipated this route and could be preparing for an attack. But Noah didn't see anything to suggest that. Of course, the preparing could be happening at their destination.

As he drove, Noah saw the small farms and ranches dotting the landscape. The houses were few and far between here, and from his research, he'd learned that River's nearest neighbor was a good quarter of a mile away. Noah passed that neighbor before River's ranch came into view.

The small house and equally small barn were at the end of a very narrow road. Emphasis on narrow. It was flanked by two fairly deep irrigation ditches, and Noah suspected when it rained, it'd make for one hard trip in and out of here. It'd be very easy for tires to slip into those ditches and get bogged down.

"Turn on your wire," Theo instructed when Noah pulled to a stop.

Noah was indeed wearing a wire, and Theo would be monitoring the feed through his earpiece. It was yet another security precaution in case all hell broke loose.

The front door opened, and River stepped out. Probably

because he'd heard the vehicle. The man was wearing baggy cargo shorts and a white tee. He was barefooted, and either he'd recently gotten out of bed or else he'd yet to comb his hair. River obviously hadn't dressed for the interview, and since there was only one other vehicle, a blue truck, that meant he probably hadn't brought in a lawyer.

"I'm Detective Noah Ryland," he said, stepping from the cruiser.

"Yeah, I figured as much," River grumbled. He raked his hand through his mop of long sandy brown hair to push it from his face.

Noah couldn't see any weapons, and since River was drinking from a coffee mug, his right hand was occupied. Still, he'd keep a close watch on him.

"I have Everly Monroe, an attorney from Silver Creek with me," Noah continued, staying put for the moment. "Is it okay if she comes in with me while we talk?"

River tipped his head toward the open door. "The more, the merrier," he muttered with a boatload of sarcasm. Still drinking from the mug, he went inside.

Noah did another check around the grounds, and when he didn't see anyone, he went to the passenger's side of the cruiser and had Everly get out. He kept her close, ready to drag her to the ground if it became necessary.

"Move fast," Noah instructed her in a whisper. "If the killer's out here, I don't want to be easy targets."

Everly did as he asked, and once they reached the doorway of the house, Noah moved in front of her until he had a good visual of River. The man was sitting in a recliner. When Noah didn't spot any weapons, he got Everly inside and shut the door.

"I tried to call Daisy about getting that membership list,"

River said, eating from a bag of microwave popcorn, "but she didn't return my call. Anyone else get it for you yet?"

Noah shook his head. "No, but I have a few names. Who's Bobby?"

"The red card guy," River said without hesitating. "I don't know. And FYI, I don't trust him."

"Why?" Noah immediately asked.

River lifted his shoulder. "The guy just sits there and listens. Hell, he might not even need to seek any peace. Some people get off on that, listening to other people's grief and stories about their misery."

"You really think that's what he's doing?" Noah pressed.

Another shrug from River. "He could be, and now that somebody killed Megan's scumbag mother, I guess you're thinking it could be him."

"Or someone else in the group." Noah paused, his stare drilling into River.

River finally cursed. "You think I killed somebody?" But the man didn't wait for an answer. "Well, I didn't."

"We've read your social media posts," Noah spelled out for him. "You're pretty angry about what your mother did."

"Damn right I'm angry. No justice. But that doesn't mean I'd turn killer." He spat out more profanity and looked at Everly. "What about you, Miss Lawyer From Silver Creek? Do you believe I killed someone?"

She didn't jump to answer, and she met River's intense stare. "I don't know, but we need to stop anyone else from dying. That's why the membership list is so important. Who else is in the group?"

River sank back against the recliner and sighed. "Jared Jackman. The only reason I remember his last name is because in one of the lighter moments in the group, he joked about not being related to Hugh Jackman. He's all right, I guess. No red card, anyway. He's there because some careless driver put him in a wheelchair. If you think I've got anger issues, mine are a molehill compared to his mountain of them."

"Oh?" Everly said, and it was obviously enough to prompt River into continuing.

"Yeah, big-time anger issues. Now, that's a guy who could kill. I mean, if he wasn't in a wheelchair and all."

Noah had picked up on that vibe, too, and Jared had been the one who'd pointed the finger at River. He made a mental note to dig deep into Jared's financials to see if he had the resources to hire a killer. Noah would do the same for River, though if the man had money, he obviously wasn't using it to make improvements to the ranch.

"That said," River went on, "if Jared had killed that woman who put him in the chair, then she would have deserved it. I mean, she ended his life, and there's that whole eye-for-an-eye deal."

"Does that mean you would have killed your mother had you gotten the chance?" Noah asked.

That earned him an eye roll and a huff from River. "No."

Noah continued to stare at him, hoping he was making the man nervous enough to spill something he'd rather not spill. "Tell me where you were early yesterday morning," Noah insisted.

"Here," River supplied. "And no, I can't prove that."

"Did you do some work? Because if so, maybe the work file will give me the time you accessed it."

River's mouth went into a flat line. "I didn't work. I'm not exactly a morning person so I usually don't start until around lunch. I keep at it until about dinner time."

Well, that definitely wouldn't give him an alibi for the time of Daisy's murder or for the boxes left for Everly and him.

Noah threw out another date and estimated time. This one for Jill's murder. "What about then? Where were you?"

River's stare became as flat as his mouth. "I was here. Look, before you rattle off more dates and accusations, the only place I usually go is to the Peace Seekers meetings. I hit the grocery store on my way back from those, and sometimes I hang out with friends at a bar in town."

The man paused, leaned forward. "Has it occurred to you that the real killer knows I wouldn't have alibis and is trying to set me up?" River didn't wait for an answer. "Who in the group told you about me? Who gave you my name to put you on my trail?"

Noah had no intentions of divulging that, but it was possible River might be able to figure it out, and Noah made a mental note to contact Jared and ask if he wanted police protection.

"I'm collecting information from a lot of sources," Noah settled for saying. "Not just the Peace Seekers. You've made a lot of angry posts on social media, and according to what you just said, you don't have alibis."

River cursed again, but he didn't get a chance to add anything else because of the sound of a car approaching. With River's attention on the window, Noah checked his phone. He'd silenced it before coming in for the interview, but he saw Theo's text on-screen.

Someone's coming, Theo had messaged. Can't see who yet.

Noah went on full alert. He stood, getting Everly to her feet so he could put her behind him. River got up as well, went to the window and muttered something under his breath that Noah didn't catch.

"It's Megan," River relayed to him.

Megan might have that airtight alibi for her mother's murder, but that didn't mean she hadn't brought the killer with her. Or that she wasn't there to assist River in trying to murder Everly and him.

Noah and Everly waited inside while River went onto the porch, but Noah watched through the window. Megan came to a fast stop behind the cruiser, and without looking inside, she hurried toward River. Her hands were empty; she wasn't even carrying a purse, and her face was red as if she'd been crying. The moment she reached River, she threw herself into his arms.

"Daisy's dead," Megan sobbed out. "Somebody killed her."

Noah continued to watch, noting River's and Megan's reactions. Megan's shock and grief seemed like the real deal. *Seemed.* Over the years, Noah had learned that people were often very good at putting up facades.

River's response wasn't tears, grief or even shock, but he did go visibly stiff. Maybe because he was genuinely surprised at the news or because he wanted them to think he was surprised.

"Is Detective Ryland here?" Megan asked.

River nodded, slipped his arm around Megan's waist and led her inside. Megan's teary gaze went straight to Noah.

"Why didn't you stop this?" Megan demanded. "Why did you let that monster murder Daisy?"

Noah had already steeled himself up for the accusation. "I'm here to try to stop anyone else from being murdered. If you want that, too, then you'll cooperate. You, as well," he added to River. "And you'll tell us everything about the Peace Seekers."

The fresh shock went through Megan's eyes. "You think River and I could be targets?"

Noah went with the honest answer. "You could be. Anyone who could know the killer's identity could be." He slid his cop's gaze from Megan to River. If River was the vigilante, that might stop him from murdering Megan. "Tell us everything about the group," he repeated.

Megan wiped her eyes, made a choked sob. "Bobby Marshall. That's the name of the red card member you were asking about. I didn't remember his last name until this morning, but then I recalled him telling Daisy that was his name when they were exchanging contact information."

"Bobby Marshall," Everly repeated, and she took out her phone no doubt to start a search on him.

"Was that common for Daisy to exchange contact info with group members?" Noah asked.

River and Megan looked at each other, shook their heads. "It sounded though as if Bobby was trying to set up private counseling sessions with her."

That would have given the man access to Daisy, and it would explain why her phone and laptop had been taken. Then again, River would have had access to Daisy as well. If he'd shown up at her apartment, Daisy likely would have let him in.

"That's why you asked me where I was early yesterday morning," River muttered. "You wanted to know if I had an alibi for Daisy's murder. I don't," he added with a groan. "But I wouldn't kill her. She was trying to help us."

True, but for a killer covering his tracks, Daisy would have been a huge liability.

"What are you going to do to keep us safe?" Megan demanded, drawing Noah's attention back to her.

"Do you want police protection?" Noah asked her, glancing at River to let him know the offer applied to him as well.

All in all, it was a good offer, and Noah watched to see their reaction. Megan quickly nodded, but River's forehead bunched up. Either giving that some thought or trying to figure out how to decline it and not look guilty as hell.

"I don't want cops watching my every move," River finally said. "But I'll lock up at night and watch my back."

And that response put River at the very top of his list of suspects. Of course, Noah didn't have enough to arrest him, but he should be able to convince a judge to get them a search warrant to go through River's house and vehicle. Slashes to the femoral artery would have created a lot of blood loss and spatter. A careful killer would have made sure he didn't bring any of that spatter home with him, but maybe River had gotten sloppy.

"Have either of you recently received any packages you weren't expecting?" Noah asked them.

"No," Megan said. "What kind of packages?"

Noah had no intention of spilling that. "Just something you hadn't expected," he confined himself to saying.

Megan repeated her no, and after a few seconds, River shook his head. "No. Does that have to do with the killer?"

Yeah, it did since the other victims and both Everly and he had received the boxes. It was a good sign that Megan hadn't, even though the killer might break pattern with her as well if he thought she knew too much.

Noah sent a text to Detective Jake O'Malley and asked him to make the arrangement for Megan. When he finished and got the okay from O'Malley, Noah turned back to Megan.

"When you leave, I want you to go straight to SAPD headquarters in the public safety building," he instructed. "Use the interstate to get there, not the back roads." Unlike Silver Creek, it would be a fairly straight shot for her to get into the city since the interstate was only a couple of miles away. "When you arrive at headquarters, see Detective Jake O'Malley. He'll make sure you have police protection."

"Thank you," Megan gushed out, and the relief seemed to wash over her. She gave River a quick hug and hurried out the door to her car. Noah didn't think Megan was at high risk, but he hoped she'd do as he had lain out for her.

"You're sure you won't take protection?" Noah asked River after Megan had gone.

"Positive," he said but then paused. "Look, I'm sorry about Daisy, but I'd rather put some distance between me and the cops. The way I see it, if the killer thinks I'm cooperating with you, then he might come after me."

Possibly, but that kind of logic wouldn't lower the man on the suspect list. Noah left River his card, figuring he'd see how the rest of the day played out, and then he'd have River brought into headquarters for another interview. He would keep applying the heat and hoped that it caused River to break. Then again, even intense heat might not break a cold-blooded killer.

With Noah and Everly keeping watch, they went back out to the cruiser and got in. River didn't come out onto the porch, but he stood at the window watching them as Noah turned around in the driveway.

"I've got a friend in the Bulverde PD," Theo said, staying

down on the floor of the cruiser. "You want me to ask them about getting a search warrant for this place?"

"Thanks, but I'll take care of that," Noah replied. He wanted someone he knew, hopefully Jake O'Malley, in charge of the search. O'Malley wouldn't miss anything important.

Everly had put her phone away when they'd hurried back out to the vehicle, but she took it out now while Noah started the drive back to the ranch. "Using variations of the name— Robert, Robbie, Bob—there are a lot of Bobby Marshalls in Texas," she explained. "At least a dozen of them are in the San Antonio area. I'll look at social media posts to try to narrow it down."

Noah made a sound of agreement, but it was possible this Bobby had continued his "red card" silence on the internet. That would have been the smart thing to do. Not rant and make noise as River had done. Instead, do nothing to draw attention to himself. That way, he could plan his kills and carry them out.

"I can help with that search," Theo volunteered, and once they were away from River's house, he got off the floor and back on the seat. He stayed low though, a reminder that until they were back at the ranch, they were all still in danger.

"So, do you believe River told us the truth about everything?" Everly came out and asked while she continued her search on the phone.

Noah was already mulling that over. "Hard to say. He certainly doesn't seem scared that he could be on the killer's hit list."

"True," Everly muttered. Then, paused. "This might be something." She continued to volley her attention between her phone and their surroundings. "Bobby Marshall from

San Antonio. It's a social media post with the phone number for a mental help service. He didn't add anything to it,
but maybe that's our guy."

Noah didn't answer. That's because his attention zoomed
into what he saw ahead. Right in the middle of the road.

A large box, the size of a refrigerator.

And there was blood running down the side of it.

Chapter Seven

Everly froze when she saw the bloody box. It was a lot larger than the one left on her porch, but she had no doubts that this one, too, was from the killer.

"I can't drive around it," Noah said in between cursing under his breath. "I'll end up in the ditch. I can't risk ramming into it because I don't know what's in there. Someone could be inside."

Oh, mercy. Everly hadn't even gone there, but she wouldn't put it past the killer to have put a body inside. Or worse. Someone alive who might be killed if a vehicle hit it.

"I'll call Bulverde PD and Grayson," Theo said. "I'll get someone out here as fast as possible."

Everly had no doubts that Grayson and the others would respond, but they wouldn't get there in the next fifteen minutes, and that meant they had to do something to make sure another driver didn't slam into that box. Along with making sure the murderer didn't use this "roadblock" to try to kill Noah and her.

Noah hit the switch for the lights and sirens, and he pulled as far as he could to the side of the road. "Look in the ditches and make sure no one is hiding in them. I didn't see anything or anybody on my side."

Her heart was already beating way too fast, but that kicked it up even more. Everly did as Noah had asked and thankfully saw nothing but murky water and weeds. If the killer was hiding down in that mess, then he'd need some kind of breathing equipment.

From the backseat, she heard Theo ease up, probably so he could swivel around to check the portion of the ditch he could see.

"There's another box about ten yards back," Theo relayed. "It's about the size of a shoebox, and I don't see any blood on it so it might not be part of this. It might be something that just got tossed."

Since the box was obviously in her blind spot, Everly started to unhook her seat belt so she could maneuver for a better look, but Noah stopped her by touching his hand to hers. He also drew his gun.

"Stay buckled up in case we have to get out of here fast," Noah insisted.

She managed a nod, and because she knew he was right, Everly glanced around to see if she could spot a trail they could use to get off the road. Nothing. But there were plenty of trees, and the ground was uneven in spots, creating a bunker-like slope that could be used for hiding.

Even though it was hard to do, Everly forced away the panic that was starting to slide through her. She tried to make herself think of what could end up happening here. Since she had no doubts that the killer or someone helping the killer had put that box in the road, it meant they were likely now being watched.

Maybe they were even in the sight of a sniper.

"The windows of the cruiser are bulletproof," she heard Noah say, obviously reading her expression.

She picked up on his expression, too, and Noah was obviously trying to figure out what to do. He couldn't go forward, and even backing up wasn't much of an option. The road was not only narrow, but there was also a sharp curve directly behind them. In front of them as well. And that was the reason the killer had no doubt picked this spot.

Everly didn't say it aloud, but she had to wonder if Megan was in that box. If so, the killer had worked fast to get her since she'd only had a couple of minutes start ahead of them. Then again, if the killer had all of this planned in advance, then those couple of minutes might have been enough.

"Grayson and two deputies from Bulverde are on the way," Theo informed them. "The deputies are about ten minutes out."

Ten minutes. That would seem like a lifetime or two, but waiting was the safest option. Maybe, just maybe, this was simply another nonlethal threat like the box that had been left on her porch. Of course, the killer had also put a body in her backyard so she doubted this was just some tactic to remind Noah and her that they had a killer breathing down their necks.

"Call Megan," Noah told her, and he handed her his phone since it had the woman's number in it.

While continuing to keep watch around them, Everly pressed the number and waited. With each ring, her stomach sank even more. On the fifth ring the call went to voice mail.

"Maybe Megan doesn't answer when she's driving," Everly muttered, and she left a message for the woman to return the call the first chance she got. Maybe Megan would be able to do that.

Everly heard Noah curse under his breath, and she knew he was beating himself up about letting Megan go off alone.

It wouldn't do any good for her to remind him that the woman could be safe and sound. After all, she'd headed in the opposite direction than they had. Besides, the killer was far more likely to focus on Noah and her—his primary targets. While that didn't comfort Everly exactly, at least it was better than thinking Megan might already be dead.

"Hell," Noah muttered.

Everly's head snapped in his direction, and she followed his gaze to the road ahead. There was a large dark blue pickup truck coming around the curve, and it was going way too fast. Apparently though, the driver saw the box and the whirling cruiser lights as well because she heard the squeal of brakes on the asphalt.

But it was too late.

Everly watched as the truck tried to swerve to avoid hitting the box, but with the narrow road, there was no way to do that. The truck slammed into the box.

And all hell broke loose.

There was a thundering boom, a deafening blast that roared through the air and shook the cruiser. Debris went flying. So did white smoke. It billowed out from the box and created an immediate cloud, but there was still enough visibility for Everly to see something that caused her heart to jump to her throat.

The truck was coming right at them.

The collision had caused the vehicle to go into a skid, and the blast had broken the glass on the windshield. Even if the driver had been able to see them though, there's no way he or she could have stopped.

"Brace yourself," Noah managed to say a split second before the truck crashed right into them.

She heard the slam of metal against metal. Felt the whiplashing jolt. And the airbag deployed, ramming into her face and chest.

The flashbacks came. Mercy, did they. Of the other collision when a woman had died, and Everly could feel the panic slicing through her, ready to spiral her out of control.

"Everyone okay?" Noah asked.

Everly latched on to the sound of his voice and let it yank her back from the panic. His question let her know that he was alive. Theo, too, because he muttered an okay from the backseat.

Afraid of what she might see, Everly looked over at Noah and got some much needed relief. Noah had a few nicks on his face from the airbag, but he was already batting that away. Everly did the same. Not easy since it was like trying to get out from beneath a huge balloon, but she was finally able to get enough of it away from her face for her see the windshield. The safety glass had cracked and webbed, making it hard to see. But not impossible.

Mercy.

The truck had not only crashed into them, it also landed on top of the front end of the cruiser, pinning them down.

"You think that's the killer in the truck?" Theo asked.

Noah had punched down his airbag as well and peered through the damaged glass of the windshield. He shook his head. "Can't tell. I'll keep watch. You run the license plate." Noah lifted his gun, taking aim at the truck, but he also started firing glances all around them.

Those glances gave Everly a much needed jolt, a reminder that the killer could be about to try to finish them off.

The truck's front license plate wasn't hard to see since it was practically right in their faces, and from the back seat, she heard Theo clicking away on his phone. There was no need for them to call in the crash since Grayson and the Bulverde cops were already on the way.

"The truck's registered to a George Millard," Theo relayed several moments later. "He lives just up the road."

So, maybe the crash hadn't been intentional. Then again, the killer could have stolen the truck. But Everly immediately rethought that. If the killer had been the one behind the wheel, he likely wouldn't have wanted to risk colliding with a cruiser.

"Hell," Noah muttered again.

Everly didn't have to ask why he'd said that or why there was a mountain of fresh concern on his face. It was because she saw, and smelled, something.

Gasoline.

It was coming from the truck. Either the crash had caused the gas tank to rupture or else someone had tampered with the vehicle to make sure it would do that.

Since the truck was blocking her view, Everly could no longer see what was left of the box, but she could smell something else. Smoke. She remembered the white billows coming from the box when the truck had collided into it. Sweet heaven. Had the killer put something in there that would start a fire?

Obviously, that horrible thought occurred to Noah, too.

"We have to get out," Noah insisted. *"Now."*

NOAH DIDN'T ESPECIALLY want Everly, Theo and him to be out in the open where they could be gunned down, but if they stayed put, the truck could explode and take the cruiser right along with it.

He could see the flames now shooting from the remains of the box. The killer had probably added some kind of incendiary device inside. One that could quickly turn deadly if the fire reached the gasoline.

What Noah couldn't see were any signs that there'd been a body inside with that device. If there was a silver lining in all of this, it was that. Of course, the killer might be planning on having bodies today by murdering Everly and him.

But Noah had no intention of letting that happen.

Theo opened the back door of the cruiser, and with his gun drawn, he glanced around. He motioned for them to do the same. Not exactly an all clear because there was no way Theo had that kind of visibility what with the smoke, but this was a risk they still had to take.

When Everly got out, Noah climbed across the seat to get out right behind her. Other than the airbag scrapes on her face, he couldn't see any visible injuries, thank God, so he got her moving as fast as he could manage.

Hooking his arm around her waist, he jumped the ditch with her in tow, and they landed on a soft patch of grass on the other side. Because of the uneven ground and probably because she was still unsteady from the wreck, Everly stumbled, nearly falling before Noah caught her.

Noah fired his gaze all around them, at the pasture and the woods while he tried to look for any signs of danger. Impossible to do because of that damn smoke, but he could still smell the gasoline and the fire and knew at the moment that was a greater threat than a killer would be.

"The driver of the truck's getting out," Theo reported to them.

Noah had already geared up to start running with Everly, but that caused him to stop and curse. Even though he heard the sharp sound of fear that Everly made, he couldn't take the time to reassure her that they would get out of this. No. He just had to focus on making sure they didn't die.

Positioning Everly behind him, Noah hunkered down so he wouldn't be an easy target, and he took aim when he saw the driver opening his door. His body braced for the threat.

To shoot if necessary.

And he waited, the precious seconds ticking away. Even at this distance, Everly and he would likely be killed from a blast. Theo and the driver of the truck would be for sure, but if the driver hadn't been the one who'd set all of this into motion, they couldn't leave him to die.

"Wait here," Noah warned Everly. "And get all the way down on the ground. Cover your head with your hands."

It was the best he could have her do while he tried to assist Theo. Noah couldn't tell Everly to run and hide because that might be exactly what the killer was waiting for them to do. If they got separated, that would make it easier for someone to pick them off one by one.

The door of the wrecked truck creaked open, and more of those seconds crawled by before a man with gray hair and a scratched-up face practically fell out of the cab and onto what was left of the front bumper of the cruiser. Noah had only gotten a glimpse of the truck owner's DMV photo, but he was certain this was the local rancher, George Millard. The man had likely just been caught up in the chaos.

Theo must have thought the same thing because moving fast, he helped the still stumbling, dazed man to the tiny space between the vehicles and the ditch. Then, because Theo was all cop and clearly wasn't going to risk them being gunned down, he frisked him.

"No weapon," Theo muttered.

The words had barely left Theo's mouth when Noah got

himself and the man moving as well. Noah hurdled across the ditch, dragging George along with him, but the man's right leg fell in, causing the muddy water to slosh up around them. Theo didn't miss a beat. He took George's left arm, and Noah took his right. They ran toward Everly, and all the while Noah prayed he could get her out of harm's way in time.

In the distance, Noah heard the wail of the sirens. That was both good and bad news because it meant backup would soon be there. But it was bad as well since the lawmen could be riding straight into an explosion.

"I'll take the driver," Theo assured Noah. "You get Everly."

Since that would get them on the move the fastest, Noah went with it. Thankfully, Everly was already getting to her feet and they hurried, ducking behind one of those bunker-like hills. Knowing that Theo would be checking their surroundings for any signs of danger, Noah took out his phone and made a quick call to the Silver Creek dispatcher to alert Grayson and the Bulverde cops about the danger on the road.

"Oh, God," Everly said, her voice trembling.

Noah still hadn't put his phone away, but he snapped toward her to see what'd caused that reaction. She had her attention frozen on some papers that they'd obviously stepped on when they'd dropped down on the ground. Except it wasn't papers, he realized when he had a closer look.

It was photos.

At least a dozen of them. Specifically, black-and-white photos of Everly's car. Ones taken after the accident that'd killed Helen. Whoever had put the pictures there had enhanced them, coloring the dark splotches of blood a bright red. Helen's blood. It had been on the road after the EMTs had rushed the dying woman away.

Noah felt his own slam of memories and knew it had to be even worse for Everly. Added to everything else that was happening, he thought this might spiral her into having a panic attack.

"This is what the killer wants," Noah told her. "He wants you so upset that you can't think straight."

She looked at him, their gazes connecting, and she nodded. It wasn't a particularly strong nod, but it was confirmation enough that she was likely going to pull herself together.

Noah continued to keep watch, all the while hoping the dispatcher had managed to get in touch with whoever was in the cop car that he could hear getting closer. Closer. But he continued to brace himself for an attack. One that could come from many directions. He was especially worried about a group of thick trees about thirty yards away. It'd be a perfect place for a sniper to hide.

That thought had barely had time to cross his mind when Noah heard the sound. Not gunfire. No. This was much louder, and he could have sworn it shook the ground beneath them.

With his gun ready, he peered over the embankment and saw something he sure as hell hadn't wanted to see.

The truck and cruiser had just exploded.

Chapter Eight

While Grayson drove Noah and her toward the Silver Creek Sheriff's Office, Everly sat in the backseat of his cruiser and balled her hands into fists to stop them from trembling. She silently cursed her reaction. Cursed even more that she'd nearly crumbled when she'd seen those blasted photos.

She'd left the Ryland ranch to go to the interview with River, knowing that the killer could use the trip as a chance to come after them.

And he had.

The bait had worked. Not as they'd planned though. It had drawn out the killer all right, but instead of Noah and her catching and stopping him, he'd come very close to ending four lives. Plus, the lives of the two Bulverde cops who'd been in the approaching car at the time of the explosion.

In this case, hindsight was her enemy because it was causing all of this to eat away at her. She couldn't help but think if Noah, Theo and she had stayed put just one more minute in the cruiser, or if it'd taken slightly longer to rescue the driver of the truck, they would have been blown to bits along with the two vehicles.

Thankfully, none of them had gotten any serious injuries, though the truck driver had been taken to the hospital for a possible concussion. Theo, Noah and she had made it out with just a few scrapes and bruises, none of which had required medical attention. They'd gotten lucky.

But they hadn't gotten the killer.

He was still out there, no doubt trying to figure out another way to come after them. That's why Grayson and Noah were continuing to keep watch around them. Everly was, too, but with her rattled nerves and the adrenaline still firing through her, it seemed as if every fence, tree and ditch could be hiding a killer.

At least Ainsley and everyone at the Ryland ranch were safe as well. Everly had called Noah's mom as soon as her voice had been steady enough to have an actual conversation. There'd been no sign of trouble there, thank goodness, but Darcy had obviously been shaken after hearing about the collision.

Megan was safe as well. Shortly after Grayson had arrived on the scene, Noah had gotten a call about that from Detective O'Malley who'd informed him that the woman had arrived safe and sound and was now in protective custody.

Since Noah had opted to ride in the backseat with her, no doubt to try to make sure she didn't lose it, he reached over and took her hand. Something he'd been doing a lot since this whole ordeal had started. Everly didn't mind. In fact, she welcomed it. Noah and she were in this together, and he was probably the only person in Silver Creek who totally understood what she was feeling.

Too bad her feelings weren't limited to just their dangerous situation.

This closeness with Noah was stirring other things, too. The heat, yes, but it was more than that. Once, she'd been in love with him. That'd been years ago and when they had been teenagers, but she had loved him. And she had to make sure that didn't happen again. She just couldn't see them having a future together since it would only trigger the nightmare memories for both of them. They were responsible for a woman's death, and that wasn't ever going away.

Grayson's phone rang, and Everly saw Theo's name pop up on the dash. Theo had stayed behind to assist the Bulverde cops so maybe they had found something to help with the investigation. There wasn't much left of the box, but the photos were intact. She seriously doubted the killer would have been careless enough to leave his prints on them, but he might have left something of himself behind.

"You're on Speaker," Grayson immediately informed Theo.

"Just wanted you to know that the bomb squad arrived shortly after you left, and they're doing a search now to see if there are any other devices. They'll send the pieces of the device that were in the box to the lab. They could get a signature from it."

A signature could maybe help identify who'd made the explosive. Even if that wasn't the killer himself, it might lead to him.

"CSIs are here, too," Theo went on, "and the road is closed so as to not compromise any possible evidence. They spotted footprint impressions in the grass leading to the spot where the photos were left. Not the prints any of us left. These were farther to the side of where we'd hunkered down. Unfortunately, they aren't actual prints, but they can estimate the size of the shoes. They're estimating a size ten."

So, they had likely been made by a man. That would help

narrow down the membership list to Peace Seekers. If they ever got a list, that is.

"Do they have any idea how the box got in the road?" Noah asked.

"Not yet, but they'll check for tire tracks. As you well know, the road isn't wide enough to do a U-turn. He could have parked on a trail, but the box was big."

"So he likely just stopped on the road, positioned the box and drove a safe distance away," Noah finished for him.

"Yeah," Theo agreed. "But he could have used a ranch trail after that so he could watch what was happening."

Now it was Noah who voiced an agreement. Everly silently echoed one, too. The killer obviously loved to taunt and torment so he wouldn't have wanted to miss them being killed. He'd probably hoped they'd be close enough to the box to make sure that happened.

"I'll forward any reports from here as soon as I get them," Theo added. "You'll be at the office for a while?"

"A while," Grayson confirmed. "I'm meeting with the medical examiner in about an hour. He's already done the autopsy on Daisy Reyes so he might be able to tell us something. After that, I'll drive Noah and Everly back to the ranch."

Grayson met her gaze in the rearview mirror, and he seemed to be trying to figure out if she was steady enough to be around her daughter. Everly knew she was nowhere near steady, and Ainsley might indeed pick up on that, but she was hoping to use a little more time to level herself out.

She was certain they all breathed a little easier when they finally arrived at the sheriff's office. "Use my office," Grayson immediately told them once they were inside the building. "I can use the break room to make some calls, and then I'll leave for the appointment with the ME. I can FaceTime that meeting with him if you want to ask him any questions," he offered.

"Do that," Noah said, adding a thanks, and he ushered Everly past the deputy on duty and into Grayson's office.

The moment Noah had her inside the office, he shut the door, and in the same motion he pulled her into his arms. At first, she thought he'd done that because she looked so shaken, but then Everly realized he needed this just as much as she did. A hug like this was a definite risk what with the heat between them. However, with everything they'd just been through, she welcomed it.

"I'm sorry," Noah muttered, tightening his grip on her for just a couple of seconds before he eased back. He didn't let go of her but instead looked down at her.

"You don't owe me an apology," she assured him. "The plan was my idea."

"And I agreed to it," he pointed out just as fast. "I'd thought the killer would want to get close and then I could stop him. This breaks pattern for him."

It did indeed. Still, if the blast or the collision had killed them, the vigilante probably wouldn't have minded that he hadn't personally been able to deliver the fatal blows as he had by slicing into his previous victims.

"The box wasn't there when we drove to River's," she observed. Everly hoped by saying all of this aloud, she'd be better able to work it out in her own mind. "So, River couldn't have put it there. He could have hired someone to do it though."

"Absolutely," Noah agreed. "So far, the killer hasn't shown that he has any bomb-making skills. That doesn't mean he doesn't have them, but if he had that particular experience, why didn't he use it before now? It would have been easier to set a car bomb than it would to take the risk of abducting his victims where someone could have seen and reported him."

True. He could have set a car bomb at night or when the victims' vehicles weren't out in plain sight.

"So, he broke pattern with us," she concluded, "because he likely thought this was the only way he'd be able to get to us. And if the killer is River, he could have not only hired someone to make the bomb but also plant it."

Noah nodded, and then he stared at her a long time. "It's too risky for you to be bait," he finally made clear.

Everly had no trouble figuring out what Noah hadn't added to that decree. "But it's not too risky for you to continue to be bait." She huffed, knowing that's what he was planning.

He slid his hands up her arms to take hold of her shoulders, and he looked her straight in the eyes. "I have to stop him. Every minute he's out there means it's a minute where you're not safe."

Everly was on the verge of spelling out to him that he wouldn't be safe either. Especially if he intentionally put himself in the path of this vicious killer, but Noah lowered his head and brushed his mouth over hers. It was only a touch and barely qualified as a kiss, but mercy, it still had a punch to it. Of course it did because after all, this was Noah.

Her body responded. A different kind of adrenaline hit that mixed with the heat. Noah no doubt saw that heat. He must have felt it in his own body as well, and he didn't step away from it. Instead, he kissed her again. This time, he sank in, pressing his mouth harder against her, causing the heat to continue to build.

But then it stopped as quickly as it'd started.

Noah let go of her and backed away as if that heat had scalded him. "Sorry," he muttered. He groaned and scrubbed his hand over his face. "That wasn't smart."

"No," she softly agreed. Not smart. But since she hadn't resisted and because her body was burning for even more, she gave Noah an out. "A weak moment for both of us. We'll pretend it didn't happen."

She'd have an easier time pretending there wasn't a killer out there, but she didn't want Noah taking on the guilt for this. Not when they already had enough of that to deal with.

There was a knock at the door, and Noah took a moment, no doubt to rein in his composure, and when he finally opened it, Everly saw Deputy Lawson.

"We have a visitor," the deputy said. "He says he's Bobby Marshall, and he claims to know both of you."

Bobby Marshall? Everly had thought they'd have to try to track down the man, but instead he'd come to them. That was good, but she had to mentally shake her head about the claim of knowing Noah and her. She didn't believe she'd met anyone by that name.

Deputy Lawson stepped to the side so that Noah and she would be able to see the man who was pacing across the reception area. He had pale blond hair, a lean build. And his head whipped up. His gaze zoomed in their direction.

And Everly felt as if someone had knocked the breath out of her.

Judging from the sound Noah made, he was having a similar reaction. That's because they did indeed know this man. It'd been fourteen years, and he'd only been eleven at the time, but there was no mistaking who he was.

He was the stepson of the woman Everly had killed fourteen years ago.

Although Everly hadn't known him as Bobby Marshall back then but rather Robert Fleming.

"Detective Ryland," Bobby greeted, then shifted his attention to Everly. "Miss Monroe. I understand you've been trying to locate me."

There was no hint of anger in his voice or in his cool blue eyes though there had been plenty of that fourteen years ago. Everly recalled him glaring and yelling at her outside the courthouse after the hearing where she'd learned her fate. That she wouldn't be serving any time for the crash.

You killed my mother, the boy had shouted. And he had continued to shout it until his father had finally dragged him away.

"I assumed you'd want to interview me," Bobby said, walking toward them.

"He's been through the metal detector," Deputy Lawson assured them. "And I went ahead and frisked him as well."

Everly was thankful for the extra security measures. Especially since Bobby was obviously now a prime suspect for the vigilante killings.

"Could you do a background run on him for me?" Noah asked the deputy, and he didn't lower his voice.

"Will do," she assured him, and she went to her desk.

Bobby didn't seem offended that Noah would have wanted the deputy to do that. Then again, since he was here, he likely knew that he was a person of interest.

With Bobby following right behind them, they went into Grayson's office. Noah maneuvered Everly to the desk chair and had her sit. Probably because he knew this had shaken her. Also maybe because the desk acted like a barrier between Bobby and her. Noah no doubt recalled the angry boy who'd shouted at her all those years ago.

"How did you know we wanted to talk to you?" Noah came out and asked. Bobby took the visitor's chair, and Noah sat on the corner of the desk.

"I knew about Jill Ritter's murder. Megan talked about it during the last meeting. So, when I heard that Daisy had been killed as well, I assumed you'd be talking to everyone in Peace Seekers."

Everly found herself studying the man, trying to detect any venom. She didn't hear any in his voice, but the glance he gave her definitely had some ice in it. And for good reason. She'd killed his stepmother, and judging from his reaction years ago at her hearing, he'd been close enough to Helen to be very upset about her.

Or maybe the upset had been because her killer hadn't gotten any jail time.

"I'd like a list of the members of Peace Seekers," Noah told the man after a long pause. She didn't think it was her imagination that Noah was studying Bobby, too, so he could figure out if they were now face-to-face with the vigilante killer.

Bobby shook his head. "I don't have one. And I only know the names of a few members. Megan Ritter, of course, and two guys, Jared and River." He paused as well. "I didn't participate a lot in the group."

"Why is that?" Noah asked, taking the question right out of her mouth.

Everly was glad he'd asked it. In fact, she needed to take a backseat and let Noah do most if not all the questioning.

After all, Bobby hadn't aimed that anger and hatred at Noah way back when. It'd all been aimed at her, and he might clam up if she pressed him for information.

"Why?" Bobby repeated on a heavy sigh. "I heard you ask the deputy for background on me. Maybe if I tell you what I've been through you'll understand why I'm looking for peace. I thought maybe I'd find it in the group."

Noah didn't waste any time jumping right on that. "What have you been through?"

No sigh this time, just a long breath. "I don't know how much you remember about my mom, but I loved her. I was crushed when she died."

Now, Bobby looked at her, and yes, the venom was still there. The seething kind of venom that didn't go away. And that meant he could have used all that anger to kill in the name of justice.

"Helen was my stepmother," Bobby went on, "but I lost my birth mom when I was five so Helen was my mother in every way that counted. I can't say the same about my father," he added, taking his voice down a notch.

Here was more pain, more venom, and Everly recalled someone mentioning that shortly before her death, Helen had filed a restraining order against her husband, Isaac Fleming.

"My father was abusive to my mother," Bobby continued several moments later. "After her death, he didn't shift the abuse to me, but he neglected me, and I was eventually sent to foster care." His jaw tightened. "If my mother hadn't been trying to get away from my father that night, she wouldn't have been on the road. She wouldn't have died. But she was in her car because he'd beaten her."

Everly recalled that as well. Whispers about the woman's previous injuries.

"Helen didn't try to take you with her that night?" Noah asked.

Bobby's eyes filled with fresh anger. "She couldn't. She was running for her life, and when she tried to take me, my father kicked and punched her. He told her he was going to kill her so she ran. She wasn't a coward," he added in a snarl. "Once she got someplace safe, she would have gotten me out of there. But she never made it to someplace safe, did she?"

All of this had apparently lit a very hot fuse for Bobby. It had brought a slam of the horrible memories for Everly. But she forced herself to hold back anything she was feeling because after all, Bobby had a right to his anger.

"Why did you change your name?" Noah asked, obviously shifting the conversation to a different direction. Good thing, too, because it looked as if Bobby was on the verge of storming out.

Bobby seemed to settle, and he drew in a long breath through his mouth before he answered. "I didn't want any connection to my father, and Marshall was my stepmother's maiden name."

Everly hadn't known that. Then again, she hadn't exactly been thinking clearly after the fatal car crash, and she definitely hadn't sought out personal info on Helen.

"I changed my name," Bobby went on, "and started calling myself Bobby because my father always called me Robert." He stopped, sighed. "The past can eat away at you. The memories."

Yes, Everly was well aware of that. "And that's why you joined Peace Seekers?" she asked in a murmur.

Bobby nodded. "Even though I used the red card, I was

getting a lot out of the meetings. Not a misery loves company thing. It was just helpful to hear that people had gone through bad things and survived."

Everly tried to pick through that to determine if after hearing those *bad things* that Bobby had decided to do something to right the scales of justice. Maybe. But she'd gotten just as much of a guilty vibe from River as she was getting from Bobby.

There was a quick knock at the door, and when it opened, Deputy Lawson stuck her head in. She made eye contact with Noah before she handed him a piece of paper. "The report you requested," she said and closed the door when she left.

Since this was the background check on Bobby, Everly had a look and saw something highlighted. *No experience on record with explosives.*

Of course, that didn't mean he hadn't hired someone who had that experience, but if that had happened, there could be a paper trail for the payment.

Everly glanced over the rest of the report and saw that Bobby had had an arrest for assault but the charges had been dropped.

"I'm guessing that's about me," Bobby said, drawing her attention back to them. If he was worried about anything that might be in the report, he wasn't showing any signs of it. "You're looking to see if I'm the person who could have killed Daisy and Megan's mother. I'm not," he tacked onto that.

Noah lifted his gaze from the report and looked at Bobby. "Then, who in the group has a warped sense of justice and could have killed?"

Bobby's mouth tightened for just a second. No doubt

because he objected to the way Noah had worded the question. Bobby probably wouldn't see these killings as warped.

Bobby's expression relaxed, and Everly thought she saw grief or something cross his eyes. "Daisy was a good person. I hate she got caught up in all of this."

Noah made a sound of agreement, but he was likely mulling over the way Bobby had put that. "Then, who killed her?" Noah pressed.

"I don't know the who, not for sure, but I'm guessing the reason she died was because she was suspicious of someone in the group, and that person might have thought she could expose what was happening." Bobby shrugged. "Of course, she had other clients, those not in the group, so it could have been one of them."

"Go back to the first part of that," Noah insisted. "You said you didn't know for sure who killed her. But you suspect someone?"

Bobby's next pause was even longer, and with his jaw muscles working against each other, he seemed to be having a debate with himself about how much to say. Or how little.

"If you believe someone might be a killer, then you need to say something," Noah said, sounding all cop. "What if this killer goes after someone like Megan? Or you? What if—?"

"Jared," Bobby blurted out.

Everly certainly hadn't expected Bobby to say that name. She'd figured if Bobby pointed the finger at anyone, it would have been River.

"Jared?" she repeated, and yes, she sounded skeptical. "He's in a wheelchair."

"Maybe," Bobby muttered.

That got both Noah's and her attention. "Are you saying Jared's not paralyzed?"

Bobby met Noah eye to eye. "At the last meeting, I happened to glance at Jared's shoes, and I saw mud on them. How did mud get there if he can't walk?" But Bobby didn't wait for an answer. "I'm saying you need to take a closer look at him because if I had to put money on who's killing in the group, it'd be Jared."

Chapter Nine

Jared.

The moment Bobby had left Grayson's office, Noah had dived right into starting a deeper background check on Jared. On Bobby as well. And Noah had also called Jared to insist he immediately come back in for another interview. Jared had balked, no surprise there, but after Noah had made it an order, Jared had finally agreed that he would make a repeat trip to Silver Creek. He'd assured Noah that he would get there within the hour.

That agreement was somewhat of a victory since it had saved Noah the paperwork of having someone in SAPD pick up Jared and bring him in. However, Noah had also reminded himself that this could be a huge waste of time and Bobby could be a liar.

Worse, Bobby could be the vigilante killer.

If so, that was going to give Everly and him the mother lode of flashbacks. The mother lode of guilt, too.

Of course, the guilt had always been there. *Always.* It was impossible to reconcile that they'd been responsible for the death of a woman. But if Bobby was killing to get so-called justice for the woman he considered his mother, then it would only add to that guilt. Everly and he had been the ones to set all of this in motion. No way for him to get around that, so he had to focus on getting to the truth and stopping the killer from claiming anyone else.

"Helen was trying to get away from the abuse," Everly muttered, drawing Noah's attention back to her.

Not that his attention had strayed too far from her. No. He'd been keeping a close watch on her since Bobby had left, and he knew that all of this was taking jabs at the old wounds they shared.

"The car wreck was an accident," Noah said, hoping to remind both her and himself.

Since Everly didn't react to that and because she still looked on the verge of having the old grief consume her, he set aside his computer search for a couple of minutes, stood and went to her. Everly was at the window, staring out, but he doubted she was actually seeing anything outside. She was almost certainly trapped in those nightmarish images of the past. Noah took hold of her shoulder and eased her around to face him.

"The car wreck was an accident," he repeated.

This time, she acknowledged what he'd said with a nod and a murmured, "I know," but as he'd expected, it did nothing to ease any of the guilt.

Noah considered telling her that because Helen had been on the run from an abusive husband, that she might have been distracted. The woman was darn sure speeding. The cops had determined that. But putting any portion of the blame on the victim wasn't going to help. A hug might not help either though that didn't stop Noah from gently drawing Everly to him.

"We're going to find this killer and stop him," he muttered, putting his mouth close to her ear. "In a way, stopping him will be the right kind of justice for Helen. I refuse to believe she'd want anyone committing murder because of what happened to her."

Everly didn't voice any kind of agreement or give him a nod, but she did sigh and moved closer to him. Until they were body to body. Even with his mind wracked with guilt, that didn't stop the heat. Noah cursed it and then added another curse word for what he was about to do next.

He brushed a kiss on Everly's cheek.

It was a mistake. He'd known it would be because that brief touch yanked him back to a different set of memories. A time when Everly and he had done more than just cheek kiss. A time when they'd been lovers.

Noah hated that the images of that night were now mixed together with the car crash. He could pick through them and latch on to the ones of them together. The kisses, the touching, the urgent need clawing its way through them. But he doubted Everly could remember one without the other.

But he rethought that when she eased back and looked at him.

He saw the old attraction in her eyes. Felt it in the buzz of her body. Felt it in his own body as well. Noah knew certain parts of him didn't always make the smartest decisions, and he got proof of that.

When he leaned in and kissed her.

If the cheek kiss had packed a punch, the mouth to mouth was more like an avalanche of fire. It raced through Noah, bringing back much better memories. Ones that would surely rob him of any common sense. And that couldn't happen.

Noah silently repeated that to himself.

It didn't bring the kiss to an immediate stop. No. He lingered several more moments, taking the heat and pleasure that he had no right to take or feel. He finally managed to force himself to pull back from Everly.

Their eyes met, and he saw the desire in hers. The confusion, too, and it was something he definitely understood. No way in hell should that have just happened. They were in Grayson's office where someone could have walked in on them, and even though that wouldn't have been good, it was the least of the concerns here. So was the fact that he should be working on the investigation.

The biggest concern—and it was a huge one, all right— was that a kiss could trigger enough of the past that it would make it impossible for them to be together even for the sake of the investigation. That couldn't happen. They needed to stop the killer, and that had to happen while he kept Everly and Ainsley safe.

"I'm sorry," they both said at the same time.

That caused Noah to smile even though he knew there wasn't much to smile about. Still, it felt good for Everly and him to be on the same page despite his body urging him to believe that the kiss hadn't been a mistake at all, that they should kiss some more. But Noah knew this was one instance where he was going to have to overrule everything but his cop's instincts. The investigation had to come ahead of his need to take Everly as if she were his for the taking.

She wasn't.

He mentally repeated that to himself and shifted his focus by moving away from her and going back to his computer. Noah heard her draw in a long breath and figured she was doing some refocusing as well because she returned to her own computer searches.

Noah frowned though, when he saw the email reply from

Detective O'Malley. Immediately after Bobby had left, Noah had fired off a quick email to O'Malley, asking him to help expedite the paperwork to get access to Jared's medical records. Noah had hoped for the best but had known the reality of getting that kind of access. Especially getting it when he didn't have any evidence other than hearsay from another suspect. Still, Noah had hoped. That hope dimmed considerably when he read O'Malley's response.

"The request was immediately denied," O'Malley had informed him. "Give me anything you can get from the interview, and I'll try again."

Noah seriously doubted that Jared was just going to hand them something they could use to get into his medical records. Well, unless the man truly had nothing to hide. But even if Jared was innocent, he might not want cops poking around in his personal files simply for the sake of proving that innocence especially since Jared didn't have a lot of goodwill when it came to the police.

Hopefully, Jared would change his mind about that access though, if Noah applied enough pressure. The kind of pressure to let Jared understand that Everly and he weren't just going to back off until they'd gotten to the truth. That included ruling out any suspects or persons of interest.

"What's wrong?" Everly asked.

Noah hadn't realized he'd made any sound, but then he heard himself grumbling under his breath while he replied to O'Malley. "It might take a while for us to get into Jared's medical records," he settled for saying. No need for him to spell out that it might never happen.

"Yes," she quietly agreed.

He could hear in her voice that she knew this was a slim-to-none shot with what little evidence they had. After all, she was a lawyer, and she would have fought this sort of thing for any of her clients. It was far easier to get financial records on a person of interest than it was to get anything related to medical history.

"Do you believe Bobby could be right about Jared being able to walk?" Everly asked.

"I think it's possible, but there are other reasons why the mud could have been on his shoes," he admitted. "He could have dragged them through mud while he was moving himself out of the wheelchair and into his vehicle. He does have a car adapted so he can drive, and we don't know where he parks that vehicle."

Though that was yet something else Noah would find with the deeper background check he was running. He turned to that search now and saw that Jared rented a townhouse in San Antonio, and he glanced through the info. The info about the type of vehicle Jared owned as well. It was a van.

"Jared has a garage," Noah relayed to Everly. Of course, that didn't rule out that he'd parked his vehicle elsewhere for a visit. Maybe a visit where he'd dumped a body. And that got Noah thinking. "Even if he can't walk, it's possible he could still be the killer. He looks strong so he could have maybe even lifted the victims himself. Or lured them into his van."

That comment got Everly shifting her attention to him, and after a couple of seconds, she nodded. "Like Ted Bundy. He would feign an injury to lure in his victims." She paused. "And someone like Daisy might not have even needed to be lured. She would have known and perhaps trusted him."

Noah agreed. "And none of the victims had large builds. If Jared could have gotten them close to the back of his van or even parked next to their vehicles, then it would have been easier for him to disable them and shove them inside."

Saying it out loud though led Noah to a big concern about that theory. All of Everly's neighbors had been questioned now, and none of them had reported seeing a van or any other strange vehicle in the area.

People in small towns would notice something like that.

The killer could have worked around that though. If he'd researched Everly, and Noah was positive that he had, then he would have known when her neighbors were most likely to be around. In other words, that didn't rule out any of their suspects.

His phone dinged, and he saw it was a text from Grayson, which he read aloud. "'The medical examiner had to delay our meeting because he had a family emergency. A sick wife,'" Grayson had added. "'I'll reschedule, but in the meantime, you could start going over the financials that just came in. I had Theo email you copies.'"

Noah immediately checked his inbox and spotted the financial reports on Jared, Bobby, River and even Daisy. He sent Grayson a quick thanks and got started.

"I can look through some of them to help speed things up," Everly offered.

He didn't even have to debate that. Yes, it bent the rules, but Noah was willing to venture into a gray area to find something that could stop this threat to Everly. He forwarded her the files for Daisy and Bobby, and while she got to work on those, Noah went straight to Jared's.

Jared had a checking, savings and another account for investments, and Noah could see the man's monthly disability payments deposited to his checking. The money wasn't coming from social security or any other government agency but rather a monthly payout from private insurance Jared had obviously had at the time of the accident.

Nothing looked out of the ordinary with the deposits and withdrawals. Ditto for the man's savings, but there was a surprise in his investments. The man had a little over a half of a million dollars invested in various mutual funds. A lot considering Jared hadn't come from money, but Noah could see that the account had been started with a lump sum payout from Winona Billings's insurance company. After that, Jared had made conservative but steady investments with few withdrawals.

One withdrawal, however, stood out.

"A week ago, Jared took ten grand out of his investment account," Noah relayed to Everly. She immediately turned to him. "He withdrew the funds in cash."

"Cash?" Everly repeated, and judging from her tone, that was a red flag for her, too. "Any indications what he used the money for?"

"None." Noah had moved on to scanning the man's credit card. Since it was set up as an automatic payment from his checking account, the money wouldn't have been used to pay off some purchase funneled that way.

But it could have been used to pay someone to set that explosive.

Or dump the bodies.

If so, that meant there was someone out there who could maybe ID Jared as the killer.

After he'd had a harder look at Jared's credit card, Noah moved to River's. The man wasn't nearly as financially well off as Jared, and only had a checking account. According to the deposits, River made good money at his job, but he also spent most of it. Judging from the charges on the credit card linked to the checking, River was into online video games.

"I found two things that stand out," Everly said after she'd been at it for about fifteen minutes. "On the first, there might be something suspicious in Bobby's accounts. Might," she emphasized. "For weeks, he's been withdrawing three hundred dollars from an ATM. I can't see how he's using it since he pays for everything else on his credit card."

Noah understood why she'd added that *might*. There were a lot of legit reasons why a person used cash over credit, but since they were dealing with a murder suspect, the withdrawals would need to be investigated. That would mean interviewing Bobby again.

"And the second thing you found?" Noah asked.

"A questionable deposit in Daisy's account. Ten grand deposited a week ago."

That grabbed Noah's attention. "The same date as Jared's withdrawal?" he asked, giving her the exact day.

"Yes," she verified. Everly sighed and sat back in the chair while she slid her gaze to his. "You think Daisy could have maybe gotten suspicious of Jared, and he paid her off?"

"Yeah, that's exactly what I'm thinking." And Noah immediately began to flesh out that possibility. "Blackmail. Not smart or safe especially when dealing with a killer. But maybe Daisy worked it out so she thought the killer wouldn't know the identity of the person he was paying."

Everly's nod was quick. "But it still wouldn't have been smart. If the killer is any one of our suspects, he'd suspect the blackmailer was someone in the group."

"Definitely." Noah paused. "Is there anything else in Daisy's financials to indicate she made a habit of this?"

Everly's attention went back to the financials. "No," she

answered several moments later. "But if she took payment this one time, it means she knew who the killer was."

It did indeed, and with Jared's withdrawal matching Daisy's deposit, that pointed to Daisy having known Jared was responsible.

"Daisy might not have wanted to turn in the person who helped get justice for her mother," Noah added. "And it was possibly more than that. The payment might not have been blackmail money but rather payment to the person who helped with the explosives."

Everly sighed again. "If that's true…" She trailed off, not finishing that, but Noah knew what she was thinking. If Daisy had indeed helped a killer, then the woman had played with fire and had gotten burned. It'd ended up costing Daisy her own life.

Noah's phone dinged with another text from Grayson. "The CSIs have finished processing your house and yard," he told Everly. "They've given you the okay to go back."

He watched to see her reaction. Relief, yes, but then came the reality. "Home," she muttered, and on a sigh, she added, "I'll have to go back."

"You could wait until the killer is caught," Noah quickly pointed out. "Ainsley and you are welcome to stay as long as you want."

"I know," she said, and Everly repeated it in a whisper. One filled with worry and frustration.

Noah knew what that sigh was all about. The kiss and the attraction were playing into this. Everly likely thought it was wise to put some distance between them. And it probably would be, so it wouldn't be so easy to give in to the temptation of another kiss. One that might land them in bed.

"I would like some things from there," she went on.

"Some extra clothes for Ainsley and several of her favorite toys. And I need to think about security. Even after we catch the killer, it would be hard to stay there if I didn't take some extra precautions."

It twisted at him to think of her leaving, but Noah knew that's exactly what would happen. Sooner or later, Everly would be going home, and she'd start putting up those barriers between them again.

"I can have Hudson go over to your place and give you recommendations," Noah offered. He nearly reminded her that no system, though, would be foolproof, but there was no need for it. It would no doubt be a long time before Everly rested easily in her own home.

Everly nodded, thanked him and turned back to the research on the financials. Noah wrote a text to Hudson, asking him to come to the sheriff's office so he could go with them to Everly's. He'd just sent the text when he heard the sound of a man's booming voice.

"Detective Ryland," Jared called out.

Noah didn't have to see the man to know he was riled to the bone. He could hear the anger raging in Jared's voice. Well, Noah wasn't exactly in a pleasant mood either, and one way or another, he was going to get some answers from Jared.

Noah got up and went to the door to see Deputy Lawson checking their visitor for weapons, but Jared wasn't looking at her. His narrowed gaze went straight to Noah.

"What the hell do you want now?" Jared snarled.

Noah decided not to wait to jump right into one of the things he wanted to know. "It's come to my attention that you don't need that wheelchair," he threw out there, and he watched for Jared's reaction.

Jared's eyes narrowed even more, but Noah thought he saw some surprise now mixed with the venom. "Who told you that?"

"A very reliable source," Noah lied. He kept his cop's gaze pinned to the man, and he added another lie. "I've already requested a medical exam to be conducted on you to verify what that reliable source said."

The seconds crawled by, and then Jared grumbled some raw profanity under his breath. With Deputy Lawson, Noah and Everly watching him, Jared clamped his beefy hands onto the armrests of his wheelchair.

And the man stood up.

Chapter Ten

Everly watched as Jared struggled to get to his feet. But he not only managed it, he also waved off Deputy Lawson when she moved in to help him. The man stood and faced Noah and her with a hot glare.

She'd expected Jared to deny having any mobility in his legs especially since he'd spat out his bitterness about his condition during his last visit. Everly definitely hadn't thought he would just admit it because an admission like that would make him a prime suspect as the vigilante killer.

"Are you satisfied?" Jared snarled, aiming his disgust at Noah. "Yeah, I can stand up. I can even walk a few steps. That sure as hell doesn't mean I'm a killer."

"You lied during an official interview," Noah pointed out just as fast. He motioned for Jared to follow him back to Grayson's office. "I'd like to hear why you did that, and then you can try to convince me why I shouldn't charge you with making a false statement to a police officer, obstruction of justice and anything else I can think of to tack on to that."

Jared huffed, but after dropping back down into his wheelchair, he followed them into the office. "Why the hell do you think I lied?" the man snapped the moment they were inside, and he didn't wait for Noah to answer. "Because I knew you'd be looking at me for these murders. Murders I didn't do."

Noah looked him straight in the eyes. "Then, you should have told the truth. You should have done everything possible to help me stop the killer from striking again. Instead, you withheld a very big truth, and I have to think you did that because you have plenty to hide." He leaned in and upped his glare. "Lie to me again. Give me a reason to toss you into a cell."

Jared opened his mouth as if to return verbal fire, but then it seemed as if he changed his mind as to what he'd been about to say. He huffed, and some of the anger drained from his face.

"I've already read you your rights," Noah reminded him. "Do you want me to repeat them?"

"No," he snapped, and then went quiet. "I haven't told anyone I regained some mobility," Jared finally said. "And like I told you, I can only manage a few steps."

Noah made a circling motion with his index finger, indicating that he wanted Jared to continue, and he didn't ease up one bit on his cop's glare. Everly totally understood why he was riled to the bone. They were in danger. Others likely were, too, and Jared could be responsible.

"I didn't want anyone in Peace Seekers to know," Jared went on when Noah and she stayed silent. "Hell, I didn't want anyone to know because I wasn't sure it'd last. I saw my doctor, and he's doing more tests, but he doesn't know if I can continue to regain movement or if all of this is temporary."

Everly wished she had ESP, or his medical records, so she could tell if he was lying. It would definitely be to the man's advantage if the cops thought he wasn't physically capable of carrying out the murders.

"I want you to give me signed permission to speak to your doctor," Noah insisted after a long pause.

That tightened Jared's jaw again. "If I say no, you'll think I'm guilty." He paused, his gaze still locked with Noah's. The moments crawled by before Jared cursed. Then, he nodded. "I'll call my doctor's office and let them know you can have access. Can I go now?"

"No," Noah was quick to answer. "First tell me about the ten thousand dollars you withdrew in cash from your investment account a week ago."

Jared cursed again, and Everly could see the fierce battle he was having with his temper. "It was a gift to a friend."

"To Daisy," Noah supplied.

Jared shrugged but not before Everly saw the fresh surprise go through his eyes.

"Lie to me," Noah repeated when Jared stayed silent, "and you'll find yourself in a cell."

More seconds ticked off. "Yeah, it was Daisy," Jared finally admitted. "I gave it to her."

Noah kept up the rapid-fire pace, tossing out a question the moment Jared finished his sentence. "Did you give her the money because she was blackmailing you?"

Jared frowned. "No. No," he repeated, shifting in his wheelchair. "She mentioned that she wanted to do a fundraiser to help the family of the dead man who'd killed her mother. I met her after the meeting and told her I'd give her the money."

Of all the explanations Everly had thought the man might come up with, she hadn't thought of that one. "Why would Daisy want to help them?" Everly asked.

"Because she was a good person." Jared closed his eyes a moment and actually shuddered. "I hate that she's dead."

His reaction seemed heartfelt. Seemed. But it occurred to her he could be feeling that way because he'd been the one to kill Daisy. Maybe because he'd felt he had no choice if she was blackmailing him. Or if she'd simply figured out he was killing in the name of justice.

"Did Daisy give you any kind of receipt or thank you note for your generous gift?" Noah pressed, and yes, there was plenty of skepticism in his voice.

That caused Jared to pull back his shoulders, and he was glaring again. "No," he growled. "And I think it's time for me to call my lawyer. According to the Miranda you recited, that's my right," Jared smugly added.

"It is." Noah stepped back, but he didn't ease up on his expression. "Make the call."

"I will, but I can't wait around here today for him to show up. I've got a doctor's appointment. I'll have to come in tomorrow with him."

Noah stared at him a long time as if trying to figure out how to handle this. As a lawyer, Everly could have told him that the evidence he did have was circumstantial. Jared's lawyer would no doubt say the same thing. There wasn't a single shred of physical evidence to link Jared to any of the crimes, and they didn't even know for certain if he had the mobility to have carried out the murders.

"Tomorrow morning at nine," Noah said. "Be here then or I'll issue a warrant for your arrest."

Getting a warrant was a definite long shot. Well, for murder anyway. But Noah could indeed bring a suspect in for questioning. Especially a suspect who'd already lied during an interview.

"Tomorrow at nine," Jared growled like profanity, and he turned his wheelchair around and left.

Jared wheeled past Deputy Lawson who was chatting with a tall dark-haired man wearing jeans and a black tee that showed the sleeve tat on his right arm. He wasn't heavily muscled like Jared, but he had a solid build that reminded her of a lightweight boxer.

The man tipped his head in greeting when he saw Noah, and Noah held up his finger in a wait-a-second gesture. He took out his phone, and she saw him press Detective O'Malley's number.

"I need a search warrant for Jared Jackman's residence," Noah said the moment he had the detective on the line. He rattled off the address after looking at the background check of the man.

"You have probable cause?" O'Malley immediately asked.

"Oh, yeah," Noah verified. "Jared handed that to me when he told me he couldn't walk. He can. He also admitted to giving ten grand to our latest victim, Daisy Reyes. She could have been blackmailing him, and there might be something to prove that in his apartment. Might be some links to the explosive that was in that box, too."

"All right. I'll get right on this," O'Malley assured him. "I'm guessing you're still in Silver Creek?"

"I am." Noah checked the time. "I'm taking Everly out to her place right now so she can get some things and go over options for a new security system, and then we'll be going back to the ranch."

Everly had another look at the man in the waiting area and realized this was probably Hudson Granger, the person in charge of security for the Ryland ranch. He didn't live in Silver Creek. She would have known if he had. But she realized she'd definitely seen him around.

Noah finished his call with O'Malley, put his phone away, grabbed his laptop and handed her the one she'd been using before he got her moving out of Grayson's office. "We can continue the research on the financials on the way."

Since her house was a very short drive, they wouldn't have a lot of time to do that, but they would when en route to the ranch.

"Do we need a backup deputy to go with us?" she asked.

"No. Hudson will fill in on that." Noah stopped, made introductions and then added. "Hudson was Special Ops."

She would have guessed he had a background in law enforcement since those sharp green eyes had seemed all cop to her. Cop with maybe a dark edge. He looked more than capable of providing backup. Everly only hoped it wouldn't be needed.

They hurried outside, not to a cruiser but to a sleek black SUV that was parked directly in front of the door. "It's bullet resistant," Hudson explained as he got behind the wheel. Noah and she got in the backseat.

"Hudson provides a variety of security services," Noah added when he no doubt saw that she had questions.

This definitely wasn't an ordinary SUV. The dash seemed more like something that would be in the cockpit of a fighter jet.

Hudson made a sound of agreement to confirm that *variety of security services*, and he gave a voice command to send a file to Noah. "Grayson asked me to work up a list of possibilities for the person who built the explosive device in the box left on the road," Hudson explained as he drove away from the sheriff's office.

Noah used his laptop to bring up the file, and Everly watched as the list loaded. There were several dozen names.

"Those are known explosives experts in the area," Hudson explained while he drove. She saw that the monitors on the dash were showing all angles of the road. "I've highlighted those with drug habits and such since they might be desperate for money and might not object to helping a killer."

The highlighted ones were at the top, and both Noah and she started to scan through not only the names but the brief bios that Hudson had provided. Judging from those bios and their run-ins with the law, these were not model citizens.

"How much would it cost to hire someone to build explosives?" Everly asked. "I'm thinking about that money Bobby's been withdrawing weekly," she added to Noah.

"It doesn't cost as much as you might think," Hudson answered, his attention on the road and his monitors. "Someone needing drug money might be willing to do it for a grand or two. I checked with the bomb squad about the specs of the explosive in that box, and it wasn't a sophisticated device. It was rigged so that someone nearby with a remote could have detonated it."

That sent an icy chill through her. *Someone nearby.* The killer who'd no doubt been watching them.

Everly had to push away those images, and she did that by continuing to focus on the list. And she saw something.

"Freddie Barker," she said, tapping the screen before she opened the laptop and went to the social media pages she'd researched earlier. Everly quickly found what she was looking for. "He commented on one of River's ranting posts."

Noah scowled when he read aloud Freddie's comment. "'The SOBs should all die.'" He whipped out his phone and requested that SAPD immediately pick up Freddie and bring him in for questioning. He'd just finished getting the okay on that when Hudson pulled into her driveway.

Even though she wanted to scour the rest of the list Hudson had compiled, Everly looked out the window at her house. She got another icy chill. One she silently cursed because she didn't want to feel that way about her home. She definitely didn't want to see images of a dead body and a bloody box.

But she did.

Mercy, she did.

Even though she didn't say anything, her expression must have shown what she was thinking because Noah took her hand and gave it a gentle squeeze. "You don't have to go in there now if you're not ready," he offered.

Everly shook her head because she didn't think putting this off was going to make it easier. Just the opposite. Sooner or later, she had to face this, and she was going with the sooner option.

Hudson parked in front of her porch, and he pressed something on the monitors. "I'm scanning the house and the area," he explained. "No one is around, and I'm not picking up on any kind of explosives," he added several moments later. "But why don't Noah and you go ahead inside, and I'll get started on setting up some cameras."

The man hauled an equipment bag off the passenger's seat and got out. Noah and she did the same, and when she used the app on her phone to unlock the front door, they hurried onto the porch.

Everly glanced around them and then up at the bruise-colored sky. A storm was moving in, a bad one from the looks of things, so she was glad the CSIs had finished processing the yard.

Leaving Hudson on the porch, Noah shut the door behind them when they went inside. But Everly only made it a few steps before she had to stop. She dragged in a deep breath, hoping it would steady her nerves.

It didn't.

What did help though was when Noah took her hand and gave it a gentle squeeze again. A reminder that she didn't have to do this alone. Good thing, too, because she wasn't sure she could have managed it.

"It'll take time," she muttered, speaking more to herself than to him. "I just have to remember how much I love this house." *Loved*, she silently corrected, but Everly pushed that aside. She couldn't let the killer take this away from her.

"There's a suitcase in my closet," she said, and Everly headed in that direction.

Noah went with her, of course, but instead of actually going into her bedroom, he stopped in the doorway, bracketed his hands on each side of the jamb and watched her.

"I won't ask if you're okay," he volunteered. "But I will ask if there's anything I can do to make it better."

It surprised her that the image that flashed in her mind this time had nothing to do with killers or attacks. It was the memory of Noah kissing her. Everly thought that another kiss from him would definitely get her mind off the bad things, but it would be like playing with fire.

The corner of Noah's mouth lifted as if he knew exactly what she was thinking. Probably because he, too, was feeling this damned heat between them.

Angry with herself and the heat, Everly dragged out the suitcase and started toward the nursery across the hall so she could pack Ainsley's things. But she halted directly in front of Noah. She couldn't stop herself from doing that. And on a heavy sigh, she leaned in and touched her mouth to his.

Playing with fire indeed.

It was so wrong of her to take comfort like this from him, but he seemed to welcome it. Well, welcome it with restraint anyway. He took hold of her shoulders and turned the kiss into more than a mere touch. It was deep but short, and when he eased back, she saw the regret in his eyes. Not regret that the kiss had happened though. No. It was because it couldn't be a whole lot more.

Everly cleared her throat, hoping it would do the same to her head, and she knew that soon she'd have to deal with these feelings for Noah. Feelings that she was scared went beyond the desire. That definitely wasn't a good thing since caring deeply for him again would only ignite the old guilt. Even if they fell in love with each other again, Everly doubted they could ever have a life together because of that guilt.

She forced herself to move even though it meant walking past Noah. Touching him, too, when her body grazed him.

He noticed.

Everly heard the husky sound in his throat. A sound she had no trouble interpreting. It was a hungry ache that wanted to be sated. But Noah didn't act on it. Didn't pull her to him for another kiss. He merely followed her to the nursery while she began gathering what she'd come to get.

She packed some extra clothes for Ainsley. The moisturizer she preferred to use on her daughter after her bath. Also, three small stuffed animals that Ainsley liked to cuddle when she slept. All things that would hopefully make Ainsley's stay at the ranch a little more comfortable. She glanced at the baby monitor camera and considered taking it as well, but she recalled one already being in the nursery that Noah had set up at his house.

Everly added a few toiletries from her own bathroom. Some makeup as well, though she silently cursed herself for caring about such things when they had a killer after them. Still, they might give her the same comfort as Ainsley's things would give her.

It hadn't taken her long to pack—and kiss Noah—but when they opened the front door, they saw that Hudson was on a small ladder that he'd obviously had in his SUV, and he was mounting a camera on the far right side of the porch.

"It has two lenses so it'll cover the entire porch and the right side of the house," Hudson explained while he continued to work. "I've already put up one in the back, and I've positioned it so it'll cover the left side of the house as well. They're motion activated, and I've emailed both of you the link so you can view the feed on your laptop and set up an account to check it on your phone. You should do that now so you'll know if you've had any unwanted visitors."

Everly figured it hadn't been difficult for a man of his expertise to get her email address so he could do that. "Thank you," she said, and she meant it.

"It's a start," Hudson explained. "After I get you back to the ranch, I'll have someone deliver more equipment. What kind of internal security system do you have?"

Everly lifted her phone and showed him the app for the one she used. "There are sensors on the doors and windows. It should trigger an alarm if someone breaks in. I know it works because a couple of times I've forgotten to disengage it before I've opened the door. It's not a loud alarm, but it's enough to get my attention."

Hudson made a sound that could have meant anything. "I have something better that I can install. Something that'll be a lot harder for anyone to tamper with. What about any cameras inside?"

She shook her head. Then, shrugged. "Nothing except for the baby cam in the nursery."

"It's motion activated?" he asked.

"Yes, but it doesn't set off an alarm. I have a monitor app on my phone so I can check on Ainsley after she's gone down for the night or a nap. I also have a monitoring unit for the baby cam that I keep on my nightstand. I have the volume on high enough that I wake up if Ainsley starts fussing." She stopped, feeling another round of worry. "Do you think I need interior security cameras?"

"It doesn't hurt," Hudson said, and he must have seen the worry on her face because he added, "When the killer left that box and Daisy's body, he didn't break in."

True, and it would have been so much worse if he had put Daisy's body inside Everly's house. Everly shuddered at the thought, and while she hoped she wouldn't have to worry about such things much longer, she would get several more nanny cams and position them around the house.

"How far of a range is the nanny cam you have in the nursery?" Hudson asked.

It took her a moment to recall that info. "About a thousand feet. It covers the entire room since Ainsley plays in there a lot, and I like to keep an eye on her if I'm in another part of the house." Though she never left her daughter alone for very long despite the house being childproofed. "I mounted the camera on the wall so I can see if she goes out into the hall."

In hindsight, Everly wished she'd put an actual camera in

the hall, too. She usually kept her bedroom and bathroom door shut, but since Ainsley was learning to turn the knobs, she might get into something she shouldn't be getting into.

Hudson got down from the ladder, and he glanced up at the sky though and cursed. "If I hurry, I can maybe beat the storm. I looked at the forecast, and things could get rough."

"Tornados?" Everly immediately asked.

"It's possible," the man added with a nod while he folded up the ladder.

"My house on the ranch has a tornado shelter," Noah explained, looking at the forecast on his phone.

She had one as well that could be accessed through a hatch in the floor of the laundry room, but she hoped it wouldn't be necessary to use it.

They were still in the doorway when his phone rang, and she saw River's name on the screen. Obviously, Noah had added it to his contacts.

"Detective Ryland," Noah answered, but he shifted his attention around the yard, doing a sweep of the area. Maybe because he thought this call could be some kind of distraction.

"I'm on my way to the Silver Creek Sheriff's Office," River blurted out, his words and breath rushing together. "I have to see you right away."

"Why? Has something happened?" In contrast, Noah's voice was steady.

"Yeah, you could say that," River snarled. "Somebody just tried to kill me."

Chapter Eleven

Noah cursed, and because he didn't trust River any more than he did their other suspects, he nudged Everly back inside her house.

Hudson went with them, and taking out a Glock from a slide holster in the back of his jeans, he checked the camera feed on his phone. If there was anybody out there in their line of sight, Hudson would spot them.

"FYI, you're on speaker," Noah spelled out to River. "Now, who tried to kill you?" Noah not only shut the door, he made sure Everly wasn't standing directly in front of it or the windows.

"I think it was Bobby," the man readily said. In the background, Noah could hear what he thought were the sounds of River driving.

"Bobby," Everly repeated on a rise of breath. She'd obviously heard what River had said and would be listening to the rest of the conversation.

"You actually saw Bobby try to kill you?" Noah pressed.

River groaned, the sound of fear and frustration—both of which could be faked. "No, but Bobby was at my place earlier so it must have been him."

Noah had to do a mental double take. "Why was Bobby at your house? You claimed you didn't even know his last name."

"I didn't," River insisted, and then he paused. He muttered some profanity. "I left a message for him on the bulletin board outside the room where we meet for Peace Seekers. I didn't use his name. I called him Red Card and added my number. He saw it and called me."

Noah did some groaning of his own, and he wondered how the heck the SAPD had missed such a note. Then again, maybe it hadn't been there when they'd searched the room.

"When Bobby called," River went on, "I gave him my address, and he came right over. I told him I was scared, that I thought Jared was the killer and that he might try coming after us. You know, to silence us 'cause I was pretty sure Bobby had seen the mud on Jared's shoes, too."

Noah didn't volunteer anything about Jared being able to walk. Instead, he pushed for more details of this so-called attempt to kill him. "Tell me what happened when Bobby visited you."

River took a deep breath. "He asked if I knew for sure that Jared was the killer, and I told him no, that it was just a gut feeling. He said I should be careful and not tell anybody else my suspicions because it might get back to Jared. And if Jared wasn't the actual killer, it might get back to the person who was."

Maybe it had already gotten back to the *person who was* because the killer could be Bobby. Then again, all of this could be a ruse set up by River to take suspicion off himself.

"Anyway, Bobby didn't stay long," River continued a moment later. "He left, and after he'd been gone about ten minutes, I heard this loud boom, and I looked out the window and saw that my front porch had blown up. I mean, there were pieces of wood everywhere."

Noah considered that and wondered if the explosive had even been meant to kill. Maybe it'd been a warning.

"Did you hear me? I said I think Bobby could have put a bomb there," River insisted.

Even though Noah figured he already knew the answer, he asked the question anyway. "Did you see Bobby do that?"

"No, but I left him alone for a couple of minutes while I went to the bathroom. He could have planted it then."

True, but that would have been gutsy to the point of being careless to do that since Bobby wouldn't have known how long River would be gone. If Bobby had indeed planted an explosive, it was more likely he'd just tossed it there when he arrived or when he was leaving.

"I'm guessing you didn't call the local cops to tell them about the explosion?" Noah asked.

"No. I didn't want to wait around for them. It would have taken them minutes to get out there, and Bobby could have come back while I was waiting on them. I ran to my truck and started driving. If you're not at the sheriff's office, you need to meet me. I'll be there in about five minutes."

Now Noah sighed. He really didn't want Everly stuck in the sheriff's office for heaven knew how long while he worked all of this out with River and the Bulverde cops who'd have to be called in to investigate the explosion. Even if she wanted to hear anything else River had to say, she probably wouldn't want to be away from Ainsley that long especially since he could fill her in on the details later.

"All right," Noah finally said. "I have an errand to do first, and then I'll head to the sheriff's office. Go straight there," he instructed River just in case the man was truly a target, "and wait for me."

Noah ended the call and turned to Everly. "Hudson and I can take you to the ranch. You can maybe work on the financials and that list Hudson gave us while I deal with River."

Until he added that part about the financials and list, Everly had been shaking her head, but she must have realized she could still help with the investigation while also being with her daughter. She finally nodded.

Noah felt the instant relief that came with knowing she'd be tucked away safely at the ranch. Not alone with Ainsley either. He'd make sure some of the ranch hands were guarding the place, and there'd be no visitors or deliveries until he'd made it back from the sheriff's office.

He turned to Hudson who was still watching the security feed on his phone. "Do you see anyone?"

Hudson shook his head. "But I can't promise that no one is out there. I can get the infrared from the SUV, but that won't extend but about fifteen yards."

In other words, if someone was lying in wait across the street or behind the house, he wouldn't be spotted. And that's why Noah drew his gun. He had to be ready in case the worst happened.

"Move fast," he instructed Everly. He didn't want to waste any time getting her into the SUV so they'd be behind the bullet resistant sides and windows.

Hudson went first, and with Everly between them, they started out of the house. Noah closed the door, figuring that Everly could lock up with her phone once they were inside the vehicle. However, they hadn't even reached the last step on the porch when he heard an odd swishing sound.

His first thought, a really bad one, was that someone had

just fired a bullet through a silencer. Obviously, it was what Hudson thought as well because he yelled "Get down."

Hudson ran toward his SUV, throwing open the door and using it for cover while he fired glances all around them. Noah did the same, and his heart dropped to his knees when he saw the small dart syringe sticking out of Everly's neck.

"I've been hit," she murmured, her eyes already going glassy, and she practically tumbled into his arms.

Noah silently cursed every word of profanity he knew, and he frantically yanked out the dart so he could feel for a pulse. It was there, thick and throbbing, but Everly's eyelids were fluttering down. She was losing consciousness.

"Call an ambulance," Noah shouted to Hudson, and as the last word left his mouth, Noah caught the movement from the corner of his eye.

A blur of motion from someone running away.

He hadn't even gotten a glimpse of the person's face, but Noah thought it was a man. Maybe the killer.

Noah had a fast debate with himself as to what to do, and he hoped he made the right decision. "Get Everly inside the SUV," he told Hudson, giving him the dart so it could be tested, "and call for an ambulance and backup."

Knowing that Hudson would do as he'd said and that he'd protect Everly with his own life, Noah took off running in the direction of where he'd seen that blur of motion. Yeah, it was a risk. Anything he did at this point could be, but he figured he could outrun any of their suspects, and he didn't want the SOB to get away so he'd have the chance to come at them again.

The raindrops began to spatter on his face as Noah tore his way across the side yard and into a thick row of hedges and shrubs that divided Everly's property from her neighbors. Hedges and shrubs that led to a greenbelt and some trees. Way too many places for someone to hide, and this area would have been out of range of Hudson's scanner.

Noah kept checking over his shoulder to make sure no one was coming to attack Hudson and Everly. And he tried not to think of Everly. Tried not to see that blood on her neck from where the dart had slammed into her. But he thought of her and saw it anyway. Maybe, just maybe, the killer had used only a sedative, something designed to knock her out but not do any real damage.

He couldn't lose Everly.

He just couldn't.

Noah glanced over his shoulder, and he saw that Hudson had thankfully gotten Everly in the SUV. That caused Noah to breathe a little easier, and he turned his full attention back to the hunt for a killer. He still didn't see anyone, but even over the thudding of his own heartbeat in his ears, he was almost positive he could hear running footsteps.

Using his forearm to shove aside some low-hanging branches, Noah broke out into a small clearing just in time to see someone duck behind one of the huge oak trees that dotted the landscape. Thankfully, the person wasn't going in the direction of the house, but it was possible he was heading to a road on the other side of the thick greenbelt. If he'd left a vehicle there, and he almost certainly had, then he could get away. Or rather try to do that. But Noah had every intention of making sure that didn't happen.

"I know you're there," Noah called out, hoping to get the idiot to leave cover and show himself.

It didn't work, but he heard footsteps again. The killer had gone back on the run so that's what Noah did, too. Not easy to run though, with the rain now stinging his eyes and while trying to fight off the worry about Everly, but the stakes were sky-high, and he needed to stop this guy.

Noah caught another glimpse of a black shirt sleeve, but he had no idea which of their suspects this could be. Maybe Bobby, but heck, it could be River, too, if he'd lied and hadn't actually been heading to the sheriff's office. River could have been calling him from right here in Silver Creek. In fact, he could have faked the explosion so it would give him a motive for coming here.

But Noah didn't rule out Jared either.

This guy was flat-out running, something that Jared had led them to believe he couldn't do, but it was possible Jared had lied as well about just how mobile he was. In fact, it was possible there was nothing physically wrong with the man. He could have used that wheelchair to make them believe he was innocent.

The rain was coming down even harder now, and a crack of lightning jabbed through the sky. The quick round of thunder that followed told Noah that the lightning had been close. Too close. Not good because he was running through trees that could be struck at any moment. Added to that, the killer could have set explosives along the way to make sure anyone in pursuit wouldn't be able to catch him.

That didn't cause Noah to turn back though. He just kept running and shoved through the thick underbrush into another small clearing.

And that's when he saw it.

Not the killer but the phone lying on the wet ground. Since it could be a lure to draw him out so he could be gunned down, Noah shifted directions. He skirted around the phone and went toward the road.

The sound he heard had him cursing.

A vehicle. Not the soft idling of an engine either, but the roar of someone gunning it. There was the squeal of tires on the wet gravel surface which meant the killer was trying to get out of there fast.

Noah ran even harder, and he rammed his way through more underbrush to leap out onto the road. He immediately took aim in the direction of the sounds of that engine.

But he was too late.

He caught just a glimpse of a black truck as it sped away. A truck with no license plate.

Hell. There was no way to trace it. No way for him to see who was behind the wheel, but he yanked out his phone and called the Silver Creek dispatcher. He gave a description of the truck and asked for immediate assistance in locating it. They might get lucky.

Might.

However, Noah figured the killer had already mapped out his escape before he'd ever fired that dart at Everly.

At the thought of her, Noah turned and hurried back toward the house. Since the rain would no doubt wash away any tracks or trace evidence, he stopped and used his handkerchief to pick up the phone. That definitely wasn't standard procedure, but if there was something on it that could help them ID the killer, he didn't want the phone to be ruined by the water.

He slipped the phone in his pocket, and Noah kept his gun ready while he made his way back through the greenbelt. He heard the sirens, and the moment he reached Everly's side yard, he spotted the ambulance pulling into her driveway. A Silver Creek cruiser was right behind it.

Hudson stepped out of the SUV, his attention going straight to Noah. Noah shook his head to let him know he hadn't caught the SOB, but at the moment that wasn't even his main concern.

"Everly?" Noah asked.

"She's still conscious. Barely," Hudson added. "But her vitals are good."

Noah had to see for himself, and while the EMTs and Deputy Lawson hurried out of their vehicles, Noah went straight to the SUV. Everly was there on the backseat, and she was muttering something.

His name, Noah realized.

"I'm here," he told her, leaning in so she could see his face. And so he could see hers. Her eyes were unfocused, but she turned to the sound of his voice, and she lifted her head off the seat.

"You're alive," she muttered, her words slurred. The breath rushed out of her, and her head dropped back down.

"I didn't catch him," he let her know. "I'm so sorry."

But he wasn't even sure Everly heard him because her face went slack. For one horrifying moment, Noah thought she'd died, and his fingers were trembling when he checked for a pulse. She was alive, thank God, but whatever had been shot into her body had obviously knocked her out.

"This will need to be tested," Hudson told the EMTs, giving them the dart. "So you'll know what drug was used on her."

Noah stepped back so the EMTs would have access to her, and he took out the phone to hand to Deputy Lawson. "I found that when I was in pursuit of the person I believe is the vigilante killer."

The deputy's eyes widened a little, and she reached into her back pocket to pull out a small plastic evidence bag. "I'll get this to the lab right away," she assured him. She glanced around, and like the rest of them, the rain was soaking through her clothes. "On the drive here, I heard the description of the truck. Somebody might see it."

She didn't sound especially hopeful about that. Neither was Noah. The storm would keep a lot of folks inside. It would also cut down visibility, and the realization of that ate away at him because he knew what this meant. The killer had gone back to his hole and could plan another way to come after Everly and him.

The EMTs loaded Everly onto a gurney, and Noah followed them to the ambulance. So did Hudson. Deputy Lawson hurried to her cruiser.

"I'll lock up the house," Hudson told him, "and then meet you at the hospital. Are you okay?" he tacked on to that.

Noah was far from okay, and that wouldn't get better until he was certain Everly would be all right. "I need to catch this snake," Noah muttered, climbing into the back of the ambulance with Everly.

"I'll help with that in any way I can," Hudson assured him. "FYI, I called Grayson, and he's on the way out here. I thought you'd want to know though that River never showed up there."

Noah cursed and took out his phone to put an APB out on River. Because if River wasn't a victim of foul play, then he was most likely the killer.

Chapter Twelve

Everly was trapped, and the jumble of images and sounds came at her nonstop. The sound of her car slamming into Helen's. The storm with its loud thunder and slashes of lightning.

And the blood.

Helen's blood.

It turned her stomach, knifed at her as fast and lethal as those lightning strikes, and Everly had to fight hard to push it all away. To come to the surface.

She sucked in a hard breath, and that caused some movement around her. Footsteps that made her heart race. Sweet heaven. Had the killer come for her here? Wherever *here* was.

"Everly," someone said. Noah.

She latched on to the sound of his voice and opened her eyes. Not easily. She had to force it, and things didn't immediately come into focus. It took several moments and some fast blinking before she finally managed to see his face.

His *very worried* face.

And it all came back to her. The feel of the dart slamming into her neck. The drug almost immediately starting to slide through her. The memory of watching Noah run in pursuit of the killer.

"You're okay," she managed to say, and even though she couldn't show a lot of relief about that, Everly felt it bone deep. Noah was all right. He hadn't been hurt. The killer hadn't gotten to him.

He nodded. "How do you feel?"

Not great, her head was still spinning, and her throat was as dry as dust, but she was alive. So was Noah. Considering the killer had gotten close enough to fire that dart, it also meant he'd been close enough to gun them both down.

"Did you catch him?" she asked though she could already see the answer in his weary, troubled eyes.

"No," he said. The guilt coated that single word, and she reached out for his hand. That took some effort as well, but Everly was finally able to clutch it.

The feel of him jolted back more memories. More realizations. Of being put in an ambulance, and now she was in a hospital bed. Not an actual hospital room though. This was the ER, and she was in one of the exam rooms.

"Ainsley," she said, trying to get up. She had to get to her daughter.

But Noah eased her back down onto the bed. "She's fine. I've been getting regular texts from my mom, and she says that Ainsley is playing with some of her new toys." He looked her straight in the eyes. "Ainsley is safe. My parents won't let anyone get near her."

She searched his eyes to see if Noah was trying to minimize any possible threat to her child. He wasn't. He was telling her the truth, and that made her breathe a whole lot easier. She obviously had plenty to worry about, but Ainsley was at the top of the list of her worries.

"What happened?" Everly asked, and that would be the first of many questions. "What drug did the killer shoot into me?"

The muscles in his jaw were as hard as iron. "We'll have to wait for tox results, but the doctor who examined you thinks it was some kind of strong pain medication meant to knock you out. Your vitals are good," he quickly added. "And you're awake a lot sooner than he thought you would be. He thought you might be out for another hour or so."

Maybe that meant the killer had given her a small dose. One not meant to kill her but rather incapacitate her enough so he could... What?

Grab her and run?

That likely wouldn't have happened with Noah and Hudson right there so maybe the killer had intended to drug them, too, and something had gone wrong. Then again, this could have been meant just to scare her. A reminder that he could get to her whenever he wanted.

That tightened every muscle in her body.

"If Ainsley had been with me today at the house, she could have been hurt," Everly muttered.

"She wasn't with you," Noah quickly pointed out, and when Everly sat up again, he didn't stop her. Instead, he pulled her into his arms. "She wasn't with you," he repeated.

Everly took comfort from his hug. Took more comfort, too, with his words and the soft kiss he brushed on her cheek. But the comfort couldn't last. Not when she had to ask him one very hard question.

"Do you know who the killer is?" She met Noah's gaze. Waited.

He shook his head. "I'm sorry about that. I went after him, but I didn't catch him. He got away."

The guilt had gone up some considerable notches, and Everly put a stop to it by kissing him. Obviously, Noah needed some comforting, too, because he groaned and sank into the kiss for some too-short pleasurable moments. When he eased back, he pressed his forehead to hers.

"River never showed at the sheriff's office, and he's not answering his phone," he said, his voice a low murmur now. "I have an APB out on him. Both Jared and Bobby are coming in tomorrow morning for interviews."

That was a necessary step in the investigation, but she doubted either of them would just up and confess to being a killer.

"I did find a phone in the greenbelt behind your house," Noah went on. He finally pulled back but stayed close. "The killer might have dropped it, and if so, the lab might be able to get something from it."

That was good. Maybe a critical mistake that would help them catch this monster before he struck again.

"SAPD is still searching Jared's apartment," Noah continued. "Nothing's turned up so far."

That wasn't a surprise. If Jared was the killer, he would have known he could become a suspect, and he probably wouldn't have left anything incriminating for the cops to find.

Even though there were no windows in the exam room, she could hear the storm outside. It sounded as bad as predicted.

With her head clearing a little, Everly moved her legs off the side of the bed and glanced down. She was still wearing her own clothes, and she didn't have on a hospital bracelet.

"The doctor wants to keep you overnight for observation," Noah volunteered before she could ask. "It'd be a good idea if you did that."

She was shaking her head before he even finished. "I don't want to be a sitting duck here. There are too many entrances and exits in this place."

Noah didn't argue with that. Couldn't. Even if they used every deputy in Silver Creek, it wouldn't be enough to guard the entire building, not with the darkness and the storm.

"What kind of side effects will I have?" she asked, and Everly let Noah take hold of her arm when she stood. The wooziness hit her, but she stayed on her feet.

"Fatigue, light-headedness. You'll need an exam, too."

"An exam that can wait," she insisted.

He opened his mouth as if to argue with that, but Everly gave him a look. One that reminded him if their situations were reversed, he wouldn't have wanted to wait around for an exam either.

"Is someone available to ride with us to the ranch?" she asked.

Noah sighed, nodded and then took out his phone. "Hudson has already gone back to the ranch to help keep an eye on things there, but Grayson is in the waiting room. I'll let him know you're ready to leave."

However, before he could text Grayson, his phone rang, and he scowled when he saw the name of the caller. "River," Noah snarled. He answered it, and in the same motion, he had her sit on the edge of the bed.

Everly didn't object. She was indeed experiencing that expected light-headedness, and she preferred to be able to focus on this call. Especially since River could have been the person who'd shot her with that tranquilizer dart.

"Where are you?" Noah demanded. "And by the way, I'm putting this call on Speaker."

"I'm nowhere near Silver Creek," was the man's answer.

River's evasiveness caused Noah's scowl to deepen. "You told me to meet you at the sheriff's office. Where were you when you asked me to do that?"

"I was driving there," River said without hesitation. "I got there and waited just up the street. You didn't come."

"No, because someone tried to kill Everly," Noah snapped. "What the hell do you know about that?"

There was no quick answer this time. "I had nothing to do with that."

"But you know about it," Noah argued.

"I heard about it after the fact. I saw the cruiser come barreling out of the parking lot of the sheriff's office, and I figured there was trouble so I called a friend who keeps tabs on police scanners and such. He said something was going on at Everly's house, that both the cops and an ambulance had been called. I didn't think it'd be a good idea for me to hang around and find out what it was."

Noah's grip tightened on his phone. "Why should I believe that? You call and say you're coming to Silver Creek, and minutes later, someone attacks Everly."

"You should believe me because I'm telling the truth," River practically shouted. "I didn't have anything to do with an attack. Remember, someone blew up my porch. If I was the killer, why would I have done that?"

"Because you might have thought it would remove you as a suspect. It doesn't," Noah stated, and his voice was as hard as the muscles in his jaw. "It. Doesn't," he repeated. "Now, where are you?"

"I'm not sure. That's the truth, too," River snarled when

Noah huffed. "The storm's bad, and the road leading to my house was flooded. I tried to get to a friend's place in San Antonio, but I ended up pulling onto a trail because it was too dangerous to drive."

Everly could hear the rain. Thunder, too. But that didn't mean River was on a trail somewhere. He could be in the parking lot of the hospital.

"I know you've got it in for me," River went on. "You think I'm the vigilante killer, but there's no proof whatsoever of that, and there never will be proof because I'm innocent."

"If you're innocent, then explain the weekly withdrawals for cash you've been making," Noah fired back. "Did you use the money to hire someone to help you with the explosives?"

Good question, and Everly very much wanted to hear the answer. Because that could indeed be the evidence to link River to the murders.

"What money?" River demanded, but then he stopped and muttered, "Oh, that. It has nothing to do with murder or explosives."

"Then, you won't mind explaining it," Noah insisted.

River groaned and muttered something she didn't catch. "I took out a personal loan. I'd overextended myself and had to pay the taxes on the ranch or I would have lost the place."

Noah didn't miss a beat. "I want the name and contact info for the person who loaned you the money."

River's next groan was even louder. "I don't have his name. It's a friend of a friend sort of thing."

"A loan shark." Noah rolled his eyes.

"I guess you could say that. High interest, but I'm paying it all back."

"I want his name," Noah pressed.

"I don't know it. He said I was just to call him Freddie, and I meet him once a week at a coffee shop in Bulverde to give him the payment. He's a big, mean looking guy so I'm never late. I'll have the loan all paid off in a couple of months."

All paid off with plenty of interest, no doubt. Well, if River was telling the truth. Everly wasn't so sure that he was.

"Look, I told you about the mud on Jared's shoes," River went on. "I'm trying to help you find this killer because, hey, I could be a target."

Noah made a noncommittal sound. "Be at the sheriff's office tomorrow morning at nine," he ordered. "If you don't show, I'll have you arrested."

With that, Noah ended the call and looked at her. "I got a glimpse of the person in the greenbelt. It could have been River." He shook his head, cursed. "But it could have been Jared or Bobby, too."

Yes, and so far the killer hadn't made a big enough mistake to help them catch him. Maybe the phone at the lab could help with that.

Noah sent the message to Grayson to let him know they were ready, but then his phone dinged with a text that came too soon for it to be a reply from the sheriff. Everly braced herself for bad news, but the corner of Noah's mouth lifted when he looked at the screen. He turned it to show her the photo. One of Ainsley asleep in the crib Noah had set up for her at his place. Her little girl looked so peaceful.

Sleeping like a baby, Darcy had texted with the photo.

Everly couldn't help it. Despite everything else that was going on, she also smiled, and she knew she was going to owe Noah's family a huge thanks when this was over.

They'd not only kept her baby safe, but they were also taking good care of her.

There was a knock at the door, and a moment later, Grayson opened it and peered inside. His attention went straight to Everly, and he frowned. Maybe because he didn't approve of her being up without waiting for agreement from the doctor.

"I'm okay," Everly told him, and that was more or less the truth. She still felt a little woozy, but she was already a lot better than she had been when she'd first woken up.

Grayson made a sound as if he didn't quite buy what she'd said, and he turned to Noah. "There's a problem. Not with any of the suspects or another attack," he quickly added when Noah groaned. "Some of the roads between here and the ranch are flooded."

That was not what Everly wanted to hear. "I need to see Ainsley," she insisted.

Grayson nodded. "One of the hands was trying to drive back to the ranch, and he reported the Silver Creek bridge is completely covered with water. It's too dangerous for you to try to use it."

Her stomach sank, and the dread washed over her. She'd held on to the hope of seeing Ainsley tonight. Of holding her. Because she thought just being with her child might soothe some of her raw nerves.

"The ranch is secure," Grayson went on. "Everything is on lockdown and the security systems are all set. Nate, Darcy and two armed hands are at your place," he added to Noah.

Everly fixed the image of her peacefully sleeping baby in her mind. The image, too, of the Rylands and the ranch hands standing guard to make sure no one got to her. That soothed her some, but there was nothing soothing about being in the hospital, especially since the killer would almost certainly know she'd been brought to the ER.

"I don't want to stay here," Everly heard herself say. She expected Grayson to argue with that. He didn't.

"I agree," Grayson said without hesitating. "Way too many places for someone to slip into his building and lay low to wait for an opportunity to strike. The two of you can come back with me to the sheriff's office and bunk in the break room. There's no bed, but you could take the couch."

"And where will you sleep?" Noah asked.

"My office," he answered.

Those arrangements didn't seem especially comfortable, but she doubted any of them would get much sleep anyway.

"I need to get Ava off shift since she's been at this for about fifteen hours straight," Grayson continued. "She should be able to get to her house if she leaves soon, and I can stay on duty." He paused. "Another option would be for the two of you to go to your place."

It took Everly a moment to realize Grayson had added that last bit for her. "Is it safe?" she had to ask.

Grayson lifted his shoulder. "As safe as it can be. I've had one of the reserve deputies watching the place for the past couple of hours, and after he had the equipment delivered, Hudson beefed up your security system. He said to call him if you had any questions."

Of course, the images of the latest attack came, and Everly silently cursed them. She hated to have all this dread and fear mixed with her home. Hated that the images only added more worry that she had no idea how long Noah, Ainsley and she would have to live like this before the killer was finally caught.

"The reserve deputy will be staying?" Noah wanted to know.

Grayson nodded. "It's Roger Norris. I sent him over after Hudson left."

Noah and she had gone to high school with the deputy, and she knew he'd served in the military. Along with running his family's ranch, he was a good cop, but Everly still wasn't convinced about going. Until she considered something.

Something that Noah wasn't going to like.

"Maybe it'd be best if the killer came after me," she said, "and he might be willing to do that if I'm home."

Noah huffed. No, he didn't like it. "Bait. I don't have to remind you about what happened when we tried that by going to see River."

No reminder was needed. The killer had nearly succeeded in blowing them to bits. But there was a huge silver lining in that attack.

"Ainsley wasn't with us then," Everly murmured. "And she wouldn't be with us at the house."

Grayson didn't huff or curse, but he looked a long way from being convinced that this was a good idea. He would have no doubt laid out some reasons as to why it wasn't a safe idea, but at the sound of the footsteps behind him, Grayson whirled around, automatically sliding his hand over his gun.

Next to her, Noah did the same, and he moved in front of her to stand side by side with the sheriff. Everly peered over their shoulders, steeling herself up in case this was the start of another attack. But it wasn't any of their suspects.

It was a woman.

Everly gasped and dropped back a step. She thought she

was seeing a ghost or that the images from her nightmares had come to life. Because she was looking at the face of Helen Fleming.

The woman Everly had killed fourteen years ago.

Chapter Thirteen

Noah stared at the woman who was making her way toward them. Even though he'd never actually met her, he had seen enough photos of her to know who she was.

Or rather who she appeared to be.

"What the hell?" Noah heard himself mutter, and he glanced back at Everly to see how she was handling this.

Not well.

The color had drained from her face, and she was no doubt having the mother lode of nightmarish memories of the car crash that had claimed this woman's life.

Helen, or whoever the heck this was, continued to walk toward them, her steps slow and cautious while she kept her attention on them. She was wearing a black raincoat and carrying a now closed umbrella. Water slid off both, dropping to the floor in soft splats.

"I know this must be a shock," she said and stopped when she was still several feet away.

That was a huge understatement. A shock which could also be some kind of trick. A distraction set up by the killer. Yes, the woman looked like Helen Fleming, but the killer could have found a close match and be using her so he could then get close enough to try to finish what he'd started with Everly.

"Don't come any closer," Noah warned her, and he went ahead and drew his weapon.

The woman's eyes widened, but she didn't panic. She sure didn't turn around and run out on them.

"I'm sorry," she said. "On the drive here, I considered how to do this. If I should call first, but I figured no matter how I made first contact that this was going to be...difficult."

Again, that was a huge understatement. Behind him, Noah could hear Everly's breath coming out in quick gusts, and he hoped she wasn't on the verge of a panic attack.

"Who are you?" Noah came out and asked.

The woman sighed. "You know who I am. Helen Fleming, but I don't use that name anymore. These days, I'm Helen Markham, and I live at 471 Pine Lane in Dallas. I'm fifty-one now and work in Pretty Petals, a downtown flower shop."

"Keep an eye on her," Grayson instructed, and he took out his phone. Probably to do a background check on that name and find out if anything she was telling them was the truth.

"We should talk," she said while Grayson got to work. "I need to explain some things to you." She paused, swallowed hard. "I need to tell you how sorry I am for letting you believe I was dead."

Everly's breath didn't gust. It broke, and the burst of air that left her mouth wasn't from humor. No. The reality of this was starting to sink in for her. For Noah, too. If this woman was truly Helen Fleming, then she'd let them live through hell for the past fourteen years.

"Is there some place we can sit down and talk?" the woman asked.

"Right here works," Noah said, and he didn't bother to tone down the snarl in his voice.

Even though this wasn't an ideal location with the ER waiting room and doors to the parking lot just a few yards away, there was the possibility that anyone could come walking up at any moment. Still, he had no intentions of letting their visitor into the exam room where she'd be right next to Everly.

The woman sighed again and nodded as if that was the exact answer she'd expected. "I don't know how much you know about what was going on with the night of the car crash," she said.

"I know everything," Everly snapped. The anger was now in her voice, too. "I remember everything. I've lived with this nightmare for nearly half of my life."

Another nod, and the woman glanced up at the ceiling as if hoping for divine help before her gaze slowly lowered back to Everly. "If I'd stayed with my husband, he would have killed me. I say that with absolute certainty. He'd already beaten me badly enough to put me in the hospital twice. And that night he told me I was going to die, that he would bash in my head."

Noah recalled reading Helen's statement, then those of the neighbors who'd verified the abuse. He was sure help had been offered to her when she'd landed in the hospital those two times, but she hadn't taken it. She'd gone back to her abusive husband. He knew that was often the case with battered spouses, and it ate away at him. However, at the moment the fact of what she'd done to escape ate at him even more.

"I was trying to get away from my husband," she went on. "I was hurt, terrified and desperate. But I didn't plan on the car crash," she quickly added.

"What did you plan on?" Everly demanded.

The shock was wearing off, and the anger was starting to take over. Noah got that. He was riled to the bone, but he stopped Everly from moving past him so she could go closer to confront the woman.

"Helen Markham didn't exist until fourteen years ago," Grayson relayed to them.

She made a sound of agreement. "I had help getting away from Isaac and starting a new life."

"I saw your body," Everly argued. "Your blood was on the road."

"Yes." And that was all the woman said for several long moments. She seemed snared in those same horrible memories.

Maybe she was.

But Noah was certain her memories couldn't have reached the level of horror that Everly's and his had.

"The blood was real. I was hurt in the crash, but obviously my injuries weren't fatal. My plan was to escape that night," she went on. "I'd connected with a group who assisted people like me, and I was driving to meet one of them at a convenience store just off the interstate. I was on the phone with that person when the car crash happened, and she told me to pretend to be unconscious."

The pretense had worked, but obviously that wouldn't have been enough to pronounce her dead.

"According to the records from the ER, you died shortly after arriving at the hospital," Noah pointed out.

She confirmed that with a nod. "The group I was working with arranged for a doctor to tell everyone that I hadn't survived."

Noah thought back to that time, to the doctor who would have done that. There'd been a lot of chaos, especially since Everly and he had been brought in for treatment, too. He recalled a young female doctor who'd been in Silver Creek on some kind of service program that provided specialists to small towns.

"Dr. Jones," Noah threw out there.

"Smith," the woman corrected. "She pronounced me dead, did the paperwork and then she and others in the group set me up with my new life in Dallas. And, no, I can't give you the actual names of Dr. Smith or those who helped me because I never knew who they were."

Noah knew there were groups out there like those. An underground network to get women and families out of violent situations, and he'd heard there were members who were doctors and such. However, he'd never heard of one of them faking a death to cover the victim's tracks.

"This could have happened?" Noah asked Grayson, and he saw that his uncle was reading over the death certificate for the woman they'd thought had been killed.

"Yeah, it could have happened," Grayson verified. "I believe she is Helen Fleming."

Even though Noah had already come to the same conclusion, it still felt like a hard punch to the gut, and he had no doubts that Everly was feeling the same thing. She took hold of his left arm, leaning into him, probably because it felt as if her legs were ready to give way.

Grayson took his attention off his phone and put it back on Helen. "Why are you here?"

Good question, and Noah didn't think it was because she'd finally wanted to clear her conscience and give Everly and him some peace.

"I heard about the murders," she murmured and then dragged in a long breath. "It's all over the news, and when I saw that Everly and Noah had been nearly killed in an explosion, I thought that maybe what was happening was connected to me, to the car crash."

"Is it?" Everly demanded.

"Maybe," she admitted, but her expression said it was a lot more than just a maybe. "I found Bobby's address, and I went to his place first, but he wasn't home so I called him. He'd put his number on one of his social media pages."

Everly made a soft sound of surprise. "Bobby knows you're alive?"

She nodded, and a fresh wave of weariness spread over her face. "He didn't believe me at first, but when I gave him personal details of our lives that only I would have known, he realized I was telling the truth." She paused. "He didn't take the news well. He was upset. Rightfully so," she quickly added.

"Rightfully so," Noah spat out.

Part of him knew he should have some sympathy for this woman who'd endured the abuse at the hands of her husband. But another part of him wasn't sure he'd ever be able to forgive her for what she'd done. Bobby likely felt the same way.

And that led Noah to another thought.

If Bobby was the vigilante, how was he reacting to the news that his *beloved* stepmother was actually alive? Would he stop killing now that his motive for going after Everly and him was gone?

Maybe.

Or maybe this would just enrage him so much that he'd start a killing spree that would include this woman who'd let him grieve and suffer all these years.

"How long has Bobby known the truth?" Noah pressed.

"Only a couple of hours. I told Bobby I was going to come clean with Everly and you," Helen went on. "Since Isaac's in jail and can't hurt me, I intend to come clean with everyone. No more hiding."

Noah nearly blurted out that her confession fell into the too little, too late category, but that would just be the anger talking. It was possible that once all of this sank in and they had the killer behind bars, that Everly and he might be able to find the peace that they hadn't had since that night when they'd thought they had ended a life. They might finally be able...

Noah stopped and let that play out in his mind. Without the strangling guilt, they might finally be able to look at each other the way they once had. He had to push that aside though. Couldn't let himself dwell on that. Yes, the guilt might be gone, but there was still a killer at large.

"How did you know Everly and I would be here?" Noah asked, going back into the cop mode.

"Oh," Helen muttered, and she paused before shifting to the change in subject. "I stopped for gas just at the edge of town, and the clerk mentioned there'd been some trouble, that Everly had been hurt."

It didn't surprise him that there was already talk about the latest attack. Things like that didn't stay secret for long, which was the very reason Everly had been so anxious to get out of here. Of course, she'd been willing to do that so she'd be bait, but that was something he'd need to talk to her about after he had finished this conversation with Helen.

"I decided to come to the hospital first and check," Helen went on. "If you hadn't been here, then I planned on going to the police station." She glanced over her shoulder in the direction of the ER doors. "The storm's getting worse, and I wasn't sure I could make it out to the Ryland ranch. And I didn't have Everly's address."

Noah searched the woman's eyes and expression to see if all of that rang true. It did. That didn't mean, though, he was simply going to trust her. He seriously doubted she was responsible for the murders and attacks, but since they were almost certainly linked to the car crash fourteen years ago, then it meant the killer likely had a connection to her. Just as that last thought crossed his mind, proof of his theory came hurrying in through the ER doors.

Bobby.

Unlike Helen, the man didn't have a raincoat or umbrella, and he was soaked, his clothes clinging to him. One look at him, and Noah saw the anger that'd tightened his face.

"Don't come any closer," Noah warned him, and even though he didn't take aim at Bobby, the man stopped. Good thing, too, since the small Silver Creek hospital didn't have metal detectors, and Noah had no idea if the man was armed.

Noah hurried to Bobby who lifted his hands in the air, and Noah frisked him. No weapon. Well, no actual one anyway, but Bobby was sporting a lethal glare. Not aimed at Everly and him. No. This glare was for Helen.

Tears sprang to the woman's eyes, and she angled herself so she could face him. "Bobby, I'm so sorry—"

"Don't," he snapped. "I don't want to hear your lame excuses for why you left me with that SOB."

"He was going to kill me," Helen muttered. She didn't wipe away her tears, and they spilled down her cheeks like rain.

"You left me with him," Bobby repeated in a shout.

The shout got the attention of the nurse at the check-in desk, and Noah didn't stop her when she reached for her phone. She was probably calling for the lone security guard who manned the hospital, but Noah doubted they'd need him. Grayson and he were both armed and ready to respond to the situation if Bobby tried to attack Helen.

"Do you know what my life was like with that monster?" Bobby went on. "It was hell," he provided before Helen could respond. Not that she was capable of saying anything. The woman was outright sobbing now.

"You ruined my life." Bobby lowered his hands to fling an accusing finger at her, and then he pointed to Everly and Noah. "Their lives, too." His voice broke, and he, too, began to cry. "You ruined so many things."

Noah was in agreement with Bobby on this, but he also felt the relief rise up in him. The hope, too, that knowing the truth might eventually help them get on with their lives.

"Did you kill those people and attack Everly and me because of all the things Helen ruined?" Noah came out and asked Bobby.

Bobby's head jerked toward Noah, and while the tears were still there, so was the fresh anger. "No." He repeated the denial in another shout. "I told you I didn't have anything to do with that."

Helen stared at him as if trying to decide if that was true. Despite the tears, there was hope on her face as well. Maybe she thought she would eventually get Bobby to forgive her for what she'd done. And he might. After all, Helen had had a good reason for trying to leave her old life behind, but she should have tried to get Bobby out of the hellish situation. Even if she couldn't have taken him with her that night, she could have had someone in the underground group try to rescue him.

Helen took a few steps toward Bobby. "Can we go somewhere and talk?" she asked in a whisper.

"No." Bobby didn't hesitate with that answer, and his glare returned with the vengeance. "I wish you'd just stayed dead."

Bobby turned and sprinted toward the exit. It all happened fast. The automatic ER doors swished open, and Bobby bolted outside.

Noah moved to go after him, and then he remembered just what a bad idea that could be. In fact, all of this, including Helen's visit, could be a setup to distract them or lure Noah away so the killer could try to grab Everly.

"Stay here and call for backup," Grayson insisted. "I'll go after him."

Noah didn't have time to argue that plan before Grayson sprinted out into the storm.

Chapter Fourteen

Everly watched the lightning bolts flash through the night sky. Not just one but clusters of them that in turn triggered rounds of booming thunder that seemed to shake the cruiser Noah and she were using.

There were no tornado warnings yet, but the rain was coming down so hard, the windshield wipers couldn't keep up, and the wind gusts were battering the vehicle. That was the reason Noah was driving at a snail's pace, and that in turn meant what should have been just a very short drive would turn into something much longer. Something much longer where she had time to think.

Everly had so many thoughts going through her head that it was hard to latch on to just one. The remnants of the tranquilizer probably weren't helping with that, but even without the drugs, she would have had to deal with the whirl of memories mixed with what Noah and she had just learned.

Helen was alive.

They hadn't killed her all those years ago.

Soon, she would need to try to come to terms with that, but for now, she had to put it on the back burner and deal with some more immediate things. Things that could get Noah and her killed if they weren't careful. That was the thought bearing down on her as Noah drove through the storm toward her house.

Yes, toward her house.

Grayson, Noah and she had had an intense discussion about that after Grayson had returned from his failed attempt to find Bobby. After Helen had left, too, saying that she intended to check into a room at the inn since it was too dangerous for her to try to drive through the storm to get back to Dallas. In the end, Noah and Grayson had reluctantly agreed to go with the bait ploy.

Bait with lots of security.

Grayson would need to man the sheriff's office, but one reserve deputy would remain parked out front of her house while another deputy would be positioned on the road behind the greenbelt in case the killer tried to make a return trip using that route. They'd be visible which would likely cause the killer to try to sneak around them, but it wouldn't be easy what with the storm still raging. The road to her house wasn't flooded, but the ditches soon would be if they weren't already.

Another security measure was that Noah would be armed, of course, and they'd monitor the cameras that Hudson had installed on the porches.

Locked doors, cameras and weapons might not be enough of a deterrent though. And if the killer was River or Jared, they still had the motive that might spur them to continue the murders.

Noah's phone dinged with a text, something it had done several times on the short drive from the hospital, but this time Noah didn't frown when he saw the message that popped up on the screen on his dash. It was from his mother, and she'd sent them another picture of a sleeping Ainsley.

Everly locked on to that image of her precious child, and it gave her a dose of resolve that she needed. The killer might have his own motive for what he was doing, but keeping her baby safe was a powerful incentive to make sure Noah and she succeeded at catching and stopping this monster.

"If Bobby's the killer, and he stops," she said as they pulled into her driveway, "you'll continue to look for evidence to put him away." It wasn't a question, but she wanted to hear Noah spell it out.

"I will," he assured her. "The killer isn't going to get away with what he's done."

No, he couldn't because as long as he was out there, he was a threat. He might not be out to seek justice, but he could want them or someone eliminated to make sure he was never ID'd.

Noah drove past the reserve deputy's dark blue SUV, and he pulled to a stop in front of her house and checked the next text he got. "Grayson put an APB out on Bobby," he said, reading the message. "No sign though of him or River. Jared's not at his apartment either."

"Is SAPD still searching the place?" Everly wanted to know.

He shook his head. "They finished and found nothing. They called Jared and told him he could return home, but he hasn't shown up yet."

Maybe that meant he was here in Silver Creek, trying to figure out the best way to get to Noah and her. A couple of hours ago, Everly would have thought the killer coming after them was a certainty. But maybe Helen had changed all of that. Well, it would change things if Bobby was the killer. His motive for seeking justice would be gone, and… she stopped as something occurred to her.

"Do you think Bobby might try to hurt Helen?" she asked.

"It's possible." Noah didn't hesitate, which meant this had already occurred to him. "Grayson called the inn and told them to make sure everything was locked up. Helen refused police protection," he added.

Everly hadn't known about that, but then Grayson had made some calls after he'd returned from his search, and he'd also sent several text updates to Noah.

Noah turned to her, and even though the only illumination came from dash lights and her porch, she had no trouble seeing the worry on his face. "You can change your mind about this," he reminded her. "We can stay in the break room at the sheriff's office."

The debate she'd been having with herself came again. "I want to stop the killer, but I don't want to do something to put you in danger."

The corner of his mouth lifted in a quick smile. "I could say something cocky like danger's my middle name, but I'm not worried about me. It's you."

Their gazes met, and even though she knew what he meant, it sounded like what he would have told her way back when. *It's you*, as in we were meant to be together. Years ago, before Helen and before that night, he'd said things like that to her, and she had believed them. That's why she'd given herself to him, why she had thought they'd be together for a lifetime.

Oh, yes. She definitely had some rethinking to do.

"We can't go back and erase the pain of the last fourteen years," she muttered.

"No," he quickly agreed.

His gaze stayed locked with hers for several more moments before he cursed under his breath. She thought he might say more, about them moving beyond the past to see where the future would take them, but he glanced away, looking at her house instead. Everly saw the shift. Saw the cop now instead of just the man, and she knew this was the way it had to be until the killer was caught.

"You'll unlock the door with the app on your phone," he instructed, gathering up the computer bag he'd brought with them. She knew he'd put two laptops in there and had covered it with a plastic garbage bag to protect the computers from the rain. "We'll run inside the house. Run," he emphasized. "Don't turn on the overhead lights and stay away from the windows. If the killer is out there, I don't want to make this easy for him. Besides, he might not use a tranquilizer dart the next time. He might decide to go for a straight kill."

That gave her a jolt of just how bad things could get. And they could get bad. Somehow though, what seemed worse than an attack was not having this resolved. Until it was, she'd never be able to get back to her life with Ainsley.

"Hudson sent me a text about the updates he was able to make before the storm got so bad," Noah went on. He showed her the new app on his phone. "The exterior cameras will now trigger an alarm so I'm going to have to pause them so we can get inside."

She was glad Hudson had managed to add that much, and it would hopefully work with what she already had. That way, they didn't get blindsided by someone sneaking in.

Everly did as Noah had instructed and unlocked the door while he hit the pause button on the cameras. She didn't even consider using an umbrella because with the howling wind, it would just slow them down and wouldn't stop them from getting wet. Instead, Noah and she focused on moving as fast as possible from the cruiser and onto the porch.

Once they were inside the house, she shut the door, locked it and used her phone to set the security system. It wasn't easy to do because her hands were wet, but it was a necessity. Since all the windows and doors were part of the system, an alarm would sound if someone tried to break in.

The AC wasn't running at the moment, but the air in the house was cool because of the storm. Her hair and clothes were dripping wet so she felt the chill slide over her, causing her to shiver. Her nerves didn't help with that. They were right at the surface, and every muscle in her body was knotted.

It wasn't exactly pitch-dark inside, but it was close enough, and it took her eyes a couple of seconds to adjust. Everly glanced around, looking for any and everything out of place. She didn't see anyone lurking in the shadows, but her attention landed on the piece of paper on the table in the foyer.

With his hand positioned over the hilt of his gun, Noah set the computer bag aside and rearmed the security cameras. He, too, was soaked through and through, but he didn't stop to dry off. He started looking around as well while Everly used the flashlight on her phone to read the paper.

"It's from Hudson," she relayed to Noah. "He apologized for not being able to finish doing the security updates, but he wanted us to know that he added dead bolts to the doors."

Everly immediately used the dead bolt on the front door and heard Noah do the same to the one just off the kitchen. "Because someone could jam the security system," she muttered under her breath.

She suspected Hudson had installed the best equipment possible, but nothing was foolproof.

Turning off her phone flashlight, Everly trailed along behind Noah as he glanced through the bedrooms. There were some things out of place, objects that'd been moved on her dresser, for instance, but she'd already noticed those items earlier when she had come to pack the suitcase. She suspected the CSIs had done that when they'd searched the place.

She paused in the doorway of the nursery and felt the mix of feelings wash over her. Part of her felt guilty for putting herself at risk like this because her daughter needed her and here she was making herself bait. But she also needed Ainsley to be safe, and this might make that happen.

Might.

The next round of thunder shook the glass in the windows, and she had to wonder if the killer would venture out in this. He would if he wanted them badly enough.

She checked the weather app on her phone and saw that the storm was predicted to start tapering off around two in the morning. A time when the killer might believe Noah and she would be asleep. They wouldn't be. Everly seriously doubted either of them would be able to sleep tonight, but the killer might pick that hour to come after them.

Everly took two towels from the guest bathroom and handed one to Noah. He used it to dry his face, but there wasn't much he could do about his clothes.

"I don't have anything here that would fit you, but I could put your jeans and shirt in the dryer," she suggested.

Everly wished she'd given that offer more thought or that she hadn't met Noah's gaze at the moment she said it. Because if his clothes were in the dryer, he'd be naked. The corner of his mouth lifted again in that blasted smile that had a way of making her forget, well, pretty much everything.

"Got a hair dryer?" he asked.

She shoved aside the effects of that smile, the effects of Noah himself, and nodded. Everly went to her bathroom, got the dryer and handed it to him.

"I'll change in my closet," she muttered, heading that way.

When she'd first thought of using herself as bait, she hadn't considered one of the hardest parts of this would be having Noah so close. Of course, she knew how he could make her body burn, but she'd thought the danger would have been enough to keep the heat in check.

She was wrong about that.

Everly hurried to her closet and grabbed a casual cotton dress from a hanger. It was loose to the point of being unflattering. Something she wore for comfort on the weekends when she'd been playing on the floor a lot with Ainsley. But a big advantage was that it had pockets so she could carry her phone and be able to hear if anyone triggered the cameras on the porches. Of course, Noah would be listening for that as well, but it didn't hurt for them both to be aware of what was going on.

From the guest bathroom across the hall, she heard him using the hair dryer, and thanks to a night-light near the sink, she could see him.

Mercy, did she.

When she glanced in, she saw that he'd taken off his shirt to dry it. He was doing that while he kept his attention on his phone that he had put on the vanity. Probably because he'd been concerned he wouldn't be able to hear the alarm over the sound of the dryer.

He looked up when he spotted her, and their eyes locked again. Locked for a couple of seconds anyway before he slid his gaze down her body. Apparently, Noah didn't find the dress as unflattering as it was because she saw that flash of need in arousal on his face before he shut it down. Not completely though, but he managed to put a leash on it.

"Is everything okay?" he asked, shutting off the dryer. "Let me rephrase that. Is everything okay with the house?"

She nodded and considered holding back on what was whirling through her mind. Not the desire this time. That was whirling, too. But this had to do with, well, everything.

"We'll have to rethink the past fourteen years," she said.

"Yeah," he agreed, and setting the dryer on the vanity, he stepped out into the hall to go to her. He hesitated though, and she knew why. It was hard to leash the heat if they touched.

But that's exactly what Noah did.

He pulled her to him, and in the same motion he brushed a chaste kiss on her temple. "It's going to be hard not to hate Helen for what she did," he said.

Everly made a quick sound of agreement. The woman had changed everything for them and had put a wedge between them that had lasted all these years.

But suddenly that wedge was gone.

It had been dissolving since the killer had put them in his sights, but Everly felt the last shreds of it fade away. All she could feel now was Noah, and while taking what he was offering was probably a mistake, Everly went with it anyway.

She put her mouth to his and kissed him.

NOAH HAD KNOWN the kiss was coming, but he realized he hadn't steeled himself up nearly enough. Then again, it was impossible to do that when the kiss was coming from Everly. Especially this kiss.

So much need.

So much heat.

They'd had their lives turned upside down again and were having to face the past. The guilt of what they thought they'd done was gone, but now there was a void that was filling up fast with this aching need and the realization that they might have never lost each other had they known the truth right from the start.

He tried not to go beyond that thought, beyond this moment, because he shouldn't be thinking of a possible future with Everly and Ainsley when their future was so uncertain. Noah just focused on the kiss. The way her mouth fit to his. The taste of her. And the way her body brushed against his bare chest. Everly had been the only woman to ever make him feel this way.

Only Everly.

He didn't tell her that now. Noah knew she might not be ready to hear it. Might never be. So, he just took the kiss and made it long and deep. Of course, it caused the attraction to soar, but thankfully it didn't rid him of common sense.

Without breaking the contact, Noah tightened his grip on her and maneuvered her into the bathroom where his phone was on the vanity. The bathroom had no windows, and since it was an interior room, it was one of the safest in the house. Just in case the killer decided to start shooting with the hopes that the bullets would make it through the walls.

Noah figured that Everly would point out that what they were doing was a Texas-sized mistake. But she didn't. The moment he'd closed and locked the bathroom door, she deepened the kiss even more. The silky sound of pleasure told him that she wasn't stopping.

Good. Because he didn't want to stop, either.

There was just enough light for him to see the arousal on her face when he lowered the kisses to her neck. He remembered this, and the thrill of touching her was just as strong as it had been all those years ago. It was like coming home and Christmas all rolled into one.

He found the sensitive places on her neck. Then again, he'd had a lot of practice finding them. Before they'd made love that one time, Everly and he had made each other plenty hot with their make-out sessions, some of which had stopped just short of sex. When they'd finally "gone all the way," it had finally given them both the release from the need.

The need that was building, building, building right now.

Noah turned her, leaning her against the edge of the vanity, anchoring her so he could slide his hand over her breasts. Again, familiar ground, and he swiped his thumb over her nipple. Judging from her quick gasp of pleasure, it had been a wise move.

Everly made some wise moves of her own. Her hand went to his chest where she touched and pressed, adding the kind of pressure that made Noah realize this foreplay wasn't going to last nearly as long as he wanted.

He kissed her again, this one hard and hungry, which pretty much described every inch of him. Everly must have felt that hardness because she ground her center against his. That robbed him of his breath and any thought of not finishing this right now.

Noah took hold of the dress, pulling it off over her head, and he kissed the places that were now bare. It was damn good but soon it wasn't enough. He rid her of her bra and kissed her there, too. Then, her panties. He would have gone to his knees to give her a kiss to satisfy both of them, but Everly stopped him by going after his jeans.

"Please tell me you have a condom," she muttered. Her voice was mostly breath and had little sound, but he heard her loud and clear.

"In my wallet," he assured her. Noah yanked that out while Everly got him unbuckled and unzipped.

But she did more than that.

She touched him, running her clever fingers the entire length of him. Noah cursed and could have sworn he saw stars. The good kind. And he was about to see a whole lot more of them.

He got off his jeans, boxers and boots. Somehow managed to get on the condom as well even though Everly didn't make that easy for him. She tongue kissed his neck all the while pulling him closer and closer.

When Noah could take no more of the torture, he sat her on the counter, hooked her legs around him and he pushed inside her. The passion slammed through him. So strong that he had to take a moment just to catch his breath. Everly did the same, and in the pale gold light, she looked him in the eyes.

She didn't say anything. Didn't need to. She just started moving, beginning the strokes that would give them a whole lot of pleasure before it sated this need.

He was starved for her and slipped right into the rhythm that would draw out every bit of that pleasure. The rhythm that would put an end to this.

Noah held on to it, moving deeper, harder, faster. He kept holding on, causing Everly's need to climb until she could take no more. Until she gave way, and he felt her body close around the hard length of him. That was his cue to finish this, to let Everly give him release.

So, Noah let go.

Chapter Fifteen

Everly wanted to stay put with her naked body pressed to Noah's. She wanted to just keep letting the aftermath of the pleasure wash over her. But she forced herself to remember that was a bad idea.

Noah and she had stolen these moments, but it had to stay just that. Moments. They couldn't linger because sex was the ultimate distraction, and they needed to stay diligent.

Even though she could still hear the storm raging outside, that didn't mean the killer wasn't trying to sneak his way past the reserve deputies and into the house. Of course, the alarms would sound when and if that happened, but it was best that Noah and she not be standing around naked if this turned into a showdown.

Noah must have come to the same conclusion because he eased away from her. He also kissed her before she could say anything.

Not that Everly had a clue what to say.

He was well aware that their being together like this wasn't a wise decision, but both also knew it hadn't been a decision at all. The heat had taken over, and they'd both needed—yes, needed—the comfort of being with each other in this most intimate way.

"Let's go ahead and get dressed," Noah muttered, brushing one last kiss on her mouth. "And then I'll check in with the reserve deputies to make sure all is well. Do you think you're up to taking another look at the financials on our suspects?" he tacked on to that.

She nodded because she was more than up to it. Everly wanted something to cause her to focus on the investigation and get her mind off Noah and what had just happened.

After picking up her dress and underwear, she went back into her room to put on her clothes. Of course, that was probably silly since Noah and she had just had sex, but Everly had wanted a moment to gather herself. Noah obviously needed a little time, too, because he stayed in the bathroom. Neither of them took long, and as he'd said, he sent messages to the deputies as soon as he came into the bedroom. The replies were fast, within seconds.

"They're both good. They haven't seen anything suspicious," Noah relayed to her. "Let me get the computer. You want to work in here?"

She tipped her head to the seating area but then realized the two chairs were directly in front of a large bay window. It would have been a good place to work if there hadn't been a killer out willing to shoot through the glass.

Noah obviously saw the position of the chairs as a problem, too, because he dragged them to the other side of the room next to the bathroom door. "I'll get the laptops," he said, heading toward the living room.

Everly went into the kitchen and grabbed two bottles of water and two cans of Coke. Even though she wasn't anywhere near being sleepy, she figured they could use the jolt of caffeine because it was going to be a long night.

Maybe a night that would lead to nothing.

Well, nothing to do with catching a killer anyway. Noah and she had definitely crossed some personal lines, and sooner or later, they'd have to deal with the consequences of that.

He came back with the laptops, handed her one and thanked her for the drinks. They sat, both of them pulling up the files on the financials. She'd study those, but first she had another look at the list of explosives experts that they'd gotten from Hudson. Everly had barely started on that when Noah's phone rang.

"It's the Silver Creek dispatcher," he explained, "and I'm putting the call on Speaker."

"Detective Ryland, this is Carlene Banks at Dispatch. I have a woman, Helen Fleming, on the line, and she wants to talk to you. Should I put the call through or do you want me to take a message?"

"Put it through," Noah instructed.

"Have you seen Bobby?" Helen asked the moment she was connected to Noah. Everly had no trouble hearing the desperation in the woman's voice, and she knew something bad must have happened.

Judging from Noah's sudden scowl, he was no doubt bracing for bad news as well. "Not since he came to the hospital. Why?"

"Because he called me. At least I think it was him. It was his number, but he wouldn't talk to me when I asked what was wrong. He just stayed on the line, and after what felt like an eternity, he whispered that I should leave if I wanted to stay alive. Detective Ryland, I'm not sure it was actually Bobby. I think it was someone pretending to be him."

"And why would someone do that?" Noah pressed.

"Maybe to scare me," Helen readily provided. "Maybe

to make me think Bobby had killed those people. I don't believe he did. I think someone is trying to set him up for the murders."

That was possible, of course, and Everly found it interesting that of their three suspects, Bobby was the only one who had had no suspicious withdrawals from his account. It was possible he was just more careful in covering his tracks than the others, but Everly couldn't dismiss the idea that Jared or River would indeed do something to set Bobby up.

"Where are you?" Noah asked, and Everly knew the reason for his urgent question. In the background, Everly could hear what she thought were the slap of windshield wipers and a car engine.

"I'm driving around, looking for Bobby," Helen admitted.

That caused Noah to groan. "You shouldn't be out in this storm. Go back to the inn and lock the door."

"I can't do that. I have to find Bobby. If he's in danger from someone pretending to be him, I have to try to save him. I can't just abandon him again."

Noah cursed under his breath. "You can work that out with him after we've arrested the vigilante killer. You're in danger just by being on the road. Do you want to cause an accident?"

Everly figured Noah had worded his question that way to make the woman stop the search and get back indoors. And it seemed to work. Helen made a hoarse sob.

"I need to make Bobby understand," Helen said through those sobs. "I need him to forgive me."

"Then go back to the inn so you'll live long enough to try to repair things with him," Noah insisted.

"You really think I can do that, repair things with him?" the woman asked.

Noah wasn't so quick to answer that time, maybe because he was asking himself if he'd ever be able to forgive her. "I don't know," Noah finally said. "Just go straight back to the inn and don't forget to lock the door. If you do hear from Bobby again, let me know."

"I will," she said, but there wasn't a lot of conviction in her voice.

Everly thought about the woman driving around in this storm. Helen could indeed get into an accident, and she hoped that wasn't what Helen had in mind by looking for Bobby. Maybe Helen intended to end her life the way everyone believed it had ended fourteen years ago.

Noah ended the call and then reconnected with Dispatch to give authorization to immediately put through any other calls from Helen. In this case though, no news would be good news because it would hopefully mean she'd gotten herself to safety.

"You really think Jared or River could have made that call to Helen?" Everly asked him when he'd finished with the dispatcher.

"Possibly, but if so that means they probably have Bobby. How else could one of them have gotten his phone? And if one of them does have him, then it means the likely plan is to set him up to take the blame for the murders."

True. Bobby would make a good scapegoat. If he wasn't the actual killer, that was. But if he was the vigilante killer, he could have made that call to Helen though, just to taunt her.

"I'm going to try to get a trace on Helen's phone," Noah said. "That way, I might be able to figure out where the call from Bobby came from."

Everly nodded and was about to turn her attention back

to the financials, but she glanced at the nightstand at the tiny bead of red light on the baby monitor that she kept by her bedside.

"What's wrong?" Noah asked, obviously noticing that something had alarmed her.

"It's maybe nothing." Or rather she hoped it was nothing. "Notice the light on the baby monitor. That comes on when it's been triggered. The camera's in the nursery, and it's motion activated. Maybe one of us set it off when we came in the house. It would have sounded with a little beep, but we might not have heard it."

The bad feeling came, twisting at her stomach. Because they'd been listening for sounds, any sounds, and even if they'd been several rooms away, Everly thought she would have heard the beep. It was the one surefire way to get her attention and would have even snapped her out of a deep sleep since it normally meant Ainsley was awake and had moved around enough to set it off.

Noah stared at the monitor. "Does it record what activated it?"

"Yes. It keeps the feed for about twelve hours." She stood to go to it, but Noah motioned for her to stay seated, and he eased across the room toward it.

It occurred to her then that the monitor was almost directly in front of a window. The blinds were closed, but she recalled the infrared Hudson had used. If the killer had that, then maybe he'd set off the monitor some way, maybe with a remote, and was waiting for one of them to go near it so he could shoot them.

Noah had obviously also considered the same thing because he drew his gun and then stooping down, he went to the nightstand. He snatched the monitor up and brought it back to her.

Everly steadied her hands enough to take the monitor and look at the bottom to see the time when it had been activated. Her stomach tightened even more.

"Judging from the time, it was triggered shortly after I was taken to the hospital," Everly managed to say.

Noah stayed quiet a moment. "Hudson came back here to install the locks a couple of hours after that. Maybe it happened then. I let him use your phone to get into the house, and he dropped it back at the hospital right before you finally woke up."

The relief came. Yes, that had to be it. Hudson had come inside to install the two dead bolts, and even though neither of those locks had been near the camera in the nursery, he might have checked out all the rooms in the house.

Everly hit the button on the monitor to view what the camera had recorded, and she didn't see Hudson.

However, she did see something that sent her heart to her knees.

She watched, her gaze frozen on the small screen as a man jimmied the window in the nursery. Everly couldn't see his face because he was wearing a dark hooded raincoat, and he kept his head down.

Everly saw the man climb through the window and into her daughter's room.

"OH, GOD," Everly muttered, her voice trembling. She stopped the recording, the image of the intruder frozen on the screen. With the dark hood and hulking posture, he looked like some monster from nightmares. "Oh, God."

Noah drew his gun and was silently repeating the same

thing. He had to force himself not to jump to some really bad conclusions. Conclusions like the killer had gotten in and planted a bomb.

A bomb that could go off at any moment.

Or that the killer was still inside the house. He battled his instincts to grab Everly and get her out of there fast.

Because that might be exactly what the killer wanted them to do.

The vigilante had cut the femoral arteries of his other victims. Hands-on, personal kills. Rather than blow Everly and him to bits, that's what he would no doubt prefer. For them to run so he could hit them both with tranquilizer darts, and then he could get close enough to slice them up.

Everly stood as if ready to bolt, but Noah took her arm and moved her to the corner of the room. Far away from the windows and even the door.

Noah had another look around, and even though the only illumination came from the night-light in the bathroom and the screen of the baby monitor, his eyes had adjusted enough that he could see the room clearly. Nothing seemed out of place, and he didn't hear any unusual sounds. Then again, the storm would block out anything like something breathing or approaching footsteps. Added to that, Noah's pulse was at a gallop now, and he could hear his own heartbeat crashing in his ears.

"The window wasn't open when we got here," Everly muttered, her voice just as shaky as the rest of her.

"No, it hadn't been." He'd checked all the windows, and they'd been locked. He'd done a cursory check of the house, too, looking for any signs that a killer was around.

There hadn't been any such signs.

But the guilt slammed into him that he hadn't checked

every nook and cranny. He hadn't made 100 percent sure that it was safe for Everly to be here.

Noah kept watch around them while he hit the button on the monitor to play the rest of the feed. On the screen, the intruder stopped and glanced around. Noah couldn't see the guy's face, but he was betting he was smirking, pleased with himself for violating Everly like this.

Had the intruder seen the camera?

Hard to tell. Noah couldn't see the guy actually looking in the direction of it, but it was right there in plain sight. Hell, he could have even seen it from the window before he'd ever stepped inside. That way, he would have known the angles he needed to avoid so the camera wouldn't capture his face.

There weren't any actual best-case scenarios of what Noah was seeing, but he had to consider this was a taunt. One that the killer had maybe been certain that Everly would see since he would figure a mother would have a nanny cam in the nursery. Even if he'd turned around and left then and there, the taunt would have been damn effective because Noah was betting it would cause Everly to never feel safe here again.

But the killer didn't leave.

With his grip tightening on his weapon, he watched as the hooded figure walked through the nursery. Slow, cautious steps without touching anything. Noah was betting though that the guy was wearing gloves.

Noah looked at the stride, at the guy's build, at the way he carried himself, and he tried to figure out if this was one of their suspects. Maybe. Probably. But he couldn't tell which one.

The man went to the doorway of the nursery, then glanced

around the hall as if trying to make sure he had the place to himself. Judging from the timing, he did. Noah noted the time and realized all of this was happening about the same time the ambulance had been arriving at the hospital with Everly.

So, the killer had shot Everly with that tranquilizer dart and had waited for them to leave before he'd climbed in through the window. A risky move since the cops were already on scene, but they'd been looking for the killer in the area of the greenbelt where Noah had heard the guy escape.

Or rather where he thought there'd been an escape.

But that had obviously been a ruse, too, and the killer had doubled back to do this break-in.

"How long ago did Hudson come back here to install the dead bolts?" Everly asked in a whisper. She seemed to be holding her breath. Noah knew how she felt. He was doing the same thing.

"It would have been at least a half hour, maybe more, since he had to wait for one of his crew to bring him the locks." Which meant the killer could have already broken in and left before Hudson had arrived.

Noah thought of something else that could have happened.

Something that caused every muscle in his body to go on alert.

He fast-forwarded the button on the feed, watching—no, he was praying—that the killer would have his look around before going back out the window and closing it behind him.

But that didn't happen.

The killer had a look in the hall, and even though his back was to the camera now and they couldn't see his face, Noah knew the snake was staring into Everly's room. Probably smiling again. No doubt fantasying about killing her. Then, the guy turned, went back to the nursery window.

And he closed it.

What was left of Everly's breath shuddered, and again, she would have bolted had Noah not kept her in place, positioning his body so that he was in front of her like a shield. He continued to watch. Silently cursing. Silently dreading what he now knew he'd see.

The killer stepped out of the nursery and disappeared out of camera view as he headed toward the main living area of the house. Noah didn't figure he was leaving either. No. Even though he couldn't see the direction of where the guy had gone, he was betting he'd scoped out the rooms for the best place to hide.

Noah hit the Pause button on the monitor, handing it to Everly, while he fired off a text to Hudson. When you came back to Everly's to install the locks, did you use the infrared scan on the house like we talked about?

It seemed to take an eternity, but it was only a couple of seconds before Hudson responded. Yes. Like you said, Everly hadn't had a chance to engage the security system before she got hit so you were worried somebody could sneak in. I didn't spot anyone, though there were some cops and a CSI in the yard.

The tightness in Noah's gut eased just a little until he recalled Everly saying something. Did you scan the tornado shelter?

Hudson's response wasn't so fast this time. I used it on the whole house, but if the shelter's surrounded by reinforced concrete blocks, it could have thrown off the scan.

Yeah, it could have. Also, if the killer had seen Hudson use the infrared scanner after they'd first arrived at the house, he might have been prepared with something like a Mylar blanket. Or even something simpler like aluminum foil that he could have taken from Everly's kitchen.

You need backup? Hudson asked.

Noah thought of the two reserve deputies. No. But the killer got in Everly's house. Might still be here in the storm shelter. Will keep you posted.

He dashed off quick texts to the reserve deputies to let them know there was a possible problem but to stay put for now. The one in the front yard, Deputy Cruz Molina, would be able to get to the door in less than a minute. Unfortunately, with the dead bolt, it would mean Noah would have to manually unlock it for him, but at least he'd have ready help if they needed.

The deputy in the back, Nelline Rucker, wasn't nearly as close, and with the storm still raging, it could take her a good five minutes or more to respond. Still, he wanted to keep her in place because if he was wrong about the killer being in the tornado shelter, Noah didn't want to leave the back of the house unguarded.

"The reserve deputies are both good cops," Noah reminded Everly. Reminded himself, too. "And this could all be a scare tactic."

That last part was wishful thinking though. If the killer had taken the risk to get inside the house, he was probably still here, not waiting to scare them.

But to kill them.

Noah heard Everly gasp, and his gaze flew over his shoulder to her. He expected to see her terrified gaze on something, or someone, in the hall. But no. She was looking at the monitor.

And Noah saw the reason for that gasp.

About six minutes after they'd first spotted the cloaked intruder climb through the nursery window, he appeared on the screen again. Noah cursed when he saw what the guy was holding. Not a weapon, though he could have easily had a gun or two in the pockets of the raincoat.

But what he had in his hand was a box of aluminum foil.

Everly made a strangled sound of fear, and Noah split his attention between continuing to keep watch around them and the monitor.

And he saw it.

One of the worst-case scenarios that had filled him with a sickening dread. Because the killer didn't go into the nursery and back out the window. Nor did he head back in the direction of the kitchen where he'd gotten that foil.

No.

With only his back visible because of the angle of the camera, Noah watched as the man walked into Everly's room.

Right where Noah and she were right now.

Everly didn't gasp this time, but because his back was pressed against her, he felt her muscles brace. Ready to fight.

Because the camera had caught the killer waving toward the camera and then getting on the floor. Onto his back. Where he had maneuvered and slid until he was out of sight.

The killer was under Everly's bed.

Chapter Sixteen

It was all Everly could do to stop the panic from taking over. But that was next to impossible. She wanted to scream. To run. To get out of there.

Because there was likely a killer beneath her bed.

A killer who'd been there for hours. Hiding, listening and waiting so he could kill Noah and her.

Noah didn't panic. Keeping his body in front of her to shield her, he took aim at the bed. "Come out or die," he snarled.

Everly braced herself for a reply. For movement. For gunfire. For any and everything, but the killer didn't respond. The only sound she could hear was the rain battering the windows.

Was the killer waiting there for Noah to come closer?

Maybe, but if so, why hadn't he just attacked when Noah had crossed the room to get the monitor? Or worse, why hadn't he broken down the door of the bathroom where Noah and she had had sex? They'd certainly been distracted then and would have made easy targets. The killer could have simply opened the door and murdered them where they stood before Noah could even get to his gun.

Noah was almost certainly thinking about that now,

thinking about how the killer could have heard their most private moments, and he was mentally beating himself up about that. Later, she would do that as well, but for now Everly knew she needed to focus on getting Noah and her out of this alive. The killer had already claimed too many victims, and she didn't want them to be his next victims.

Her heart was beating too hard, too fast, and Everly had to try to rein that in. It wouldn't help things now if she gave in to the panic. In fact, that might be exactly what the killer wanted her to do. Panic and run, and then he could get the added thrill of seeing her fear before he struck.

"Last chance," Noah snapped, with his gun still aimed at the bed. "Come out or die."

Again, Everly waited, trying to steel herself up for whatever was about to happen. But there was no response.

"Put your hands over your ears," Noah whispered to her. "I'm going to fire a warning shot."

Everly somehow managed to do as he said despite the fact that she was still holding the baby monitor and her hands were trembling. She silently cursed that trembling. Cursed that she was so unsteady at a time when she needed a clear head.

Noah gave her a couple of seconds, and he fired, the sound of the shot blasting through the air. The bullet slammed into her headboard and sent bits of wood flying. What it didn't do was send a killer scrambling out from beneath the bed.

His phone dinged with a text, but Noah kept his attention and his aim on the bed. "It's probably one of the deputies," he whispered. "Take my phone from my pocket and see."

Since her hands were shaking even harder now, it took Everly more time than she wanted to get out his phone. "It's Deputy Molina," she relayed to him. "He heard the shot."

"Text him back and tell him the killer might be in the house. I want him to hold his position for now and be ready to respond if he hears another shot or any signs of trouble."

Noah's voice was a lot steadier than hers, and since he hadn't hesitated with his response, it meant he'd already given that some thought. If the killer wasn't under the bed, then he was likely somewhere else in the house, and he might gun down the deputy if he tried to come in.

She sent the text and got a quick reply. "Should I contact Grayson?"

"Not yet," Noah said after she showed him the screen. "The storm's still bad, and this might be some kind of ruse."

"Is there anything else on the monitor to show what the intruder did after he got under your bed?" Noah asked her after she'd sent the second text to Deputy Molina.

Everly certainly hadn't forgotten that she was still holding the monitor. She'd had to shift it in her hand to reply to the deputy's text, and she shifted it again now so she could see the screen. She hit fast-forward until she spotted Noah checking out the nursery after they'd come here from the hospital. Everly watched, too, as Noah had gone into the bedroom where they are now.

Where the killer had been.

The camera stayed triggered for thirty seconds after Noah had gone back into the front of the house where she'd been waiting for him. Then, nothing.

"There isn't anything else on the feed except for you going in the nursery," she explained. "That triggered the camera. The killer could have maybe crawled out of the bedroom to keep from triggering it again."

And if so, that meant he could be anywhere in the house.

Noah took his phone from her and shoved it into his

pocket before he reached down and pulled out a small gun from a boot holster. "My backup weapon," he continued to whisper. "You know how to shoot, right?"

"Yes," Everly managed to say. She'd taken shooting lessons after a former client had threatened her when she'd lost his case. She had managed to hit the targets, but she wasn't so sure she could shoot another person.

But she immediately rethought that.

She'd kill if she had to protect Noah or Ainsley. She would kill to stop the vicious snake who was after them.

"What are you going to do?" she asked, reaching out for Noah when he took a step away from her. "Please tell me you're not going to check under the bed."

"No," he assured her. "If he's under there, I'd be an easy target to gun down. But I want us closer to the front door."

Everly started to ask why, and then it occurred to her that they might have to run for their lives. That definitely didn't help tamp down the panic, but she knew Noah was right. They had to be prepared for whatever the killer tried to do to them. Plus, if one of the deputies had to get in, they'd need to release the dead bolt.

"Stay right next to me, and when we get away from the wall, I want us back-to-back," Noah instructed. "You keep watch behind us, and I'll cover the rest."

She nodded and wished there was time to say something. Everly wasn't sure what that something would be, but she knew she couldn't bear the thought of losing Noah. She blamed the sex for that.

But then she had to mentally shake her head.

It wasn't the sex that had brought them closer. It was the *feelings* they had for each other that had led to sex. She had always cared deeply for Noah. Had once even been in love with him. And Everly could feel that love returning.

"What's wrong?" Noah whispered. "You groaned."

Yes, she had, but it hadn't had anything to do with the danger. It'd been because this was not a good time for her to realize just how much Noah meant to her.

"I'm okay," she settled for saying. It wasn't anywhere close to the truth, but it got Noah moving again.

As he'd instructed, they went back-to-back once they were away from the wall, and they began to make the trek across her bedroom. She tried to listen for any and all sounds that they were about to be ambushed.

But there was nothing.

It seemed to take a couple of lifetimes to reach the door, and of course, every shadow looked menacing. Especially the bed. Everly obviously had a too-vivid imagination because she could practically see the killer there. Unfortunately, she couldn't put a face on him, but she had to wonder if it was Jared, River or Bobby who was playing these mind games with them right now.

Noah and she stepped into the hall, and while Everly glanced around, she made sure some of those glances were at the bed. She steeled herself up in case the killer came rolling out from there, ready to fire shots at them, but she saw or heard nothing.

Where was he?

And how did he plan to finish this?

That question froze in her mind when Everly heard a sound. Not inside the house. But rather outside. Out front. There was a slash of headlights in the window, followed by the sound of a car engine.

Maybe Deputy Molina or Hudson had called Grayson.

If so, Everly knew he wouldn't just come charging toward the house where he could be gunned down. He was a veteran cop which meant he'd know how to handle a situation like this.

She heard the sound of voices and thought one of them belonged to Deputy Molina. The other, however, was a woman.

"Bobby?" the woman shouted.

Both Noah and Everly groaned because the woman who'd just yelled was Helen. Sweet heaven, what was she doing here? And better yet, how could they get her to leave fast because it wasn't safe for her to be here with the killer nearby.

Noah's phone rang, causing him to curse, but the call wasn't a surprise since it was probably from Deputy Molina. Probably. But it also occurred to Everly that it could be the killer trying to dole out another distraction. In fact, if the killer was Bobby maybe he'd lured Helen here with the intention of not only letting her be that distraction but also killing her.

Cursing under his breath, Noah maneuvered her so that her back was against the wall in the living room, and he became her human shield again. With his position, he could also keep watch of the hall in case the killer came at them from there. Noah then answered the call, keeping his phone in his pocket and putting it on Speaker, no doubt so it could keep his hands free in case they were attacked. It was a risk, since the killer might hear them, but it was also critical that they find out what Deputy Molina had to say.

"What's going on?" Noah asked the moment he had the deputy on the line.

"This woman just showed up, and she won't leave. She says she's looking for her stepson, that he could be in danger," Molina added, his words rushed together. "Should I have Nelline drive around so she can take the woman to the sheriff's office?"

"No. Because the woman, Helen Fleming, could be a decoy to get us to do just that." Noah huffed. "I want to talk to Helen."

It didn't take long, only a couple of seconds for the deputy to do that, and Everly heard Helen's frantic voice. "I can't find Bobby anywhere, and I have a bad feeling that he's been hurt. Is he here? Is he in the house with you?"

The answer to that was a Texas-sized maybe, but Noah didn't come out and say that. "Helen, you need to get in your car and go back to the inn. It isn't safe for you to be here."

"But I have to find Bobby," the woman sobbed. "Please help me find him."

The words had just left her mouth when Everly heard the blast. Felt it, too, because it shook the floor beneath them. Not a bullet. Not that.

But an explosion.

THE IMPACT OF the explosion knocked Everly and him back against the wall. Slamming them into it and knocking him off-balance. He had to fight to stay on his feet. Fight, too, to get past the slam of adrenaline and figure out what the heck had just happened.

Noah heard the crashing sounds of things falling, and the sounds were coming from Everly's bedroom. Judging from the smoke that started to seep from the room and out into the hall, the killer had put a bomb in there.

Hell.

The snake could have killed them, and there might be more than one bomb. Since the killer had had plenty of time in the house before they'd gotten back from the hospital, he could have set multiple explosives on timers, maybe set to go off when he thought Everly and he might be asleep.

The bomb must have rattled some windows in the bedroom enough because Everly's security system went off. Not a loud blare of noise, just the pulsing beeps. A warning to let them know there was trouble.

"Kill the alarm," Noah instructed her. The beeps wouldn't help them now, and they ran the risk of masking other sounds.

Because she wasn't especially steady, it took Everly a moment to get her phone from her pocket, and she silenced the alarm. Noah wished he could take a moment to try to reassure her. To let her know that he would do everything possible to get them out of this, but there wasn't time. Later, he'd try to make up for the huge mistake of allowing her to come here.

"What happened?" Noah heard Helen shout.

But Noah ignored her and ended the call. He didn't want the distraction of the woman's wails especially since those wails could be masking the sounds of a killer. He didn't believe Helen was a willing participant in the murders, but that didn't mean Bobby, Jared or River wouldn't use her in some way to make it easier to get to Everly and him.

"We need to get out of here," he told Everly though she was already well aware of that. Judging from the smell, the explosions had also set off a fire in her bedroom. "When we get to the front door, you stay to the side. I'll unlock it and let Molina know we're coming out."

Noah didn't want Everly and him hit with friendly fire, and the explosion had likely put Molina on edge. He'd need to call out to the deputy to let him know they were coming out of the house.

That had huge risks.

Because the killer would hear him as well. But it couldn't be helped. Even a text or phone call to Molina could be an alert, too. Noah suspected the killer was out there, waiting. Maybe to see if the explosives would end their lives or if he'd try to do that with a secondary attack.

It was impossible to pick out the sound of something like footsteps. Not with debris and maybe even the roof falling in the bedroom. Added to that, the storm wasn't cooperating. The rain was still coming down hard which might turn out to be a blessing though, if there was indeed a fire. It could mean Everly's house might not end up burning to the ground since there was no way Noah could risk calling out the fire department right now.

After some long moments where too many bad thoughts fired through his head, they made it to the front door, and Everly automatically moved to the side. She also started firing gazes around the living room and kitchen. Looking for a killer who might be on the verge of ambushing them.

An ambush could certainly happen, but Noah was betting this vigilante wanted them outside. If not, why not just gun them down when they returned from the hospital? Or hell, when Everly and he had been in the bathroom? No, this and the explosive were part of some plan, and Noah had to be ready for, well, anything.

He unlocked the door and eased it open. The headlights to Helen's car were still on and were cutting through the slashing rain, but Noah didn't see the woman.

Molina was nowhere in sight either.

Noah already had a bad feeling about this, but that bad

feeling soared when he heard the engine. Not Helen's car. But Molina's SUV.

The SUV started toward the house.

"Stay back," Noah told Everly, though that, too, was a risk if another explosive went off.

"Molina?" Noah called out.

No answer. Not from a person anyway. But the driver of the SUV revved the engine and sped right toward them. The big SUV had a reinforced bumper that plowed right through the wooden porch.

Noah jumped back, trying to push Everly out of the path. But he was too late. The SUV slammed into the house. Glass and wood flew, but that didn't cause the biggest jolt. No. That had come from the back of the house.

From another bomb.

There was a loud thundering boom, and the roof caved in on them.

Chapter Seventeen

One second Everly was standing, and the next second, she found herself on the floor. Or rather what was left of the floor. Her house was literally falling down around them, and that wasn't all.

There was another explosion.

This one came from the rear of the house, from the direction of the back porch. Mercy. The killer was trying to bury them alive.

Everly shoved away some of the debris from her face, and she tried to get up so she could find Noah. Hard to do what with the rain now pouring through what was left of the ceiling. The rain ran down her face, stinging her eyes. The smoke wasn't helping either. Despite the rain, there was white smoke billowing through the house.

Groaning, she managed to sit up, and she silently cursed when she didn't see Noah. Or the gun he'd given her. She'd dropped it in the fall, and she was very much afraid she might need it.

She heard Noah make a sound of sharp pain. A hoarse groan. And Everly tried to clear her head and her eyes so she could see him. The relief came when she felt the hand take hold of her arm and yank her from the debris.

Then, the relief vanished when she saw it wasn't Noah.

This was the man in the dark raincoat, the one who'd crawled through the window.

The killer.

She couldn't see his face because he had on a ski mask beneath the hood, but Everly did get a glimpse of the hypodermic needle that he pulled from his pocket. She put up her hand to stop him.

But she failed.

Everly managed to push him away, some, but not before he managed to get some of the drug into her. When she knocked away the needle, he started dragging her out of the house.

She called out for Noah so that he'd hear where she was. So that he might be able to help her stop what was happening, but in case he couldn't get to her in time, she started fighting.

Everly kicked out at the man, the heel of her shoe connecting with his shin. He made a sharp sound of pain and snarled something she didn't catch. His voice wasn't loud enough for her to make out who he was. He seemed to shake off the pain and kept dragging her onto the porch.

Everly tried to punch him, but she could already feel the effect of whatever drug he'd given her. Another of those tranquilizers that would soon make her unconscious. That couldn't happen because if she didn't stay awake, if she didn't fight him, he would kill her.

"Stop," she heard Noah shout, and she caught just a glimpse of him as he rose from the piles of debris. His head was bleeding, and there were cuts on his face, but he'd managed to hold on to his gun.

He pointed it at her attacker.

That didn't stop the man. He merely shifted her so that she was in front of him, and he made his way down the steps to the open door of the SUV. She continued to fight, trying to punch him or knee him in the groin, but he latched on to her hair.

The pain shot through her, causing her breath to go thin. The dizziness had already started, and that only made it worse. He shoved her into the front seat of the SUV, and she spotted the person on the backseat.

Helen.

The woman was lying on her side, and there was a swatch of duct tape over her mouth. Her hands and feet were tied, and even in the dim light, Everly could see her glassy eyes. He'd obviously drugged Helen, too.

Everly turned in the seat to try to punch the man again, but he whipped out a gun, and he pointed it. Not at her though.

But at Noah.

The killer didn't spell out the threat. Didn't have to. If she fought him, he'd shoot Noah. It was possible Noah would be able to duck down in time and get out of the way of the bullet, but he looked dazed from that head injury, and that might cut down on his response time.

Noah could die.

She could lose him right here, right now.

Everly stopped fighting, but she wasn't giving up. Obviously, this monster was going to try to take her elsewhere so he could kill her. So he could kill Helen, too. And somehow she'd have to stop him.

The engine of the SUV was already running, and the man threw it into Reverse and sped down her driveway. Noah came barreling off the porch and took aim. But he didn't have a clean shot. And the killer knew that because she heard him laugh.

The anger tore through her, and she wanted to claw out the man's eyes. She wanted to make him pay for all the lives he'd taken, but she had to wait until Noah was no longer an easy target.

Helen moaned, obviously trying to say something, but her eyes were more than just hazy now. She was already losing consciousness, and Everly knew the same might happen to her. The killer hadn't managed to get the full contents of the syringe into her, but it might have been enough to knock her out.

The killer sped past Helen's car and the cruiser that Noah and she had used, and Everly caught a glimpse of the man facedown on the ground. Her heart sank because this was probably Deputy Molina. She prayed he wasn't dead, but they were dealing with a man who'd already killed and probably wouldn't hesitate to do it again.

"If you try anything stupid, the woman dies," the man growled in a low whisper. He still had the gun even though he was now griping the steering wheel with both hands.

Everly tried to pick through that warning and figure out who was behind the wheel, but she still couldn't tell. If it was Jared though, this was proof that he had no mobility issues because the man was having no trouble driving the SUV.

For once the storm was working in her favor though, because the rain sheeted over the windshield, making it impossible to see much of the road. The killer slowed, some, but not nearly enough, and the tires of the SUV shimmied when he plowed through one of the deep puddles on the asphalt. If he kept this up, he'd kill them all.

"I need to buckle her in," Everly insisted.

It surprised her more than a little when the killer didn't stop her. Everly located the seat belt and fastened it around Helen. She put on hers as well and hoped it would be enough if they crashed.

"Where are you taking me?" she asked, wanting to hear his voice again. Not that it would necessarily help if she knew who she was fighting. But if it was Bobby, she might be able to use Helen to try to reason with him.

"Shut up," he snarled, again using that low growl.

Everly blinked hard, trying to stave off the dizziness, and she noticed something. She wasn't losing consciousness as fast this time as when he'd shot her with the dart on the porch. Maybe because she'd been right about him not being able to get a full dose in her. It was also possible this drug wasn't as potent as the other had been. And she could think of a bad reason why he wouldn't want her completely knocked out.

He might want her awake and aware when he killed her.

Or rather when he tried to kill her. Because Everly had no intentions of making this easier for him.

He took the road away from Silver Creek, probably because he knew someone had called Grayson by now, and that the sheriff would be responding from that direction. Noah would realize that, too, and that's why he would know which way to come after her.

However, there was a problem. The road away from town was narrow and filled with sharp curves. Not a good combination considering the storm.

Which meant the killer likely didn't intend to go far.

Maybe he had plans to turn onto a ranch trail. There were plenty of them out here. He could pull the SUV into some trees so he wouldn't be visible from the road, and Grayson or Noah might drive right past them.

In the distance she heard the howl of a siren. Noah probably. Hopefully, she silently amended. Maybe that head injury hadn't been so bad that it prevented him from driving. Then again, this was Noah. Nothing short of death would prevent him from coming after her.

And that meant the vigilante would have a chance to kill him, too.

That caused an ache inside her that went all the way to the bone. She didn't want to die. She wanted to live a long life with her daughter. But she didn't want that life to come at Noah's expense.

When she saw the killer glancing to the sides of the road, she knew she'd been right about him looking for a trail. He'd soon find one which meant she had to do something before he pulled off.

But what?

Her first thought, a terrifying one, was she could cause them to wreck, and just the thought of it gave her a hard slam of flashbacks. The crash, the blood. The horrible anguish she'd felt because she had believed she had killed a woman.

But she hadn't.

And Everly used that to try to anchor herself, to fight both the panic and the dizziness. She had one shot at this, and she had to take it before the killer got her off the road and into the woods. He could kill her there and then use her to draw out Noah.

That wasn't going to happen.

Everly said a quick prayer, and with the cruiser lights flashing on the dark road behind them, she drew back her elbow and rammed into the killer's ribs. He cursed her and tried to hit her in the face with the gun, but Everly latched on to his hand as if her life depended on it.

Because it did.

Hers, Noah's and Helen's.

She held on even when he pulled the trigger, and the bullet slammed into the windshield. She dug her fingernails into his hand, causing him to howl in pain. Then, she gave him a second jab with her elbow.

He turned, trying to fight her off, but the SUV went into a skid. The killer tried to grab the wheel, but there wasn't enough time. The SUV flew off the road toward a fence.

The killer cursed, not a low growl this time, but in his actual voice.

Everly knew, she finally knew, who the vigilante killer was.

Just as the SUV slammed into the fence.

FROM THE MOMENT that Noah had started chasing the SUV, he'd known that this could turn deadly. The roads were in the absolute worst condition for a car chase, and even if the killer had a plan to take Everly to a secondary location so he could murder her, that didn't mean the snake wouldn't kill her by wrecking the SUV.

Noah tried not to think of that. Tried to focus only on getting to Everly before she died.

But then he saw the SUV fishtail on the slick road. The tires skidded through the water, and Noah's heart dropped when he realized the driver was out of control. Maybe Everly had something to do with that because even though he couldn't see her, he was betting she was fighting for her life. If she was capable of fighting, that was. It was possible she was already unconscious from the drug the SOB had managed to pump into her again.

"I'm not far behind you," Noah heard Grayson say through the speaker on the dash of the cruiser.

Noah had called him the moment he'd started the pursuit because he'd known he would need the backup. Had known, too, that Deputy Molina would need medical attention since he'd seen the deputy lying on the ground outside Everly's. Grayson had already called for an ambulance, and he might need to call for another.

Because ahead of him, the SUV flew off the road and plowed into a barbwire fence.

He tried to assure himself that the impact hadn't been nearly as bad as the killer ramming the SUV into Everly's house. Everly could survive this, and he had to hold on to the belief that she had.

Noah fought to keep control of his own vehicle, and he managed to come to a stop about twenty yards away. Before he could even get out, the driver's side door of the SUV opened. The man wearing the dark raincoat barreled out.

Not alone.

He had hold of Everly's hair and dragged her out with him. Thanks to the headlights on the vehicles, Noah got a glimpse of her face. The terror, yes, and she had some cuts, but she was alive and fighting. She was trying to get away from the killer. Her struggling stopped though, when the killer turned and pointed a gun at the cruiser.

Noah didn't stay put. He got out, and using the cruiser door for cover, he took aim even though he knew he couldn't risk firing. Not with the way the killer was holding Everly. If Noah shot now, he could end up hitting her.

"It's over," Noah called out to the killer. "Everly didn't

kill Helen in that car crash fourteen years ago. There's no reason for you to dole out so-called justice."

He knew that wouldn't stop the man, and it didn't, but he wanted to try to get the guy to say something so he'd know who he was dealing with. Not that it mattered. He would do whatever it took to stop the killer from claiming another victim. But if he knew the killer's identity, he might be able to come up with something he could use to distract him.

The killer turned and started running toward some trees, and he dragged Everly right along with him. Noah left the cruiser, and he ran to the SUV to use it as cover. He cursed though, when he heard the moans coming from inside.

Helen.

Hell, she was tied up on the backseat.

Noah didn't smell any gasoline, and with the rain coming down, there wasn't a high risk of fire, but he sent a quick text to let Grayson know the situation. And that he was going in pursuit. He couldn't wait for his uncle to arrive because if the killer made it to those trees, he'd have way too many hiding places where he could hide and gun them down.

It might also give him enough time to go ahead and kill Everly.

Right now, he was using her as a shield, but the killer wouldn't need that once he was out of the path of any bullet Noah could fire at him.

Noah started running, knowing he might have to drop to the ground at any moment, but he had to keep the killer and Everly in his sights. Hard to do though, the farther he got away from the headlights. The storm helped some with that due to the lightning strikes that lit up the night sky. It was possible one of those strikes would hit him. Or Everly.

But at the moment neither of them had a lot of choices. They both had to stop the killer.

Behind him on the road, Noah heard the wail of Grayson's cruiser, but he kept running. Kept his attention nailed to Everly. She stumbled, maybe on purpose, and thanks to a lightning bolt, he saw her glance back at him. The moment seemed to freeze with their gazes connecting.

He had to save her.

He couldn't let this SOB kill her and take her from Ainsley. And from him.

"It's River," Everly shouted.

River. So, now Noah knew who he was dealing with. The man who Jared had said was angry with the world. So angry that he obviously didn't care if he hurt an innocent woman.

"You're not killing now for justice, River," Noah called out to him. "You're killing to cover your tracks." Which, of course, meant River intended to try to kill him as well now that he knew his identity.

"It's all justice," River spat out.

"No, it's covering your butt," Noah muttered.

Noah cursed when River made it to the first of the trees, and he ducked behind them with Everly. River crouched down so he wouldn't be an easy target, and he didn't waste any time firing his gun. However, since Noah had figured that's what would happen, he'd already run to the side and had then dropped down into the sopping-wet pasture. The bullet that River fired missed.

Well, hopefully it had.

It could have gone into the SUV.

Noah had to push the possibility of that aside, and he started to belly crawl his way to Everly. His crawling stopped though when he heard the sounds of the struggle.

Everly didn't scream, but she made a grunting sound that let Noah know she was in a fight for her life.

He got up and started running.

He had to get to her in time, and Noah wouldn't consider any other possibilities. As long as he had breath in his body, she wasn't going to die.

Noah ran as if everything in his life was at stake. Because it was. And he knew at any second, River could fire a fatal shot at him. Noah soon learned the reason why River hadn't been able to do that though. When he reached the end of the trees, Noah saw Everly kicking River. She also had a death grip on the man's wrist, and that grip had almost certainly prevented him from firing.

But not for long.

River punched her with his left hand, and it was enough to off-balance her. Enough for River to take advantage of that. He grabbed Everly and dragged her in front of him, putting the gun to her head.

Noah ducked behind one of the trees and looked for the angle of a shot he could take. There wasn't one. But there was a silver lining to this. River likely wouldn't shoot Everly because he wouldn't want to lose his human shield.

"It's over," Noah repeated to him.

River laughed. "I guess you think you can talk me into surrendering."

Noah figured he had no chance of that so he just kept looking for the right angle for a shot he would take if he got the chance. "I've heard confession's good for the soul. Especially good for relieving a guilty conscience. You murdered Daisy, and she did nothing wrong."

"She was going to turn me in," River snarled. "I had to stop her. That's self-defense."

In his warped mind, it probably was. "And Everly? More self-defense?"

"Damn right." Because Everly was trying to squirm out of his grip, River moved. Not enough though.

"You can't cover all your tracks," Noah tried again. "You'll be arrested."

"No." River's denial came fast. "Bobby will be. I've planted enough evidence that he'll take the fall for this. He could probably get off with an insanity plea, but he'll still be locked up, and I won't be."

"Maybe." Noah made sure he didn't sound convinced of that at all, and the sarcasm was obviously enough to light River's temper.

River cursed. "I should have just waited in Everly's house and killed you both." He got to his feet, keeping Everly in front of him. He was obviously planning on trying to run with her again.

"Why didn't you?" Noah shifted, too, getting ready to follow River wherever the hell he was going.

"Because when I was under her bed, it occurred to me that you might watch the monitor right away and just start shooting. So, I got out and stayed out of camera range so I could hide my little surprises, including one under the bed with all the foil I left behind. I figured that little blast would get you two running out of the house so I could grab at least one of you."

"Did Jared or Bobby help you with those explosives?" Noah asked, hoping the sound of his voice would mask his movement. He shifted behind the tree, looking for that better angle.

"Hell, no. You were right about the money I was withdrawing each week. There are lot of people out there who feel the same way I do about scum escaping justice so I got it all done for a discount."

Once this was over, Noah would be tracking down that explosives expert who'd helped River do so much damage.

"Did you kill your mother, too?" Noah asked to keep him talking.

"Yeah, so what? She deserved it because she killed my dad."

It sickened Noah for River to speak almost casually about ending a life. Now, River wanted to do the same to Everly.

"I gotta hand it to you," River said. "You figured out the withdrawals, and that's when I knew the distraction of blowing up my own place wasn't going to put you off my scent. That's why you're both here right now."

Noah tuned out what the man was saying because River was on the move again, dragging Everly toward another cluster of trees. Noah knew that behind those trees was a small ranch where there'd no doubt be vehicles that River could use to try to escape.

That wasn't going to happen.

Knowing he had to act now, Noah darted out from cover, and as he'd hoped, River stopped and turned the gun in his direction. River fired.

And missed.

Noah didn't. Both his hands and his aim were steady, and he took advantage of the way River had shifted his body to get off that shot. Noah put a bullet in the man's shoulder, the only part of him Noah could shoot without the risk of hitting Everly.

Everly took advantage as well. She jabbed her elbow at River, using the momentum to push herself away from him. She scrambled to the side, and when River turned to shoot her, Noah made sure he pulled the trigger first. Not a shoulder shot this time either.

Noah fired two rounds into the killer's chest.

River dropped like a stone, and with Noah's gun still aimed, he ran to him to kick his weapon out of the way. He glanced at Everly, just a glance to confirm that she was as okay as she could be, considering just how close they'd come to dying. Then, Noah turned his attention back to the killer.

"You're a dead man," Noah told him. Not a taunt. The truth. River was bleeding out fast and didn't have even a full minute left.

River's face was etched with pain, but he managed a forced smile. "Oh, it's not over," he said, his eyelids already fluttering down. "You didn't win, *Detective Ryland.*" He said Noah's name like venom and used his dying breath to add, "Wonder if you can live with killing Helen. For real this time. Because you won't be able to get to her before she dies."

Noah didn't have time to text Grayson. Didn't have time to do anything. Before the blast tore through the night.

Chapter Eighteen

Everly's heart sank when she heard the explosion. Sweet heaven. Not this. Not after everything they had all been through.

"When River got me out of the SUV, he took something from his pocket and tossed it onto the backseat," Everly managed to say while Noah pressed his fingers to River's neck to make sure he was dead. He was.

Noah nodded, and he went to her, pulled her into his arms. There was so much emotion in that embrace. So much relief. Emotion and relief that Everly felt, too, and later, she would tell Noah just how thankful she was that they'd both made it through this. For now though, they had to try to save Helen.

"River drugged you?" Noah asked her. He hooked his arm around her waist to get her moving.

"Yes, but I knocked away the needle before he could give me the full dose."

That was yet something else she was thankful for. She was light-headed, but it could have been a whole lot worse. If she hadn't been conscious, she wouldn't have been able to get away from him so Noah could take that kill shot.

With Noah's firm grip on her, they started threading their

way out of the trees. "There was no reason for River to kill Helen. He didn't show his face in the SUV, and I'm almost positive she didn't know who he was."

Noah made a sound of agreement and kept moving, but she knew what he was thinking. River hadn't tossed that explosive in the SUV because Helen could have ID'd him. No. This was one last jab at Noah and her. River might not have been able to kill them, but they would have to live with how all of this had played out.

Everly heard sirens. Both police and an ambulance from the sound of it. Her first thought was "Good," but then she realized that Grayson or the EMTs could have been close to or actually in the SUV when the bomb went off. That got her moving as fast as she could.

Sweet heaven.

How many people had River killed with his parting shot?

As if Mother Nature decided to give them a break, the rain let up some as Noah and she came out of the trees and into the pasture. The water was still stinging her eyes, but she spotted the two vehicles on the side of the road. Noah's and Grayson's. She'd been right about the ambulance, too. It was right behind the second cruiser.

But her heart skipped some beats when she saw the SUV.

Or rather what was left of it.

The bomb had obviously worked because the SUV was a mangled heap with white smoke spewing from the radiator.

"Grayson," Noah muttered.

For one horrifying moment, she thought Noah had seen his uncle's body. But no. Not his body. Grayson was on the side of his cruiser, in a position of taking cover. He wasn't alone either. There were two EMTs with him.

And Helen.

Grayson was holding the woman in his arms.

"She's alive," Grayson called out to them. "I got her out right before the SUV blew up."

The relief hit Everly so hard that her legs gave way. Noah was right there to catch her though, and he scooped her up, cradling her against him as he made his way through the pasture and toward Grayson.

"Any idea if there are other explosives?" Grayson asked, studying them with those cop's eyes. No doubt looking to see if they were injured.

"I don't think so," Everly managed to say. "I saw River throw only one thing onto the backseat."

"River," Grayson repeated. He handed off Helen to the EMTs, and they took her in the direction of the ambulance. "I heard the shots. I'm guessing he's dead?"

Noah nodded, and once they reached Grayson, he set Everly on her feet. He didn't let go of her though. "I'll do a full report, but River was the killer, and when he tried to escape with Everly, I shot and killed him."

"Good," Grayson muttered, but he was still giving them the once-over. "Your faces and hands are nicked up. Is that the worst of your injuries, or are there more?"

"The worst of them," Noah and she said in unison.

It was true, and that was yet something else they could be thankful for. River had tried his best to kill them, and Noah and she had escaped with only minor injuries. Of course, they'd have to also deal with the nightmare of memories the man had created, but Everly thought with time, those nightmares would go away. Especially since River wasn't going to be able to claim any other victims.

It was over.

The danger was gone.

Her head had no trouble accepting that, but she still jolted when she saw the approaching headlights of the vehicle. Grayson reacted, too, and he drew the gun he'd just put back in his holster.

"I'm not expecting anyone," Grayson said, and that caused Noah to step in front of her again.

Like Grayson, Noah took aim, and the EMTs scrambled to get Helen into the ambulance.

"Don't shoot," the man shouted as he barreled out of the car. He lifted his hands in the air, no doubt to show them that he wasn't carrying a weapon. "It's me."

Bobby.

Thanks to the illumination from the headlights, Everly could see that he also had some cuts and scrapes on his face. "River's the vigilante killer," Bobby blurted out. "He asked me to meet him, and when I did, he drugged me and tied me up. I think he was planning on setting me up to take the blame for the murders."

So, River had left another witness behind after all.

"You got away," Grayson said, going to the man to frisk him. "No weapon," he relayed to Noah.

"Yeah, once the drugs wore off, I managed to get untied." Bobby's gaze went to the SUV, and he groaned. "River said he was going to blow up Helen." He swallowed hard as if he wasn't sure he could handle the truth. "Did he?"

It was Grayson who answered. "No. She's in the ambulance. She's hurt, but I don't think her injuries are bad."

The breath seemed to swoosh out of Bobby, and he dropped to his knees, pressing his hands to the sides of his head. "Thank God."

"The last time we saw you, you were very upset about Helen being alive," Noah pointed out.

Bobby nodded. "I was, but I was more upset when I realized the SOB was going to kill her." His groan was long
and filled with both relief and regret. "River had no right
to do that."

"No," Grayson agreed, "and now he's dead. I'll want to
take your statement about how he took you captive, but for
now, you can see your stepmother if you want."

Bobby practically sprang to his feet, and he started toward the ambulance. However, he stopped just as fast as
he started. "She might not want to see me after the things
I said to her."

"Bobby?" Helen called out before any of them could respond. "I want to see you. I love you."

That got Bobby moving again, and he ran to the back
of the ambulance for what Everly was certain would be a
welcome reunion. It might take Bobby a while to forgive
Helen for what she'd done, but it seemed to Everly that the
forgiveness had already gotten started. It would probably
help, too, once Bobby learned that Helen had risked her life
to search for him.

"I'll wait here for the CSIs and the morgue guys," Grayson volunteered, glancing up at the sky that had finally
stopped spitting rain. "If you're okay enough to drive, you
can go to the ranch and see Ainsley. She's fine," he quickly
added. "I just thought it'd do you good to see her after you've
cleaned up a bit."

Everly knew that Noah and she would definitely need the
cleaning up. They were soaked to the bone, and some of the
small cuts on his face were bleeding. She suspected her own
cuts were doing the same. But Grayson was right. It would
do her plenty of good to see her daughter. She thought it
might do the same for Noah.

Noah slipped his arm around her, though it wasn't necessary for him to help her walk. She was plenty steady now, and she could feel her nerves leveling out even more with each step. She got into the front passenger's seat of the cruiser, and Noah got behind the wheel. He didn't start the engine though. He pulled her to him and kissed her.

Suddenly she didn't feel so steady after all, but it had nothing to do with fear or nightmarish memories. It had to do with the intense need she felt in his kiss.

And the love.

Of course, the love might all be on her part, but Everly was going to take a risk and pour out her heart to him.

She pulled back, catching on to his face to frame it with her hands. "We can't make the past go away, but there's plenty we can do about right now. About the future."

The corner of his mouth lifted, and then he winced a little because his lip was cut. Still, he chuckled. "I like the sound of that. What kind of future do you have in mind?" But he didn't wait for her to answer. "Because I want a life with Ainsley and you. A life where we're a family. Where I can tell you every day how much I love you."

Everly didn't mind one bit that Noah had beaten her to saying all of that. Because it was exactly what she'd intended to tell him.

Exactly what she wanted.

"Well, you can say the *I love you* right now," Everly offered. "And I'll say it right back to you."

Noah smiled. Kissed her. "I love you."

Everly managed to say her own "I love you, Noah Ryland" before he kissed her again and stole her breath.

* * * * *

MURDER AT
SUNSET ROCK

DEBRA WEBB

Tennessee has been my home for twenty of the past forty years. From the birthplace of rock 'n' roll in Memphis to the Great Smoky Mountains of east Tennessee, it's a wondrous state.

I hope you'll enjoy this second installment of the Lookout Mountain Mysteries. Sunset Cove is a fictional community I hope you will enjoy!

Chapter One

Olivia Ballard's fingers tightened on the steering wheel as she slowed for the final turn.

Firefly Lane.

She'd grown up here. At four, when her mother died, her grandparents had carried on with raising her. There was no one else. Her father had disappeared the year before. Olivia drew in a deep breath and made the turn that would take her home. Except was it really home anymore? Everyone was gone.

A fresh wave of tears burned her eyes. Her grandmother—Gran, she had called her—had passed away when she was only nine. Grieved herself to death, Willy, her grandfather, had explained. She never got over losing her daughter, her only child. As much as Gran had loved Olivia, and Olivia had no doubt that she had, her heart had been fractured beyond repair.

Pushing away the memories, Olivia focused on maneuvering forward. Somehow the long gravel road that cut through the thick woods seemed narrower than the last time she had visited. The thick canopy of trees blocked the sun, leaving the road in an eerie twilight. Half a mile later, the trees parted and the landscape opened up into a lush clearing, rich with the colors of nature. Olivia braked to a stop at the end of the road, which was actually the driveway. Willy's cabin was the only house on Firefly Lane, and it sat at the very end. His land stretched from the road, several acres wide, through the dense forest, over the cliffs and spiraling downward to the world below. As a young girl, Olivia had dared to hike along that cliffside—too close, her Gran would say. Willy would chuckle and tell her to be careful.

Willy, she smiled sadly at the memory of the man she had adored and depended on for everything as an adolescent with no mother or siblings and no grandmother. Everyone had called him Willy—his name was William, after all. No matter how her gran had attempted to prod Olivia into calling him Grandpa or Papa, she had refused. He was Willy. Her father and grandfather all rolled into one. The man who took care of scraped knees and prom dresses and everything in between.

How could he be gone?

Grabbing her cell, Olivia emerged from her car. She tucked the phone into the pocket of her jeans and surveyed the yard. Willy had bordered a full acre around the cabin with a stacked stone fence nearly three feet high. She smiled and shook her head at the idea of just how many stones were required to build that fence. He'd teased her gran often, saying the stone fence was really more of a decoration— remembered from long ago visits to faraway places. Gran would remind him that she had agreed to spend the rest of her life in this mountain cabin of his, but only if he turned it into the cottage of her dreams.

To Olivia, it was very European. With the multitude of flower beds, there were more blooms than grass. A post-and-wire fence surrounded a vegetable garden that would be the envy of gardeners anywhere. Vines snaked up every possible vertical space, including the walls of the house. The place looked more like a hundred-year-old English cottage than a cabin in the woods of Tennessee. Her gran had spent decades creating exactly that look. Even as a little girl, Olivia had known Willy was right about the stone wall being decorative. But that touch had made her gran immensely happy, and Willy would have done anything for her.

Willy's vintage Land Rover Defender was parked next to the house beneath the shade of a massive white oak. A trembling smile tugged at her lips. God, how he'd loved that old thing. He said it made him feel as if he were on safari. Truth was, he carried parts of the world they had visited in his heart too. There were times and places that stayed with you, he would say.

"I should have come back sooner." The words tasted bitter on Olivia's tongue and sank deep into her gut, where they sat like blocks of concrete.

She reached back into the SUV for her bag, then slammed the car door shut, frustration and anger—at herself—burning away the softer emotions. Olivia hadn't been home since Christmas. Christmas! How could she have waited over five months? She and Willy had talked two or three times each week, but that wasn't the same, no matter that they used video chatting most of the time. She should have been *here*.

Now her dear grandfather was dead.

Olivia swiped at the tears that would no longer be held

back. Her first stop when she had arrived in Chattanooga had been the Hamilton County Medical Examiner's Office, where she'd insisted on seeing her grandfather's body. Sheriff Arnold Decker, Willy's close friend, had already identified his remains, but Olivia had needed to see for herself that he was really gone. He'd always been so strong and confident. How had this happened?

Her chest tightened with the image that played over and over in her mind. Multiple broken bones and a devastating head injury, the attendant had explained. Her grandfather had fallen, the report said. From Sunset Rock.

Even now, she could hardly believe it was true.

For the past twenty-four hours, Olivia had been operating on autopilot. Late yesterday, the call had come from Sheriff Decker explaining that Willy's body had been found by hikers on Bluff Trail. The assumption was that he'd fallen from the overlook, Sunset Rock. Olivia had heard the words, but her brain had stopped working after the word *dead*. *Willy is dead*.

On the seemingly endless drive from Bozeman, Montana, she'd repeatedly berated herself for allowing 159 days to pass since she'd hugged him. Since she'd inhaled the familiar woodsy scent of him. She had mentally ticked through each of those days and what she'd done on them, and none of it had been excuse enough not to have visited the only family she had left in this world.

She stared at the house, told herself to move toward it. She was tired. She'd been driving all night—not that sleep would have been possible. Every minute of every hour she'd played Sheriff Decker's words over and over. *I'm so sorry to inform you that your grandfather is dead. When you get here, Liv, you let me know if there is anything I can do to help. I am so, so sorry. He was like a brother to me.*

She had thanked him then ended the call. She hadn't been able to talk...how could Willy be dead?

Even twenty-odd hours later, the little girl in her wanted to crumble to the ground in a sobbing, miserable heap. But she was no little girl anymore. She was thirty years old. A geologist in Bozeman. She owned a townhouse with a mortgage and an SUV. Had work friends.

And no one else. Not a single other person connected to her by blood or anything stronger than the shallowest definition of friendship.

Olivia closed her eyes and forced the horde of debilitating emotions away. She had things to do. When she'd called her boss, she had already been on the road and hadn't been able to say when she would return to work. She had weeks and weeks of unused leave. Her work was well ahead of the rest of the project. It wasn't like she couldn't take a few weeks off. She squared her shoulders. She owed it to Willy to take care of him and his home properly—the way he would want it done.

She dug in her bag for her keys. "No putting this off any longer, Liv."

Forcing one foot in front of the other, she walked to the porch, climbed the three steps and crossed to the door. She poked the key into the lock, took a deep breath and turned it, then opened the door. The scent of home filled her lungs. Her eyes closed with the weight of sensory overload. Didn't matter that she hadn't lived here in a dozen years. Not since college. This would forever be home.

Forcing her eyes open, Olivia stepped inside, closed the door and came to an abrupt halt.

The house was a wreck.

Not merely untidy or cluttered…someone had ransacked the place. Her heart charged into a gallop.

Olivia held her breath. Whoever had done this could still be in the house.

Her icy fingers dove into her bag and closed around the small can of pepper spray Willy had insisted she carry starting the day she left Hamilton County. The spray would be no help against a gun, but it was the only weapon at her disposal just now. She glanced at the shotgun on the rack above the mantel. She listened intently. No sound. Okay, she should make her way to the fireplace and grab that shotgun.

Easing soundlessly in that direction, she kept her gaze roving side to side, checking each door that exited the main room that was living, dining and kitchen all in one. Beyond the first of those doors was a short corridor that led to the bedrooms and bath. The only other door led to a small laundry room and mudroom as well as the back door.

Since the front had been locked, whoever had done this must have entered and, hopefully, departed from the rear of the house.

Olivia made it to the fireplace. Still no sound. No movement. No unexpected odors.

Keeping her attention focused on her surroundings and the spray poised in her right hand, she reached up with her left and clutched the long, cold barrel. She lifted the shotgun from its resting place and drew it down to her side. The pepper spray went back into her bag, which she eased down onto the floor. Then she readied the shotgun with both hands, the business end leading the way as she moved away from the fireplace. She didn't have to wonder if it was loaded; Willy had kept it loaded at all times.

The cushions had been pulled from the sofa. Chairs over-turned. The drawers of her gran's sideboard stood open haphazardly, the contents spilled onto the wide-plank wood floor. The cupboard doors and drawers were open as well, utensils and spices spewed over the countertop. Photographs and paintings that had once hung proudly on the walls lay on the floor, tossed aside like trash.

Fury whipped through Olivia. Her grandparents' beloved work. Willy had been the photographer, but it was Gran who had created amazing paintings of his work—paintings that had sold for thousands of dollars. Between their talents, they had amassed a small fortune. Though one would never know it based on his demeanor. Willy was never one to brag or to show off. His only remotely lavish purchase that Olivia was aware of was his Land Rover Defender—the vehicle he'd had since before she was born—and donations to charities focused on saving the planet. His and Gran's worldwide travels had convinced him the environment was on the verge of extinction.

Olivia paused before continuing into the hall. She tucked the butt of the shotgun firmly into her shoulder, rested her cheek against the stock and snugged her finger around the trigger. If someone was hiding in the house, he had better hope he could escape faster than she could lock in on him.

Unlikely.

With the curtains open on the windows, enough sunlight filtered in to prevent the rooms from being in shadow.

First room, her old room, was clear. Like the main living space, the room had been searched with no care for the value of anything or where it landed. Same in her grandparents' bedroom and the third bedroom—the one her parents had used. Her gran had insisted on keeping the room exactly as it was when Olivia's mother died. She hadn't been in the room in years. Once she'd surveyed the space, she closed the door and moved on. Even the single bathroom had been scoured for whatever the intruder had hoped to find.

Olivia relaxed the tiniest bit.

Weapon still held in a firing position, she moved back into the main living area and headed for the mudroom. Still no sound or abrupt movement. If anyone had still been in the house, she'd given him opportunity to flee by starting with the bedrooms. At this point, she felt fairly confident the house was empty. But she wasn't letting down her guard until she was certain.

The small mudroom was empty, but the back door was open.

Arms shaking from the extended tension, she lowered the shotgun. She started to reach for the door to close and lock it but stopped herself. There could be finger prints. She needed to call the police.

Olivia blinked, steadied herself. Whoever had ransacked the rest of the house had searched this room too.

She leaned against the shelves of canned goods and dug her cell phone from her pocket. Rather than tie up a 911 dispatcher, she called the sheriff's office directly. The woman who took Olivia's call assured her she would let the sheriff know and someone would be out shortly.

Deep breath. She tucked the phone into the hip pocket of her jeans and dared to close her eyes for a moment to gather herself. Willy was dead. Someone had come into his home and searched for something. But what?

Olivia opened her eyes and pushed away from the shelf-lined wall. She had no idea, but she damned well intended to find out. She marched over to the front door, her steps full of new purpose. There were a number of outbuildings, a barn and big old shed Willy had turned into a darkroom for himself and a studio for Gran. While she waited for the sheriff or one of his deputies, she should check those places too. What kind of person took advantage of a death to ransack a man's home? The question sent a new surge of outrage roaring through her.

Focus on what needs to be done.

Willy had taught Olivia how to search for lost things. How to take an area and divide it into a grid and cover those individual sections without missing a single square foot of the overall area. There were no footprints to be found. Apparently, it hadn't rained in several days. Moving on, she searched the barn first. The big old structure was basically untouched. The garden tools and tractor were just exactly as they were the last time Olivia had reason to go into the rambling space. The shed was a different story. The place had been turned upside down.

What in the world had the intruder been searching for?

Money? Willy certainly hadn't kept much money lying around the house, but even a small amount might seem like a lot to someone desperate enough to do this.

However, Olivia suspected the perpetrator had left utterly dissatisfied if the goal had been cash or items easily converted to cash.

The one thing she hadn't spotted so far was Willy's camera. Not just any camera either. It was a rare vintage Nikon. More important to Olivia than the monetary value was the sentimental value. The camera had been like an extension of Willy. Wherever he was, the Nikon was. He went absolutely nowhere without it. Though it was likely worth several thousand dollars, selling it would be a problem. The thief would need to find someone with a keen interest in photography to land anywhere near what the camera was worth. Otherwise, it would go for very little. She walked back to the house and propped the shotgun behind the front door. She stared at the mess and, despite her best efforts, cried again.

By the time an SUV bearing the sheriff's department logo arrived, Olivia had pulled herself together once more and gone through the house again in search of the camera. It was not there, which made sense since Willy would not have left the house without it. Why hadn't the Nikon been found with him? If he'd had it with him, and he most assuredly would have, then it had to be in the vicinity of where he had been found. Seemed like a very good question to ask the deputy climbing out of the SUV. It wasn't the sheriff, which was fine by her. She wasn't ready to see anyone who had been that close to Willy.

Olivia braced herself. So far she'd gotten through the search without falling completely apart, but she'd been on a mission. Adrenaline and anger had been fueling her. The anger had fizzled out at this point, and the adrenaline had faded. Her bravado was sinking fast.

Hold it together a little while longer.

As the deputy walked toward the porch, he removed his cap and gave her a nod. "Liv." When he reached the steps, he glanced down, gave his head a shake. "I am so sorry about Willy."

Maybe it was her mind's decision to zero in on the neatly pressed button-down shirt that seemed to barely contain broad shoulders and the faded jeans hugging long legs that threw her off. Or the baseball cap with the gold star emblazoned on it that he held in his hands—hands she knew

as well as her own—that caused her to suddenly lose the ability to speak. No. It was none of those things. It was *him.*
Huck Monroe.

What was he doing here? Had he heard about Willy's death already? Had he driven all the way up from Miami? Wasn't he a sheriff's deputy there? Despite the circumstances, she almost laughed out loud. Huck Monroe had never visited. Not once that she was aware of in ten damned years. Why would he bother now?

"What're you doing here?" she demanded.

Her brain was playing tricks on her, obviously. She hadn't been able to read the identifying letters on the cap as it hung from his hands. But the Hamilton County SUV was sitting in the driveway, the lettering large and easily readable. Yet that made no sense. Huck had taken off for sun and sand and whatever else in south Florida that had attracted him forever ago.

He offered a sad smile. "I live here now." Hitched his head toward the SUV. "I'm a detective with the sheriff's department."

Wait. What? "When?" It was the only word she could force past her lips.

Why hadn't Willy told her about Huck coming back home? Maybe because she had made it clear she did not want to hear that name ever again.

She blinked away the memory of shouting those words at Willy.

What did it matter and why would she care? Particularly at the moment. The fissure in her heart widened. Her grandfather was dead.

Maybe she swayed the slightest bit, or her face paled. Whatever the case, Huck reached for her.

"You okay?" His hand clamped around her arm to steady her.

No. She tugged away from his grasp. She couldn't do this. Not right now. "I need someone else." Her move to get away turned into more of a stumble back a couple of steps. The worry that clouded his face turned her confusion to renewed anger.

No. This was not acceptable.

"Why don't we go inside and have a seat?" he offered, ignoring her demand. "Then you can tell me what's going on?"

What she wanted was to call the sheriff's office and ask that they send someone else, but even in her current emotionally charged state she understood that would be petty and silly. She simply needed to pull herself together and get this done. When the words and images whirling in her head had calmed and her heart had stopped twisting, she could think more clearly. She had to make that happen sooner rather than later. This was not the time for childish behavior.

Deep breath. "Fine."

She turned and walked into the house. He followed.

"Wow." Huck gave a long, low whistle.

Yeah, she thought. Wow.

"Have you had a look around?" he asked as he surveyed the mess. "Noticed anything missing?"

"I looked around, yes. I can't find his Nikon." She rested her hands on her hips to prevent the shaking that had started there. What was wrong with her? Even her knees suddenly felt rubbery.

Shock. This had all been too much for a person who'd had no sleep in more than twenty-four hours and, now that she thought about it, hadn't eaten.

"His camera is missing?"

"I think so. At least, I haven't found it." She nodded, feeling overwhelmed. "I tried not to touch anything once I was beyond the front door." She glanced back in that direction. "Other than Willy's shotgun. I carried it with me through the house and when I checked the barn and shed."

"You were smart to be careful." He gave a nod. "We'll get our crime-scene investigators out here to check for prints."

The swell of emotions was back. Fierce and insistent, like a swarm of bees expelled from their colony and searching for a new hive. Another idea, one far more sinister leached into her soul. Her eyes didn't know where to land. Her heart was unsure of how to slow down and efficiently pump. She felt on the verge of collapse, and yet she wanted to run screaming through the woods.

This could not be happening.

"They said he fell." Her gaze settled on him… Huck— the boy she'd fallen in love with at fifteen. The boy with whom she'd thought she would be spending the rest of her life. The man who had decided not to wait for her. The man who had left and never looked back.

She sank into the closest chair. She was exhausted. The call from the sheriff had come at two yesterday afternoon. She had left work, rushed back to her townhouse, thrown a few things into a bag and hopped into her car. She had literally driven all night, stopping only for gas. Her brain was no longer functioning properly; otherwise, she would know exactly what to say and do next. She was generally far more collected and self-assured than this.

Willy was dead.

Gone forever.

She surveyed the chaos left behind in his home.

And someone had done this…it was no accident.

Huck was suddenly next to her, crouched down and looking her directly in the eyes. "The medical examiner found
nothing to suggest foul play. Nothing at all suspicious." He
surveyed the carnage in the room. "But unless you believe
your grandfather made this mess himself or we can find
something more that's missing, we need to determine if
there's a connection between his fall and what we see here
that would suggest a different conclusion."

Was he proposing that someone had killed Willy?

"This—" she waved her hand at the room "—makes you
think someone may have pushed him?"

Who would do such a thing? For the most part, Willy had
been a hermit in his later years. He and her gran traveled
the world in the early days, as much time on the road as at
home. At least until Olivia's mother reached school age, and
then they'd had to give up so much traveling to raise their
daughter. Not once had her grandparents ever spoken of a
single regret. They had loved this place. A lump swelled
in her throat. He was gone. The last member of her family.
Tears burned her eyes all over again.

She blinked and glared at the man who hadn't answered
her question. "What are you saying?" she demanded.

"This," he said, "is the definition of suspicious circumstances."

Chapter Two

Huck Monroe kept an eye on Olivia. She looked ready to fall to pieces. She'd lost her grandfather, her last remaining family. Worse, now there was reason to believe—at least in Huck's opinion—foul play may have been involved.

The crime-scene unit had arrived an hour ago, but they were far from finished. Though the Ballard cabin wasn't very big, the old man had kept a lot of stuff. Huck wouldn't call him a hoarder, but he definitely wasn't one to let go of anything easily. Too many memories, he would always say. There were more photographs in the house than anything else. But then William Ballard had been a photographer with a long, much celebrated career and numerous prestigious awards.

Huck's gaze slid back to the swing hanging from that big old tree where Olivia had sequestered herself. The massive oak had always been her favorite. His too really. They'd climbed it enough times. Her grandfather had hung that swing when Olivia's mother was a child.

She looked so alone. His gut clenched. His first inclination was to comfort her, but they no longer had that kind

of relationship. Ten years was a long time not to speak to
someone, but Olivia hadn't forgiven him yet. He doubted
she would have spoken to him today if not for the terrible
circumstances.

She hadn't been home in months. Willy had told him
she was home last Christmas. Oddly enough, Huck had almost driven over to see her. He'd moved back to Hamilton
County earlier in the fall. Willy had been only too happy to
have Huck back in the area. He'd welcomed him as if nothing bad had ever happened.

Obviously, he hadn't told Olivia about Huck's return.
Probably hadn't wanted to deal with the backlash. Olivia
didn't talk to or about Huck, Willy had explained. Never
wanted to hear his name again. At least that was what she'd
said the last time, according to Willy, that he'd mentioned
Huck. She hated him for leaving. Refused to consider or
even hear his reasons.

Huck walked back into the house. He couldn't keep standing on the porch staring at her, no matter that he wanted
to. He'd repeatedly suggested she let him take her somewhere else—his place, a hotel, any place so she wouldn't
have to watch this painful but necessary step. She had refused, of course.

He really couldn't blame her. She had every right to feel
the way she did, even if he hadn't wanted to admit it a decade ago. Time had changed his mind, made him see his
own mistakes in what happened. The truth was, he'd had
no good reason for leaving. Other than the fact that she'd
gone to Atlanta for college and seeing her only every other
weekend had made him restless and more than a little jeal-
ous. He'd lasted more than a year, nearly two. Managed to
get through the academy and start work as a sheriff's dep-

uty. He'd been happy for a while, then he'd made a mistake he couldn't take back. He'd decided on a surprise visit to see her in Atlanta. Her schedule was so hectic they'd had to plan any visits. He'd known this well, but he'd gone anyway. The certainty that she would somehow outgrow him had planted deep roots in his psyche. Had made him doubt her.

Then he'd seen her with friends. Study friends, she always explained. Whenever she spent the whole weekend studying and other people were involved, she called them study friends. He'd seen her and those friends gathered around picnic tables in a park near the university. Huck had started toward the group, but then he'd noticed the guy who seemed particularly taken with Olivia.

His real mistake had been in not walking over to that picnic table and introducing himself. Instead, Huck had spent the entire weekend shadowing Olivia and her friends. The closeness, the comradery he'd seen had been like a flash from the future. He would never be like those people. He hadn't gone to college, had no plans to. He didn't drive a sports car or wear the latest fashions.

He just didn't fit in with the life he saw happening for Olivia. The last thing he wanted to do was hold her back. He had remembered vividly all the conversations about traveling the world and exploring the possibilities out there. By twenty-one, he had realized his possibilities were far more limited than hers.

He hadn't wanted Olivia to ever feel in any way limited. So he'd left. Taken a job as a deputy in Miami-Dade County. Olivia would be better off without having to worry about him. He'd left without a word to her or to her grandfather.

She hadn't forgiven him.

He'd made a mistake.

He considered the painting of Olivia one of the techs was processing. It had hung over the fireplace, just above that shotgun rack, for as long as Huck could remember. Incredibly, she was even more beautiful now than she was as a young girl and that was saying something. Never married. Traveled the world. Worked in places he'd never even dreamed of visiting. Then a year ago, she'd taken a more permanent position in Montana. Willy figured she had decided it was time to settle down.

Huck wondered if there was someone. He shook his head. None of his business.

He'd given up that right better than ten years ago.

Funny, when he was near her, it felt like only yesterday that they had last kissed. That her fingers had caressed his jaw and her long, silky hair had whispered against his skin.

He shook off the thoughts and focused on the work. Something had gone down in this house, perhaps before Willy went over that cliff. Huck intended to find the truth. He owed the man. Not only because he had forgiven Huck and welcomed him back as if he'd never left, but because he had always treated Huck like family. Huck would not fail him now.

He wouldn't fail Olivia either.

A walk through the house gave him a good idea of how much more time was needed, then he headed outside to update Olivia. She should decide where she intended to stay for the night. He didn't see any reason she couldn't return to the house in the morning, but that wasn't happening tonight.

As he approached, her head came up. "Have they found anything?"

He hadn't thought about it until that moment, but she hadn't said his name. Not once in the past couple of hours had she called him Huck. Clearly, she still hated him. It wasn't like she didn't have every right to.

"We won't know until the analysis is complete. In any home, there are lots of prints. Screening the ones that should be there from the ones that shouldn't takes time. So far, nothing that shouldn't be here has been found."

She nodded, opened her mouth to say something and then closed it.

"This is a really tough time for you," he said, softening his voice despite the tension humming inside him. "To get this kind of news and then come home to a scene like this one. It's hard. As difficult as it is, the best thing you can do is get a good night's sleep and come back in the morning. You'll see things more clearly then."

Olivia stared at him, her dark eyes digging deep into him, making him want to hug the hell out of her. He imagined she wouldn't be too happy if he tried.

"You're right." She looked away. "I should go to a hotel and get some sleep." She stood, leaving the old wooden swing to sway listlessly in the air. "I'll be able to digest all this better tomorrow."

An urgency plowed through him. The strangest thought that maybe if he let her get away, he wouldn't see her again for another ten years accompanied the sensation.

"Look," he said, his voice rough, "I know this might sound a little crazy, but I moved into the old homeplace. It's a big house. There's plenty of room, and I'll probably be here for most of the night, so you'd have the place to yourself."

She stared at him in something that resembled confusion or astonishment.

Rather than give her the chance to consider what he was

saying, he dug out his keys, pulled the one for the house free and thrust it at her. "Go. You'll be safe there."

Then he managed a half smile, turned and headed back into the house. She didn't call after him. Didn't tell him to go to hell and fling his key at him. When he reached the front door of the cabin and dared to look back, she had walked to her car and climbed in. Relief washed over him. He watched until she was gone. It was the least he could do. Before he could go inside another vehicle arrived. Sheriff Arnold Decker himself.

Huck walked down the steps and headed toward his boss. Decker had turned the big seven-oh last year, but he had no plans to retire anytime soon. The citizens of Hamilton County loved the guy. He was a good man. A damned good sheriff. He'd been voted in by a landslide after the county's beloved Tarrence Norwood's ill health had forced him to retire.

"Monroe." Decker nodded. "What've we got here?"

The sheriff was far too busy to show up at every crime scene, especially one that hadn't been confirmed as of yet. But William Ballard wasn't just any victim. Back in the day, he had been one of Chattanooga's biggest and most beloved celebrities. Fact was, he and Decker had spent plenty of time fishing together. The two had been good friends for as long as Huck could recall.

"Olivia came home and found the house and shed a wreck."

Decker would know the shed wasn't just some place to store tools. It was Willy's darkroom and workplace. The space where award-winning photos had been developed. His wife's art studio was in there as well. She and Willy had turned that old building into an artist's work retreat before sheds were in for that sort of thing.

Decker settled his hands on his hips. "The ME's report said he fell." He shrugged. "An accident. No suspicious circumstances."

Huck nodded. "But the house and shed suggest a different story."

Decker swore, shook his head. "Let's have a look."

Chattanooga and the surrounding area might be Tennessee's fourth largest metropolitan area, but communities like Sunset Cove gave the area a small-town atmosphere where folks knew their neighbors. Huck had kicked himself repeatedly for ever leaving. He'd given up on Olivia and that had been the biggest mistake of all. Even Willy had worried that it might be too late to ever repair the damage. God knows they had discussed it many times.

Willy was gone now. Olivia had no reason to ever come back after this.

Huck's gut clenched with despair. Maybe it was too late, but damn it, when he'd seen her standing on her grandfather's porch, he'd felt like there might still be hope. Or maybe that had been wishful thinking. But he couldn't let her leave again without trying, could he?

Focus, pal.

Decker surveyed the chaos. "What the hell?" He shook his head, then turned to Huck. "You could be right," he admitted, "but we could also just be looking at someone who heard about his death and decided to capitalize on the situation. There's some pretty desperate folks out there with the state of the world these days."

Huck nodded. "I considered that too. But then I noticed the things that hadn't been taken. Mrs. Ballard's jewelry is still in the bedroom. Some of it looks pretty valuable. There's a small gold coin collection and various household goods that could be easily sold or traded for drugs." He shrugged. "So far, I haven't found a thing that's missing other than his camera. Olivia noticed it first. Unless it was found with his body, and I just haven't heard, it's gone."

Decker blew out a big breath. "Well, hell." His fierce gaze settled on Huck. "I want you to get to the bottom of this, Monroe. Willy was more than just a friend. If someone did this to him, I want to know."

"Yes, sir." He was preaching to the choir. Nobody in this county cared more about William Ballard than Huck.

"You let me know if you need anything," Decker went on, "and take care of Willy's granddaughter. He'd want us to make sure she's okay." He shook his head. "If she'd told me when she was arriving, I would have gone to the ME's office with her. Damn it."

Huck understood. He would have done the same. If he hadn't been in Nashville for that deposition, he would have been here anyway. But he hadn't heard the news until this morning. He'd wanted to call Olivia, but he didn't have her new cell number. She likely didn't want him to have it.

"You don't need to worry about Olivia, sir," Huck promised his boss. "I'll take care of her."

Huck intended to do everything in his power to make sure Olivia had whatever she needed for however long she was in town. She would be Huck's top priority. Maybe in the process of getting through this tragedy there was some way he could convince her to forgive him. And whoever did this to Willy, assuming it wasn't an accident, had better hope someone else found him before Huck.

Twilight Trail, 7:00 p.m.

OLIVIA SAT IN her car staring up at the house for a long time before she even attempted to talk herself into climbing out.

This farmhouse had been her second home growing up. Huck's parents had been like the aunt and uncle she had never had. Willy and her gran were both only children, and her mom had been their only child.

She sank deeper into her seat. How sadly ironic that both her parents were only children. Her father had been a drifter until he landed in Nashville and met Laura Ballard during her freshman year at Vandy. She'd stolen his heart, he'd claimed. But after only a few short years, he'd disappeared. Then, Laura had died. In the span of one year Olivia had lost both her father and her mother.

For as far back as her memory went, no one ever talked about her father. As Olivia had gotten older, her gran had told her the few things she knew about him. Only child, drifter, etcetera. Huck had asked his parents about her dad, and they'd told her some things like the part about her mother having stolen his heart and how the two of them were away for weeks at a time even after Olivia was born. Her father's work, Gran had explained.

Olivia looked exactly like her mother. Same dark hair and eyes. Same everything, really. Looking at a photograph of her mother was like looking in the mirror. There were only a few photos of her father. He'd had sandy blond hair and blue eyes.

Like Huck.

Olivia closed her eyes to slow the whirlwind of thoughts and emotions. Huck had left her the same way her father had left her mother.

"Enough." She opened the car door and forced her feet on the ground and pushed herself into an upright position. It wasn't until she turned back for her overnight bag that she realized she'd left her purse at the cabin. Whatever. She was too tired to care. Huck would bring it. Maybe. They had exchanged cell phone numbers before she left. Apparently, Willy had done as she'd asked and never given him her newest number. She reached into the back and grabbed her overnight bag, then shoved the car door shut. Forcing one foot in front of the other, she walked to the house.

Unlike the cabin, Huck's family home stood two stories, with a basement and a huge attic. They'd explored every square inch of that attic as well as the basement. From ghost-hunter clubs to detective partnerships, they had played every imaginable game. Huck was only a year older than her, so they'd had a tremendous amount in common. If she told the truth, she would admit she'd loved him since they were kids. That love had just blossomed into something different as they grew older.

"Fool," she griped at herself for going down that road.

She climbed the steps. Couldn't help smiling at the pair of rockers that still sat on the porch. It seemed to Olivia that on hot summer evenings Huck's parents could always be found rocking on this porch. His dad had died suddenly late last year, and only a few months later his mom had moved to Knoxville to live with her older sister, who was also a widow. Didn't take much imagination to recognize she wouldn't have wanted to stay in this big old house alone. She probably hadn't expected Huck would ever come home. Olivia was shocked still that he'd decided to do so *after* his mother left.

Willy had made comments about folks in Sunset Cove,

including Huck, even when Olivia hadn't wanted to know, particularly about Huck. She had been well aware Willy had always hoped she and Huck would find a way to work things out. Even after ten years, he'd held onto that foolish optimism.

Olivia hadn't had the heart to tell him that was never, ever going to happen.

She unlocked and opened the door. The familiar scents filled her senses. The aftershave Huck had always worn lingered in the air. How, in a house this large, could she smell *him* first and foremost? And why hadn't he started using something else? She didn't want to smell that scent.

Just stop.

Her grandfather was dead...the only person in this world who was biologically part of her. She was weak right now. Shaken by the idea that someone may have hurt him. Of course, she couldn't be expected to maintain her usual defenses. She was only human after all.

She closed the door, locked it and decided she needed a shower. Desperately.

She was almost to the stairs when a framed photo on the hall table stopped her.

Sam. Samson, the big old sweet Labrador that held a place in her fondest memories.

She dropped her bag. Picked up the frame and touched the image of the black dog.

He'd died the year after Huck had moved to Miami. He'd been seventeen at the time. This dog had been on a multitude of camping trips with Olivia and Huck. She'd never been able to have a dog of her own because this sweet animal had ruined her for any other pet.

She held the photograph to her chest and cried. Couldn't

stop the tears. She collapsed onto the bottom step of the staircase. She cried for Willy and how she missed him so desperately. She cried for all the things that should have been and never would be. Mostly, she cried because she felt hollow and lost...adrift.

When she had cried herself out, she struggled to her feet. She steadied herself and placed the photograph back on the table. She remembered vividly how after her grandmother had died, she'd suffered with sudden crying bouts for months. She expected it would be the same this time.

She trudged up the stairs. Passed the bedroom that had belonged to Huck's parents and the one that had been—probably still was—his. She went to the room that had been a guest room for as long as she could remember and plunked her bag on the bed. She took out the nightshirt she'd brought and clean underwear. Then she made her way to the hall bathroom.

Blindly, she retrieved a towel from the shelf and climbed into the shower. It wasn't until the hot water had filled the cubical with steam that more of the scents she couldn't bear closed in on her. The soap she had smelled on his skin even though he'd barely touched her today. The shampoo he used. Emotion engulfed her once more, and she sank into it, embraced it. As painful as it was, at least it was something real.

She needed something, anything, to cling to right now.

Chapter Three

Olivia brushed her hair and pulled it into a ponytail to get it out of the way. This was her preferred hairstyle when in the field. Today it was about not having the strength to care. She stared at her reflection in the hazy mirror over the antique dresser. In time, the hurt would pass on to a more manageable level. She could do this. She was strong.

She closed her eyes and drew in a deep breath. Huck had been up for a while. First thing, when he got up, she'd heard him walk down the hall and stand outside her door. He hadn't knocked or said anything. She supposed he'd considered one or the other but changed his mind.

As much as she appreciated his generosity, she was glad he'd gone downstairs.

Going downstairs was something she had waffled back and forth about since the moment she woke up. Doing so meant facing him…on his home turf. It wasn't that she didn't feel completely at home here. She did. She had played in this house. Had dinners in that kitchen. Romped in the yard…had her first kiss in his bedroom at the ripe old age of thirteen.

She shook her head. The kiss had startled them both.

He hadn't initiated it any more than she had, it just happened. They were listening to music and suddenly their faces were coming together. It hadn't happened again for a very long time. But they had held hands a lot after that. Running through the woods. Walking along the sidewalk in town. Watching movies. It was like they were connected and there was no way to separate one from the other. Her every thought and plan started and ended with him. What would Huck think? Do? When would he be over? What were they going to do today? When would they kiss again?

When she'd left for college, she hadn't once considered there would ever be life without Huck. They would be together forever just like they always had been.

Except they hadn't.

Olivia forced her head out of the past and grabbed her cell. She needed to charge it before heading out for the day. There was a lot to do, and she was woefully unprepared even after a good ten hours of sleep.

Steeling herself, she left the refuge of the borrowed room. The smell of burning toast accompanied the sound of swearing as she descended the stairs. Her lips lifted in a little smile. The idea that his morning didn't appear to be going so well helped her to relax just the tiniest bit. Maybe she wasn't the only one feeling utterly awkward.

She paused at the kitchen door and watched for a moment. He popped two slices of bread into the toaster and leaned down to adjust the browning control. On the stove, steam rose from a frying pan. Eggs more than a little overdone, she decided based on the odor wafting from that direction. Beyond those unpleasant scents was the smell of coffee. Now that mustered her attention.

Olivia moved into the room. "Good morning."

Huck straightened and turned to face her. "I hope I didn't wake you with all my…" He waved a hand at the mess he'd made. "I've never been much of a cook. Mom never let me near the kitchen, and in Miami it was too easy to hit a drive-through to bother with honing any chef skills." He shut off the stove eye and considered the eggs. "We should probably do that today in fact."

"It's okay. I'm not really hungry." She glanced toward the sink. The coffeepot still stood next to that big old farmhouse-style sink tucked beneath a double window. Huck's mom had always said staring out that window with her cup of coffee each morning before anyone else was up was one of her favorite parts of the day. "Coffee, I need desperately."

He grinned. "Good thing I do that quite well."

He walked to the counter, grabbed a mug he'd already placed there and poured the brew. "Black, right?" He turned, offered the steaming mug to her.

"Right." She crossed the room, accepted the warm cup. "Thanks."

He swiped at his blue T-shirt as if suddenly feeling underdressed. "I brought your handbag from the cabin. It's on the sofa."

"Great. Thank you. I need my charger."

He held out a hand. "Give me your phone, and I'll put it on my charger." He hitched his head toward the door. Sure enough, one of those handy charging stations sat on the counter by the back door. "I put mine on the charger every evening when I come home."

She slid her phone from her hip pocket and placed it in his broad hand. "Thanks."

Olivia pulled out a chair at the table and took a seat. After he'd put her phone on the charger, he poured himself a cup of coffee and joined her. His every move—the way he'd reached toward her, the way he turned, even the way he sat down—were all as familiar to her as breathing. She knew him as well as she knew herself, and yet after ten years apart, they were strangers now.

Some things, she supposed, were too deeply engrained to be erased even by time.

She was pretty sure she recognized the faded blue tee too. Vintage for sure. All the way back to when they were teenagers and in love with classic rock. But the logo wasn't why she remembered the tee. It brought out the perfect blue in his eyes. Made her want to lean closer to make sure she wasn't imagining such a pale, pale blue color. People he met always commented on the unusual color of his eyes. The body-hugging jeans were, of course, classic Huck.

How was it that she hadn't thought of him in years and suddenly she was here, with him, and her entire being felt as if she had missed him desperately every minute of every day for more than a decade? Felt as if the part of her that had been missing was suddenly right in front of her.

She was emotional, she told herself. Losing Willy had broken her defenses. Made her weaker than she'd expected. Made her frantic for human connection.

She sipped her coffee and somehow managed to keep the emotions that attempted to crowd into her chest under some facsimile of control.

Huck looked up from the cup he'd been staring into. Maybe he was struggling with the situation as well. "It's good to see you, Liv, no matter that I'm sorry as hell for the reason you're here. You know I loved Willy."

She did know. Just like that, here came those damned tears again, burning her eyes. She blinked at them, attempted a smile. "I know." She swallowed at the lump clogging her throat. "We talked several times every week." Her smile was boosted at the memory of his voice. "He was still taking photos even at seventy-two. He detailed his every foray on the trails he knew I loved so much. It was almost like I was still here."

If she walked those trails now, she wouldn't be surprised at nature's changes. He'd kept her updated on every single detail. Olivia had decided that he had missed his second calling by not writing a book or two. His ability to describe the landscape and capture its full beauty in words as well as on film had been inspiring.

"The man was healthy, strong. Went hiking every day." Huck shook his head. "He knew those trails better than anyone."

Images from the house and shed populated her brain like files on an awakening computer screen. "I can't believe he would have gotten too close and fallen." She squeezed her eyes shut and shook her head. "He was too careful to make that kind of mistake." She took a deep breath, opened her eyes once more. "I realize anyone can make a mistake—stumble—I get that…but Willy was well versed in all the ways to recapture one's balance. To handle the unexpected."

"That's what I told the sheriff."

"He and Willy were friends," Olivia said aloud, remembering all those fishing trips and all those tales of adventures as young men. "What does he think?"

Huck shrugged. "He believes the case could go either way. Willy was old, like him, he said. Sometimes you lose your balance unexpectedly."

The ravages of age affected everyone, but Willy would

have borne that in mind. He hadn't been fool enough to believe otherwise. "So, he believes it was an accident?"

"He did," Huck admitted, "until he saw the cabin. He said I should do whatever it takes to determine what happened either way."

Olivia studied him a moment. The tension in his shoulders. The restlessness in his hands as he turned the mug around and around. "What do you think happened?" she asked, needing to know for sure she wasn't in this alone.

His eyes connected with hers, the weight of worry heavy. "I don't know, but I'm leaning toward the idea that it was not an accident, and I damned sure intend to find the answer one way or another."

Fighting a renewed burst of emotion, she said, "Willy didn't have any enemies that I know of."

Huck shook his head. "No way. Everybody loved him."

"Except whoever pushed him." The words twisted in her gut like barbed wire.

Their gazes collided again. "We'll figure this out."

"I want to go there." She drew in a deep breath. "To Sunset Rock. I need to see it." She needed to breathe the air...to feel what he'd felt in those final moments. Her heart thudded harder with the weight of pain.

Huck nodded. "I'll take you."

Sunset Rock, 10:30 a.m.

HUCK INSISTED THEY grab something to eat on the way. Olivia had been certain she couldn't possibly eat, but when he'd come out of the diner with that bag of buttered biscuits with bacon, she'd eaten.

To reach their destination, they had parked at Point Park and proceeded on foot along the trail. Willy would have done it that way. He'd done it thousands of times. So had Olivia. So had Huck. It was the most inspirational route. Besides, Huck had already said his Defender had been parked there. The sheriff had driven the vehicle back to the house after his body was recovered.

This place was nothing short of awe-inspiring. The vast, long mountain ridge cut through Alabama, Georgia and Tennessee, rising far above the Cumberland Plateau. Hikers, trail runners and climbers loved it. The trails in the area never got old, not even to the folks who had lived here their whole lives. She was lucky to have grown up in the Lookout Mountain area. Considering the stunning views, the place was aptly named. Oh, and the caves. So many caves. As a kid, Olivia had tagged along on many cave explorations with Willy. When they were old enough, she and Huck had explored plenty on their own as well.

Willy had only one rule about her and Huck venturing into this beautiful yet dangerous terrain: always provide someone a thorough plan for your trip before you leave. The exact route, departure time and anticipated return time. It was the golden rule, particularly for those hiking alone.

Had Willy told anyone where he was going that last day? Or had his number one rule been only for others?

Nearly two miles from where they parked, they reached Sunset Rock. High above the Tennessee River and the world below. The sheer drops from Sunset Rock were sudden and steep. It was no place to be distracted. The unprotected drops were far too dangerous not to use extreme caution no matter how often you visited.

And no matter the danger…no matter the hurt this place now wielded for her, Olivia lost her breath as she took it in.

"It doesn't matter how many times you see it," Huck

said, reading her mind, "it's beautiful in a way that's difficult to explain."

"This is the last thing Willy saw." The idea gave her a sense of peace and at the same time stabbed deep into her chest.

They stood there for a very long time, experiencing the solitude, soaking up the beauty. They hadn't met a soul on the way up or when they arrived, so they were completely alone in this vast, stunning terrain. The silence felt right. For Willy, she decided. This was the perfect place to remember him. No matter where his body was, his soul would be flying here.

After a time, Huck said, "Do you remember what we used to do sometimes?"

She turned to stare up at him, wondering if he meant the same thing she had just recalled. Then he reached for her hand, and she knew he did.

"Just close your eyes," he said softly as his fingers curled around hers.

Olivia closed her eyes. She didn't have to look to know Huck did the same.

Back when they were together...before...they would come up here, ease as close to the edge as they dared, and then stand very still with their eyes closed. It was like floating high above all else...like being the only people on earth with unseen forces drawing them closer and closer.

When she couldn't bear the silence or the pull of him any longer, she opened her eyes and tugged free of his hold. His eyes opened, the pain there not unlike her own.

"I want to see where they found him."

He nodded. "Okay."

The trek down was quiet, somber. Olivia drifted into a

kind of numbness she hoped would get her through the part that came next.

When Huck led her off the visible path, there was no crime-scene tape, no evidence markers. But when he stopped, she recognized the place. There was evidence of disturbance amid the plant life. Grasses smashed by the landing. Trampled by rescuers. Rocks pushed aside. Blood.

Olivia blinked. Stared at the stain on one fairly large boulder.

The point of impact.

Her stomach dropped, and she felt sick.

"Are you sure about this?" Huck was next to her, his hand on her arm.

With effort, Olivia pushed the frailer emotions aside. "They didn't find his camera."

If it wasn't at the house or in the shed, it had to be here. She had checked in the Defender and it hadn't been there either.

Unless...someone took it.

"I doubt the rescue crew would have known to look for it," Huck offered.

Valid point. Olivia looked up, her eyes searching for the most likely place where he would have gone over the edge. Her guts tied into knots, but she had to do this. It was too important. If someone caused Willy's death, he couldn't be permitted to get away with it.

"Let's spread out, but be careful." Huck studied her a long moment. "I'm guessing you haven't done this in a while."

He was likely assuming as much based on the sneakers she wore. Her hiking boots were back in Montana, and he was right; she hadn't done this in a while. Her promotion to project manager had sentenced her to more time in the office.

"I'm good," she said rather than admit the truth in his words.

Beyond the well-traveled trail, the brush was thick. The terrain rocky. Treacherous in places. But she kept going. Creating a grid of sorts around the point of impact.

She shuddered each time the words echoed through her brain. Somehow the more technical term wasn't as awful as "the place where he died."

Willy was dead.

Hurt made breathing difficult, but she kept going. She prowled through the greenery, poked around between the rocks. Memories from the hundreds if not thousands of journeys she and Huck had made along these trails kept intruding on her thoughts. There was a cave, more a narrow crevice in the rocks upon first glance, somewhere around here. She and Huck had tucked themselves away there so many times. Reading. Talking about the future. Stealing kisses.

As if her thoughts had led her there, she found that secret place. Probably not really secret but not easily seen or found. She slipped beyond the crevice and into the wider part of the space created by the rock walls that had split apart eons ago. Digging out her cell, she used the flashlight app to study the walls. Found what she was looking for and traced her fingers over the slight indentions in the rock. Huck had spent hours slowly chiseling their initials into the rock.

"A million years ago," she murmured.

She leaned her head against the cool rock. All those years ago, who would have thought this was where they would be now. Torn apart. Her heart battered. Maybe his too. Willy gone.

Olivia closed her eyes and breathed through the pain. Life would never be the same. She thought of all the things she wished she had said to Willy the last time they had talked just three days ago. Had she told him she loved him? That she missed him? That she wished she had stayed closer all these years?

It was sadly true. So many times in the past decade she had considered that she'd made a mistake traveling the world with her work rather than being close to home. Egypt. Mexico. Peru. Chile. Greece. Had those weeks and months spent at archaeological sites been worth it?

She had thought so at the time. Willy had loved hearing all about it. He'd told her about showing off the pictures she shared with him. She'd sent him endless treasures from her adventures.

But none of those were the same as spending time with him.

"I wondered where you'd gotten off to."

Huck's voice had her opening her eyes. His cell phone light was pointed at the ground but provided enough illumination for her to see him.

Unlike when they were kids and the space was enough to comfortably accommodate the two of them, his broad shoulders required that he turn slightly to fit now. The air in the space felt suddenly lacking. Not nearly enough. His scent...his presence filled it up. Closed in around her.

"I'd forgotten about this place." She looked around, anywhere but at him.

"I come here sometimes."

She frowned. Confused. Couldn't *not* look at him then. "You do?"

"Sure. We spent so much time here it feels like a place I don't want to forget."

The way she had.

"Why?" she asked.

"Why what?"

It was too dark to see his face well enough for her to read his expression, but the confusion was quite clear in his voice.

Maybe it was the darkness or this place that gave her the courage to delve into the until now forbidden subject. "Why did you come back to Sunset Cove?"

He didn't answer for a while. Maybe a whole minute.

"Mom was moving to her sister's. Aunt Gloria couldn't stay home without help, and there was no one else." He shrugged. Olivia didn't so much see the move as hear his shoulders scrape the rock. "To tell you the truth, I think she hadn't been happy in the house since Dad died."

"I'm sorry," Olivia said, suddenly realizing that she owed him an apology for not attending his father's funeral. "I was in Peru when your father died. Communications at the dig site were minimal. I didn't get the word that he'd died until a week later."

"Willy told me."

"He was like my second father," she admitted. "I loved him."

The silence went on for too long. She'd said more than she should have.

"Anyway," Huck said abruptly. "Mom was ready for a change, but she didn't want to abandon the place. She said I should take the place and make it my own. So that's what I did."

"That was very noble of you." She didn't believe for a moment he'd left his life in Miami behind and come back here just because someone needed to take care of the house. Or maybe it was just easier to believe that since she had stayed gone too.

"Not really," he said. "I was ready to come home. I'd been considering moving back for a while when she asked."

The idea that Olivia had been struggling with the same feelings hit too close. This was too much. Way too much.

"Do you mind? I'm feeling a little claustrophobic?"

Without a word, he slipped away. For a moment she waited in the near darkness, her heart hammering at having abruptly lost the closeness.

Big breath. Don't think about it.

Olivia followed the path he'd taken. Once they were back on the trail, he said, "I don't think we're going to find his camera. Either he didn't bring it with him, or someone took it."

Like his killer.

Deep inside, Olivia shuddered. "He never went anywhere without it. You know that."

"Yeah." He surveyed the landscape. "I do."

Which left only one option.

Someone took it. After viewing the scene, Olivia couldn't see how the camera would have survived the fall. The film with whatever pics he'd taken may have been salvageable but not the camera. Which made the idea that someone had taken it even more ludicrous.

Unless he took it before Willy fell. The scenario played out in her head. Willy trying to hang on to the camera... losing his hold...falling...

Olivia forced the images away.

The possibility brought up another question: Was there something on the camera that mattered to the person who took it? Something important enough to kill for?

Uneasiness slid through Olivia. "Do you think he may have taken a photo of something or someone that made him a target?"

"I guess it's possible." Huck glanced at her. "You're thinking someone just passing through? Maybe Willy came upon some sort of trouble?"

Olivia didn't respond right away. She kept walking, heading back. Huck did the same. "It could happen."

"It could. Wrong place, wrong time sort of thing."

"Or maybe someone he knew from his traveling days. Someone who wanted money or whatever from him?"

"Had he mentioned having any visitors?"

Olivia shook her head. "But he did seem distracted the last time we talked."

"When was that?"

"Sunday. We talked that morning." Olivia considered the conversation. "It was shorter than usual. Willy said he had a lot to do." Looking back, his rush to get off the phone had seemed more urgent than she'd realized at the time. Or perhaps his death only made it seem so.

"What about his cell phone?" Olivia had only just thought of the device. Willy generally took his cell with him. To him, it wasn't as essential as his camera, but over time he had come to see that it was immensely handy.

"It should be in his vehicle," Huck said. "Sheriff Decker drove the Defender back to the house. I'm sure he would have left it in the vehicle as long as it was found and not needed for evidence."

"It could be evidence," Olivia argued. She didn't remember seeing it when she'd looked for the camera but, honestly, she hadn't even thought about the phone.

"Now that we have suspicious circumstances," Huck confirmed, "that's correct, and I've ordered his cell phone records, which will show us all calls or messages, even those that may have been erased from his cell. So if we don't find it, we can still determine who he was in contact with."

"We should check the Defender and see if it's there," Olivia said, needing to see it. To know something now.

"We'll do that first, then I think we should go through the house more thoroughly," Huck suggested. "This is my case, and I intend to focus solely on it until we figure this out. Decker said I should take all the time I need."

Olivia paused. "Thank you. I'm sure you could have passed off the case, but I appreciate you doing this personally, Huck."

Her breath caught. She hadn't said his name out loud in so, so long. It felt foreign and yet somehow normal...natural. She had known this man her whole life...knew every part of him by heart just as he knew every part of her. Strangely, for once it didn't hurt to say it.

He gave a curt nod and kept walking.

By the time they reached the parking lot, Olivia decided she had overstepped. The thick silence had been evidence enough. Although she didn't see how he had a right to be put off by anything she might feel or say. After all, he was the one to leave and start a new life. Given his leaving and staying gone so long, it was reasonable for her to feel his offer of help was unexpected. Over the top even. She would not feel guilty for saying what needed to be said.

By the time they had reached his SUV, she decided to just be honest. If they were going to work together to find the truth about what happened to Willy, honesty was important. All this tension and subterfuge would just be in the way.

Being the gentleman his daddy had taught him to be, Huck opened the passenger-side door for her.

Olivia hesitated before climbing in. "Look, all I was trying to say back there is that, after all this time, I do appreciate your decision to go the extra mile."

He turned to her, anger or maybe frustration radiating from him. "First," he said tightly, "Willy was like family to me. I would do anything to help. Second..." He stalled, took a breath. "It's my job."

Olivia felt oddly calm. Maybe it was the calm before the storm, but she was grateful for the ability to speak evenly. "You're right. Still, it's above and beyond. You were gone a long time. Never reached out. Didn't drop by if you ever visited your folks. I would understand if you'd chosen to pass."

He held up both hands. "Wait. You're saying my help is unexpected because *I* left ten years ago?"

Her own anger and frustration stirred. "That's right."

"You left first."

The three words were heavy with accusation.

Olivia's mouth dropped open. "I went to school. I—" she slapped her chest "—was coming back when I graduated."

He bit his lips together so hard she wondered how his teeth didn't crack. When she would have launched her next barb, he spoke again, "I don't know where you got your information, but I visited Willy whenever I was in town. Called him at least once every month."

His words stunned her. Seriously? Why would Willy not have told her that part?

Because you didn't want to hear anything about Huck.

"I called you." The words were out before she could recall them. Humiliation swaddled her, suffocating and frustrating. But she'd said it. She couldn't unsay it any more than he could unhear it. "Over and over. In the beginning, I mean. Left messages for you with your parents. You never once called back."

"We should get going." He reached for the SUV door.

She glared at him. And there it was. The truth of the matter. He'd left, and even when she called, leaving countless messages for him to please, please call her back…he hadn't.

He just left without looking back.

Olivia settled into the passenger seat and buckled her seat belt. She would take his help if it meant finding out what happened to Willy.

But she would never, ever forgive him.

Chapter Four

Firefly Lane, 12:00 p.m.

Huck parked behind Olivia's car. Putting aside their personal issues, they had agreed that the next step was to more thoroughly search the cabin and the shed. He'd taken her back to his house to get her car and overnight bag. She'd insisted. He had a feeling that decision had something to do with not wanting to be committed to going back to his place at the end of the day.

Nothing he could do about that. She was a grown damned woman. He watched her climb out of her car and walk to the porch. He'd thought she was the prettiest girl he'd ever seen when they were kids, but that didn't begin to describe her now.

As angry as she made him, she was a beautiful woman. Just looking at her...listening to her voice undid him.

Get your head on straight, man.

He climbed out of his vehicle and headed toward the house. He stopped at the Defender and checked for Willy's cell phone. It wasn't in the vehicle. Good thing he'd ordered his phone records. As he headed inside, he considered how much easier it might be if he just told her the reason he'd taken off all those years ago. But it wouldn't change any-thing. The fact was he'd eventually realized that he'd made a mistake, but by then there was no turning back. Why tell her what an idiot he'd been? How his immaturity and in-security had ruined their lives? That his ego disguised as concern for her had been leading him? It wouldn't change one damned thing.

What was done was done.

No looking back. That motto had helped him survive losing her.

Forward—he had to keep pushing forward or lose his sanity altogether.

The crime-scene investigators were finished with the property, so he and Liv were free to do as they pleased. Considering how much stuff Willy had, going through it all thoroughly would take some time.

His gaze landed on Olivia, who stood in the middle of the living room. Huck just hoped they got through the journey without her hating him even more. He wasn't sure he could survive another stab to the heart.

She turned to face him, and the air rushed out of his lungs. His hopes died a sudden death. He would not sur-vive this either way.

"I appreciate you taking me to…where it happened." She drew back her shoulders, lifted her chin. "But I've got this part from here."

While he recovered from her unexpected statement, she surveyed the room and went on, "I mean here—in the house. I've got this. I'm sure you have plenty of police work to do on the case without hanging around with me."

"There could be evidence *here*," he said, finding his voice and a reasonable comeback.

"If I discover any evidence, I'll call you." She walked past him and to the door, opened it. "Thanks again."

He felt the knife slice deep between his ribs. He wanted to shake her and demand to know why it had to be this way. Couldn't they at least be friends? Get along like two people who had known each other their whole lives minus all the emotional stuff?

But he said none of those things. He made his way to the door. Should have walked on out. Shouldn't have paused even for a second. But, apparently, he wasn't that smart.

He stared down his shoulder at her. "It doesn't have to be this way."

She looked up at him, her expression firm, her lips tight. "*This* is the way it is."

Maybe it was the fire in her eyes—the absolute blazing determination in her voice—but he felt the burn on his back when he walked out all the way to his SUV.

He swung open the driver-side door and slid behind the wheel, his frustrated gaze still on that damned door. She stood there, watching him. She wanted to ensure he left. Wanted to watch him go.

On autopilot, he started the engine, shifted into Reverse and peeled away without taking his eyes off her. He could watch too, by God.

He slammed on the brakes, hit Drive and roared away.

Yeah, he was a fool. He slowed his speed. Pounded the steering wheel with the heel of his hand. He was thirty-one damned years old, and he'd just acted like a rebellious teenager.

Olivia Ballard was the one person in this world who could turn him inside out that way. Make him want to tear something apart…like the life he'd spent a decade building—the one without her.

His chest tightened to the point he could scarcely breathe. Ten years was a long time but not nearly long enough to forget her. He'd kept hoping someday she would hunt him down and tell him she'd never stopped loving him. That he'd made a mistake when he left and she was tired of waiting for him to admit it. But that was a fantasy that only worked in his dreams.

The warning that he'd failed to put on his seatbelt finally punctured the haze of anger and frustration blurring his good sense. He slowed, yanked the belt across his lap and snapped the buckle.

"Idiot," he growled.

His cell vibrated, and he dragged it from his pocket. *Sheriff* flashed on the screen. He hit Accept. "Monroe."

"Huck, I've asked the medical examiner to have a second look at Willy. He says he can do it today and release the body tomorrow. Pass that on to Olivia, would you?"

"Yes, sir." The idea of having to go back and talk to her had his throat going completely dry. "We had a look around at Sunset Rock and along the trail where his body was discovered. Didn't find anything. Olivia is going through the house and shed again to see if she can determine if anything besides his camera is missing."

A sigh echoed across the line. "We may not find any answers, but I'm afraid this is the best we can do."

The sad truth was the sheriff was right. Sometimes the answers just couldn't be found.

When the call ended, he put one through to Liv. He was too much of a coward to go back and face her again. Mostly because he was damned afraid of what he might say. She didn't answer, so he left a voice mail.

In the end, she was right. There was plenty he could do that didn't involve being in that cabin with her. Willy had friends. Huck intended to interview each one. To stop in all the places he frequented. Talk to anyone who had seen him in the past two or three weeks. What was on his mind? Did he mention any issues? Any trouble with anyone? If Willy had been murdered, murder rarely happened in a vacuum. Someone somewhere had seen or heard something.

All Huck had to do was find that needle in a haystack.

Firefly Lane

As much as she didn't want to, Olivia felt bad for sending Huck away. But she had known that spending so much time with him would have driven her over an edge she might not be able to come back from. It was better if she did this alone. She needed time and space to grieve.

She had decided to start in Willy's bedroom. The room wasn't that large, but it was filled with Gran's treasures. She'd collected flowers, pressed and framed them. They covered a good portion of the walls. Olivia had always loved them. One of the quilts her gran had made covered the bed. Olivia dragged her fingers over the soft, worn cotton. Her grandmother had been a very talented woman. She wondered if her mother had been the same. Olivia remembered glimpses of her mother. She actually had very few memories at all. Gran had talked about her sometimes. Willy said she didn't like talking about Laura because it hurt too much. Olivia hadn't really understood until Huck left. Losing a child was far worse than losing a boyfriend, but afterward Olivia had understood the kind of hurt her gran had suffered.

She picked up the framed photograph of her mother that had sat on the dresser in her grandparents' bedroom for as long as she could remember. Olivia looked so much like her mother. Willy had said she was like Laura's twin. Olivia traced the shape of her mother's face, the silver chain with its tiny sunflower pendant. Willy had given that necklace to Laura on her sixteenth birthday. She'd worn it ever since.

Olivia didn't remember the necklace other than in the pictures of her mother. Laura hadn't really raised her at all. After Olivia was born, Laura had spent more time traveling with Kasey—Olivia's father, though the two had never married—than at home with her new baby daughter. She would put in an appearance, Willy had told Olivia because she certainly didn't remember, only to leave again.

When Olivia was three, her father had left and never come back. Willy said he'd sneaked away, leaving a devastated Laura behind. She was never the same after he left. Then a year later, she died. Photos were Olivia's only real memories of her parents, and she couldn't be sure if she actually recalled those moments or if they were lodged in her subconscious because her grandmother had described the events of each photo to her. As she grew older, Olivia had decided that since Kasey left her, he wasn't worth remembering anyway.

Willy was the only man Olivia had ever loved who hadn't left her.

She closed her eyes and battled a rush of emotion. He would be here now if not for whatever happened up on that ridge. Damn it!

Olivia placed the photograph back where her gran had kept it. The woman in the photo was a stranger, just like the man who'd played the part of her father for just a little while.

One by one, she picked through the drawers in the dresser and bureau as well as the bedside tables. She checked under the bed, under the mattress and in the closet. She straightened up the mess the intruder had made as she went along. Olivia found many things that made her smile, others that made her cry and so many things with which she would never be able to part.

She made up her mind right then that she would leave this cabin exactly as it was. Whenever she was home, she wanted to stay here and be surrounded with all these things.

With a deep, reaffirming breath, she moved on to the bathroom, which was a piece of cake compared to the bedroom. Next, she stared at her own bedroom door. Decided it could wait. She'd spent enough time thinking about Huck the past few hours. Looking at and touching all the things she'd kept from their shared childhood was more than she could deal with just now. Her mother's room was up then.

Olivia opened the door and turned on the light. She moved through the room, checking drawers and shelves. Beneath pillows on the bed and under the mattress. She set to rights the items that had been tossed aside.

When she opened the closet door, her mother's scent, whether real or imagined, filled her nostrils. Her dresses and blouses hung just as they had for more than a quarter century. Shoes lined the closet floor. Olivia slipped her foot into one. She smiled. Fit as if they had belonged to her. A photo of her mother and father together sat on the bureau. It was one of only two or three photos of her dad. She studied the face of the man who had decided she wasn't worth the effort of being a father. Handsome enough. Tall, slim.

Olivia found nothing she hadn't seen before. Noticed

nothing missing. She left the room, closing the door firmly behind her.

"Now, for this." She surveyed the main room.

For a moment, the task felt overwhelming, and the idea of where to begin was lost on her. She decided to start with the fireplace and that big old painting of her as a young girl.

Logs were stacked in the fireplace. Even at this time of year there was an occasional cool evening that prompted the need for a cozy fire. She removed the stack, checked beneath the grate. Then moved onto the damper. Nothing except soot.

Using a chair, she reached above the gun rack and hung the painting back in its rightful place. She touched her gran's name where she'd painted it across the bottom right corner. A smile tugged at her lips. Olivia hadn't inherited her grandmother's talent for drawing and painting. She had a pretty good eye when it came to taking pictures but nothing like Willy's.

She climbed down then restacked the logs.

The rest of the main room was still a mess from whoever had ransacked the place. Like in the bedrooms and bath, she straightened up as she went along. She would be staying here until this investigation was over. When she left, she couldn't leave Willy's home in this condition.

Willy hadn't been a focused housekeeper. The dust was a little deep. Olivia grabbed a dust cloth and cleaner and decided she'd better take care of that issue as she went along. Gran would have been appalled. Willy would have said he had other, more urgent matters that needed his attention. Like wandering the trails he so loved.

Olivia understood. Being out there was a calling she

couldn't deny either. She loved her work the same way Willy had loved his.

Taking her time, Olivia searched, cleaned and tidied. By the time she was finished, it was nearly six. Then she whizzed back through the bedrooms and did a little dusting too. Made herself go through her own room. It wasn't until she'd put her cleaning supplies away and washed her hands and face that she realized she hadn't eaten since breakfast. She went back to the fridge and picked through the cheese offerings. Willy had loved cheese, which was good since Olivia loved it too. Crackers were a given. No cheese lover ever allowed himself to run out of crackers.

She hadn't realized she was starving until she dug into the cheese and crackers. While she ate, she thought of the past few conversations with Willy. If there was a problem or if he'd been having trouble with someone, why hadn't he told her? Beyond a bit of noticeable distraction, he'd sounded exactly like he always did. Maybe he hadn't recognized whatever danger was close. He hadn't been a young man anymore.

The thought speared her with pain. She should have come home more often, then she would have seen what he'd obviously hidden from her. Something had been very wrong.

The idea that Father's Day was this month and she'd intended to visit him for that weekend nagged at her. She shouldn't have waited. Something from Sunday morning's conversation nagged at her. She'd mentioned coming for Father's Day, and he'd suggested she shouldn't. He'd made some excuse about air travel not being as safe as it once was and that they should wait until her birthday in September.

She replayed the conversation. Looking back, it felt off, totally un-Willy-like, that he had urged her so adamantly not to go to the trouble of visiting this month. Why wouldn't he want her to visit?

Tossing her paper plate and napkin into the trash bin, she told herself there must have been a problem. He loved her visits. Hurt twisted inside her at the idea. Maybe it was nothing related to her, but something…related to the person who killed him.

Olivia had to stop herself. Couldn't bear the idea. She would revisit the possibility later. Right now, she needed to finish going through Willy's things. She readied herself to start with the outbuildings. The sooner she was finished, the sooner she could consider whatever she found or felt after having verified what was here and what was not.

Outside, the sun had settled on the treetops, leaving shadows here and there. Olivia started with the barn since that would be easiest. This was where Willy had kept his lawn mower and gardening tools—none of which appeared to have been disturbed. Gran had turned what likely was once a tack room into her personal gardening shed. Her gloves still waited on the wood table where she'd last left them. Her tools and seed pots were perfectly organized. Even the wide-brimmed hat she'd worn faithfully when working outside hung on its hook. She'd repeated the rules of proper outdoor work attire to Olivia a thousand times. Sunscreen, a hat, gloves, good jeans and sturdy shoes.

Olivia touched the gloves but didn't pick them up. Willy wouldn't have wanted her to move them from that exact spot. The dust gathered around them was proof he'd been very careful not to disturb those gloves either.

Nothing in the barn that hadn't always been there. Nothing missing.

The shed was next.

Olivia had been inside it already when she'd had a quick look to see if anything was missing, so the multitude of familiar scents didn't hit her quite so hard this time. She focused on Gran's studio first. It was on the south side of the shed, with windows on three sides facing south, west and east. Until darkness fell, some amount of light filtered into the large room. Willy had given his wife the larger portion of the shed. The brushes and materials she had used lined the shelves along the walls beneath the windows. A large work table held court in the middle of the room. Gran's easel stood near a wall of windows. Waiting on the easel was a nearly finished painting of a scene in Coolidge Park—one of Chattanooga's most beloved places.

A customer had commissioned the painting and would gladly have taken it without the final touches remaining, but Willy had refused to part with his wife's final work. Olivia was glad he hadn't. It looked perfect standing on the easel in Gran's studio. She was very grateful the painting had not been overturned or damaged during the intruder's rampage of a search.

Olivia prowled through the drawers in the wood table. She opened wooden boxes Gran used for storage and checked behind every single item cluttering the endless shelves in the studio. She tidied any mess made by the intruder as she went along. Nothing unexpected was found. Nothing missing as far as she could determine. On to Willy's side of the structure.

Willy's workroom and darkroom were closed off from the rest of the shed. The only entrance into the shed led into a small sort of foyer where there was a bench and a place to hang a coat or umbrella. A fridge stocked with water and soft drinks sat in one corner. There was a small bathroom.

Straight ahead was the set of French doors that led to Gran's studio. On the north side was the single door to Willy's work area. The space beyond was plain, no frills. A typical photographer's studio sans the backdrops since he never did personal portraits. A high table extended the length of one wall. Willy's computers and printers sat humming, ready to wake up with a single touch. Two stools, one at each work station, waited. Filing cabinets and shelves lined another wall.

This tidying and in-depth search were going to take some time.

Olivia started with the computers. She scanned the folders on both. Found nothing but the usual landscape photos. Willy didn't do people. If a person was in the shot he wanted, he waited until they moved on before taking it.

Nothing unexpected in his email.

She checked the shelves, reorganizing as she went. Moved the few items that hadn't been disturbed and carefully placed them back where they belonged. Then the file cabinets. She opened drawer after drawer, reviewing the contents of each folder it contained. Nothing she hadn't expected to find. She was very grateful the intruder had not slung files all over the room. He'd apparently run out of steam by the time he reached the shed. His search had cooled noticeably.

The darkroom was next. It was small, so maybe it wouldn't take so long.

She reached for the narrow door. It was locked.

She shook her head. Of course it was. Willy always kept that room locked. She took a moment to remember where he kept the key hidden.

A grin stretched across her face. "Oh yeah."

She walked back to the more vintage of the two computers, picked up the keyboard and there was the key. Taped to the bottom of the keyboard. Willy kept one in his pocket, but he also kept this spare just in case he lost the one he carried around all the time.

She walked in, turned on the light. There was nothing out of place in here since the door had been locked. The darkroom was divided into two parts, the dry side and the wet side. The dry side, enlarger and cutter along with the paper storage area were straightforward, easy to scan. The wet side was a little more complicated with its various trays. Developer, stop bath, fixer and water and then the drying area.

Olivia found nothing beyond the expected.

Until she reached the end of the drying area, where Willy had hung what were likely his most recent photos. Or at least the ones he'd taken and then developed before his death.

The photos were all hanging backward with the plain white paper side facing out instead of the image captured by the film.

Why would he do that? He always hung them so he could view the images.

Olivia reached out and turned around the first of the row of six photos. The image appeared to be in downtown Chattanooga. It was taken at night, but she could see a bar in the background. Not the kind she would imagine Willy ever visiting. But the most surprising part was the person—a man—near the entrance of the bar. She couldn't make out his face. Tall. Thin. He wore a T-shirt and jeans and a baseball cap.

She turned the next photo. Same general area. Same man based on the tee and cap. The photo was of him coming out of the bar. His face was still too blurry to make out. All six of the photos were of this man. The final one showed him climbing into a black car parked along the street. Unfortunately, the license plate was not visible.

Heart thumping extra hard, Olivia removed the photos, placed them in a stack. These definitely warranted additional consideration. Before leaving the darkroom, she checked the shelves under the tables. Moved the jugs of chemicals around to see anything else that might be stashed there. Nothing.

On her way out of the darkroom, she grabbed the loupe.

The thought occurred to her that she should call Huck, but she couldn't go there just yet. She needed a little more distance.

Outside, it was dark now. She hurried across the backyard and entered through the mudroom door. Closing the door with her foot, she still managed to lose her hold on the photographs, and they flew across the floor.

"Oh damn." She set the loupe aside, flipped on the mudroom light and dropped to her knees to gather the potential evidence. As she did, she scolded herself for forgetting to lock up the darkroom. She'd have to go back.

A solid thud echoed from somewhere deeper in the house.

Olivia froze.

Had she locked the front door before going out to the shed? No, of course not. Other than the darkroom, Willy rarely locked his doors as long as he was home. She'd grown up with the idea that it was safe to leave your doors unlocked, and although she didn't do that in Bozeman or any of the other places she had lived, being back here had her falling into old habits.

Big mistake.

Someone was in the house.

Her heart launched into her throat. Her fingers loosened

on the photographs she'd started to pick up. Slowly, she pushed to her feet. Listening intently for any other sound. Maybe when she'd closed the door she caused something to fall...

But she hadn't closed the door that hard...had she?

The silence throbbed in time with her rising respiration. A slam made her jerk.

Door.

Front door.

Someone had either gone out...or come in.

Olivia grabbed the knob on the back door and twisted, opened the door and rushed out into the darkness.

She hid next to the steps, crouched and pressed against the stone foundation. *Listen! Listen*, she told herself, forcing her heart to slow and the roar of blood to quiet.

For a very long while, she remained in that crouched position. Listening. Not one thing disrupted the usual night sounds. Crickets. Frogs. The hoot of an owl. The whisper of a rare breeze.

When enough time had passed that she felt it was safe to move, Olivia dared to rise. Her legs were stiff from squatting for so long.

Slowly, she moved around the house, peering into the darkness. No other vehicles except her car and the Defender. No sounds beyond the ones she had long minutes ago identified.

Holding her breath, she climbed the steps to the front porch. A creak from the last one made her freeze.

When nothing or no one moved or made a sound, she crossed the porch. The door was closed. She reached for the knob but froze.

Someone had been in the house. Not the wind. Not some animal.

A person. One capable of opening the door and then slamming it shut.

She opened the door and stepped inside. The house was dark save for the dim mudroom light reaching through the kitchen. She felt her way to the corner behind the door. When her fingers closed around the cool steel of the shotgun, relief washed through her.

Shotgun in hand, she moved to the switch and flipped on the light.

Olivia blinked rapidly to adjust her eyes to the brightness. She surveyed the main room. Everything looked exactly as she'd left it.

Her first deep breath since hearing that thud filled her lungs.

"Okay." She closed and locked the front door. Walked straight to the mudroom and closed and locked that one. She gathered the photographs and loupe and moved back to the main room. She placed the potential evidence or whatever it was on the table and did what she had to do.

She lifted the shotgun into firing position, then progressed through the rest of the house to ensure there was no one hiding inside. She didn't expect there was, but she had to be sure. A quick look into closets and under beds... behind the shower curtain confirmed her conclusion.

Then she got angry.

What the hell was going on here?

She stamped back to the table where she'd left those photographs.

Olivia placed the shotgun on the table in easy reach, then she sat down and spread out the six eight-by-tens. She picked up the one that showed the man's face and grabbed the loupe. Still, his face was too blurred to make out. Willy must have taken the photos from quite a distance.

She moved from photo to photo, scanning each closely with the loupe.

Going back to the photo that showed the man's face the clearest, which wasn't clear at all, she studied the rest of him. The tee he wore sported a football team logo. His button-down shirt with its multicolored checks was open, worn more like a jacket. She traced over his face again.

She stared at the bar front in the photo and what she could see of the street. Why would Willy have been following some guy around in a not-so-good part of downtown?

Didn't make a lot of sense.

But neither did his falling from a place he loved and had visited thousands of times.

She turned to the front door.

Had the man in these photos been in the house tonight?

Were these photos what he was looking for? If so, why not go to the shed and break into the darkroom?

Or maybe he didn't know about the photos and had come back to look for whatever he'd been searching for when he tore the house apart.

He would have seen her car and how the house had been straightened up, but that hadn't deterred him.

Ice slid through her veins.

She reached for her phone and called Huck.

As much as she didn't want to, she needed him.

Chapter Five

Firefly Lane, 9:30 p.m.

Huck barreled down the drive and slid to a stop. He was already opening the door when he shoved the car into Park and shut off the engine.

Olivia stood in the open doorway, that old shotgun hanging from her hands. He ran toward her, fear—no, terror—about what could have happened pounding through his veins. He shouldn't have left her here alone.

He wasn't letting her out of his sight again.

Not until this was done.

"Whoever was here," she said as he strode toward her, "he's gone now."

Relief that she was okay almost buckled his knees. "I need to double check."

She nodded. "I'll just..." She backed up, moving deeper into the room and then to the wall next to the door. She leaned against it. "I'll wait here."

He closed and locked the front door. "I'd feel better if you stuck with me."

Another feeble nod.

Damn. She was scared to death. He could understand

why. This cabin was basically in the middle of nowhere. No neighbors for miles.

She couldn't stay here. He would not allow her to stay here. Not alone. Whether she liked it or not—whether she agreed with him or not, she was not spending another moment alone.

He moved through the house. Checked each room. She'd put things back in order. Terror still stabbed at him whenever he thought of her being here alone and someone coming in the house. Willy would have been as mad as hell at him for leaving her here alone. He should never have allowed that to happen. But she'd insisted. Wanted him to go. Damn it.

The house was clear. Relief rushed through him. She was okay, and that was what mattered. He wouldn't make that mistake again.

He hesitated in the kitchen. "Stay put. I'll check the shed and barn. Keep the doors locked and don't open them for any reason—not unless I tell you to."

She stared at him a moment as if she might argue with the order, then she said, "Okay."

His reached for the door when what he really wanted to do was hug her and promise her everything would be okay, but he couldn't make that promise just yet. He flipped a pair of switches at the back door and headed out. He waited on the steps until he heard the lock turn.

Willy had installed a few outdoor lights decades ago, but the illumination was minimal. His wife had insisted she didn't want anything interfering with her ability to see the stars.

"Stars are about the only thing you can see," Huck muttered as he navigated the darkness. He pulled the handgun from his waistband and held it, barrel down, as he moved forward.

It wasn't like crossing the backyard was a straight shot. The flower and vegetable gardens Olivia's grandparents had cultivated over the years spanned the distance between the house and the tree lines on the property. Little fences and stone borders created a damned maze. Huck had known this place like the back of his hand before.

But that had been a long time ago. Now he had to pay attention to each step to prevent himself from tripping and falling into a mass of thorny rose bushes or a vine-covered obelisk. The gate to the small fenced area around the barn stood open. At one time, there were chickens and goats. When Huck had moved back last fall, he'd asked Willy about the critters—as he had called them—and Willy had chuckled and said he'd managed to outlive them all.

Anger sparked deep inside Huck at the idea that someone had ended the man's life. The world needed more folks like Willy.

The barn was clear. Huck stayed alert to the slightest sound or movement as he headed for the shed. Inside, he turned on the lights. Maybe two minutes were required to determine there was no one hiding out there either.

It appeared Olivia was right. Whoever had been here was gone now.

He weaved his way through the gardens and to the back door and gave it a knock. "It's me. You can open up now."

The lock released and the door opened immediately. "Did you see anyone?"

He shook his head as he stepped inside. "Whoever it was is either long gone or hiding out there in the darkness somewhere." He tucked his weapon away, closed the door and locked it. "I didn't notice any vehicles on the side of the road as I drove here and I didn't meet any outgoing vehicles, but that doesn't mean someone didn't park on one of the side roads along the main route and walk over."

"There's something you need to see." She propped the shotgun against the wall and walked to the table. "I found these hanging in the darkroom. They must be the last photos Willy developed."

Huck picked up one and then the next. He recognized the area. "Downtown. Not the sort of places I'd expect Willy to venture into."

"He was watching that man, I think." She picked up the loupe. "His face is not clear enough for me to make out. Maybe you'll recognize him."

Huck used the loupe to study the images of the man, particularly his face. Olivia was right; it was impossible to ID him. He placed the final photo and the loupe on the table. "Why would Willy be following some guy—anyone, for that matter?"

Olivia shook her head and settled into a chair. "I have no idea. He never took photos of people." She shrugged. "I mean, besides family and that wasn't as often as one would think given he carried that camera with him all the time and everywhere. It was like part of him."

Huck lowered into the seat at the end of the table. "I don't think I ever saw him without it."

Olivia rubbed at her eyes and exhaled a weary breath. "I don't understand what's happening."

"We'll figure this out," he promised, knowing he might not be able to keep that promise. "Tomorrow, we'll drive to the bar in the photos and have a look around. Maybe talk to the owner or manager."

"I don't want to wait." She stood. "I'm going now."

Oh, hell. He'd figured that was what she'd say. He pushed to his feet. "I know better than to try and talk you out of it."

"Thanks."

"So I'm going with you."

"I don't need a bodyguard," she countered, anger or frustration in her voice.

"Maybe not," he said, pushing in his chair, "but this is my case, and that means I'm in charge."

The stare-off lasted a full fifteen seconds.

"Fine." She walked over to where she'd left the shotgun, picked it up and returned it to its resting place above the mantel. "Just make sure you don't get in my way."

There was the Liv he knew and...

The thought trailed off. "We'll play it by ear, how about that?"

She didn't answer, just grabbed her bag and started for the front door.

Outside, she locked up and headed for his SUV. She opened her own door and climbed in. Huck shrugged, walked around the hood and got in on his side. She'd never liked him playing the part of gentleman. *I can open my own door*, she'd scolded. *I can close it too. I'm not helpless, Huck.*

Olivia hadn't been the kind of girl who wanted anyone doing for her what she could do herself. Apparently, that hadn't changed.

But she definitely wasn't a girl anymore.

He glanced at her as he drove through the night, heading down the mountain.

Willy swore she hadn't had a single serious relationship since Huck left. But maybe the old guy had only told Huck what he wanted to hear. As far as he could see, her personal life had remained personal. Her social media was all about work. He'd been cyberstalking her for years. At first, he hadn't been able to bear seeing her even online. Eventually, his curiosity or need—maybe both—had gotten the better of him, and he'd found her. His own social media account was just a page he'd opened in order to see her. He never posted anything. Had no desire to interact with anyone else. She had been the one and only reason he'd bothered.

"Willy said you don't do relationships."

Her words startled him. He'd been in his own thoughts so long, his focus on driving, he'd almost forgotten he wasn't alone. "What?"

Had she asked Willy about him?

"You know Willy," she said, her attention remaining straight ahead. "He never stopped seeing you as part of the family. Sometimes he'd just start talking about you."

Huck got it now. "Even when you didn't want to hear it."

Her silence was answer enough.

"He talked about you all the time." Huck smiled. He couldn't tell her how much he'd loved hearing about her adventures. Even before he moved back, the phone conversations he and Willy had always somehow found their way to the subject of Olivia.

"I miss him."

Her voice sounded so desolate, so weary. It took every ounce of willpower he possessed not to reach for her hand. But she wouldn't appreciate the comfort. Not from him.

"You didn't answer the question."

He glanced at her profile. "You didn't ask a question."

"Is it true, you don't do relationships?"

He'd known that was what she meant, but he wasn't sure confirming or denying Willy's statement would be a good thing. As strong as Huck wanted to believe he was, he did have feelings, and if there was anyone on this earth capable of making him weak or causing him pain, it was her.

"Define *relationship*," he said instead.

She gave a dry laugh. "Seriously, you can't just say yes or no?"

She was looking at him now. He felt her gaze burning through him. When he braked for a red light, he dared to meet her fierce glare. "Does it matter?"

She blinked, turned her head to stare forward once more. "Not at all."

And there it was, a blade to the heart. "Enough said."

The rest of the drive was made in silence.

Even on a Tuesday night, traffic was frustrating. Chattanooga was a beautiful city with numerous tourist activities and plenty of old South charm, but it also had its share of problems, including traffic and road work. And like any other large metropolitan area, there were areas that were far less safe than others. Their destination, Rick's Bar and Grill, was in one of those areas.

He parked on the street, half a block from the bar. Based on the view from there, Willy had been parked in the same general area.

"I want to go inside."

He'd seen that one coming. "Chances of catching our unidentified subject in there aren't that good."

She turned to him. It was too dark to make out her expression, but he felt her glare. "I snapped pics of the guy in Willy's photos. Maybe someone in there, a bartender or waitress, will recognize our unsub." She stared at the bar. "I've watched my share of cop shows too."

Now she'd gone and ticked him off. "First of all," he

pointed out, "this is not the kind of place where folks willingly ID each other." She started to argue, but he held up a hand cutting her off. "Secondly, I *am* a cop."

Rather than toss a biting comeback, she surprised him by simply getting out of the vehicle.

"Damn it." He grabbed the badge from his console and got out. "Hold up, Liv." He tugged his shirttail from his jeans to cover the weapon tucked at the small of his back. Slipped his badge into his front pocket.

She didn't wait.

He hustled to catch up with her. "You need to cool down."

"I'm fine."

He snagged her by the arm, pulled her to a stop. She shot him a how-dare-you look. "This is not some mountainside where ancient civilizations once resided, or some valley where parts of a lost city are thought to be, this is a place where people hook up for drugs and other commodities, make the kind of deals no one wants to know about. The kind of place where people end up dead."

She jerked her arm loose from his grip. "I'm not naive, Huck. I know what happens on the streets in crime-infested areas." She glanced at his untucked shirt. "I also know that weapon, as well as the badge you're carrying, makes you a far bigger target than me."

With that she stalked away. He followed. Anything else he might have said was irrelevant considering she wouldn't listen.

The vibration of the music shook the air well before they reached the entrance. Inside, the joint was packed with bodies and the music was even louder than he'd expected. The tables were full, the stools at the bar as well. The rest of the crowd filled the space between the bar and tables. No doubt several city ordinances were being broken, including local fire codes.

A big sign over the bar announced the grill part of the establishment was no longer operating. No surprise there. Food wasn't the moneymaker in a place like this.

Olivia slipped through the crowd as if she did this every day. She reached the bar, and he moved in behind her. She stiffened at his nearness, but she didn't look back or say anything. Not that he would have heard her or that it would have done her any good.

She waved down the first of two bartenders. Showed him the photos. He shook his head. Huck stood by while she repeated the process with the other bartender. Then they moved to the end of the bar where the waitresses picked up their orders. Olivia did the same with each one. Got a similar head shake in response.

Huck watched the waitresses. Only one captured his interest. Blond. Skinny. Pamela, according to her name tag.

Pamela had recognized something about the pics. Huck had spotted the tells when she looked at the pics and then shook her head. She'd lied straight up.

Luckily, a couple of stools at the bar became available. Huck slid atop one first, his gaze clocking Pamela's movements.

The bartender arrived, and he ordered beers.

Olivia shot him a look and leaned close enough for him to hear, "I still don't like beer."

He turned to her, putting his face so close to hers their noses almost touched. Heat seared through him, but he managed to deliver the necessary question. "Does this look like a wine kind of place to you?"

She leaned away and faced forward.

The bartender plopped two bottles of beer on the counter. Huck picked up one and pushed a bill toward him, then turned back to his study of the waitress. She noticed him watching and smiled. He smiled back.

Half a beer later, she had left her tray at the end of the counter and headed down a corridor marked Restrooms and Emergency Exit.

Huck leaned toward Olivia. "I'll be right back."

She jumped as if his voice had startled her. She turned toward him. "Where are you going?"

He nodded to the corridor where Pamela had disappeared. "Bathroom. Do not move from this barstool. Stay put right here where the bartenders can see you."

She rolled her eyes. "Where would I go?"

"Seriously, Liv," he pressed her with his eyes, "don't move."

She picked up her beer and took a sip. Made a face. "Go."

He slid off the stool and shouldered through the crowd of patrons. The corridor was empty. The emergency exit was propped open with a rock. Huck figured that was where she'd headed. Maybe for a smoke break.

As much as he didn't like leaving Liv at the bar, he suspected the waitress wasn't going to talk if they both appeared to gang up on her.

He glanced beyond the crack that separated the door from its frame. Sure enough, the waitress was leaning against the wall, sucking on a cigarette. He put his shoulder into the door, opening it and surveying right and left as he did. The back side of the establishment was fairly well lit, and he spotted no other warm bodies in the vicinity.

He walked to where Pamela stood and propped his back against the wall, matching her stance.

"Your friend didn't come with you?" She turned to Huck, blew smoke in his face.

He waved it away. "You know the guy we're looking for." Not a question. She recognized him.

She turned her head, staring at the back of the row of businesses that faced the next street. "I saw him a couple of times."

"You know his name?"

"Nope." Another long drag. "Only saw him here twice."

"Did you talk to him?"

"Maybe."

"Was he with anyone?" Huck resisted the urge to warn her that he could haul her in for questioning if she didn't cooperate.

"Nope."

"What will it cost me to find out what you talked about?"

She grinned. "Your friend wouldn't be happy if you gave me what I wanted." She glanced at his lower anatomy.

Huck chuckled. "Is there a compromise?"

She threw down her cigarette. Smashed it out with the toe of her high-heeled shoe. Then she turned to him. "He was looking for a woman."

The answer could mean a number of things.

"A particular woman?"

She nodded. "From his description and the photo he flashed me, I'd say he was looking for your friend."

Pamela stepped around him and went back inside.

Huck surveyed the alley again and then did the same. His mind screamed at him that she couldn't be right. Why would some random guy come here looking for Olivia? She hadn't lived in the Chattanooga area in more than a decade. And she had never been to a place like this one.

He cut through the crowd and found his way to the bar. But Olivia wasn't there.

His heart punched his sternum. He twisted around, scanned the crowd. Swore. Where the hell was she?

He plowed through the crowd, searching for her white blouse. The one that he'd tried not to notice stretching over her breasts and molding tightly around her waist. The one he'd wanted to tear off her.

Fear rose like a snake ready to strike as he searched face after face. No Olivia. Damn it!

Long dark hair. White blouse.

He spotted her talking to a guy not ten feet from the front entrance. His fear turned to fury.

He strode straight up to her and took her by the arm. "We have to go."

She glared up at him. "What are you doing?"

The other man stepped forward. Huck cut him a look and warned, "Don't even think about it."

The other guy held up a hand then dissolved into the crowd.

Smart man.

"Let's go."

She ranted at him as he ushered her toward the door, but he couldn't hear the words over the music.

As soon as they were outside and the doors closed, muffling the volume of the music, she dug in her heels. "What the hell, Huck?"

"We'll talk in a minute." He started forward again.

She didn't budge, forcing him to stop.

"What did the waitress say?"

Maybe she had watched a lot of cop shows. "Not here," he urged.

This time she complied and started walking again.

He watched the street, the sidewalk and storefronts as they moved quickly to his SUV. He touched the passenger-side door handle and the lock disengaged. Thankfully she didn't make a fuss, so he opened the door for her to climb in. Then he closed her door and hurried around to the driver's side. He slid behind the wheel but didn't start talking until they were back on the road and heading up the mountain. He focused on driving and ensuring that no one had followed them.

When her patience reached its limit, she turned to him. "What did she say?"

"How do you know I spoke to anyone?" He really wanted to know the answer. He was curious.

"The mirror behind the bar. I saw you watching her. Saw her watching back. Obviously, the fact that she had to go to the bathroom at the same time as you was no coincidence."

He grinned. "Pamela and I met out back."

"That's not sketchy at all," she muttered.

Was that jealousy he heard in her voice? He wished. "I recognized she was lying when you asked her if she knew the guy in the photos."

"And?"

"She didn't know his name, but she'd seen him at the bar a couple of times. She said he was looking for someone."

Olivia shifted in the seat. "Who? Not Willy. I can't see him at a dive bar."

Huck wasn't sure how to tell her the rest. "A woman. He was looking for a woman."

"Did *Pamela* know the woman's name?" Olivia demanded. "Good grief, are you purposely trying to be evasive?"

Huck braced himself. "He didn't give a name, just a description."

"How is that helpful?" She sank back into the seat. "I do not understand what's happening. None of this makes sense."

The solitary answer he hadn't given her yet wasn't going to help her understand any more than the revelation had him.

"So tell me," she insisted, "what did this woman he was asking about look like?"

Huck braked at the four-way stop. He turned to her and prepared to say the words that, he feared, wouldn't help at all yet would somehow change everything.

"You. The waitress said the woman he asked about looked like you."

Chapter Six

Firefly Lane, 11:50 p.m.

Olivia didn't speak again until he parked in front of her grandfather's cabin.

She had never been in that bar. She did not know the man in the blurry photos or the waitress named Pamela. Why on earth would the man—this stranger Willy had been watching—have gone to that bar looking for *her*?

It made absolutely no sense. Willy would never be involved with whatever this stranger was up to. Willy would have gone to the police if there was trouble he could pinpoint and prove.

Her mind stumbled on the thought. Then why watch the guy?

What she and Huck had learned tonight hadn't provided any answers...only more questions.

"We should get your bag," Huck said, his voice too soft, too quiet. "You can't stay here."

Olivia glared at him even though he wouldn't see her in the dark. She wanted to yell at him, but she was too emotionally drained. "No. If he—whoever he is—comes back, he'll come here. This is where I need to be."

Huck stared out the windshield for a moment, then turned to her, his expression unreadable in the darkness. "If you're staying, I'm staying."

What could she say to that? She was the one who had called him for help. Even if she so, so wanted to do this without his or anyone else's help, she understood she could not do this alone. Only a fool would pretend otherwise.

"Fine. You can sleep on the couch."

She pushed the door open and got out. She might have to be under the same roof as him, but she didn't have to look at him or endure the scent of him. It was driving her mad.

She did not want to feel that hunger...that need for him.

It had taken her years, but she had finally broken herself of that need. Like an addict who'd survived the pain of withdrawal, she'd put that craving behind her. He was no longer her first thought when she woke in the morning. No longer her last thought before she went to sleep at night. No longer a part of every breath she took.

She refused to become that person again—the one who could hardly bear to live without him.

No. No. No!

She unlocked the door and left it open since he was right behind her. Didn't look back. She went straight to her bedroom and slammed the door shut. Collapsing against the door, she squeezed her eyes shut to block the renewed flood of emotions.

She would not cry anymore. No amount of tears would bring Willy back or solve the mystery of his death. Being strong was the only way to move forward, and damn it, she intended to move forward. To find answers. Strength was the only weapon she had against whatever was happening here.

Willy always told her she was one of the strongest people he knew. She could not let him down now.

Olivia opened her eyes and felt for the switch. She flipped it, and light filled the room. Her childhood room...the one where she'd always felt safe and loved. The one she'd tidied and dusted only a few hours ago.

She blinked, looked again at the wall over her bed where a poster of her favorite rock band had resided since she was seventeen. The poster had been torn away and now lay draped over her headboard with only one corner left clinging to a strip of tape on the wall. Words had been painted on the bared wall:

I knew you'd come back.

Feeling as if she were in a bad dream, Olivia moved toward the bed, her gaze holding to the words. She reached out, touched the black letters that had obviously been spray-painted above her headboard.

Dry. They had been there for a while. An hour at least. Whoever had done this had come into the house while they were gone. Unlocked the door and then locked it back. Surely, he wouldn't have dared to do all this with Olivia right outside in the shed cleaning up his mess...her heart pounded harder. Either way...he had been back.

"Huck!"

His name erupted from her in a final wail before every ounce of remaining strength and will poured out of her. She wilted against her bed.

What was happening?

The door flew open, banged against the wall, and he was suddenly at her side, staring at the ominous message. "What the hell?"

"We locked both the front and back doors." Olivia turned to the man standing next to her. "He must have Willy's key."

"You shouldn't stay here tonight, Liv."

A blast of fury shored up her failing strength. "I'm staying."

He exhaled a weary breath. Reached for his cell. "I have to call this in. Get someone from the CSI team out here."

Olivia left the room and moved through the rest of the house. Had anything been taken? Had he returned to the house for something he'd hoped to find that he hadn't found last time? Or only to leave her a message?

When she felt satisfied that nothing had been moved, she went to the kitchen and readied a pot of coffee. Obviously, sleep would have to wait.

Huck joined her as she leaned against the counter, waiting for the coffee to brew.

"It'll be about an hour before someone can get here."

"I can't imagine what they'll find," she said, frustrated beyond all reason. "Obviously this guy is smart enough to cover up his tracks."

"Maybe so but we have to look all the same. I need to have a look around outside. I'd prefer it if you stuck with me."

"Let's do it." She'd already looked around inside. He'd done the same after making his call. Beyond the two of them, there was no one in the house.

Huck headed outside, she followed.

"Stay close," he warned.

"I know the drill." By now she was becoming an expert at this sort of thing.

The shed was first. If anyone had been inside, they hadn't moved anything. Hadn't touched anything. Olivia followed him to the barn, her mind mulling over the details of the photos. If the man's face were clearer, maybe Huck could have run the image through some sort of system that would ID him. He likely had a driver's license, possibly a criminal record. Then again, that might only happen in fiction.

The idea was irrelevant when considered against the question that had just occurred to her.

Willy was a true professional—an artist. How had he taken such a bad shot six times? Olivia had never known him to fail to home in on any scene he chose. The photos of the man at the bar were wrong. So, so wrong.

When Huck was satisfied no one was lurking in the shed or barn, they returned to the house. The guy from the crime-scene team arrived earlier than expected. The smell of coffee summoned her as they went back inside. Huck and the other guy, Sergeant David Snelling, got straight down to business. Snelling was a large man, six three or four, broad shoulders. Dark hair peppered with gray. Most importantly, he appeared very thorough.

Exhausted, Olivia poured herself a cup of the coffee and waited. She sipped the brew and mulled over the myriad questions whirling in her brain. Why hadn't Willy told her there was something going on? Then she reminded herself that he never complained. Never talked about feeling bad or getting old. He'd insisted he was going to live forever. He'd been telling her that since she was nine, when Gran died. He would never leave her. He would live forever.

Except he hadn't.

The burn of tears rimmed her eyes. She squeezed them shut and focused on the rich, hot coffee. She had to use whatever was necessary to keep herself grounded. Someone had pushed Willy. She was certain. She had to find that person. Had to ensure he paid for what he'd done.

It wouldn't bring Willy back, but it was the right thing to do. Willy deserved justice.

Olivia inhaled a deep breath, forced the thoughts away for now. She finished her coffee, left the mug in the sink and went to the bookcase that sat beneath the television. She sat down on the floor and pulled out the family photo albums her gran had made when Olivia was a kid. Willy never did photo albums. No matter that he took thousands of photographs. They were either on the wall or neatly tucked away in chronological order out in the studio.

She opened the oldest one first. Photos of her grandparents and her mother filled page after page. Willy had been an extraordinarily handsome man in his youth. Still had been, in Olivia's opinion. She wondered why he'd never dated or even sought out companionship after so many years. Especially after Olivia moved away. She remembered asking him once if he was lonely. Willy had laughed and said that loneliness was only a state of mind. He filled his life with the beautiful things around him and with capturing that beauty on film.

Had he only been saying what she wanted to hear? That he was fine without her?

She stared at the photos of her mother. She had been so much prettier than Olivia. Everyone who saw the photos always said she and her mother looked alike, but Olivia had never seen herself in that league. Her mother had been stunningly beautiful. There weren't that many photos of her father. Only the two. He'd been quite handsome as well, with a wide, teasing smile.

Olivia hadn't really thought about him since she was

a child, but she considered him now. Where did he live? Was he still alive? Why had he left them? Her grandparents hadn't talked about him either. Whenever Olivia had asked, they would only say that he'd been a drifter. Had no family except for Olivia and her mother. Unfortunately, his inability to form roots had caused him to drift on when Olivia was still a toddler.

She wondered if her mother had grieved over being left behind by the man she loved. Had she grieved herself to death the way Gran had after she died? Olivia wasn't convinced of the idea, but she couldn't deny there appeared to be scientific evidence that dying of a broken heart was indeed possible.

Turning the page, she studied the photos of herself growing up. So many included Huck. She smiled. Couldn't help herself. They'd fallen in love as kids even before they had a clue what that kind of love was. She moved to the final album. The photos there took her breath. The two of them were always together. She had thought they always would be.

The front door closed, and Olivia jumped.

"He'll get back to us if there's any news," Huck said.

She hadn't realized he and Snelling, who had obviously just left, had even walked through the room where she was sitting, deep in the past.

Emerging fully back to the present, she tucked the photo albums away. "Good." Then she stood. "I've been thinking—"

Huck said the same thing. They looked at each other and laughed. "You first," he insisted.

"There has to be some sort of personal connection to all this." Her heart squeezed at the thought of sweet Willy lying in the morgue on an ice-cold slab. She blinked away the image. "Whoever hurt Willy had an agenda. Wanted something. Whatever that something was, only Willy could provide it, which is why I believe the killer was someone Willy knew. Maybe even trusted considering they were on that ridge together when he fell."

"Assuming Willy went there willingly on the day of his death," Huck countered.

Olivia gave a nod. "It kills me to look at the possibility in that light, but you're correct."

Huck went to the coffee pot, picked up a mug and filled it. "Bearing in mind tonight's message," he set his attention on her, "my guess is whatever the trouble was—it was about you."

The concept ripped through her. "I've been skipping all around that scenario, not wanting to land on it."

"You haven't lived in the area for a long while now," he said as he propped a hip against the counter, "which suggests it probably doesn't have anything to do with anyone here."

"No one here would hurt Willy," she granted. Not possible. Willy had no enemies.

"I agree," Huck confirmed. "I interviewed several people today, and no one was aware of Willy having any sort of trouble. All said the same thing: Same old Willy. Good man. Nobody was aware of any issues."

She nodded. "It's hard to see anything else at this point."

"Which makes me seriously nervous," Huck said, "about you staying here."

"We've settled that already," she reminded him, not going there again.

"Got it," he assented.

She thought about those last conversations she'd had with Willy and that message left on her bedroom wall. "I told Willy I was coming to visit for Father's Day, but he was adamant that I shouldn't come. He came up with all the reasons it would be better if I didn't. I didn't think too much about it at the time, but now I don't know."

"Whatever was going on," Huck said, "Willy didn't want you involved or didn't want this person to be able to get to you."

Several things clicked in Olivia's brain just then. "Wait." She rushed over to the refrigerator, searched the notes secured to the door with magnets. "It's not here." She turned to face Huck. "Willy had my cell number and address on the fridge, just in case he got sick…or something happened. I insisted that he keep it there. It's gone."

Coffee forgotten, Huck joined her at the fridge and scanned the notes there as well. "Where else would he have had something about where you live now?"

She rushed to the drawer where envelopes and postage stamps were kept. There was an old address book there too. Gran had kept it there for as long as Olivia could remember. She flipped to the page where her name and information would be and it was gone. Torn out.

She showed it to Huck. "He was hiding my contact info."

The idea that Willy was murdered to ensure Olivia came back tore through her like an axe to the chest.

"What do you know about your father?" Huck asked before she could voice the terrifying idea.

Olivia shook her head, mostly because she couldn't bear the scenario circling her brain. "No more than you, really. He and my mother met when she was away at college. She got pregnant with me, dropped out and brought him home with her. When I was three, he disappeared and then she died." Olivia struggled to keep her throat from closing with the emotion swelling inside her. She couldn't be the reason Willy was dead. How would she endure that?

"Willy never heard from him again?" Huck tilted his head, eyeing her as if he suspected she was on the verge of breaking down. "No letters? No pop ins? You were his daughter, after all."

"Nothing that I know about." She swallowed at the tightness growing in her throat.

Huck scrubbed a hand over his jaw. "Was there ever any legal paperwork done about you? Custody papers? Adoption?"

Olivia moistened her lips, struggled to stay calm. "My parents never married, so I didn't have his last name. But his name is on my birth certificate. Kasey Aldean. There was never any other paperwork to my knowledge."

"We need to see if we can find him." Huck shrugged. "Rule him out."

"I guess so." She drew in a deep breath. Somehow managed to calm her heart. "I can't see why he'd come around after all this time."

"You never know. He may have been in jail most of the time he's been gone. He was aware Willy was quite the famous photographer. Maybe he wanted money. Or maybe he just finally grew up and wanted to know his daughter."

"That's a lot of maybes." Though she hadn't really known her father, she doubted he'd suddenly felt the urge to be a father and get to know his daughter.

The thought had her considering how Willy might have reacted had the man showed up. He would not have been happy…he would have taken measures to protect Olivia. Like hiding her contact information.

"The real question," Huck said, "is if the guy did show up, why didn't Willy tell you?"

"What if he was trying to protect me?" That fear pounded in her veins again. "What if he's dead because of me?"

"Don't do that to yourself, Liv."

Olivia didn't see him move, but he felt closer somehow. "But if—"

"You're tired," he interrupted her. "We should call it a night. I'll blockade the doors and be on the couch if you need me."

Whether it was out of a need to distract herself from thoughts she couldn't bear or sheer stupidity, she asked, "Why did you come back? Really?"

He searched her eyes, her face. "Does it matter? Really?"

Rather than answer, she forged on, "Did you have a bad breakup? Couldn't see your way past it to hang around in Miami? Let's face it, that's a big move just to take care of the homeplace. Weren't you up for a promotion or something?"

Those blue eyes of his narrowed suspiciously.

She'd said too much. She hadn't meant to reveal how Willy kept her up-to-date on Huck, even when she hadn't wanted to hear it. Damn it. She should have shut up and gone to bed. She should have let the awful possibilities haunt her rather than end up standing here having said what she said. Damn it.

"Why *didn't* you come back?" he asked.

She held steady, didn't look away as that piercing gaze bored into hers. If she evaded the truth, he would know it. Obviously, he'd honed that skill in his work. "I've thought about it the past couple of years." She looked away then, couldn't endure his probing any longer. "In the beginning, my work was exciting. I moved around a lot, so there was never time to dwell on anything but work. Then the opportunity in Montana came along, and I took it, thinking I would be happy."

"Permanence," he said. "Willy thought you'd decided it was time to settle down."

Her gaze snapped back to his. Had Willy also told him about her suddenly feeling incomplete? Needing more than just work? A life outside her career? A family? She wanted to be annoyed, but she loved Willy too much to care what he'd allowed to slip. Whatever he said to Huck, it was only because he loved Huck too and still harbored a deep-seated hope that the two of them would end up together eventually.

"Lots of people feel that way at my age." She shrugged, blowing off the notion. "The isn't-there-supposed-to-be-more syndrome." For her, it had started right after her twenty-ninth birthday. Suddenly all she could think about was the plans she and Huck had made when they were just silly kids. College first, get married. Travel the world and then settle down to begin a family at thirty. Here they were, thirty and thirty-one. Where was the more?

The memories tugged at her already raw emotions.

Fool.

"We had big plans for our thirties," he said.

The way he said the words or maybe the words themselves had her struggling to breathe. "That was a very long time ago."

He reached out. She froze. His fingers brushed her cheek, tucked a loose strand of hair behind her ear. The touch had her heart moving too fast.

"It was." His hand fell away. "But it was real. I haven't felt anything real since…"

"Huck." She somehow managed to look him in the eyes. "We had a classic childhood love story. It was wonderful. The problem is we were kids. It wasn't meant to last because we had no idea what we really wanted."

For a moment, she thought he might argue with her point. Instead, he just turned away. "I'll lock up."

Had he seen that lie?

Because the truth was the last thing she remembered really wanting was him.

Chapter Seven

Thursday, June 8, 8:00 a.m.

Huck had already brewed coffee when Olivia made an appearance. He'd heard her get up a while ago. She'd taken a shower, then gone back to her room for a while. At that point, he'd decided his need for food wouldn't wait any longer. He'd prowled through the fridge and the cabinets and come up with cheese toast. Thankfully, with diligent monitoring, he'd managed not to burn it.

"Good morning." She only glanced at him on her way to the coffee pot.

She'd hardly slept last night. He'd heard her puttering around in her grandparents' bedroom off and on all night. Even when he managed to doze off, the slightest sound had his eyes snapping open.

"Morning." He gestured to the table where he'd arranged the cheese toast on two paper plates. "I figured I'd play it safe this morning."

She glanced at the stove, grimaced. "I'll need a few minutes to work up an appetite."

He laughed, couldn't help himself. "I'm still waiting on mine to show up."

She sat down at the table. "I hope you slept better than I did."

He pulled out a chair and joined her. "It's hard to keep watch and sleep at the same time." No need to mention he'd heard her every movement.

"It was hard to sleep in there around all their things," she confessed. "Harder than I expected."

"Guess so." She'd pulled her hair into a ponytail, the way she had when they were kids. She'd worn it that way the past couple of days. He liked it. Wearing it like that made her look so damned young. His gaze drifted down to her tee. He grinned. "I remember that shirt."

Nirvana.

"I didn't have a lot of options since I didn't bring enough clothes. Luckily, I still had a few things in the closet." She laughed. "Do you remember when I came home with it? Willy wanted to know why I bought it?" She shrugged. "I told him because Callie Letterman had one. You remember Callie, the most popular girl in high school."

"I remember her. She's a cashier at the market on Gunbarrel Road. Married. Two kids. Her husband teaches science at the middle school over in Dread Hollow."

"Really?" Olivia frowned. "I thought she went to New York to be a model."

"I guess it didn't work out." He picked up a slice of cheese toast and took a bite. Not bad.

"Anyway," Olivia picked up the piece of toast from her plate. "Willy refused to allow me to wear the shirt until he introduced me to the band's music. He said it was just wrong to wear a band tee and not know who they were."

"I can see his point." Huck grinned. "I remember Willy liked them almost as much as I did."

Olivia nibbled at her toast. "I've been thinking about the message and the photos. Your idea that this stranger might be my father got me thinking. The man in the photos is older. His hair is kind of grayish. It could be him—Kasey Aldean, I mean."

Twenty-seven years older—that was how long he'd been gone. Huck knew what the bastard had done. Even as a kid he'd wondered who left their child like that.

Far too many people. As an adult and a member of law enforcement, he knew this well. In Olivia's case, it hadn't been so relevant. She'd had Willy. He had always been like a father to her. But not everyone was so lucky.

"Did he ever try to contact you or Willy?" Huck asked. He figured not, but it was possible there had been contact during those years he was away in Miami.

"Not that I'm aware of." Olivia nibbled her toast then set it aside as if that tiny bite had been enough. "I suppose it's possible he contacted Willy at some point, and Willy refused to pass along the message. He felt very strongly about Kasey having left the way he did. I don't think he planned to forgive him."

She was right on that one. Willy would have wanted to protect her from the father who had ghosted her all those years ago. No explanation for his abandonment would have been good enough.

"I can see if he's in the system. If he's ever been arrested or fingerprinted for any reason, I might be able to locate him."

"With that note on the wall," Olivia offered, "I suppose he's the closest thing to a person of interest we have right now. I just can't imagine why he would bother."

"Maybe he got religion. Decided it was time to make amends." Huck turned his hands up. "Or was looking for money, like we talked about."

Willy had lived a very frugal life the past couple of decades. Other than Olivia's college tuition, he likely saved most of his income from new work and royalties from older work. Huck had no idea what his savings was like, but he imagined it was sizable. Enough so to tempt someone who might feel he was owed something. After all, Kasey Aldean had left Willy his daughter. What was a daughter worth?

The idea made Huck sick. What kind of man saw his child as a negotiable asset?

"I appreciate anything you can do to find him." She reached for her coffee again. "Part of me hopes he can't be found. If he wasn't part of this, he may see Willy's death as his invitation to attempt getting to know me." She shook her head. "I don't want to know him."

Huck reached across the table and put his hand on hers. "If I find him, I'll make sure he knows that."

She managed a wobbly smile. "Thanks."

The vibration of his cell warned he had an incoming text. He checked the screen. "They're releasing the—Willy." He typed a quick response. "I asked that they send him to the funeral home. The one that took care of your grandmother."

"Thanks. I'll call Mr. Nelson and let him know Willy requested cremation."

Huck remembered the service for Willy's wife. There hadn't been a coffin since she'd chosen cremation. The service had been held at Sunset Rock. Only close family and friends had been present. Willy and Olivia had scattered her ashes in the air. It was the sort of thing that made an impression on a ten-year-old boy.

"Are you planning a service?" With all that had happened, he hadn't had the opportunity to ask her.

She moved her head side to side, sadness shadowing her expression. "He made it very clear ages ago that he didn't want any sort of service. He just wanted his ashes spread at Sunset Rock. The same way we did Gran's except without all the fanfare."

That was Willy. He felt he'd had more than his share of notoriety with his photographs. He had preferred low-key these past few years.

Olivia looked to Huck. "I hope you'll be there with me. Willy would want you there."

"Of course."

A rap on the door had Huck pushing back his chair. "I'll see who it is."

OLIVIA STOOD, sending her own chair sliding back. Had the crime-scene investigators returned to search for more evidence? Maybe they had returned with news. She watched as Huck checked out the window.

"It's Ms. Lockhart, Madeline, from the diner."

Olivia remembered Ms. Lockhart. She'd always given Olivia the largest slice of pie in the case whenever she stopped in after school. Olivia had been certain the lady thought she and Huck were special since whenever they were at the diner she spent more time with them than any of her other customers. As Olivia had gotten older, she had realized the lady had a crush on Willy. He never seemed to notice, but Olivia had seen it every time they stopped at the diner. Olivia started toward the door and Huck.

"Morning, Ms. Lockhart," Huck said as he opened the door.

"Good morning, Huck." She beamed a smile. "How's your momma?"

"She's doing great," Huck said. "She and her sister have decided to start traveling the world. They're on a cruise right now."

"That's just wonderful." The lady stepped inside, a nine-by-eleven glass dish covered with aluminum foil in her hand. Her attention shifted to Olivia. "Oh, sweetie, I'm so sorry about Willy."

Olivia accepted her one-armed hug. No matter that she'd cried a dozen times already, emotion welled in her eyes and throat. "I'm still struggling with believing it."

How did you come to terms with the loss of the one person who had always been there?

The older woman drew back. "I brought that casserole you always loved." She offered the covered dish to Olivia. "The one with the chicken and the noodles and cheese."

Olivia smiled. It was still her favorite. Whenever she'd been in the field all week with work, she made this casserole when she came home and ate it the entire weekend. "Thank you. I could never make it the way you do, though I've tried so many times."

Sadness cluttered Madeline's face. "Do you know when you'll be spreading his ashes? He told me that's what he wanted, and I'd really love to be there."

All the times this lady had flashed her brightest smile for Willy from behind the counter at the diner flickered one after the other through Olivia's mind. Had he finally taken notice? It sounded as if they'd grown closer considering he'd shared his final wishes with her. "I would love for you to be there. We'll try for tomorrow. I'll let you know the time for sure."

"Thank you." She glanced from Olivia to Huck. "I should go. I'm sure you're busy."

"Ms. Lockhart," Olivia said, waylaying her departure, "did Willy mention any trouble recently? Maybe someone who had visited him and upset him somehow?"

Her face paled. "Why, my gracious, no. He…" Her mouth slowly closed as if something besides what she'd intended to say had occurred to her. "He didn't mention anything, but I do believe something was bothering him."

"Would you like to join us for coffee?" Huck asked with a gesture toward the kitchen table.

"I would, but you know I have to get to the diner." She laughed. "Keep my staff on their toes."

The lady had owned the only diner in Sunset Cove for as long as Olivia could remember. "Something was bothering him?" Olivia prodded. "In what way?"

Madeline shrugged. "You know, as I so often say, the old gray mare ain't what she used to be, meaning at the end of the day I'm ready to collapse on the sofa and just relax. Willy…" She blinked, seemed to consider her words. "Some nights, we would relax at my house." She shrugged, her cheeks going pink. "Dinner and television. Other times, we'd come here."

Olivia smiled, her heart lifting at the idea. "I'm so glad to hear he was spending time with you and not here all alone."

Madeline visibly relaxed. "We enjoyed our time together." A frown furrowed her brow. "Last week was like any other until Sunday. On Sunday…he seemed distracted. I had this sense of him being someplace else, so to speak. When I asked, he pretended not to know what I meant."

"He didn't mention anyone or thing?" Huck pressed. "Maybe something that didn't seem so important at the time."

Madeline looked from Huck to Olivia and back. "What's going on, Huck? Are you suggesting Willy's fall was no accident?"

"Do you believe it was?" Olivia asked, her tone more pointed than she'd intended. "If you spent a good deal of time with him, did you notice his balance being off or some issue that might have made him less sure-footed than usual?"

Her shoulders slumped. "I did. I spent all the time with him I could and the answer is no." Madeline closed her eyes and drew in a deep breath. "When Decker told me he'd fallen...that way, I didn't believe him. Then when the medical examiner didn't find anything, I tried not to think about it anymore."

Olivia reached out, put a hand on her arm. "Whatever happened, we're going to get to the bottom of it."

"You have my word on that," Huck promised.

A tear slipped down Madeline's cheek, and she swiped it away. "As much as I know in my heart he wouldn't have gotten that close to the edge if he didn't feel safe, I hope the other possibility isn't true. Willy didn't deserve to die that way."

Olivia bit her lip in an attempt to hold back her own tears. "When was..." She cleared her throat and started again. "When was the last time you saw his camera?"

Madeline made a face. "The camera? The one he always had with him?"

Olivia nodded. "We can't find it. Not where he fell and not here."

"We were together on Sunday. We went downtown for lunch. He had his camera then."

"Where downtown?" Huck asked the question that pounded in Olivia's brain.

"We went to Big River Grille on Broad. We both love— loved that place."

Olivia and Huck exchanged a look. "Did you go anywhere else downtown after that?"

She shook her head. "Like I said, he seemed very distracted. Said he didn't feel well." She shrugged. "The Cajun fish tacos weren't sitting right with him, so we went home early. We were back at my place by two and he begged off dinner that evening." Her gaze grew distant as if she were remembering that day. "I watched from the window as he left—the way I always do. But he didn't turn toward home."

"He went back toward the city," Huck guessed.

"Yes." Her arms went around herself as if she suddenly felt cold. "I told myself he just took a different way home, but I'm sure that wasn't the case."

Olivia passed the casserole to Huck and hugged the woman. "Thank you for telling me this." Olivia drew back. "It's really important that we understand how Willy was feeling and anyone he might have spoken to those last few days."

Madeline nodded. "You be careful." She looked to Huck. "If someone did this to Willy, he might still be around."

"Show her the picture," Huck said to Olivia.

She hadn't even thought of the pictures. She went back to the table and grabbed her cell. She showed the photos to Madeline. "These were on the dry rack in Willy's darkroom. Other than what's in his camera—if anything—I'm assuming these are the last photos he shot."

Madeline studied each photograph, then swiped to the next one. She shook her head. "I can't see him very well, so I can't say that I recognize him or the place." Her frown deepened. "Are you certain Willy took these photos? I've never seen him do such a poor job of focusing in on his subject." She handed the phone back to Olivia. "Maybe he was aiming for something else."

Olivia thanked Madeline again and Huck walked her to her car. Olivia returned to the kitchen counter where the original photos sat in a stack of other papers that hadn't really given them anything to go on just yet. She went through the photographs, one at a time, searching for any other detail that might have been what Willy was actually looking at when he took the shot. Something that he'd zeroed in on. All six were different, confirming to some degree that Willy had been following the man as he moved from outside the bar to inside and then when he came back out again, presumably later.

The man had to be the subject, but Madeline was right, this looked nothing like Willy's work. At first, Olivia had been so overwhelmed she hadn't even considered that aspect. Of course, she'd noticed the out-of-focus work, but she hadn't really considered it. And yet, the idea made complete sense.

This was not Willy's work. He hadn't taken these shots.

"Did you find something?"

Olivia looked up. She hadn't heard Huck come back in. "She's right. Willy didn't do this."

Huck nodded slowly. "All right then, let's consider our timeline. Ms. Lockhart says she and Willy had lunch on Sunday. They were back at her place by two, and he left. She thinks he didn't go home." Huck's expression shifted to one of astonishment. "Wait. I saw Willy on Sunday." He popped his forehead with the heel of his hand. "It didn't cross my mind until Madeline said lunch on Sunday was the last time she saw him. I ran into him at the market around three-ish, maybe four. I was going in, and he was coming out."

"His camera was with him at lunch," Olivia noted. "She saw the camera. Did you see it later when you ran into him?"

"No." Huck shrugged. "But he'd been in the market. He probably left it in the Defender."

Olivia nodded. "Probably. Did he buy anything? I only ask because the fridge is basically bare. There was some cheese and a carton of expired milk but not much else."

Huck thought about the cheese toast he'd made. He'd used the only two slices of bread left in the house. "He only had one bag." He searched his memory for the image of Willy at the market that day. "There was one of those loaves of French bread. You know the kind that's always in baskets in random places so people will grab it as they go by."

Olivia nodded. "Like a baguette."

"Yeah, that's the one. Like when you're making spaghetti dinner. I saw one of those poking out of the bag and…a bottle of wine."

"Wait." She looked taken aback by that last one. "Willy never drank wine."

Huck shrugged. "Maybe it was for Madeline Lockhart."

Like him, Olivia stared at the door Ms. Lockhart had only just exited. "We'll have to ask her."

Huck nodded. "Back to the timeline. Willy was found around two on Monday afternoon. Sheriff Decker took the call himself."

"Those photos were taken at night," Olivia said, wanting to move past that horrible part in the story. "Since we know

Willy had the camera Sunday as late as two, and if he didn't take those shots, then whoever killed him did. On Monday night, I'm thinking. Came here and developed the film without fear since Willy was gone and I hadn't arrived yet."

"Since his death was considered an accident," Huck went on, "there was no reason for anyone to come here to check things out. Decker knew to call you. No need to come here looking for contact info on next of kin. But what if the wine was for our unsub? Maybe he came to dinner on Sunday night? We know it wasn't Ms. Lockhart or any of Willy's other friends I interviewed."

"Oh, my God, you're right." Olivia looked around. "At some point after three or four and maybe after dinner on Sunday night, the unsub, as you call him, was here. Did he have dinner with Willy? Did he leave and then come back later and search the house?"

"Which means," Huck realized, "the murder happened sometime after four on Sunday. And if our unsub wasn't Willy's dinner guest, he came later that night or on Monday night and searched the house. Even dared to come back while you were away yesterday and leave a message." Huck nodded, pieces falling into place. "You were right when you suggested he has a key."

Olivia's breath caught. "Where is Willy's key ring? We can confirm the key is missing if we find it. There would have been a key to the house, the shed. Everything."

Huck ran his hand through his hair, his mind—like hers—working to figure out the missing details. "Decker said the Defender was in the parking lot at the Point— where Willy always parked—so Decker drove it home the same afternoon—on Monday—when Willy was found."

He gestured to the door. "I'm guessing he left the keys in the vehicle."

Olivia was at the door by the time Huck caught up with her. She hurried to the Defender, opened the door. The heavy bundle of keys still hung from the ignition. A quick look confirmed the house, the shed and darkroom keys were missing.

"He took the keys after he killed Willy," she murmured. Her knees buckled.

Huck's arms went around her and pulled her against him. "We'll get him, Liv."

For a long minute, she allowed him to comfort her. But then she pulled free. "We should go back to that bar and talk to anyone we can find along that block. Maybe someone else saw Willy or the guy he was watching."

He had been thinking the same thing. "It's a long shot, but it's the best one we've got just now."

She nodded. "I'll get my bag."

Rick's Bar and Grill,
Chattanooga, 10:30 a.m.

THE BAR WASN'T OPEN, but that didn't matter since it wasn't their destination this morning. The street was empty around it, making for good parking. Olivia climbed out of the SUV and walked around the hood to meet Huck.

"Where should we start?" Both sides of the street were lined with businesses. Several were closed down, the windows boarded up. Others were closed until after five.

"We'll start with the nail salon just over there." He nodded to her right. "Then go around the block."

"Should we split up?" She counted seven shops that appeared to be open.

"No way. We stick together."

Somehow she had known that would be his answer.

When they reached the nail salon, Olivia fell back a step and let Huck do the talking since the two female employees studied him closely from the moment he opened the door. Understandable, Olivia admitted. Huck was a good-looking man. Tall, fit, handsome.

She banished the thoughts, pretended to check out the nail polish colors while he chatted with the ladies. Neither had seen the blurry guy in the photos or Willy. Since this shop closed around the time the bar's clientele likely started to filter in, Olivia wasn't really surprised.

The next business, a print shop, had the same answer. Not open past five, hadn't seen either man.

"To tell you the truth," the print shop owner admitted, "I don't come down here after dark. It's not safe."

The thought of Willy coming to a place like this had Olivia's nerves on edge. Willy had been in plenty of dangerous places in his life, but the danger had always been from the elements or the terrain. Never from another human.

It didn't make sense. Not coming here, not the blurry photos. She was certain Willy didn't do either of those things.

On the sidewalk, Olivia glanced back down the street at the bar. "Why would this person—this unsub—come here? Why take those shots and develop them?" Olivia wondered out loud. "Then leave them for me to find."

I knew you'd come back.

"If the goal was to leave me a puzzle to solve," Olivia grumbled, "I'm going to need a few more pieces."

"The message left on your bedroom wall," Huck said as they continued walking, "suggests Willy told whoever our unsub is that you wouldn't be coming back. He'd hidden your contact info from the bastard."

Olivia stalled, her heart bolting into a frantic rhythm. "Do you think he killed Willy because Willy wouldn't tell him where I was?" The idea had her stomach dropping to her feet.

The pain on Huck's face gave her the answer without him having to say a word.

"Oh, God." She started walking again. Had to move or risk falling into a heap of emotions that were already shattering into bits inside her.

"We can't be sure, Liv."

There he went speaking softly to her again. She wanted to scream. To hear him shout. This was wrong, wrong, wrong. *Breathe.*

By the time they reached the final shop on their side of the street, she had calmed herself to a reasonable degree.

The shop was a small market that wrapped around the corner of the block. Inside was cold. Olivia shivered after walking the block in the heat. Today was a good deal warmer than yesterday, or maybe it was just the humidity. The woman behind the counter was older, closer to seventy than sixty, Olivia guessed.

Again, she hung back, allowed Huck to do the talking. Mostly because she didn't trust her emotions just now.

Huck provided the usual spiel and showed the photos he'd added to his phone as well. The woman put on her glasses and took her time, peering closely at each pic. When she finished, she shook her head.

Olivia wandered to the wide plate-glass window and found a spot between the signs spouting one sale or the other to peer out at the street. Was it possible her father had come back after all this time? Had he carried a grudge against Willy for some reason? Maybe he'd been in prison and only recently was released, like Huck suggested. Maybe there was some terrible secret about her father that Willy hadn't wanted to tell her.

"Thank you," Huck said, drawing Olivia's attention back to him. She walked toward him when he passed the woman a card as he had the other folks they had questioned today. "If you think of anything later, I hope you'll give me a call. We would be grateful for any help at all."

The woman had stopped listening to Huck and was staring at Olivia. When Olivia stopped next to Huck, the woman said, "Are you with him?"

Olivia looked to Huck then said, "Yes."

The woman frowned, then shook her head. "You look so familiar." She snapped her fingers, a light coming on in her eyes. "Wait, wait, wait. I know why you look familiar. There was a guy in here looking for you."

Adrenaline fired in Olivia's veins. "When was this?"

The woman shrugged. "Maybe Tuesday. I can't say for sure. But he had a picture of you." Her gaze narrowed. "He just kept pushing me. Said you'd been seen in this area."

Olivia looked to Huck. "I've never been here before."

The woman set her hands on her hips. "Well, he sure thought you had."

"Are you certain the man who talked to you wasn't the one in the photo?" Huck asked.

She held out her hand. "Let me see those photos again."

Huck turned his phone over to the lady. She looked at the images for a long moment, then nodded. "I can't positively say so," she admitted as she handed the phone back to him. "But he's the right size, kind of skinny, and the height is right. And the fella asking about her did have grayish hair like the one in the blurry photos. Not the other one you showed me. It definitely wasn't him."

So not Willy, Olivia understood. The man in the photos outside the bar had come into this shop searching for someone who looked like Olivia. This was insane.

"The shoes or any of the clothing look familiar?" Huck asked, prompting her to look closer.

She shook her head. "Nah, but it could be him. For sure."

"What about his eyes," Olivia ventured. "Did you notice the color of his eyes?"

Her face scrunched up in thought. "I just can't remember. Not dark. Something lighter, but I can't say blue or gray or maybe hazel."

"He didn't leave you a card? A phone number or anything?"

The older woman frowned. "Wait just a minute." She went to the cash register, surveyed the bulletin board hanging on the wall next to it. She snatched a card from the board. "This is the one." She walked back to where they waited. "There's no name, but there is a phone number."

Huck accepted the card and immediately called the number. Olivia and the lady behind the counter watched and waited. Huck shook his head and ended the call. "Voice mail."

The lady shrugged. "Sorry but that's what he gave me."

"Thank you," Huck said again. "You've been very helpful."

As they walked toward the exit, the lady called after them, "Wait, wait, wait…"

Olivia and Huck turned back to face her once more.

"I remember something else. Something he said when he gave me that card."

Olivia held her breath, hoped it was a name...anything useful.

"He said," she went on, "if I saw you I should call that number or the police immediately 'cause you're *dangerous*."

Chapter Eight

Firefly Lane, 1:30 p.m.

Huck had called the number again. Finally, he left a voice mail.

He and Olivia had stopped at Nelson's Funeral Home to take care of the arrangements for Willy. His ashes would be ready when Nelson's opened tomorrow morning. Olivia had asked Huck to call Ms. Lockhart and the sheriff. He'd done so on the drive back to Willy's house. Both would be there. Then Decker had asked Huck for an update.

There wasn't a lot to say just yet, but the information the woman at the corner market had given basically confirmed what the message on her bedroom wall suggested: someone had been looking for Olivia. This unknown person could certainly be the person involved with Willy's death and the ransacking of his home and workspace.

So far, they hadn't talked much about the other part of what the woman had said. Olivia wasn't dangerous, and she certainly hadn't been in that neighborhood. She hadn't even been back in the state since Christmas.

Huck parked behind Olivia's SUV. He turned to her. She hadn't moved. Just sat in the passenger seat staring forward.

He understood that focusing on Willy's arrangements had helped her to get past the woman's bizarre comments for a little while, but now there was nothing to do except examine the information more closely.

"I have a friend in Miami," Huck said.

Olivia turned to him and waited for the rest.

"He's not a cop, but he used to be one. He's a PI now, and he has the kind of contacts cops aren't supposed to use. I think he'll be able to help us figure out who this number belongs to."

She nodded. "I appreciate whatever you can do."

"Meanwhile," he suggested, "how about we look through your mother's things again and see if we find out anything else about your father?"

"You read my mind." She reached for her door.

Huck got out and met her on the stone path that led to the front porch. The sun was scorching today. Above average heat for June. Life in the South, he mused.

"You know," Olivia said, "when the waitress said the guy had been looking for someone who looked like me, I thought she might be playing us." She shrugged. "But now..." She hesitated at the front door. "I just don't see how this is possible."

"It'll take time," he assured her, "but we will put the pieces together."

She exhaled a big breath, nodded.

When she would have unlocked the door, he reached for the key. "Why don't I do that?"

Without argument, she placed it in his hand.

He opened the door and took a step over the threshold. Fortunately, all looked exactly as they'd left it that morning.

"It's clear," he said, pulling the door open wider for her.

Still gun-shy, she walked in and looked around before visibly relaxing.

He closed and locked the door. "I'll do a walk-through, then, if you'd like, you can start looking through your mother's room while I make that call to my friend." He drummed up a smile. "I could warm up that casserole Ms. Lockhart dropped off. We should eat. We can't operate on adrenaline alone."

"Okay." The smile she managed was dim, but he appreciated the effort.

Olivia wasn't one to give up; he couldn't see her doing that now. She needed to be strong more than ever before, and he didn't doubt one little bit that she would do just that.

Huck did a quick walk-through, found no indication anyone had been in the house. Olivia disappeared into her parents' bedroom, and he made the call to Dex Trainor in Miami.

"Monroe," his old friend said, "I can't believe you haven't come running back by now. There must be more to that mountain than you shared."

Huck grinned. "It's home," he said. "We all know there's no place like home."

It had taken him ten years to understand that old saying was far too true.

"What can I do for you?" Dex asked.

"I have a cell number. I need to know who the number belongs to."

"Easy peasy," Dex said. "Give me the number, and I'll see what I can find."

Huck passed along the digits and thanked his old friend. They talked a minute more, with Dex giving him the lowdown on Huck's former colleagues. Huck appreciated they were all doing well, but that life was behind him now. He wasn't looking back any more than he was going back.

Huck warmed up the casserole and set the table, then he went in search of Olivia. She sat on the floor cross-legged, looking through old letters.

Huck sat down beside her. "What'd you find?"

She gestured to the pile of letters that sat in what looked like a scarf that had the wrinkles to show it had been tied around the bundle of letters. "I found these in the bottom drawer of Gran's dresser. Letters my mother had written to her when she was away with my father."

Huck picked up one of the letters and studied the graceful handwriting. "She signed with X's and O's."

"And little hearts." Olivia pointed to the hearts her mother had drawn along the bottom of her signature.

"You were just a toddler, basically, when she died." Huck passed the letter back to her. "Do you ever recall your gran or Willy mentioning any issues with your mom? Anger issues or…" He shrugged, hated like hell to say the other. "Or maybe mental health issues?"

Olivia shook her head. "Everything they ever said about my mother was positive. She was beautiful. She was happy. She gave them a great deal of joy. She loved me."

Huck considered the words used. "Never that she was a good mom or about her aspirations for what she wanted to do in the future?"

A frown worked its way across Olivia's face, and he wanted so badly to trace it with his fingertips and then smooth it away.

"They never used those specific words," she said. "I can't say that I recall ever hearing about any plans she had for the future or anything that she specifically did with me or with them." She looked up at Huck. "Do you think there was some sort of issue? Maybe she didn't die of pneumonia. Maybe she died of a drug overdose, and that's why they've always been so closed up about it."

"We could see if there was a report done by the medical examiner's office. Or check with Mr. Nelson to see if he took care of your mother for the funeral."

"Better yet, you could talk to your mother." Olivia set the letters aside. "She might know things that she's never wanted to say to avoid hurting my feelings."

Huck pushed to his feet and held a hand out to her. "Come on. Lunch is ready. I'll call my mom while we eat."

Olivia took his hand and got to her feet. "Thanks."

He followed her to the kitchen, his stomach reminding him that he was beyond starved.

"Smells good." Olivia inhaled deeply. "And I'm actually hungry."

"That makes two of us."

While she poured glasses of ice water, Huck dished up the casserole. He waited until they'd settled around the table and Olivia had dug in before making the call. He put his phone on speaker and placed it on the table.

"Huck, what a lovely surprise," his mom said in greeting. "You just caught us. We're back in New Orleans, and we'll be heading to Tennessee on Sunday."

"I hope you had a good time."

"We did, but we're tired. Glad I don't have to drive home."

"Mom, I've got you on speaker, and Olivia is with me."

"Olivia." She fell silent for a moment then launched into her regrets for the loss of Willy. Olivia swiped at her eyes but kept a smile in place at his mother's enduring words.

"Thank you, Mrs. Monroe. I'm very grateful that Huck is with me."

Wow. He hadn't expected to hear those words in this lifetime.

"I would certainly be there as well if we hadn't been in the middle of the ocean when I heard the news. I am so sorry I can't be there."

"You're here in spirit," Olivia said, "and that's what matters."

"We have some questions for you," he said to his mother.

"All right," she said. "We're resting in our rooms until dinner, so fire away."

He smiled. "I'll let Liv do the asking." He looked to her to continue.

She placed her fork on the table and squared her shoulders. "I don't really remember my mom, and I'm certain everything Gran and Willy told me about her was biased. It would be, of course. Can you tell me if there were problems? Did Mom have any issues?"

Silence strummed in the air for a few seconds. Huck braced for whatever was coming. Olivia did the same, her shoulders visibly tensing.

"Your mother," she began, "was a beautiful child and an even more beautiful woman. You take after her in that way."

"Thank you. That's very kind of you to say."

Huck wanted to tell Olivia that anyone who wasn't blind would say the same thing. It wasn't about kindness; it was just the truth.

"When she met your father. Kasey. She fell head over heels in love. She was away in college and, I'm sure you know, that's where they met."

"My grandparents didn't know him at all, right?"

"That's correct. But when Laura came home with him, she was already expecting you, and your grandparents, though disappointed as you can imagine, welcomed them both. They adapted and went on with life. It was their way. Willy had a more difficult time, I think, but Joyce never missed a beat."

"I was aware of most of this," Olivia said. "I was born a few months later."

"Yes," Huck's mom continued. "In the beginning, I was convinced that everything was working out. Willy and Joyce seemed so happy. It was more difficult to tell about Kasey. I always got a sense of deception from him. And he was gone so much. By the time you were six months old, your mother would disappear with him for a week or two. Sometimes he would stay gone for more than a month."

"Disappear?" Olivia looked to Huck. "I know they traveled a lot. For my father's work, I assumed."

Another few moments of silence. "I hate telling you this," she said, "if Joyce and Willy had chosen not to."

"Please," Olivia said, "I need to know the truth."

"It's important, Mom," Huck confirmed. "There are some things happening here that we need to better understand."

"Should I be worried?" she asked, always concerned for her son even though he was a grown man.

"I'm fine," he assured her. "It's not about me. It's about the past."

"Okay." Though she sounded skeptical, she continued. "There were many times when your grandparents had no idea where your mother was. She and Kasey would just disappear without telling anyone. If it involved any sort of work, I was never told. Worse, when Laura was home, she wasn't herself. I wasn't privy to all the details but what I do know is that Willy and Joyce worried all the time. Joyce was terrified that the next time your parents disappeared, they might take you away too. Thank God that never happened."

OLIVIA FELT GOBSMACKED. Why had Willy never told her about their fears? She could understand her gran never saying anything, Olivia had still been a child when she died. But Willy should have told her at some point.

"Did Willy or Gran ever say why they thought my mother behaved this way?" Olivia almost wanted to stop this conversation right now. It turned all that she'd believed about her mother upside down.

"Willy was convinced something happened to Laura during her first year of college. Maybe the stress was too great. It's possible she dabbled in drugs, though there was never any confirmation of this. But it was like when she came back from college after dropping out, she was a different person. There were moments when we would see the old Laura, but those were few and far between. She was short-tempered and…and violent even."

"Violent?" Olivia felt ill. She hadn't expected this complete about-face from what she had been led to believe.

"Kasey would show up with bruises and black eyes. Several times, Laura broke things. But it wasn't like that all the time, Liv. There was something wrong, I'm certain. It doesn't seem that way since she was home for parts of four years before…." She paused for a moment. "But the problems slowly escalated, and with the long absences, Willy and Joyce didn't understand just how bad it was. Kasey took off, and then, well, you know. Laura passed."

Reeling, Olivia had to ask. "Did she really die of pneumonia?" In light of all she'd just learned, Olivia no longer trusted what she'd been told. Clearly, her grandparents had wanted to protect her, but this was a lot to keep from her.

"The truth is," Mrs. Monroe said softly, "I don't know how she died, but it wasn't pneumonia."

"Christ," Huck muttered. "Why didn't you tell me this?"

Olivia shook her head. "Huck, don't go there."

"I made a promise," his mother said. "Willy asked me, for Joyce's sake, never to speak of it and never to tell a soul. I promised I wouldn't, and until just this moment, I have not."

Olivia nodded, her emotions whirling way too fast. "I understand, and I truly appreciate you telling me now. It's important that I know."

"Liv's right," Huck said. "Thank you for telling us. I know it was difficult for you to under the circumstances."

"You know," his mother went on, "your father and I were very old when we had you, Huck. We loved Laura. Willy and Joyce were so kind to allow us to enjoy her childhood as if she were part of our family too. Then, when Laura went off to school, I found out I was expecting you. It was the greatest blessing. We were very, very lucky. But sometimes things go wrong for reasons we can't understand. Joyce and Willy had to face that awful unknown, and I know they were able to face it with far less difficulty because of you, Liv. You gave them the strength and courage to carry on. Always remember that."

"Thank you." Olivia wasn't sure she could stay still any longer. She stood.

"Thanks, Mom," Huck said. "We'll talk again soon."

"Okay. I'll see you soon. Love to both of you."

Olivia was on her way to the back door before the call ended. She needed air. To walk off all these feelings.

Huck caught up with her outside. "I'm sorry, Liv. I had no idea."

"Well, at least now we know why this guy—assuming he's my father—is going around asking people about me and saying I'm dangerous. I suppose he assumes since I look like my mother, I must be like my mother in other ways."

Huck put a hand on her shoulder, turned her around mid-step. "No, you are not like the woman my Mom just described. That wasn't even your mom. That was whatever demon had stolen her life. I know you, Liv. You are the kindest person on this planet. You would never purposely hurt anyone. And I'm certain your mother was the same, but something happened to change her. As sad as that is, it wasn't your fault, and it doesn't mean it has or will happen to you."

He'd read her mind. Though her mother had been younger when this breakdown or change happened to her, Olivia couldn't help thinking about all the times she had felt so stressed. But she'd never lost touch with who she was and turned into someone else. At least not to her knowledge. What if she didn't know? Could she have come back here without telling Willy and gone to that bar?

No, that wasn't possible. She was always at work. No way.

"You're right, I know." She managed a smile for Huck's benefit. "It's just tough to hear a truth like that when you thought you'd known the truth all along."

"Maybe it was a bad idea."

"No." She shook her head. "With all that's going on, it was necessary." She reached out and took his hand. "Walk with me."

His fingers curled around hers, and he followed as she moved forward. It wasn't until she was nearly to the cliffs that she understood where she was going. She spotted the big tree and the bench that stood beneath it. Joyce and planted flowers all around the tree's massive trunk for Laura.

Laura Ballard was buried beneath that big tree.

Olivia sat down on the bench Willy had built. There was no headstone. He'd carved her mother's name into the wood.

Huck held onto her hand and stood next to her. She was glad. Despite their not-so-happy history, she was very glad he was here. She needed him maybe more than she ever had before. She stared at her mother's meticulously kept grave.

How was it that one person could leave behind so much damage?

Willy and Gran had been good people. They hadn't deserved that kind of tragic loss. But most who suffered tragedies didn't.

Olivia wondered whether things might have turned around if her father had stayed. If he had been here, maybe her mother would have managed to keep going.

If he was back, Olivia intended to find him. Maybe she would ask him why he hadn't tried harder for her and her mother's sakes.

If he had hurt Willy...well, she wasn't sure what she would do.

She squeezed Huck's hand. She hoped he would help her make the right choice.

Chapter Nine

Firefly Lane,
Friday, June 9, 9:30 a.m.

Olivia stared at her reflection. The ivory dress fit her perfectly. The light tan pumps she'd found worked well with the dress and weren't so high-heeled. The image in the mirror shook her just a little.

Somewhere in all those photos, there was one of her mother wearing this dress. Olivia had seen it a thousand times.

The memory sent a chill racing over Olivia's skin.

Though Willy never really talked about her mother, Gran had spoken of her often. She had gone through the photos of Laura many times with Olivia and talked about the moments.

Olivia turned away from the mirror. She hadn't gotten up this morning with the idea that she would wear one of her mother's dresses—there were dozens hanging in that closet—but she hadn't considered until then that she had nothing to wear this morning.

When she'd thrown those few things into her overnight bag, preparing for a memorial hadn't been on her mind.

But then Willy wouldn't have cared if she'd worn jeans. But Olivia needed to dress up for this. It was the last time she would hold any part of him in her hands. There would be no more hugs, no more smiles from him.

This day had to be special. For him.

A soft rap on her door had her heading that way. It was time to go. Sheriff Decker was picking up Willy's ashes. He and his wife were bringing Madeline Lockhart along. Olivia felt confident their attendance would make Willy happy. Because whatever he thought, his life had been worth making a fuss over.

Olivia opened the door. Huck smiled at her. He looked nice this morning. The navy shirt brought out the paler blue of his eyes. She'd always loved staring into those striking eyes. The jeans were classic Huck. They'd driven to his house last night for him to pick up a few things. She'd made the mistake of following him to his room. The framed photo of them on his dresser had stolen her breath. It had been taken at Sunset Rock by Willy. It was the day before she left for college. When he'd noticed her staring at it, Huck had mentioned that the photo was his mom's favorite.

Olivia thought maybe it was his favorite too. There was a duplicate tucked away somewhere at her townhouse.

"You ready?"

She pulled herself back to the here and now. Smiled. "I am."

They walked out of the house, locking the door for the good it would do. Huck hustled ahead of her and opened the passenger-side door.

As she climbed in, he said, "You look great."

"Thanks." She gave him a nod. "You too."

His broad grin lightened the sadness just a little.

She settled into her seat as he rounded the hood then scooted behind the wheel. When he'd turned the SUV around and was headed away, she figured it was a good time to say what needed to be said.

"I know we've spent a lot of years apart."

He glanced at her, his eyes saying it all. The pain there matched her own.

"We both said and did things…"

"There are no words," he hastened to say when she hesitated, "to explain how much I regret my actions."

"Same here," she confessed. And why not? It was true. It was time to put the past behind them. "Your being here through all this means a great deal to me. I hope, moving forward, we can be friends."

He grinned at her. "I will always be here, Liv."

He didn't exactly agree to the friends part, but she thought maybe that was implied by his words.

How could they not be friends?

Definitely they could be friends.

Huck drove to one of the parking spaces higher up the mountain, closer to their destination. Good thing, considering the shoes she wore. They might not have such high heels, but they definitely weren't made for hiking. Another vehicle was already there.

"That's Decker's car," Huck said as they passed it on the way to the overlook.

Olivia's emotions had gotten the better of her as they approached Sunset Rock, the place Willy had loved so much. Sheriff Decker and his wife waited, the small recyclable box containing Willy's ashes in his hand. Ms. Lockhart stood by, her eyes red from crying. But it was the rose-colored dress that stood out. She looked beautiful. Olivia was glad all over again that she had been in Willy's life, even if he hadn't shared the news with Olivia. Everyone deserved to have someone.

The thought had her glancing at Huck. He deserved someone too. Was the relationship they shared so long ago holding him back?

Could she say it hadn't held her back?

The idea twisted the already tight emotions inside her.

"Olivia." Decker offered the box to her.

"I thought we could each say something and spread part of his ashes." Her lips trembled on the last part.

Okay, keep it together. She didn't want to fall apart until this was done.

Decker smiled. "Good idea."

"Would you go first?" Olivia asked.

"I will." The sheriff and his wife stepped forward.

Decker talked about how much he would miss his longtime friend and avid fishing buddy. He and his wife each reached into the box and removed a portion of ashes, then allowed them to flow through their fingers. After a moment of silence, they moved back a few steps and passed the box to Olivia.

"Ms. Lockhart," she said, holding the box toward the older woman.

Madeline nodded, tears dampening her cheeks. She moved forward. "I'll miss you, Willy."

Olivia felt whatever else Lockhart had to say was most likely private and stepped back to give her a moment. When ashes had filtered from her fingers, she brought the box back to Olivia.

Olivia turned to Huck. "Will you do this with me?"

He nodded and walked to the edge with her. They had

stood here so many times. They had loved this place just as Willy had.

For a long moment, Olivia couldn't speak. She stared out over the beauty that had captivated the man who had marveled at magnificent views all over this planet and yet always came back to this one. Huck opened the box and started first.

"Thank you for always being you, Willy." Ashes floated from his fingers. "Life won't be the same without you."

Olivia smiled, fighting a flood of tears. "I love you, Willy." Ashes slipped from her fingertips. "I'll try my best to make sure all your hopes and dreams for me come true."

More than anything else, he wanted her to be happy and fulfilled. She hoped she could make all that he wanted happen. She glanced at Huck. She'd suggested they stay friends; that was a good first step.

The five of them finished giving Willy the send-off he had requested. When they were back at the parking site and Mrs. Decker and Ms. Lockhart were in the sheriff's car, Decker followed Olivia and Huck to his SUV.

"I talked to the lead investigator of our CSI team this morning. They didn't find anything. None of the prints collected were in the system."

Huck shook his head. "I was afraid that would be the case."

Decker shrugged. "Just proves our guy is smarter than the average perp."

"I'm still working on finding the guy in the photos." Huck told his boss about the woman at the market they'd spoken to yesterday, but he didn't mention the phone number or the friend he'd called for help.

Olivia doubted the sheriff would want to know about

any steps outside the usual protocol. If they were lucky, the friend would find something useful.

When the sheriff had driven away, she and Huck loaded into his vehicle. "What now?" she asked.

"Now we go back to the cabin so you can change those shoes."

She laughed, her heart still so heavy. "And the dress?"

He shot her a wink. "I kind of like the dress."

Olivia stared out the window as he drove toward home. *Home.* This would always be home. She had lived many other places, but none were engrained so deeply.

"Monroe."

Huck answering his cell had her turning toward him.

He listened for a while then said, "All right, man. Thanks. I owe you." The call ended, and he glanced at Olivia. "That was my friend from Miami. The number is registered to a burner phone."

Olivia frowned. "What does that mean exactly?" She had heard the term.

"It means someone bought the phone and the minutes without a contract. Probably paid cash so there's no way to connect the phone to him or her."

Not the news she had hoped for. "Great."

"Yeah," Huck agreed. "We'll just keep looking."

"Thanks."

He glanced at her. "You don't need to worry, Liv. Even if it wasn't my job, I wouldn't give up."

She wouldn't have expected anything else. As far as she knew, he'd only given up once.

She blinked the memory away. Reminded herself that whatever happened in the past, they could still be friends. She wasn't going back on that. Ever.

Firefly Lane, 11:30 a.m.

OLIVIA UNLOCKED THE door and walked in. The first thing she did was step out of her mother's shoes.

Huck's hand on her arm made her stop and stare at him. He nodded toward something across the room. Her gaze followed his, and on the kitchen table, positioned right in the middle, was her grandfather's camera.

"Stay right here by the door," he ordered, "until I have a look around."

Olivia leaned against the closed door, needing the support, and watched as Huck drew his weapon. He kept it with him always but rarely wore it when it was just the two of them. This morning, he'd left it in his SUV for the memorial service. Ever vigilant, he'd brought it into the house when they arrived. Good thing, she decided.

When he'd completed a walk-through of the house, he gave her a nod.

She rushed across the room and reached for the camera but stopped just shy of touching it. She looked to Huck, who stood beside her now. "I should wait until we check for prints?"

He shrugged. "I don't see the point. He didn't leave them anywhere else, why change his MO now?"

Huck was right. Olivia picked up the camera. Checked for damage. Saw none. She frowned. "Someone took photos."

"He wants you to see," Huck suggested, his face heavy with worry. "He's playing with you."

Olivia squared her shoulders. "Let him play. He's not going to win."

Huck gave her a nod. "Damn straight he's not."

"I should change before we go to the darkroom." She certainly didn't want to damage her mother's dress with chemicals.

HUCK STRUGGLED TO hang on to patience.

It took some time to develop the film. In the darkroom, he watched each step from the moment Olivia removed the film from the camera and its cassette. He watched her ready the film and the tanks for what came next. She prepared the developer mixture. Checked the temperature and then poured it into the film tank. She moved through the steps as if she'd done this just yesterday. It wasn't until after the rinse and careful soak in wetting agent that she started to remove the film from the reel she'd used for the developing process.

She unrolled it, cut it into shorter strips and hung the strips to dry.

"It's him," she said, peering at several of the shots with Willy's loupe. "This time the shots are clear."

When she reached the final strip, she gasped. Huck tensed.

"I think it's the guy from the other photographs. He's dead. Shot." She straightened and passed the loupe to Huck. "At least, he looks dead. Maybe this is part of some sick game."

Huck viewed the film strips. Definitely the man from the photos, Huck decided. He was lying on the ground, two holes in his chest. Blood pooled around him. Either someone was very, very good at staging and theatrical makeup, or the guy was dead.

He studied the scene. The man appeared to be on a porch or patio. Huck moved back to the other shots. Whoever had taken the photographs had followed the victim for a while. The shot of him walking along a sidewalk had captured a street sign down the block.

"I think I know where he is." He placed the loupe on the table and turned to Olivia. "We need to find this guy."

"His body?" she countered.

Huck nodded. "Sure as hell looks that way."

Before leaving, Huck zoomed in and snapped photos of the shots he might need. The quality wasn't the best but since the strips had to finish drying before they could be used for creating actual photos, they would have to do.

After locking up the house—for the good it would do—they headed into Chattanooga.

"Why would he kill someone, take photos and leave them for us to find?"

Huck glanced at Olivia. She stared forward, her profile furrowed with worry. "Like I said, it's some sort of game."

"What kind of person plays games with murder?"

This was the part he didn't really want to talk to her about. He could be wrong, but deep down he knew he wasn't.

"Usually when you're dealing with a killer who likes to play games, it's someone who has done it before."

"Are you saying he could be a serial killer?"

The horror in her voice had his fingers tightening on the steering wheel.

"No. I'm not saying that—I'm saying this isn't a first kill." He should consider his words more carefully, he decided. "At this point," he reminded her, "we don't know who caused Willy's death any more than we do who killed the guy in the photos. Assuming he's dead."

And that was a pretty good assumption.

"But if your unsub is him—my father," she said, "you're saying the way this looks, he could be a repeat killer."

Not a question. She got it. All that crime TV, he mused. But this wasn't TV. This was real life. *Her* life.

"Yes." He wasn't going to lie to her.

"What are the other options?" She twisted more fully in the seat. "There are others, aren't there?"

He slowed as they reached the city limits. "Yes, there are other possibilities."

"Like he could be deranged, mentally ill?"

"It's possible." He braked for a red light. "Remember, all of these are theories. We don't know anything yet."

She shifted forward again. "It's just hard to take considering I just learned my mother suffered from some sort of mental illness no one thought I should know about, and now my father appears to be a killer."

"You're not a killer and you are not mentally ill," he said, hoping to convey the certainty of his words with his eyes.

She looked away. "The light's green."

He shifted his attention back to driving. "Liv, you can't borrow trouble like this. You're already under a great deal of stress. You just lost Willy. Give yourself a break. You are not a bad person or a person with issues of any sort."

"How do you know?" she demanded, anger in her tone now. "You and I have been apart for a decade." She pounded her chest. "I could have been in and out of mental hospitals all this time for all you know."

"I know," he said, his eyes on the road and navigating the heavier traffic, "because Willy would have told me."

"He didn't tell me about my mom," she argued, the anger weakening now.

He glanced at her. "Because we talked about *you* all the time. I strong-armed him into an update after every conversation he had with you."

"Why?"

Those three little letters were crammed full of emotion.

The frustration he recognized. Impatience. And something else that sounded far too much like hurt. Damn it. He hadn't meant to hurt her. He'd been young and stupid, and he'd made a monumental mistake.

"Because I care." He hoped she would leave it at that.

"Why would you still care that much after all this time?" No such luck.

"We're here," he said, avoiding the question. He pulled to the curb and shifted into Park.

She leaned forward, peered out at the street. "Oh, my God, you're right." She pointed to the street sign at the end of the block. She released her seatbelt. "What do we do now?"

He released his own. "We start with the houses that are empty. They'll be the easiest to access and offer the most likely place for where an unreported shooting could take place."

She surveyed both sides of the street. "Looks like most of the houses are unoccupied."

"That will work to our advantage."

They climbed out, met in front of his SUV. Only two other vehicles sat along the street. Both older, both appeared as if they had been there for a while.

"It looks as if the houses have been vacant for a long time," she said as she followed Huck along the cracked sidewalk to the first house on the left.

"There's about three streets in the area that are like this." Abandoned. Forgotten. "The good news," he said as he stopped at the steps up to the porch, "is people have started buying the houses a couple of streets over and turning them into nice homes. So maybe there's hope."

"Maybe." Olivia stared at the dilapidated house in front of them.

One by one, they checked the front and back yards of the houses, first one side of the street, then the other. In the photo, the man was lying on a porch or a patio—concrete. Old and cracked like the sidewalks leading to each one.

Since the street was a dead end, there was no traffic.

City sounds floated on the air from blocks away. The distant echo of traffic played a constant background to the other faraway sounds.

The fifth house from the last on the block proved to be the one they were looking for. The smell warned Huck before his gaze traced over the body.

"Stay here," he said to Olivia, indicating the rear corner of the house. "I can still see you if you stay here, but I can't have you getting any closer. This is a crime scene now."

She nodded her understanding.

He drew his weapon, though he doubted anyone, particularly the killer, was about. When he reached the crumbling patio, the victim lay on his back just as he had in the photos. Judging by the condition of the body, he'd been dead a day, maybe a day and a half.

Huck called Decker before calling the discovery in to Chattanooga PD. Since he didn't have gloves, checking for a wallet or any other type of ID would have to wait.

If this wasn't Liv's long-lost dad, who the hell was it?

Chapter Ten

2:50 p.m.

Huck's patience was wearing thin.

He and Olivia had been waiting for more than an hour. The detective on call had arrived half an hour ago, and still they had been told nothing.

He paced the sidewalk in front of the house—the crime scene. Olivia leaned against the driver-side door. She was obviously growing more anxious with every passing moment, but so far, she had remained calm.

If the dead guy was her long-lost father...damn, Huck couldn't even imagine how she would feel. Her father had been in his early twenties when he and Olivia's mother were together. Olivia wasn't sure of his exact age. Twenty-seven years later, he would be around fifty or so. The victim looked to be in that age range.

Huck paused, stared beyond the yellow tape now draping the yard. All the activity was taking place behind the house, so he could see nothing.

"Maybe the detective forgot we're waiting," Olivia said.

Huck walked over to where she stood, propped against the side of his vehicle. "We're not a priority for him, that's for sure." And understandable. The man had a job to do. They'd given a statement to the first officers on the scene, but Huck expected there to be more questions from the detective.

"If that is my father," she ventured, her voice revealing her weariness, "I just don't get why he would be asking about me and calling me dangerous."

Huck had considered the same questions. "I'm thinking he exaggerated his story about you to get the desired reaction. People are more likely to make that call if they believe danger is involved."

He shifted his attention from the house to her. "The big questions in my mind are why look here or at that bar? Why would he think you would be in this area?"

A frown marred her smooth brow. "Maybe Willy told him to look here to throw him off track. He may have thought he was protecting me."

Which left one big, glaring question. "If this scenario is even remotely accurate, why not warn you?"

Olivia shook her head. "That's the part I can't make fit. Willy would never leave me hanging like this." Confusion deepened those frown lines. "Why didn't he go to Sheriff Decker and ask for help?"

"Or me," Huck pointed out. "I talked to him all the time. On Sunday, for God's sake…before what happened. Not a word was mentioned about trouble of any sort. He seemed just fine."

"Monroe."

Huck shifted his attention to the detective heading in their direction. *About time.* He straightened away from the vehicle. "Detective Kepler."

Kepler paused on the sidewalk next to where they waited

and flipped through his little notebook. "Tell me again what brought you here."

Huck explained about Willy and the photos. He didn't go through the whole spiel about the missing camera that suddenly reappeared. That could wait for another time. He also didn't mention the lady in the corner market. Not relevant just yet.

"And you do not know this man, Ms. Ballard. Is that correct?"

"I do not," Olivia confirmed.

Huck was glad she left her answer at that. No need to mention their suspicions just yet.

"Well," Kepler turned to the next page, "let's remedy that right now. His name is Louis Rogers. He's a private investigator here in Chattanooga." He shrugged. "Low-rent sort. No criminal record. A few minor traffic violations but basically a clean guy."

"You're sure that's who he is?" Olivia pressed. "Could he be carrying a fake ID?"

Kepler shook his head. "I've run into him on cases before. I know him, or I should say I used to know him. We went to high school together a million years ago. Anyway, any ideas on why someone would send your grandfather photos of him? Or why your grandfather took photos of him?"

"I'm sorry, I have no idea. I only came back to town a few days ago because my grandfather died. Murdered, we think."

Kepler looked to Huck then. "You said the grandfather may have been murdered Sunday night or early Monday. I'm guessing this guy bought the farm a couple days ago, give or take. The ME is on the way, and we'll know more then."

"Anything in the house?" Huck asked. He'd peeked in a few windows and didn't see anything. The place looked vacant.

"Nope. The houses on this block are all vacant. Rumor is they're all being taken down by some developer who has plans for one of those commercial housing developments."

Huck pulled a business card from his pocket. "Give me a call if you need anything else or find something that might be useful to my case."

Kepler tucked the card into his jacket pocket. "I hope you'll do the same."

"No question," Huck confirmed.

Kepler seemed satisfied with his answer and wandered back to his crime scene.

When he was out of hearing range, Olivia asked, "What now?"

"Now we go to Mr. Rogers's office before Kepler heads in that direction."

When they had settled into his SUV, she said, "Good plan."

"Let's just hope Mr. Rogers has an employee or kept good notes about his cases."

The medical examiner's van arrived as they were driving away, announcing to anyone in the vicinity that there was a body to be examined and removed.

Kepler wouldn't be going anywhere for a while.

Lee Highway, 4:00 p.m.

THE PI'S OFFICE was in a strip mall shoehorned between a now permanently closed candy store and a vacant office currently for lease.

When the detective had said low-rent, Olivia had anticipated something far sleazier. The area wasn't bad, and the offices, though old, appeared in good condition. They were in luck since a woman was in Rogers's office.

When Huck opened the door for Olivia, the woman looked up.

"We're closed," she announced. The swollen, red-rimmed eyes told Olivia she had heard the news.

Huck showed his badge. "Deputy Detective Monroe. This is my associate." He tilted his head in her direction. "We have a few questions for you, ma'am."

"You weren't supposed to be here for another hour or so," she said, clearly annoyed.

Based on the files spread haphazardly across her desk, Olivia decided the lady was hoping to get rid of any incriminating evidence before Detective Kepler arrived. Private investigators had a reputation for operating outside the law at times.

Huck held up his hands. "You have nothing to worry about from me," he assured her. "The detective who's coming next is the one who will be looking for the dirt. Also, I'm sorry for your loss, ma'am. My associate here just lost her grandfather—he was murdered too, and we need your help. That's why we're here. It's the only reason we're here."

She looked from Huck to Olivia. "Make it fast. I don't have a lot of time to tidy up."

"I understand," Huck confirmed. "Can you tell us what case your partner was currently working on?"

The woman collapsed into the chair behind her desk. "I'm—was—his assistant. He was working on a family issue related to a man named William Ballard."

Olivia's heart thumped against her ribcage. "That's my grandfather. He was murdered…"

The assistant closed her eyes and exhaled a big breath. "I was afraid of that." She opened her eyes once more and met Olivia's gaze. "I heard about Mr. Ballard's death, but there was no mention of murder." Another big breath. "Louis had been MIA since Wednesday morning. He got a phone call real early. We were both still asleep. He said he had to go, and he never came back."

So this lady was more than an assistant to Rogers. "Did you report him missing?"

She shook her head. "He told me never to do that unless he was MIA with no contact for seven days."

Olivia stepped closer, held out her hand. "I'm Olivia Ballard. I'm very sorry for your loss and even sorrier that it may have been connected to my family somehow."

The assistant stood, accepted Olivia's hand. "Gina West. Sorry for yours too."

"Can you tell us more about the case?" Huck asked.

Their hands fell apart, and Olivia held her breath, hoping for some information that would help answer the mounting questions about Willy's death. Her chest tightened at the idea that it looked more and more like it was related to her missing father.

"Mr. Ballard," Gina said, "wanted everything kept quiet. It was imperative to him that no one knew about whatever was happening. Louis never told me the details, and I never asked. When a client requests that level of confidentiality, I've learned it's best if I don't ask questions. Louis always told me what I needed to know and nothing more." She moved her head side to side. "I know basically nothing about the case, and Louis didn't write anything down."

Olivia's hopes plummeted. This could be just another dead end.

"You didn't overhear anything that might help us?" she asked.

"I'm sorry. No. Louis met with his client away from the office. It was all very secretive. I'm assuming he met with Mr. Ballard since he called it the Ballard case, but I never met or spoke to the client."

Another shake of her head. "I can tell you," she said, "that Louis may have used one or more of his sources for help with the case."

"Can you give us contact info?"

"Normally, I wouldn't…" She blinked rapidly to hold back the tears shining in her eyes. "But I guess it doesn't really matter at this point." She zeroed in on Huck. "If what you're looking for can somehow help find who killed Louis, I'm game."

Gina provided a list with three names and contact information. Those, she said, were the people her boss relied upon most often. She also promised to contact Huck if she learned anything relevant to the Ballard case.

As they drove away, all Olivia could think was that she never dreamed her family would become a murder case.

Huck insisted they stop for food while he attempted to reach out to the names on the list provided.

The diner he chose was an old one on Tremont Street in Chattanooga, but the atmosphere was casual and comfortable. The music wasn't too loud, and there wasn't much of a crowd.

Olivia picked at her sandwich. She told herself to eat, but it was difficult with all the emotions crowded into her throat.

The first two names on the list came with cell numbers. Huck's calls went unanswered, not entirely surprising, so he left voice mails with the promise of a reward for information. Hopefully that would prompt responses.

The third name had no contact number, but his employer's address was listed. A car wash only a few blocks away, which was the reason, she learned, Huck had chosen this diner.

"I just don't understand why he didn't tell me," Olivia said finally. She pushed her plate away. She hadn't been able to manage more than a bite or two. How could she? "This makes less and less sense. Willy and I always talked about everything. Why change now?"

Huck reached across the table and squeezed her hand. "He was protecting you. For me, the real question is why didn't he come to me for help?"

"Good question. I can only assume he thought he would be able to handle it on his own." She shrugged. "With the PI's help."

"Still doesn't make sense to me," Huck countered. "If he was going to anyone for help, why not me? I'm here. I'm a cop."

A sour taste rose in Olivia's throat. "Maybe because you're a cop."

Huck stared at her as if the idea had just struck him as well. "You're thinking that he didn't want me or you to know about whatever this is."

She nodded slowly, the concept settling fully. "Maybe my father is some sort of criminal, like you suggested, and he didn't want me to find out. He may have been concerned you would tell me."

Huck pulled out his wallet and left cash on the table for their food. "Let's see if we can find his guy at the car wash."

As they left the diner, Olivia considered that the spreading of Willy's ashes felt like a dream now though it had been only a few hours ago. She still found it difficult to comprehend that he would never come home again.

Had her mother felt that way after her father left? A completely different situation, of course, but the sense of emptiness must have been similar. Olivia couldn't help wondering if her work would ever be enough to fill this new void.

She glanced at the man behind the wheel as they drove away from the diner. At some point after he left ten years ago, she had convinced herself that she no longer missed him, but that had been a lie. She could see that now. Being here with him in light of all that was happening, it was easy to see just how badly she had missed him.

She looked away, stared out the window. What a mess they were. Pushing away the thought, she focused on the present. Finding the truth had to be priority one just now.

The car wash was busier than Olivia would have expected. Then again, she supposed everyone wanted their cars nice and clean for the weekend. In Montana, she rarely worried about her vehicle's appearance. Between the snow and the remote sites to which she was often assigned, keeping a vehicle clean was pointless.

"It might go more smoothly if you wait here. Keep the doors locked." He lifted the console lid and pulled his weapon out, placed it on the closed lid. "This won't take long."

Too mentally fatigued to question his decision, she agreed. "All right."

He climbed out, closed the door and waited until she hit the lock button, then he went into the car-wash office. They had no idea what this source looked like or even if he was at work today.

Half a dozen men and women were busily wiping down freshly washed cars. When those vehicles were picked up by their owners, more pulled out of the car-wash tunnels to take their places, and the whole process started over again.

Huck exited the office and approached one of the men drying a vehicle. The man's body language shouted loudly and clearly of his wariness, but he didn't take off. Olivia felt her hopes rising. The longer the two talked, the more hopeful she became.

Her pulse jumped when Huck shook the man's hand and headed back to the SUV. Olivia hit the unlock button and mentally crossed her fingers.

Huck climbed in and shifted into Reverse. "It isn't much, but it's something. Rogers gave him an address to surveil. He was to let Rogers know if anyone went in or out of the house."

"Did he see anyone at the location?"

As he pulled out onto the street, Huck shook his head. "He did not. Maybe we'll have better luck."

Vine Street, 6:30 p.m.

HALF AN HOUR with no activity had elapsed since Huck parked across the street from the address Rogers's source had provided. A real-estate sign was in the yard listing the house for sale.

The house on the right of the property appeared to be empty. A for-rent sign stood in the yard. On the left, an older lady sat on the porch in a rocking chair, rocking and fanning herself with one of those old-fashioned hand fans once given out by churches. Huck's grandmother had been so proud of hers. She'd told him repeatedly that it was a blessing not to have to sweat so in church on Sunday mornings.

"Should we peek in the windows? Sneak in the back?"

Olivia was running out of patience. Huck understood. "I think we'll start with the for-rent property and peek in windows there. Then when we're around back, I'll cross that little picket fence and have a look through some back windows of our target house. That way if no one's home and the back door is unlocked, I can have a look around without the lady in the rocking chair noticing."

"You mean *we*, right?"

He made a face. "If there's any breaking and entering, you should leave that to me."

She rolled her eyes and climbed out of the vehicle.

Somehow he'd known that wasn't going to work.

He waved at the lady on the porch as they crossed the street. She paused in her fanning but didn't wave back.

Huck snapped a pic of the for-rent sign with its contact info for the rocking lady's benefit. They climbed the steps and peeked in the front door and windows. Then they chatted about the size of the yard and the closeness to the street as they strolled around back. Huck made the first move toward the other property. He stepped across the short picket fence and walked quickly to the back door. Olivia followed close behind him.

Through the window in the door, the kitchen and part of the living room beyond it were visible. No furniture that he could see. He used his shirttail to grasp the knob and give it a turn, and the lock released with little effort. He opened the door.

He hesitated, turned to Olivia. "Don't touch anything. No need to leave incriminating evidence."

She nodded.

The kitchen cabinets were mostly bare. A few canned

goods and a box of crackers. The dining room was part of the kitchen, but there was no table. A wide cased opening led into the living room of the small bungalow. The only furniture was a portable chair like the ones people used for camping or ball games. No papers, letters or personal items lying around.

The rest of the house was the same. No furniture. There was a sleeping bag in one of the two bedrooms. Soap in the shower stall. Someone had been staying here under the radar.

Huck checked the sleeping bag. Empty.

A few minutes more of searching and they still found nothing.

"We should go," he said, "before the lady next door gets suspicious."

Olivia exhaled a big breath and nodded her agreement. They followed the same path back to the other house and pretended to discuss the property's options as they made their way back to his SUV. Olivia stared out the window as they drove away.

"I'm beginning to think we're never going to find any answers," she said, her voice distant.

Huck reached for her hand, gave it a squeeze. "We're just cutting through the weeds right now," he assured her. "We'll get to the flowers soon."

His instincts warned they were far closer than either of them understood.

Firefly Lane, 9:00 p.m.

OLIVIA WAS GLAD to be home. She was emotionally exhausted, and she just wanted some quiet time.

No. She *needed* quiet time. No thinking or talking about the possibilities in this case. Just turn it off and relax.

She climbed out of the shower and dried her body, grateful for those long minutes under the hot spray of water and away from the rest of the world.

Once her hair was dry and she'd dressed in one of her grandmother's nightshirts, she opened the door. The scent of bacon frying had her mouth watering. She wandered into the kitchen, where Huck had just set two plates filled with scrambled eggs and bacon on the table.

"It's not exactly a gourmet dinner," he warned, "but it's edible."

"Smells great."

Olivia dug in. She didn't slow down or chat until she was finished. Then she felt stuffed. "I should not have eaten all that." She put her hand to her stomach. "But it was wonderful."

Huck finished off his. "Good. Hopefully that makes up for my last disappointing attempt at cooking."

She laughed and together they cleaned up the mess he'd made. Strangely, she felt more relaxed than she had in ages. Maybe it was about having hit bottom emotionally. There was nowhere to go but up.

Huck tossed the towel he'd used to dry dishes onto the counter. "It's my turn for that hot shower."

"Go on. I think I might see what's happening in the news. I feel like I've been off the grid for forever."

Sometimes getting away from the news and social media was beneficial. Willy had insisted that social media was just another way to distract ourselves from real life. Olivia was pretty sure he was right.

She turned on the television and scanned the channels for

five or ten minutes, but her mind wasn't on the screen or the talking heads whose voices filled the air. She couldn't keep her thoughts from drifting down the hall to the man in that shower. How had she pretended he didn't exist all this time?

He'd done the same to her, she supposed.

Didn't matter. Not anymore. It was time they put that behind them and defined how they would do *this* going forward.

Friends. They could be friends. They had both agreed.

But the feelings churning inside her right now were not exactly the sort she would feel for a friend. The need was overwhelming...fierce. She needed more than just friendship. She needed to feel his arms around her and his mouth on hers.

Olivia closed her eyes and fought the building urgency.

She needed to calm down. To pull back and to...think this through better.

The sound of the door opening and his bare feet in the hall was the last straw. She stood. Threw down the remote and rushed around the sofa and toward him. He stood just outside the bathroom door with only jeans hugging his body.

Her heart beat so hard breathing was impossible. She walked straight up to him. He stared at her now, the towel he'd used slipping to the floor. She put her arms around his neck and tiptoed to reach his mouth with her own.

She kissed him hard with the urgency driving her. He held back, slowed her down, which only made her more frantic.

"Liv," he whispered against her lips, "we need to slow this down."

She plowed her fingers into his damp hair and pulled his mouth back to hers.

A blast drowned out the heavy sound of their breathing and the voices still humming from the television.

Huck drew back, his eyes going from dazed to focused in a single heartbeat. He set her aside, went back into the bathroom and returned with his gun.

"Stay put," he warned, and then he was gone.

The haze of need vanished in that instant, and Olivia whirled around.

He'd already disappeared into the kitchen or to the front door.

She rushed after him.

Another whoosh and then something like an explosion made her jump.

Huck stood staring out the window over the sink, his phone to his ear. Part of her felt frozen in some crazy dream as she heard him give the address and tell whoever he'd called to hurry.

Another sound outside had her moving forward, her gaze zeroing in on that window.

Flames.

Flames flickered high in the darkness.

Something was on fire.

Olivia shook herself and rushed closer.

The shed.

The shed was on fire.

Chapter Eleven

Olivia stood at the back steps and stared at the dying embers of Willy's beloved shed. All those beautiful photographs and the film...all Gran's paintings. Not to mention the equipment and the things the two of them had cherished. Every little thing from the paint brushes to the camera lenses.

Gone. All gone.

Firefighters had wet down the barn, the nearest trees and shrubbery as well as the cabin in hopes of preventing sparks from igniting a second fire. Olivia leaned against the wall of the cabin and watched the final steps of rolling up hoses and preparing to leave now that the fire was out. Spotlights showcased their work like dancers on a stage.

Huck and Sheriff Decker stood in the middle of the fray.

Olivia had wept like a child, but sometime after midnight resignation had set in and kicked all the other emotions aside. It was done. There was nothing she could do to bring any of it back.

Willy was gone. The biggest part of him that had remained was gone.

This place would never be the same. Never.

She closed her eyes and wished the smell of destruction would diminish. Wished the damned bugs fluttering around the porch light would go away.

"Hey."

Olivia opened her eyes. Huck stared down at her, traces of soot smudged on his face. The worry in his eyes made her wish they could go back inside and lose themselves in more of those kisses they had shared before...this. She glanced at the ongoing efforts of the firefighters. They would be leaving soon, and she deeply appreciated all that they had done, but it was a total loss. Not their fault. It just was.

"We found a couple gasoline cans. Decker will take them in for processing."

Beyond Huck, she saw the sheriff walking away from the shed carrying the two red cans. Plastic ones. Not one of the metal ones Willy had for his lawn mower.

The fire hadn't been an accident.

The resignation collapsed into something more desolate.

"You should go inside," Huck said. "Try to get some sleep. I'll be in when this is finished."

She wanted to say it was already finished, but she couldn't find her voice. Instead, she nodded and did as he suggested.

Rather than collapse on the sofa as was her first thought, she trudged to the bathroom, peeled off her smoky clothes and climbed into the shower to wash away the smoke and soot. Her hands did the work with the soap and shampoo from memory because her brain had officially shut down. She wasn't sure how long she stood beneath the spray of water, but it had turned cold when a knock on the door jarred her from the trance.

"You okay in there, Liv?"

Shivering now, she shut off the water. "Fine. I'll be out in a minute."

She found a towel and dried her skin and hair. The idea of blowing it dry was more than she could manage putting into action. She grabbed the nightshirt hanging on the back of the bathroom door. The soft cotton felt good against her skin. She stared at her reflection and couldn't help playing the words the woman from the corner market had said. *He had a picture of you...'cause you're dangerous.*

Why would that PI, Louis Rogers, have had a picture of Olivia?

And why on earth would he say she was dangerous? She had never met the man. She hadn't been in Hamilton County since Christmas.

It made no sense.

She still had no idea why Willy would have hidden her contact information. If he had hired the PI, why would he give him a photo of Olivia and have him look for her?

She was too tired to think about this anymore. She opened the door and stepped into the hall.

"You okay?"

Huck stood in the hall, hands on his hips. He looked so worried.

"I'm okay. Give the water heater a minute to catch up."

She walked into the main room without a glance beyond the windows. The firefighters and their equipment would be gone by now, but she couldn't bear to see the devastation, even lit by nothing more than the moon.

Her emotions needed a reprieve.

She went to her room, ignored the spray-painted words on the wall, tore away the old poster and then threw back the covers. She climbed into her bed. If sleep would pull her under quickly, she might just survive this night.

Instead, she lay there, eyes wide open. She heard every drop of water fall in the shower. Imagined it sliding over Huck's skin. She squeezed her eyes shut and banished the thought. Eventually the bathroom door opened, and the scent of soap and his skin drifted through the air. Her entire being longed to have him hold her.

She listened to him move through the house, checking doors and windows. When he wandered back into the hall, she held her breath, bit her lips together to prevent calling out to him.

He paused at her door. "Liv, you asleep?"

Don't answer. Don't answer.

"No." *Fool.*

"Everything is locked up. I'll be on the couch if you need me."

She told herself to say goodnight or okay...or to just keep quiet and let him walk away.

Impossible.

"Huck?"

"Yeah?"

She opened her eyes. He stood in the doorway, backlit by the dim light in the hall. Maybe if he'd been wearing a shirt...maybe if she hadn't been so weak...

"I need you here with me."

For a single endless moment he stayed right where he was.

Her heart twisted with disappointment. He was smarter than her.

Then he moved into the room. "You sure about that?"

Heart racing now, she nodded. "Yes."

She drew the covers back as he approached the bed. "I need you, Huck."

Rather than take off his jeans, he climbed into the bed, pulled the covers over himself. "I'll stay right here until you wake up."

She snuggled closer. "Hold me, please."

He tucked one arm around her and pulled her into him. "For as long as you want."

One word echoed through her, but she didn't dare say it out loud. She told herself it was the pain talking. The uncertainty. The loss. Whatever it was, that word just kept echoing.

Always.

8:00 a.m.

RINGING WOKE HER.

Olivia's eyes opened. The sound came again. A cell. Not hers. Wrong ringtone.

She threw back the cover and sat up. Her head ached. Eyes felt raw. Throat too. All the smoke, she decided. She found a pair of jeans and a shirt in her closet. The jeans were ragged, as was the style back in high school. A tee with a Life Is Good logo was the best choice. Her favorite pair of leather sandals caught her attention, and she tugged those on. Still fit. Worn comfortable. A look in the mirror over the dresser had her gasping. Her hair was a wreck. Happened when she went to bed with it wet. A thorough brushing and a ponytail holder took care of that problem. Nothing she could do about the red-rimmed eyes.

The smell of coffee had her making her way to the kitchen. Huck stood at the sink, staring out the window. At the rubble, she surmised. A stab of pain sliced through her. She walked to the counter and poured herself a cup of coffee.

He smiled at her. "Good morning."

How did he look so damned rested...so unmarred by last night's events? Staring at him, dozens of memories from spending all those hours snuggled up with him in bed flashed one after the other in her head. The feel of his bare chest...his muscled arms. A powerful thigh nestled between hers. The smell of his skin.

She blinked. "Morning." A sip of coffee made her wince. Too hot. She should have paid better attention. "Who called?"

"That was the PI's assistant. She found something she thought might help."

Olivia's mood lifted instantly.

"She spoke with one of the sources we weren't able to reach. He said Rogers had asked a lot of questions about a private mental-health clinic on Pineville Road. Right off Moccasin Bend Road. Since it's unrelated to any of his other cases, she thought it might be part of the Ballard case."

"Isn't Moccasin Bend like a state hospital?" Her mind raced to make some sort of connection to Willy or to herself. Or perhaps to her parents.

"It is, but this isn't that one. It's a private facility that just happens to be in that same area. I helped a deputy escort a patient there once. Rich guy from over in Emerald Valley."

"We should check it out."

"Drink your coffee," he suggested. "I'll have a look around outside, and then I'll be ready."

Olivia turned her back to the counter and the window over the sink. She wasn't sure she could bear to look just yet.

When she'd finished her coffee, she went back to her

room and looked for a slightly less casual shirt. She would hate to be denied entrance to the posh clinic because she looked like a vagrant. A pink wrap top. Dressed up the jeans. Good enough.

She grabbed her bag and locked up. Huck waited for her on the porch.

"You ready?" His gaze lingered on the blouse.

She wondered if he remembered it. It was that old. "I'm ready if you are."

Olivia waited until they were headed down the mountain to ask, "Any ideas on how this clinic might be connected to my family?"

"None at all." He slowed for a turn. "While I was having a look around outside, I even called my mom and asked if she recalled anyone Willy or Joyce might have known being committed for any reason. She said not that she remembered. If anything like that happened, it was kept extra quiet."

Which meant it was still possible. "Maybe my mother. But she's been dead for what, twenty-six years? I can't see how that would be relevant."

The PI's words about her being dangerous reverberated again.

"I don't know where this is going," Huck offered, "but it's possible his interest in this clinic had nothing to do with your case. The assistant can't be sure."

"She said that?" Olivia decided Huck might be couching the information in hopes of making her feel better.

"She said it wasn't related to any of his other cases."

Which meant it was related to Willy's case, Olivia mused. "That's what I thought."

"Let's not borrow trouble," Huck countered with a pointed look in her direction.

A new thought sucker-punched her. "Tell me the truth, Huck. Did I ever have any issues that for some reason I'm not remembering?"

He came to a full stop at a red light maybe more abruptly than he'd intended. "You did not."

She breathed a little easier. "Good. Thanks." With all that was going on, she couldn't help but wonder if she was the one with issues.

The drive took half an hour. The wooded area along Moccasin Bend Road was flanked on both sides by the Tennessee River and looked more like a national park. But that wasn't the case at all. At one end of the road was the well-known state hospital, and at the other was where the road became Pineville and split off toward a more industrial area. Just before that split their destination, the Pineville Institute, stood in the woods well off the road. Oddly, along the way there was at least one hiking trail, a golf course and an archaeological district. The city of Chattanooga lay just across the river. None of it really fit together, as if the various parts had been shaken and then tossed out to fall where they might.

Huck eased his SUV into a parking space. A few cars were already in the lot. Olivia hoped since it was Saturday, it was a visitation day, and that would make it easier for them to get inside.

"What's our strategy?" she asked, turning to the man who made her heart skip a beat. Not a good thing, she feared. As much as she wanted to recapture some aspect of their relationship, they were different people now with vastly different lives. Then again, it hadn't felt that way last night when she had lain in his arms feeling safe and warm…and wanting.

"We go in, mingle a bit if possible. Flash around the official pic of Rogers I snatched from the internet. If we're questioned, I flash my badge and ask to see whoever is in charge." While he talked, he tucked his weapon into the glove box and locked it.

"Let's do it then."

They climbed out. He locked the doors as they walked toward the entrance. The clinic looked more like a palatial home. Olivia could only imagine the cost of being a resident in a place like this. Judging by the vehicles in the lot, money wasn't a problem.

Inside was cool. The entrance doors opened to a large, stately lobby that reminded her of one she might find in an elegant New York City hotel. The reception desk looked exactly like a check-in or concierge's counter.

Olivia hung back as Huck approached the counter. He showed his badge. "I'm looking for whoever is in charge."

The younger man behind the counter smiled widely. "Mr. Cyrus is the deputy administrator. Though he isn't usually in on Saturdays, he is in today. He's currently in a meeting. If you don't mind waiting, I'm sure he won't be more than half an hour."

"I'll wait," Huck said.

He joined Olivia at the table in the center of the room. Large bouquets of fresh-cut flowers stood in glass vases atop the table. The smell cloying.

"Half an hour," Huck said. "The manager on duty is named Cyrus."

Didn't sound familiar to Olivia. "What are the odds he'll answer our questions?"

"Not good," Huck admitted, his gaze following the visitors moving on past a set of French doors.

"You thinking the same thing I'm thinking?" she asked, pretending to admire the flowers that basically provided great cover for their position.

"Maybe." His gaze settled on those French doors.

"You hang around out here," she suggested. "Go back to the counter and chat with the man there from time to time. I'll go on in like I'm an authorized visitor. I'll float around and see what I can find."

"I don't know about separating," he argued.

"It's a secure facility," she reminded him. "What could go wrong?"

For two beats, she was sure he would argue. Instead, he exhaled a worried breath. "Just be careful. I'll take a seat closer to the doors, right in front of that desk, where I can be seen."

Olivia nodded. "I'll mingle." When the next cluster of visitors wandered by, she joined the group.

Once she was beyond the French doors, she stayed with the group for a bit longer. Another lobby, not quite so elaborate, was on the right. Most of the group filtered in that direction, leaving Olivia with just one other woman. The woman moved farther down the wide corridor.

The next large space they encountered reminded Olivia of the conservatories she'd seen in Europe. Lots of glass and loads of enormous plants. Numerous conversation areas, some with sofas and chairs, others with larger tables surrounded by chairs. A counter on the far side was stocked with refreshments. Olivia turned away when the attendant monitoring the refreshments glanced her way.

Olivia moved on, pretending to know exactly where she

was going. The corridor split into two narrower halls. She went right. Doors lined the hall, each with a number. She wondered if these were the residents' rooms. Being in this area might get her kicked out. She scanned for cameras. Spotted two.

Damn it.

She walked faster, reached an exit door and walked out. A large patio spread out before her. Tables shaded by umbrellas dotted the space, each conversation area adorned with potted plants. Several tables were occupied. Straight ahead was a long, shallow pond that cut through the stone landscape. Koi fish glided leisurely through the crystal clear water.

Olivia turned around and decided her best option was to show the PI's photo to employees. They all wore the same uniform, blue suits, some with trousers, others with skirts.

A woman floated around the tables, smiling, removing empty drink cups and chatting. Olivia sat down at a table in her path. When the woman reached her, she flashed the photo and asked, "Have you seen this man? I was told he'd been bothering guests here."

Olivia held her breath and waited for a response. The lady in blue shook her head. Her gaze narrowed as she leaned closer.

"I haven't seen him. Are you part of the new security?" she asked. "The undercover ones? I heard they had put new people in place after what happened."

Olivia's pulse skittered. "It's state mandated."

The woman glanced around. "It's crazy. In forty-two years, they haven't had an escape until now."

Clocking the movements of the others in the room, Olivia assured her, "We intend to see that it never happens again."

"We'll all feel safer," the other woman said before progressing on to the next table.

Heart pounding with the charge of adrenaline, Olivia stood and walked away. She reentered the clinic through a different door. This one took her back to the large room with the conversation areas and the refreshment counter. She walked straight up to the woman there and asked the same question, showing the photo.

The woman's eyebrows went up. "I can't say that I've seen him." Her gaze narrowed. "Do you have reason to believe he was involved in the trouble over in D wing?"

Olivia gave a solemn nod. "It's very possible. Have you been in the area today? It's important that we monitor closely with the visitors coming in and out."

Olivia had no clue what she was talking about. She was just going with the flow and hoping like hell she didn't screw up this unexpected cover. Maybe she had missed her calling.

"I was over there a few minutes ago." She hitched her head in the direction Olivia had gone earlier. "All was quiet."

"Good to hear." Olivia glanced at the woman's name tag. "Thank you, Susan."

Olivia wandered on, following that wide corridor once more. This time when she reached the end, she went left. A side staircase waited at the end. Beyond the staircase was another exit. She weighed whether to take the stairs but decided the exit might prove more beneficial since the woman with the refreshments had said "over in D wing" not "up in D Wing." Sounded like a separate area.

Beyond this exit was a sidewalk leading to a maze of buildings. Olivia smiled. Hoped she was fast enough to avoid security noticing someone not wearing a blue suit in this area.

She passed buildings B and C and strolled straight toward D, which sat the farthest from the main building. At the entrance, the door was secured with an access panel that required a badge or other card to swipe. Unlike the other buildings, this one had no windows. She decided to walk around the building to look for other entrances. Maybe someone had propped open a side door or was standing outside to have a smoke. Though she doubted smoking was allowed anywhere on the campus.

Olivia had no idea how much longer her ruse would work. She listened for the sound of footfalls above the rush of blood in her ears. Her nerves jangled with equal parts excitement and worry. She could imagine security rushing to drag her away.

She spotted a patio at the back of the building, but this one was very different from the last. This one was austere with concrete tables and benches and a high fence around the space. No plants or umbrellas at this one. No getting beyond the fence either.

A lone woman sat at a table on the far side of the patio. Olivia walked in that direction, staying close to the fence. The woman's head came up when she noticed Olivia. As Olivia moved closer to her side of the concrete expanse, the woman grew visibly agitated. Her body tensed, her face seemed to pale. She looked older than Olivia but it was difficult to say precisely how much.

When Olivia had gotten as close as she could with the fence in her way, the woman stood, her movements stilted. She walked toward the fence, toward Olivia, her eyes growing ever wider.

"What're you doing here?" The words were hissed almost under her breath. She looked around as if she expected someone to see them.

Uncertain whether to ask questions or just play along, Olivia smiled. "Hello."

The woman's head moved side to side so hard Olivia couldn't see how she didn't get whiplash. "You said you were never coming back. Ever."

Heart thumping frantically, Olivia opted to play along. "I had to."

The woman took a step away. "You shouldn't have come back. Now they'll know."

She ran away. Snatched at the handle of the door leading into the windowless building.

Olivia couldn't move. She stood there...frozen. How could that woman possibly know her?

Firefly Lane, 12:00 p.m.

LUCKILY, BY THE time the deputy administrator, Cyrus, had warned Huck he would need a warrant to be inside the facility, Olivia had returned to the lobby. Huck had known something was very, very wrong when he saw her face.

As they had driven away from the clinic, Huck had been seriously worried about Olivia. She hadn't said a word since exiting that clinic. Not until they were across the river and headed up the mountain did she break her silence and tell him what happened. He'd struggled for something to say that would possibly explain what the woman had said to Olivia.

But there was only one explanation, and he couldn't go there...not yet.

As he parked behind her SUV at the cabin, he noted that Decker was already there waiting for them. Calling the sheriff and telling him they needed a meeting ASAP had been the only option. Something was way out of bounds here, and to tell the truth, he wasn't sure he could trust his judgment in the matter.

Decker met them on the porch. "What's going on, Monroe? I just got a call from the deputy administrator at Pineville, who says you were up there harassing residents."

"Not true, Sheriff," Huck argued. He wasn't actually surprised Decker had gotten a call already.

Olivia unlocked and opened the door. "I'm the only one who spoke to a resident," she said before going inside.

Huck waited for the sheriff to go next, then he followed.

Olivia immediately launched into the story about what they had learned from the private investigator's assistant. She didn't slow down long enough for Huck to get a word in edgewise until she was done and had confessed to getting the call, coming up with the idea to go to the clinic and going inside. She summed up her monologue by saying that Huck had only gone along to protect her from herself.

When Decker's attention swung to him, Huck shook his head. "This is not her fault. I—"

"Save it," Decker said. "We all need a good stiff drink, and then we need to talk."

To say his response surprised Huck would be a vast understatement.

Olivia gestured to the sofa. "I'll get Willy's bourbon."

Huck rounded up three glasses and joined his boss. He chose the chair opposite the sofa. Having the coffee table between them felt like the right move.

Decker said nothing until Olivia sat down on the sofa and poured the bourbon. They each tossed back the shot, even Olivia. Huck was impressed that she only winced.

Decker set his glass on the table. "I'm going to tell you what Willy should have told you a long time ago, Olivia."

Huck braced himself. Wished he was closer to her. She looked tired and exhausted and about fifteen years old again. Holding her in his arms last night had broken him over and over. Each time he'd managed to pull himself together, she moved or breathed a little more deeply, and he'd come undone again.

Olivia squared her shoulders. "I'm listening."

"Your mother, Laura, was always a little wild." He shrugged. "Looking back, we should have seen it for what it was." He shook his head. "But we didn't."

When she would have spoken, he held up a hand to stop her. "When she ran off and got involved with your father, Willy and Joyce tried to make the best of it. If she was happy that was all that mattered. But after you were born things went downhill fast."

"What does that mean?" Olivia demanded, her eyes shining with the emotion she could no longer contain.

Huck's gut clenched. He waffled between wanting to hug her and to punch Decker. He hoped to hell all this was necessary. Otherwise he might just lose his job for kicking the guy's butt for putting her through this.

"Laura was mentally unstable, Olivia," he said flatly. "We all pretended it away, but after you were born the clues were undeniable. It wasn't so easy since she and that jerk disappeared frequently. But when they'd come back, it would take her weeks to be right again."

"Depression? Schizophrenia? What are we talking about here?" Olivia demanded.

"The one diagnosis was schizophrenia." He exhaled a big breath. "But who knows. When you were three, he left without her for a while. She basically came undone. She had to be hospitalized. We took her to Pineville. It's private, so we could keep it quiet. Willy didn't want that kind of thing on her record."

"How long was she there?" Huck asked since Olivia seemed to have lost her voice.

"Three months. When she came home, he showed up again, and for a while she seemed to be happy," Decker went on. He stared at the floor a moment. "But then she did something we couldn't pretend away. That loser told her he was planning to leave again, and she lost it. Killed him. I was there. I tried to stop her."

The shock on Olivia's face forced Huck to his feet. He moved to stand next to her. "What the hell?" he demanded of his boss.

"Willy begged me to help him cover it up." Decker shook his head. "I shouldn't have done it, but Joyce was devastated. Willy was falling apart. The bastard was a drifter, had no family. No one was going to miss him. There was Olivia's future to think about. How could we let her grow up with that hanging over her head?"

Huck swore. "You helped Willy cover up a murder?"

Decker nodded. "Having Laura charged with murder wasn't going to bring him back. Wasn't going to help anyone."

Huck rested his hand on Olivia's shoulder, wished he could take her out of here, away from this horror story. "I feel compelled to tell you, sir, that you may want to stop talking at this point."

"No." Olivia looked up at him, the hollow, pained look on her face ripping his heart out. She turned back to Decker. "What happened next?"

Decker took a moment, likely to consider the ramifications of what he was doing. "We buried him and pretended nothing had happened. Laura lapsed into depression. No matter how Willy and Joyce tried, she just wouldn't snap out of it. They took her back to Pineville for a few weeks, and that seemed to help, but then…" He cleared his throat. "She went to the dam and jumped. She'd left a note at home, but by the time Willy got there, it was too late."

Olivia inhaled a sharp breath. She stood. "Thank you for finally telling me the truth."

She pushed past Huck and disappeared out the back door. He stood there, in a kind of shock. Torn between punching his boss and going after her.

"You do what you will with what I've said," Decker announced, pushing to his feet. "She needed the truth. As awful as it is. For the record, I did what I thought was best, and I'd do it again."

He left.

Huck wasn't sure there was any way on earth to fix this, but he had to try.

Chapter Twelve

Huck walked out the back door. Olivia stood on the stone path amid the hundreds of blooming plants bordering each side. If Willy were here, he would say what a perfect shot the scene would make. Her dark ponytail hanging against the pink shirt. The contrast of the silky pink against the worn blue cotton of her jeans. The multitude of colors in the blooms surrounding her and all of it facing a backdrop of blackened rubble where the shed once stood. Beauty and tragedy.

Pulling in a deep breath, Huck moved in behind her. He bowed his head, could smell the sweet scent of shampoo in her hair.

She whirled around, faced him. "Did you know any of this?"

The misery on her face made him want to pull her into his arms and promise her anything. She was too hurt and angry to allow him to touch her right now. He shook his head in answer to her question. "I can't imagine how hard it must have been for Willy to carry that burden all this time."

"He lied to me." Tears welled in her eyes. "I can see

how he rationalized this scheme in the beginning. But not now, after all these years." Her breath caught. "There's no excuse."

"You're angry," Huck said. "When you've had some time to think, you might be able to see his reasoning."

She shook her head. "I don't see that happening." She laughed then, the sound painful. "It's such a cliché. Everything I've believed my entire life is a lie."

Huck took her by the shoulders and gave her a gentle shake. "No. Willy and Joyce loved you. More than anything. Laura loved you, the best she could. I might not remember her, but you're her daughter. I can't imagine she was that different from you when you get down to the basics. Whatever illness plagued her, I'm betting she did the best she could. Everything your family did was to protect you."

She stared up at him, the tears sliding down her cheeks gutting him. "It's still all lies any way you look at it."

He had to find a way to make her see...

"I lied to you."

She stared at him. New pain settling into her features.

"When I left, it wasn't because I didn't want to be with you anymore. It was because I didn't want to hold you back."

She shook free of his touch. "What the hell are you talking about?"

"I couldn't take being apart so much. So one Saturday morning, I drove over to surprise you." He swallowed back the doubt. "I watched you and your friends all weekend. Watched the way this one guy watched you...laughed with you. I was just a rookie cop. No way I'd ever be able to offer you the kind of future that whole college scene, guys like that one, could offer you."

She held her hands up as if she felt the need to protect herself. "You didn't say a word. Why didn't you talk to me?"

"I couldn't. I just needed to let it go."

"You mean, let me go." Anger lashed across her face. "You threw us away because you…"

"I thought I was doing the right thing." Damn. This was not helping at all.

"You took the coward's way out. It was easier than fighting for me—not that a fight would have been required." She clenched her fists at her sides as if she needed to hold herself back from punching him. "You gave up and walked away when there was no reason to. That guy—the big flirt everyone in our group complained about—was just a jerk trying to get in every freshman's pants. He was no one to me. And you—" The breath shuddered out of her. "You were everything."

Before he could find the words to say, she shouldered past him and went back into the house. Well, hell. He'd screwed that one up big time. So much for his big confession. Idiot!

OLIVIA SLAMMED THE back door shut and stormed through the house and into her room. This was too much. She could not think about all the lies anymore. The most urgent issue at the moment, in her opinion—not that she was a cop—was who the hell was behind Willy's death? Who killed the private investigator? And who burned down the damned shed?

She grabbed a tee and changed from the pink blouse, which was the best one she had available here.

Dragging her fingers through her ponytail to free it, she had to ask why the hell she was still here.

Willy was dead. The shed was destroyed. She could just change the locks on the cabin and walk away.

Staying wouldn't change one damned thing.

Fury roared through her. Except she wasn't going anywhere until she found the person who hurt Willy. He'd protected Olivia her entire life—even if some of his decisions weren't the best ones. She loved him. She owed him. Nothing was going to stop her from getting this done.

She dug through her closet and found her sneakers.

"I made the wrong choice."

She turned from the closet to find Huck standing in her doorway, looking for all the world like a lost puppy with nowhere to go.

"You did." She steadied herself, tamped back the rising anger. She walked to her dresser and dug out a pair of socks, then sat down on the bed. She took her time, putting on the socks and then slipping on the sneakers. "You should have trusted me. Talked to me. Instead, you threw me away."

He closed his eyes, shook his head. "Don't say that." His eyes opened once more, and he searched hers. "I would never do that. I thought—at the time—I was doing the right thing. It was a while before I realized I was wrong."

She stalked over to where he stood still bracketed by that doorway as if it might somehow protect him from the coming storm. Not happening. "And just when did you have this epiphany? Was it after the fifth time I tried to call you? Or after I came back home and knocked on your door until my knuckles bled? Or maybe it was months after I had cried myself to sleep every damned night."

If she'd sucker-punched him, he wouldn't have looked any more damaged.

She wanted to be glad, but somehow couldn't muster the triumphant feeling.

"I was wrong, Liv. I would've done anything to make it up to you, but I realized it was too late by then."

"Coward." She pressed a hand to his chest and pushed him back from the door.

She had stuff to do.

He followed her out of the house. Let him. He wasn't going to stop her.

In the barn, she searched until she found a shovel. Then she rummaged around for a second one. When she found it behind the rakes and hoes, she grabbed it and tossed it toward him. To her surprise, he caught it.

"If you're going to keep hanging around," she said, her voice a little wobbly despite the anger, "you can help me."

"Okay."

He might feel differently if he bothered to ask what she planned to do. Since he didn't, she headed away from the barn and the house and that damned pile of charred metal that was once the shed. She didn't stop until she reached that big old oak so close to the cliffs it was a miracle its roots went deep enough to hold it in place.

She stopped next to her mother's grave. "Both my parents are dead. Willy's gone. Gran. Then who's doing this? Who would have a motive to want to hurt me or hurt the people I love? Think about it. Why wouldn't Gran or Willy want to be buried here, next to their only child—their daughter? That alone should have set off warning bells ages ago. Something isn't right about this grave."

A realization dawned and his head moved side to side. "Liv, I get what you're saying. But you can't do this."

"I can." She swallowed back the tears that crowded into her throat. "You can either help me or you can walk away. You've done it before."

He stared at the ground a moment, properly chastised. "What do you expect to find?"

She lifted her shoulders in an exaggerated shrug. "I don't know. Maybe some proof of what the truth really is."

"Decker said she's dead." Huck glanced toward the grave at Olivia's feet.

"Then why was Rogers looking for her? Why did that patient at Pineville asked me why I was back?"

"I don't know what the PI was doing, but Decker said your mother was a patient at Pineville."

"He did," she agreed. "But the woman who spoke to me was thirty-five at most. Are you telling me she remembers my mother from more than twenty-five years ago?"

Huck held her gaze for a moment. "You didn't mention that she was so young."

"It wasn't relevant until Decker's confession." The way Huck was looking at her now had anticipation zinging through her. He was thinking the same thing. If it wasn't Olivia the woman had seen…then who?

"You'll need gloves."

"We both will," she admitted.

They walked back to the barn together. No one spoke. Finding the gloves was easy because Gran had been meticulous at organization and Willy had ensured it all stayed that way.

Huck's hands barely fit into a pair of Willy's leather work gloves. Gran's gloves fit Olivia perfectly.

The walk back to that big old oak was equally quiet. They'd both said more than enough. There was nothing left to do but dig.

By the time they were standing in a hole the length of a

coffin and about waist deep, Huck paused. "We should take a break. Drink some water."

He'd long ago discarded his shirt. The tee beneath was streaked with sweat and dirt.

Olivia's tee was damp. Her arms ached. She was thirsty, but she wasn't stopping. "Not yet."

She dug her shovel into the dirt. Hit something. Probably another rock. "Damned rocks," she muttered.

Apparently convinced she wasn't stopping, Huck began digging again.

She crouched down and dragged her finger around the rock. She'd discovered that to get them out, she had to dig around the damned things until they were loosened from the soil. She alternated between prying around it with her shovel and scrapping away what she could with her gloved fingers.

White peeked from the dirt.

The color wasn't the same as the other rocks she'd unearthed. She swiped at the dirt, pushing aside a little more.

A hole in the rock appeared...then another.

Not holes. Eye sockets.

Olivia tumbled back. Let go of her shovel. The handle banked off Huck's broad shoulder.

He stared at what she'd revealed. He muttered something unintelligible as he dropped to his knees. He tore off the gloves and scratched at the dirt around the skull. Moving by rote, she joined him, scratching and tugging.

Once the skull was free, Huck sat it on the ground next to the base of the tree, away from the pile of dirt on the other side of the hole they'd dug.

More bones...fragments of fabric. The better part of a sneaker.

Olivia sat back, the sneaker's rubber sole held between

her gloved fingers. Not a woman's sneaker. Too long...too wide. This was a man's sneaker.

Her gaze collided with Huck's.

He started digging again, his movements as frantic as the pounding in her chest.

The other sneaker or what was left of it appeared. Then the parts of a belt buckle. Rivets from a pair of name-brand jeans...nothing was left of the cotton.

Olivia's fingers closed around an object...black...wallet.

She pulled it from the dirt. Stared at it a moment then handed it to Huck. She couldn't open it...no way.

He opened the wallet; deteriorating pieces fell away. His dirt-crusted fingers struggled, tugging at what Olivia hoped was an ID of some sort.

When it was free from the plastic slip, he held it out for her inspection.

Driver's license. *Kasey Aldean.*

Olivia stared at the bones spread over the grass then at the image of a young man on the driver's license.

This was her father's grave.

Her father's remains.

Then where the hell was her mother?

Chapter Thirteen

6:00 p.m.

"We wanted to save you the additional pain," Sheriff Decker explained.

Olivia wanted to scream! Instead she steeled herself against the raging emotions. "What're you saying?"

Decker stared at the bones scattered on the ground. "I told you Willy and I hid his body to protect your mother. This is where we buried him."

Huck stood next to her, but so far he had allowed her to do the talking. She appreciated his deference to her need to demand answers.

"Where is my mother buried?"

"She isn't." Decker's shoulders sagged. "You know how the waters are around that dam. We searched for days to no avail. Her body was never recovered. I guess you can say she's buried in the river." His shoulders squared then as if he'd decided there would be no more appeasement from him. He gave Olivia a firm look. "You need to stop this, Liv. You need to get on with your life. Digging around in that part of the past will never bring you the peace you're looking for. What's done is done, and some things are best left alone."

With that, he gave Huck a nod and he walked away. Huck followed him. Probably had a few things of his own to say. This news about the cover-up had shaken him too. To find the remains had been the last straw.

Olivia couldn't remember when she had felt so angry... so damned disappointed. She blinked. Realized it had been ten years ago when Huck threw away her hopes and dreams. But that had been different. This was... Olivia shook herself, couldn't quite label what the hell this was.

The sheriff. A lawman vested with the power of enforcing the law...wanted her to pretend she hadn't just dug up the remains of a murdered man.

Her father.

His skull hadn't been bashed in. She hadn't seen any sort of damage to any of the other bones. Huck hadn't noticed any readily visible damage either.

Had her mother poisoned him? Shot him?

Olivia squeezed her eyes shut. Didn't matter. She had killed him, and then she'd taken her own life. Had she not once considered how her actions would affect her baby? Or maybe she had known that Olivia would be better off with her grandparents.

She couldn't be here any longer. Olivia walked away from the shallow grave with its bones laid bare on the open ground. She needed to think. To consider all this painful information.

She'd almost reached the house when Huck met her in the middle of the backyard.

"He's gone."

Olivia considered this man—the one person she felt she could still trust. "Do you believe him?"

"Which part?"

"Any part?" Olivia surveyed the yard with all its blooms that had given her grandparents so much pleasure. "Obviously, my father is dead. I'm sure Willy wouldn't have helped cover up his murder without a very compelling reason, so I suppose it's true that my mother killed him."

Huck pulled out his cell and tapped a few keys. Olivia waited to hear whatever he had to say.

"I can find your mom's obit on here, but nothing about her death or a drowning at the dam."

Olivia shook her head. "That makes no sense. Wouldn't that have been on the news?"

Huck nodded. "Definitely. Unless they covered it up too."

"They certainly never told me she took her own life."

"Decker wasn't the sheriff then, but he was an up-and-coming chief deputy," Huck pointed out. "He could have called in a favor with a private search and rescue team."

Olivia lifted her chin and offered a scenario of her own. "What if she never jumped? What if she just left that note and ran away?"

Huck nodded slowly. "Then suddenly came back recently for reasons that worried Willy. He hires a PI to try and figure out what her game is and…well, you know how that ended."

"I have to know for sure." Olivia moistened her lips, struggled with the conflicting emotions. "If she's alive, I want to find her. If she hurt Willy, I want…"

Huck reached out, took her hand and gave it a reassuring squeeze. "We can figure that part out as soon as we determine where she is."

Olivia nodded. He was right. "We should go back to that

house, where the sleeping bag was. Maybe she was staying there, and the guy watching for her just never saw her."

"We'll start there."

Vine Street, 7:10 p.m.

THE STREET WAS QUIET. At this hour on Saturday evening, most people were probably out for the evening or inside having dinner and watching their favorite television program. They would have gotten here twenty or so minutes ago, but they'd had to clean themselves up after digging up those bones. Olivia hadn't wanted to take the time for showers, so they'd washed up, changed clothes in record time and headed out.

Huck parked at the curb in front of the house that was for rent, the one they'd used as a decoy to see the one next to it. And like before, the old lady sat on her porch rocking the evening away.

"I'm going to talk to her," Olivia said.

"We've got nothing to lose," Huck agreed. They had already been in the house and found nothing useful other than evidence that someone had been staying there.

They climbed out and headed to the lady's front porch. She stopped rocking and watched their approach.

Olivia opened the gate to her picket fence. "Good evening," she said. "Do you have a moment for a few questions about the house for rent?"

Olivia stopped at the bottom of the steps. Huck stood behind her.

The older lady surveyed them a long moment, lifted her chin as if she might banish them from her property. "I thought you were looking at the one for sale."

Huck almost grinned. She remembered them.

"Yes, ma'am," Olivia said. "We had a look at it too, but it's the rental that we're really interested in."

She grunted as if uncertain if she believed Olivia. "Well, come on up here on the porch so I can hear you better."

Huck thought she was hearing just fine, but he was grateful for the invitation.

Olivia climbed the steps and waited for Huck to join her.

"Take a load off," the lady offered.

Olivia took the matching rocker next to her; Huck settled on the swing.

"Thank you." Olivia smiled. "I'm Olivia Ballard, and this is my friend Deputy Detective Huck Monroe."

The woman eyed him suspiciously before turning back to Olivia. "I saw you before."

Huck noticed that she didn't give her name. He didn't blame her. They were strangers.

"Yes, ma'am," Olivia agreed. "When we looked at the house next door."

The woman shook her head. "Maybe your friend don't know it, but I saw you going in and outta that house like you owned the place."

Olivia frowned. "You're mistaken. It wasn't me."

The woman laughed. "You might have your deputy friend here fooled, but I watched you coming and going ever since Monday night. It wasn't even dark when I saw you creeping around."

IT TOOK EVERY ounce of willpower Huck possessed not to speak up, but he clamped his jaws shut and let Olivia run with this. Her eyes widened, and she nodded.

"Sorry, I didn't mean to bother you. I wasn't sure you

saw me, but now I know. It's important that no one finds out I was here."

The lady shook her head. "No bother. I figured you was hiding from somebody. I wasn't gonna call the police un- less you started some trouble. Thelma—" she hitched her head toward the houses farther down the street "—said she talked to you. Said you were real nice." She glanced at Huck. "I guess you found someone to help you figure out whatever trouble you're in."

Olivia nodded. "I did. I'll just check in with Thelma and let her know. Is she home?"

"If that little old red car of hers is in the driveway, she's home." She nodded toward his SUV. "You should've seen it when you parked."

"Thank you." Olivia stood. "It was kind of you not to tell anyone about me."

"You were smart to stay gone when that fella was out there watching. He stayed day and night for two whole days."

"Yes, ma'am."

As they descended the steps, Olivia glanced up at Huck. Her eyes full of uncertainty. He got it. The woman obvi- ously hadn't seen Olivia. She'd seen someone who looked like her. And from her porch, she likely hadn't noticed that the woman she saw was older.

Whatever Decker thought, Huck was pretty damned cer- tain that Laura Ballard was still alive.

Just past the rental house and the one for sale was a small bungalow with a little red car parked in the driveway.

Olivia took a big breath and started up the sidewalk to the small porch. Huck followed.

Before they reached the porch, the occupant of the

house—presumably Thelma—opened the wood door. "Are you okay?" she asked through the screen door.

"Thelma?"

The woman blinked, stepped out onto the porch. "Oh... I thought you were someone else."

"My name is Olivia Ballard," she said. "I need to ask you some questions about the woman who was staying next door."

Thelma nodded. "It's weird how much the two of you look alike." She glanced beyond Olivia to Huck. "He your husband?"

"No. He's my friend."

Huck liked that she called him her friend but...part of him wished she had said he was her husband.

"What questions?" She eyed Olivia with mounting suspicion. "They sent someone looking for her, just like she said they would. I ain't planning to help her be found if she doesn't want to be found."

Huck decided it was time he spoke up. "Ma'am, the woman you met is Laura Ballard, Olivia's mother. What she may not have told you is that she is in danger. The people looking for her may not be as worried about her well-being as Olivia and I are. If you can help us, you'll be helping Laura."

She eyed Huck with more of that suspicion. "I see from that vehicle you're driving, you're a cop. Maybe she don't want no cop to find her either."

"If someone else finds her first," Olivia added, "we may not be able to help her."

Thelma exhaled a big breath. "She escaped that place where she'd been a prisoner for most of her adult life. She said she couldn't trust anyone and that she was worried about her daughter." Her gaze narrowed again. "So that's you?"

Olivia nodded. "I've spent my whole life believing she was dead."

The woman made a face. "I ain't gonna ask how that happened, but she did say the last person she trusted got killed."

Olivia shared a look with Huck. "Did she say who that person was?"

Thelma shook her head. "I don't know. She hasn't been back since that guy was watching the house."

"Did she tell you anything else?" Olivia pressed. "Who kept her prisoner? Why she was never able to escape before?"

"She didn't tell me much, but she did say she'd been trying to get away for years, but all her attempts failed."

Huck passed her a card. "Please call if you hear anything else from her. We want to help, but we can't if we don't find her."

Thelma stared at the card then looked to Olivia. "You really should help her. They did stuff to her at that place."

Huck felt Olivia stiffen next to him.

"What sort of things?" Olivia asked, her voice thin.

"She didn't go into much, but she did mention shock treatments. She said that was one of the ways they punished her."

Olivia nodded. "Did she seem okay to you?"

Thelma looked put out by the question. "Are you asking me if she seemed crazy?"

"No," Olivia countered, "I'm asking you if she seemed calm or frenzied? Afraid or overly upset?"

"She seemed fine. Determined to find someone to believe her. But she did not seem the least bit agitated or off her meds, so to speak. She acted as normal as you or me."

Olivia nodded. "We'll do all within our power to help her."

The woman watched until they had loaded up and driven away. Olivia sat in silence as Huck navigated the streets.

"I need you to be careful, Liv," he warned, glancing at her as he drove. "We don't know the whole story. Willy would never have gone along with any part of this unless he felt there was no other choice."

Olivia turned to Huck. "I don't know what to trust anymore."

He took her hand in his. "We'll figure it out."

The question that kept ringing in his head was why the hell hadn't Decker told him Olivia's mother was still alive?

Unless he really didn't know.

Firefly Lane, 8:30 p.m.

OLIVIA STILL FELT numb as she unlocked the door and went into the house. She didn't know what to think or to believe.

She wanted to feel hurt that Willy hadn't told her whatever part of all this he knew. If, as Decker said, he'd been protecting his daughter, she could understand. But why not come clean in the past few years? Olivia was a grown woman. She had a right to know the truth.

At the window over the sink, she stared at the rubble that had been his and Gran's prized workplace. How had it all come to this?

She thought about Willy's final days on this earth. He'd had lunch with Madeline. Had he known then that something was wrong? Had Laura already escaped the facility? Was Laura the reason he'd been at the market buying bread and wine? Madeline said she hadn't seen him since lunch on Sunday...so who was he preparing to have dinner with?

At this point, the only reasonable answer was: Laura.

Was Willy who Laura had meant when she said the one person she could trust was dead?

Olivia wished she had been able to ask the woman at Pineville when Laura had escaped, but she'd run away too quickly. She went to the stored photo albums and grabbed the ones with photos of her mother. She collapsed on the sofa and started flipping through the pages, scanning each photo.

Huck sat down next to her. "What're we looking for?"

"This." Olivia tapped a photo of her mother on the beach, a glass in one hand, a bottle of wine dangling from the fingers of the other. "She was a wine drinker." She met Huck's gaze. "What if she was coming here to have dinner with Willy on Sunday night? Maybe the wine and bread were for her."

"We need to find that wine bottle." Huck shot to his feet.

Olivia put the photo album aside and stood. "Willy recycled glass."

They hurried out the mudroom door. Next to the small back porch was the large wheeled garbage can as well as several smaller lidded bins where recyclables were stored.

Olivia opened the bin for glass and picked through the few items. "Nothing here."

Huck opened the larger garbage can.

"Willy wouldn't have tossed it in the trash," Olivia said.

No sooner than the words were out of her mouth, Huck withdrew a wine bottle. His eyebrows rose higher on his forehead. "Maybe Laura tossed it in here. She may have cleaned up after their dinner."

"Maybe." Olivia joined Huck at the garbage can and surveyed the contents. The trash was picked up on Fridays, so whatever was inside would only have been from the weekend leading up to Willy's death. She hadn't tossed anything in there since her arrival. The smell of rotting spaghetti sauce made her wince. The better part of the stick of French bread lay among the noodles and red sauce. "Doesn't look like they ate much."

"Good thing the bottle was on top," Huck said.

He held it gingerly. His fingers touching only the rim of the very top.

"If you'll grab me the largest plastic bag you can find, I'll put the bottle inside and have someone come pick it up and check for prints."

"Good idea."

Olivia hurried into the house, searched the cabinets until she found the plastic storage bags. "Will a gallon size do?"

"Think so."

She grabbed a bag and held it open while Huck eased the bottle inside.

"I'll make the call. Maybe Snelling will pick it up today and put a rush on the processing."

Olivia nodded. "Thanks." She hitched a thumb toward the hall. "I'm going to shower." Truth was she felt totally exhausted. She couldn't risk falling asleep with the odor of dirt clinging to her skin.

Huck was already making the call.

Olivia rounded up a clean nightshirt and locked herself away in the bathroom. She peeled off her clothes and tossed them into the pile with the others they had abandoned today. She turned on and adjusted the water in the shower and stepped into the tub.

She washed her hair, massaged her scalp. The hot water felt good against her sore and tense muscles. Moving the soap over her skin, she felt herself slowly relaxing as she washed the horror of their discovery off her body. Had Willy and Gran known her father was buried there?

The idea that Willy hadn't told her stabbed deep. She tried to find some logic to rationalize his decision, but nothing felt big enough or strong enough to leave her in the dark this way. Why would he deny her that truth? If Laura truly had some sort of mental illness, Olivia needed to know. So many were hereditary.

The woman's—Thelma's—story about Laura being held prisoner nudged her. Of course, she would feel like a prisoner in a place like Pineville. Some patients who suffered with mental illness were unaware of the trouble. But Thelma had insisted Laura seemed fine. Normal. But even patients with extreme disorders had times of calm clarity.

Olivia couldn't think about this anymore. She shut off the water and got out, dried herself and tugged on the nightshirt. It took some time to brush out her hair, but when it was done she finally felt hungry. By the time she'd blown her hair dry she was starving.

Huck was already scouring the cabinets when she walked into the kitchen. "Looks like we may have to see if we can get something delivered."

"Any of those services available this far out?" Her stomach reminded her she needed to get something ordered now.

Huck pulled out his cell and tapped an app. "Pizza? Mexican or Chinese?"

"Pizza."

A few more taps. "It'll be on our doorstep in thirty-five minutes."

"Great."

"Meanwhile." He walked to the fridge and reached inside. "We can share a beer."

He withdrew the single can. Willy's favorite.

"We can do that."

Huck passed the can to her. "You go ahead. I'm taking my turn in the shower."

"I'll save it for you," she offered.

"Go ahead. I'll figure out something after I shower."

"Wait, is your CSI friend coming?"

Huck paused at the door to the hall. "He came. Picked up the bottle and had some interesting news."

Olivia popped the top on the can. Beer wasn't her favorite recreational drink, but right now she was fairly desperate. "Oh yeah?"

Huck nodded. "According to his wife, who's the chief deputy, Sheriff Decker has resigned, citing personal reasons."

Olivia's jaw dropped. "Are you serious?"

"Chief Deputy Snelling will be acting sheriff for now."

"Do you think all this prompted that decision?" Olivia could certainly see how he would feel compelled to do so considering that his dark secret was out now—at least with her and Huck.

"When he left, I'm fairly certain he understood how we felt about what he'd done."

"He made a bad choice." Olivia had known the man her whole life, but right was right, and he'd been wrong all those years ago. He should have talked Willy into doing the right thing, not jumped in to help him do the wrong thing.

"He did." Huck gave her a nod then disappeared into the hall.

Olivia had never been more thankful for his presence. She sighed. Feeling a sense of relief that surprised her. Her life was upside down right now, but at least she wasn't alone.

As she sipped the beer, she wandered through the living area. Studied the painting over the fireplace. Moved on to the other photographs framed and hanging on the walls. She felt such deep regret that the shed had been destroyed. So much history gone.

Had Laura done that?

Was she trying to hide something or trying to tell Olivia something?

If she was out there somewhere and knew Olivia was here, why not come to the door? Talk to her? Olivia certainly hadn't been involved in whatever happened to her. She had no reason not to talk to her and to hear her out.

And what if she is responsible for Willy's death?

Olivia pushed away the voice and that too painful question.

She walked to the door, opened it and stepped out onto the porch. Was her mother here somewhere watching? Waiting for an opportunity to talk to Olivia alone?

Or waiting for an opportunity to kill her?

Olivia finished off the beer and set the empty can on the railing. She moved down the steps and surveyed the yard. Her and Huck's vehicles stood one behind the other. Willy's Defender was parked next to the house. Gran's pots of flowers and mounds of blooming shrubs scented the air, effectively masking the lingering smell of smoke. It was cooler now that the sun had fallen behind the trees, leaving the twilight.

Olivia thought of the bones near the cliff. She should probably feel guilty about leaving them lying there. At some point they would have to call in the find, and the bones would be taken for examination. She wondered if at this point cause of death could be determined.

It happened on the television shows. She supposed it could in real life as well.

She suddenly wondered if she could ever live here again. This had been home to her. Even though she'd been gone a decade, it had always been home. But the people who had made it home were all gone.

Except Huck. He was back.

A shiver swept over her, and she scolded herself for allowing the sensation. They had been over for a very long time. In spite of what he'd told her, there were some bridges that couldn't be crossed again even if they hadn't been burned completely. But they could be friends. She wasn't losing that.

He was a good man. She couldn't deny how well he'd turned out. She'd heard about his awards and commitment to the community over and over from Willy even when she had not wanted to.

He was even better looking now than he had been as a kid. Very, very good looking if she was honest with herself.

He'd treated her with such respect...more than she had afforded him. She'd wanted him so badly last night. She would have made love with him in a heartbeat...but he'd suggested they slow things down.

She stilled. Then again, maybe there was someone else. Willy had said Huck didn't do relationships, but maybe Willy hadn't known.

She would be a fool to think he didn't have plenty of women interested.

A lump rose into her throat. She reminded herself that she was no longer interested. That she had moved on.

Except none of that was entirely true.

She dated. Had the occasional weeks-or months-long relationship...but never anything serious.

Never anything even remotely close to what she had with him.

Had their mistakes ruined the possibility of their best chance at something real...something permanent?

Whatever else they did or didn't have, he was the one person she could still count on...could still trust.

Was she going to finish this, walk away and pretend that she didn't still care about him...didn't still want him?

If she did...she would never know.

Know what? She swore at herself. Her heart pounding. Every part of her needing...*something*.

No. She did an about-face and headed back into the house. She would not—could not—walk away without knowing. Without being sure.

She locked the door and took a deep breath.

The scent of steamy air drifted to her from the hall, and she followed it there. Huck walked out of the bathroom, the towel he'd used wrapped around his waist.

He smiled. "Sorry. Forgot to grab clean clothes."

She walked straight up to him. "Look me in the eyes," she ordered, "and tell me you don't want me."

He frowned. "What?"

"Tell me you don't want me." She drew in a breath, every nerve in her body sizzling. "I want you to say it, and I'll go into my room, and I won't bother you again."

The expression that slipped over his face—a tenderness that stole her breath. "Why would you think I don't want you?"

"Then show me."

His hands came up to her face, cupped her cheeks. He stared at her lips as his descended there, and then there was nothing else. Only the taste of him...the smell of him and the feel of his body so close to hers.

He kissed her until she melted against him. Her fingers found their way to the towel and pulled it loose from his hips. He lifted her against him. Her legs circled his waist, and he carried her to her room.

Her nightshirt hit the floor, and her panties slid down her legs. He lowered her to the bed and pressed against her. Then there was no thought...there were only sensations. The feel of him inside her. His lips on her breasts. His hands on her skin.

She touched all of him, tracing, remembering all the places she had once known by heart. Her hungry mouth finding his jaw, his forehead. Legs entwined, bodies moving at that perfect, sweet pace.

And nothing else mattered.

Chapter Fourteen

Sunday, June 11, 9:30 a.m.

"You're sure about this?"

Olivia stared at the man seated in the chair across the table from her...the one who had reminded her last night of all she had lost ten years ago...his touch, the smell of his skin...the taste of his kiss. She never wanted to be far from him again.

Did Huck feel the same way? She couldn't be sure. She'd awakened alone this morning. He'd already gotten up and made coffee. Worse, he seemed somehow distant. Was he ready to bolt again? What had she done to make him feel that need? She understood now that she should have seen his concerns ten years ago. What happened was ultimately both their faults.

She did not want to make the same mistake twice.

"I'm sure." She nodded. "All these secrets have been kept far too long. I don't want any of this hanging over my head anymore." She shrugged, set her second cup of coffee aside. Going for the extra caffeine felt like a mistake now. She was jumpy...jittery. "We don't have to mention Sheriff Decker's part in all this. I'm sure the ultimate decisions were made by Willy and Gran."

"Decker should have to own his part in this, Liv."

Maybe Huck was right. The truth was she was too close to this to be objective.

"He's your boss—former boss," she finally said. "I'll leave that decision to you."

He nodded. "I'll make some calls. We'll get a team out here to finish the exhumation and collection of the bones."

"Thank you." She met his gaze, wanted to say more, but he gave her a nod and stood.

"I'll be on the porch."

She watched him go, and no matter that he seemed distant or distracted this morning, she was certain she couldn't have read him so wrong last night.

Olivia stood. She needed a walk. If only around the yard. She needed to just soak up the images and scents of home. To brace herself.

Her cell pinged with an incoming text.

Olivia tugged her phone from her pocket and stared at the screen.

Willy.

Her heart bumped into a harder rhythm. The text was from Willy's cell phone. This could be the person who had taken his life. *Breathe*, she told herself as she started toward the front door and simultaneously opened the text.

I need to tell you the real story.

Another text appeared.

It's your mom.

Olivia stalled at the front door, the bottom falling out of her stomach.

Please come to the grave.

Torn between rushing out the back door and telling Huck, her good sense won out and she stepped out onto the porch. Huck was still on the phone. She held her phone in front of his face so he could read the text messages.

His expression shifted to surprise, and his gaze collided with Olivia's. "Thanks, Snelling. Let me know when a team is headed this way."

He lowered the phone from his ear and stood. "You just got those?"

She nodded. "From Willy's phone."

He slid his phone into his pocket and reached for the weapon on the table next to the rocking chair he'd vacated. "Let's go."

Olivia didn't budge. "If it's her and she sees you, she might run."

His head was moving side to side before she finished speaking, his expression hard. "I'm not letting you go alone."

"I know," she agreed. "That's why I'm telling you rather than rushing through the woods right now."

Relief softened his face. "Okay. I'll take the roundabout path, the one we used when we wanted to ditch anyone following us."

She nodded. "I'll take the main path."

"Don't get ahead of me, Liv. Take your time. I'll be able to see you most of the way, but don't get there before I do."

"I won't. I'll take it slow. I'll go out the back, just in case she or whoever is watching."

"I'll give you a thirty-second head start by going through the barn."

She smiled. That was exactly what they used to do when they didn't want Willy and Gran to know they were going to the cliffs. They'd walk leisurely to the barn, slip out the back and barrel through the woods.

"Okay."

He took her by the arm before she could get away. "Be careful."

"You too."

Olivia left the house, strolled along the stone path. She paused at the tree line to send a response.

I'm coming.

Her pulse raced in time with the pounding in her heart. Her mother was out there somewhere. She had no doubt about that now. Whether she was deranged or dangerous, Olivia didn't know. Whether this was even her, she couldn't be sure. But the one thing she felt certain of was that whoever had Willy's phone may have been the person to hurt him.

The thought sent fire rushing through her veins. If her mother had killed Willy, Olivia wasn't sure she could trust herself in the woman's presence. Thank God for Huck.

Rather than get distracted with worries of what the facts might be, she focused on moving forward. She scanned left and right of the path, watching and listening for movement. What if her mother was armed? The thought slowed her steps. Someone had shot the private investigator.

Someone had pushed Willy...

The grave was very close to the cliffs.

Olivia steeled herself and kept moving. She had Huck. If

she stopped and looked closely enough, she would see him on that narrow little path they used to take.

Keep moving.

If she looked for him, anyone watching her would notice.

Focus forward.

By the time that big oak came into view, her nerves were jumping. Maybe it was how anxious she felt or some deep instinct that slowed her, but for the first time in a long time she paused to take in the beauty that lay before her.

Past the big tree was the view beyond the cliffs. The sky was clear. It was breathtaking.

"Olivia."

Female voice.

She turned to find a near mirror image standing a few feet away, midway between her and the unearthed bones that now lay in a neat pile rather than spread out as she and Huck had left them.

The woman who was her mother smiled. "You're so beautiful."

She stepped forward. Olivia instinctively stepped back.

Laura's face clouded. "Sorry. I didn't mean to scare you."

Olivia steeled herself. She would not be afraid. She recovered the step she had fallen back, then took another and another until she stood within touching distance of her mother. "I'm not scared."

Laura's smile returned. "I'm glad."

There was nothing in her hands. The jeans she wore fit snuggly, so unless a weapon was hidden behind her, maybe the way Huck sometimes tucked his gun at the small of his back, she wasn't carrying one.

"You wanted to talk," Olivia said rather than the barrage of other things that rushed into her head.

This was her mother.

A dozen turbulent emotions bombarded her at once.

She wasn't dead...why had Gran and Willy lied to her?

Laura's expression shifted to something fierce and bordering on frantic. "You can't trust Decker. He killed your father." Tears welled in her eyes. "He killed Willy."

Olivia stared at her, the fresh sting of pain deep and excruciating. "I don't believe you."

The sheriff and Willy had been friends forever. Why would he do such a thing? He'd even admitted to helping Willy cover up what Laura had done.

"You killed my father. Decker said so."

Laura stared at the ground for a moment. Her shoulders slumped as if she were too weary to hold them straight anymore. Fine strands of gray filtered like tiny silver threads in her dark hair. Her mother was not the smiling, young woman in the photos Olivia's gran had curated. She was much older now. Nearly fifty. She was still beautiful though, her face barely marred by age.

Her mother drew in a deep breath and lifted her face once more. "Whatever he told you was a lie. If you'll let me, I'll tell you the truth."

Olivia nodded. "On one condition."

Her mother searched her face. "What condition?"

"That you allow Huck to be part of this. We can trust him. If what you say is true, he can help you."

The fear in her expression pained Olivia more than she'd anticipated.

"You have my word," Olivia promised. "He would never betray me."

Laura nodded. "If you're sure."

Olivia sent him a text, to keep up the pretense. The longest half a minute Olivia had ever endured later, Huck joined them.

Laura eyed him skeptically at first.

"It's good to see you," he said to her.

She blinked, more tears glistening in her eyes. "Thank you."

The longer Olivia stood there watching her, the more convinced she became that this woman was not in any way unbalanced, but she reserved judgment for now.

"Start at the beginning," Olivia suggested.

Laura nodded. "Daddy and Decker were friends as far back as I can remember." She shrugged. "He was always nice to me. But as I got older, he watched me in a different way." She shuddered. "When I was thirteen, he raped me." She looked away.

Olivia and Huck shared a look. "Can you prove this?" Olivia asked.

Laura shook her head, still looking anywhere but at them. "He said the same thing when I told him I was going to tell. He said Willy would never believe me. He had just made chief deputy. Everyone loved him."

Olivia braced herself. "Keep going."

"I stopped fighting it and let him have his way. I lost count of the times. I spent hours figuring out ways to avoid being alone anywhere for fear he would show up and make me..." She let go a big breath. "But then I graduated high school and escaped. I was so grateful. I missed Mom and Dad, but the relief of never having that bastard paw me again was worth it." Her expression fell. "Then he caught me away from the university one day, and he did it again. I knew then that I'd never be free of him until I had a man who loved me who might be able to protect me." She smiled.

"I met Kasey, and everything was perfect for a while. I got pregnant with you, and we decided to come home. I knew Mom and Dad would help us get on our feet." She closed her eyes for a moment. "I never dreamed he would dare intrude again, but he did."

"He did this to you again?" Olivia said, unable to say the word, her insides twisted into knots.

She nodded. "When you were three." She stared heavenward. "He'd left me alone for three years. I thought it was over. Your dad and I had plans to start an organic farm. We hadn't told Mom and Dad yet, but we'd been traveling around nearby states searching for just the right location. Sometimes we would be gone for a few weeks, but I could never stay gone longer than that." She smiled. "I missed you too much."

Olivia felt undone. "You didn't just disappear all those times?"

Laura frowned. "Who told you that?"

"Decker," Olivia responded, looking from Laura to Huck. No need to mention his mother. She'd only repeated what she'd been told.

The pain on Laura's face tugged at Olivia's heart. She so wanted to believe what this woman—her mother—was telling her. The idea that Willy had trusted Decker made it difficult for Olivia to do otherwise. This woman was a stranger...how could Olivia be certain she was telling the truth?

"He wanted you to believe the same thing he made my parents believe," Laura said. "He twisted their concerns and made them believe things that weren't true. He was so bold that one day I was walking to town and he saw me. He almost ran over me. I ran into the woods, and he parked and came after me." She stared at the ground again. "This time, I told Kasey. He told me to set up a meeting with Decker, and he would take care of it. I did what he said. Decker didn't know Kasey would be there. Kasey told him never to come near me again or else."

"How did Decker respond to the ultimatum?" Huck asked.

Laura jerked at the sound of his voice as if she'd forgotten he was there. "He…he shot him. I tried to help him." Tears rushed down her cheeks. "He grabbed me, put the gun in my hand and then knocked me unconscious. When I woke up, I was at Pineville. I had been out of it for days. He'd given me some sort of hallucinogenic. My crazy behavior had my parents convinced of his lie that I had killed Kasey. He said we had both been doing drugs. He claimed that the times Kasey left without me were because I had been violent with him. None of that was true. But no matter what I said, no one would believe me. The doctor at Pineville kept me drugged. Finally when I was released, it was weeks before I could get off the meds and pull myself together again. I would try to tell them the truth, but the side effects of withdrawal only convinced them further that I was lying, and I'd end up at Pineville again. It took nearly a year for my brain to get right enough to understand that I would never be free again until I ran away."

"You faked your death," Olivia suggested.

"I was going to," Laura said, "but Decker caught me. He let the note I'd written stand and took me back to Pineville. My parents never knew I was alive."

"Why would Pineville go along?" Huck asked, his voice telling Olivia he was not convinced.

"The administrator, Leo Rich, and Decker go way back,"

Laura explained. "I don't know what Decker has on him, but Rich would do whatever Decker said."

"Did you kill Willy?" Olivia demanded.

Laura gasped. "Of course not. I didn't even escape until that bastard told me what he'd done and said if I tried anything else, you would be next."

"What did he mean, try anything else?" Huck asked.

Olivia needed to sit down. She found the nearest boulder and collapsed there.

"I was there for over twenty-five years," she said, her emotions getting the better of her. "Eventually, they stopped keeping me in solitary confinement. I tried making friends with people I knew would be seeing their relatives or be released. I would tell them my story and about my dad. I begged them to get a message to him when they were released, but something always happened. One fell in the shower and hit her head the day before she was to be released. Another hung herself. It was when the third one slit her wrists by digging with her fork until the deed was done that I realized no one could save me. Decker would always find a way to stop me. He and Rich had too many ears in that place."

"You're saying," Olivia spoke up, "this person—this Leo Rich—who did whatever Decker told him killed these people."

Laura nodded. "It's the only explanation."

"But you did eventually escape, obviously," Huck countered.

"It was a long time before I dared. I had resigned myself to dying there." She closed her eyes and shook her head. "I honestly don't know why he didn't kill me a long time ago. I even asked him that on one of his visits."

"He came to see you there?" Olivia's head was spinning.

Laura squared her shoulders. "Numerous times. Said he couldn't bear not to see me. He swore he'd never let me go."

"There are cameras outside the facility," Huck said to Olivia. "If he went there, we can find him on video."

"Knowing him, he will have that figured out too." She stared hard at Huck. "Whatever you believe about Decker, he's capable of anything." She turned back to Olivia. "I spent two years developing a secret friendship. We were so careful. She understood if anyone found out, she would be killed. She was released last Friday. I gave her a necklace—my sunflower necklace—that I always wore so Willy would know she was telling the truth. On Sunday morning, she drove to the cabin and told Willy the truth about where I was and what Decker had done."

"She told you she did this?" Olivia said.

Laura shook her head. "She couldn't risk contacting me back at Pineville. But I know she did because on Monday Decker came to see me. He said he knew what I had done and that my foolishness had caused him to have to kill his best friend—my father. He said if I ever told anyone else or did a single other thing, he would kill you."

Olivia turned to Huck. "I don't know what to believe."

"I knew I had to do something no matter what he said," Laura went on, her voice rising with desperation. "I couldn't trust him to keep his word that he wouldn't touch you as long as I behaved myself. So I took the chance I had been afraid to take all these years." She looked away. "I think I may have hurt one of the attendants pretty badly. I didn't mean to hurt anyone. I just had to get away."

"She may be telling at least part of the truth," Huck said to Olivia.

Olivia held her breath.

"While I was giving you that head start," he explained, "Snelling called. Decker's prints were on the wine bottle. Someone had wiped most of them, but there was one perfect print that matched Decker's."

"Decker drinks wine?" Olivia asked.

"Yes," Laura said quickly. "He and I liked the same kind, red."

Huck nodded. "She's right. Me and some of the other deputies used to laugh about having a sheriff who didn't like beer."

"He said they had dinner together on Sunday night," Laura said. "Dad had invited him and then confronted him about what he'd been told. There was a fight, and the injuries Dad got from the fight left Decker no choice but to throw him off Sunset Rock. He thought it was ironic." A sob tore from her throat. "He told me how Dad wanted to kill him for what he'd done, and then he laughed because Dad was the one to die."

"There was a private investigator," Huck said.

Olivia could no longer keep up; tears were streaming down her face, and she felt ready to curl into herself. How had he gotten away with this all these years?

"Decker hired him to find me, and he did," Laura confessed. "I told him the truth, and I think he believed me. Especially because of my father's murder. I think that was maybe the only reason he believed me. The next thing I knew, he was dead too."

"Still telling your lies, I see."

Huck whipped around at the sound of Decker's voice. The weapon pointed directly at his chest kept Huck from reaching for his own.

"Decker," Huck said carefully. "We understand what she's up to," he assured his soon to be former boss. "There's no need for you to prove one damned thing. The woman is obviously insane."

"Huck," Olivia demanded, "what're you doing?"

"I'm not crazy," Laura howled.

"Of course you are," Decker sneered. "I went to a great deal of trouble to show just how nuts you are. Like ransacking Willy's house. Burning down the shed. Taking those photographs." He shook his head. "She was always doing crazy stuff. If Willy and Joyce were here, they would tell you." He laughed. "They never had a clue I was playing them."

"We should get her into custody," Huck suggested, "and clear this up at the station."

Decker laughed. "I know about the prints, so don't try to play games with me, Monroe." He shook his head. "Too bad your crazy mother escaped and killed your lover, Olivia, the same way she killed her husband. And of course, she had to kill you too. Then herself."

"There's just one problem with that," Olivia said. "No one is going to believe you this time, and I think you know it."

Decker laughed. "Maybe. But none of you will be around to corroborate her story."

A guttural howl rent the air. Moving so fast Huck barely saw her, Laura rushed toward Decker.

Decker swung his weapon in her direction.

Huck drew his own.

Gunshots exploded in the air.

Chapter Fifteen

Erlanger Hospital,
Chattanooga, 12:00 p.m.

Olivia paced the waiting room.

Her mother was still in surgery. The shot Decker managed to pull off before Huck's shot plowed through his brain had hit its mark. Her mother had been gravely injured.

Laura had been rushed to the hospital with her vitals plummeting.

Olivia wrung her hands, paced the opposite direction. She didn't want her to die. She had just gotten her mother back.

Damn it.

Decker was dead. Thank God.

Acting Sheriff Snelling was executing a warrant at Pineville at this very moment. The last Huck had heard from one of his fellow deputies, the administrator was spilling his guts in hopes of getting some sort of deal. Administrator Leo Rich had accidentally, he claimed, killed a woman when he was in college. Decker had helped him cover up his involvement, and Rich had been paying him back since.

All of it, every single word, made Olivia sick. None of this would bring Willy back, but Olivia was grateful to have found her mother. She had been a prisoner for more than two decades. Laura deserved to have her life back—not to have it taken from her after all she had been through.

Huck came into the small surgery waiting room. "Hey. Any news yet?"

Olivia shook her head. "You?"

"Sergeant Snelling called to say his CSI team found your mother's necklace, along with photos Decker had taken over the years. Several of her in the hospital. Some you don't want to hear about."

Olivia cringed. She hated that bastard. Hoped he rotted in hell.

She steadied herself. "That's more proof she's telling the truth." Olivia felt ill at the idea that her mother had been lost and alone all these years with Willy only a few miles away.

The whole thing was insane.

The door opened and the surgeon, still wearing surgical scrubs, walked in.

Olivia's knees felt weak. Huck was suddenly at her side, his arm around her back.

"Your mother came through well," he said. "She'll need some time to heal, but I expect a full recovery."

Relief gushed through Olivia. "Thank you. When can I see her?"

"She'll be in recovery for an hour or so, and then we'll get her settled into a room. You can see her then."

Olivia thanked him again. When the door closed behind the doctor, she turned to Huck. "Thank you for all you've done. I wouldn't have gotten through this without you. I'm certain I wouldn't have found the truth without you."

Confusion lined his handsome face. "I'm concerned this sounds like goodbye."

Olivia smiled. "I will have to go back to Bozeman and pack up my townhouse. Settle things at my office. But then I'll be back."

It was impossible to miss the hope in his eyes. "For good?"

She shrugged. "Or bad, depending on how you look at it. You see, Deputy Detective Monroe, if I'm staying here, it has to be a package deal."

His eyebrows went up. "Package deal?"

"I get you in the deal."

"I'm more than happy to oblige, ma'am."

He kissed her to seal the best deal of their lives.

Deep in her heart, Olivia had always known there was no place like home.

* * * * *

COMING SOON!

We really hope you enjoyed reading this book. If you're looking for more romance be sure to head to the shops when new books are available on

Thursday 3rd August

To see which titles are coming soon, please visit

millsandboon.co.uk/nextmonth

MILLS & BOON